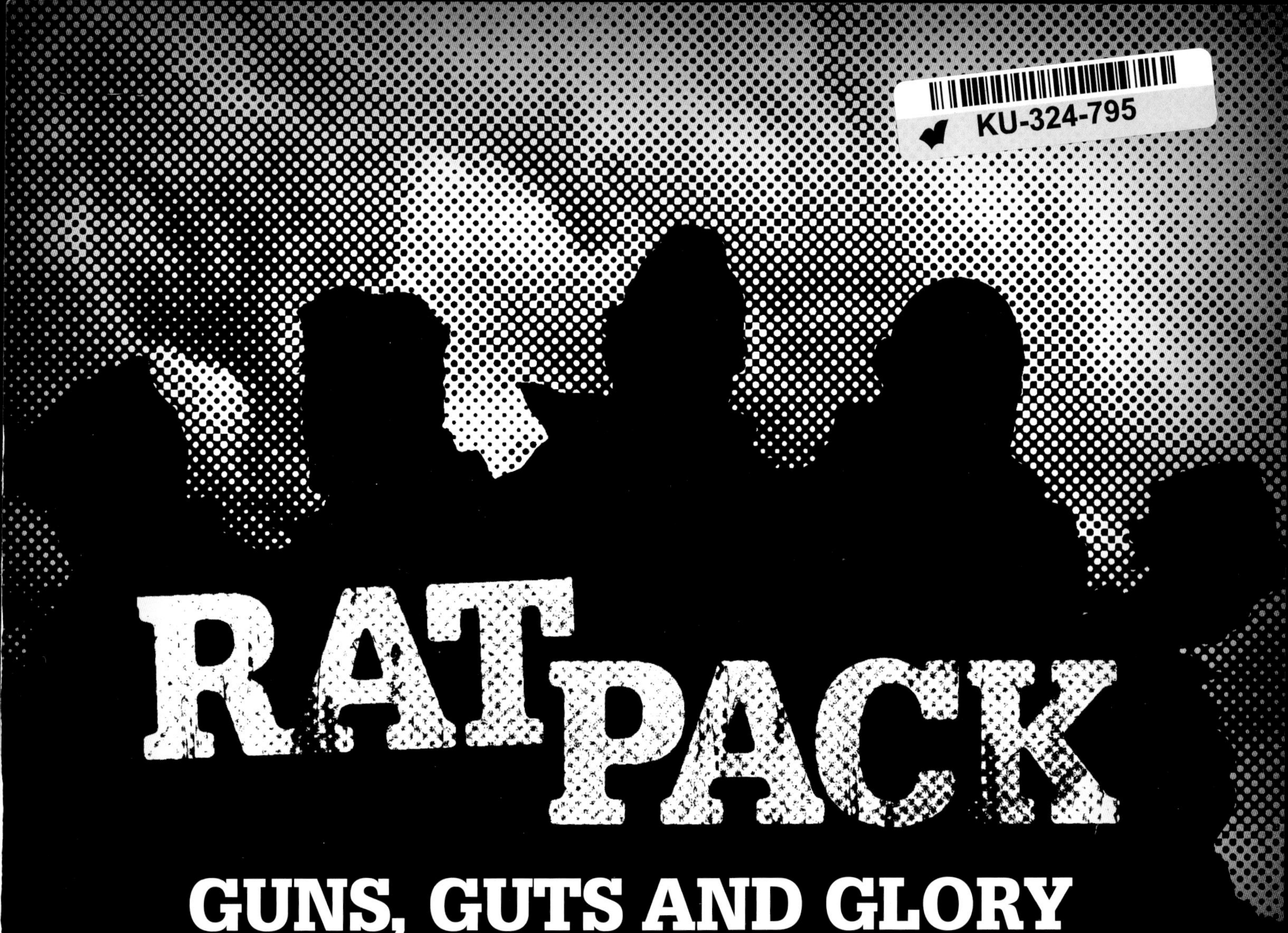

RAT PACK

GUNS, GUTS AND GLORY

TITAN BOOKS

RAT PACK: GUNS, GUTS AND GLORY
ISBN: 9781848560352

Published by Titan Books
A division of Titan Publishing Group Ltd.
144 Southwark St.
London
SE1 0UP

A CIP catalogue record for this title is available from the British Library.

First edition: August 2012

1 3 5 7 9 10 8 6 4 2

Printed in China

Grateful thanks to Moose Harris for his expertise and comic materials; Pat Mills for taking time out to be interviewed; David Leach; JP Rutter; and Melanie Leggett and Linda Beavis at Egmont UK – all of whom made the production of this book possible.

What did you think of this book? We love to hear from our readers. Please email us at: **readerfeedback@titanemail.com**, or write to us at the above address.

To receive advance information, news, competitions, and exclusive offers online, please sign up for the Titan newsletter on our website: **www.titanbooks.com**

This book is a work of fiction. Characters may have views and use language which some of today's readers may find offensive. The publisher and copyright holder in no way endorse the views expressed or language used.

Much of the comic strip source material used by Titan Books in this edition is exceedingly rare. As such, we hope that readers can appreciate that the quality of reproduction achievable can vary.

www.titanbooks.com

CONTENTS

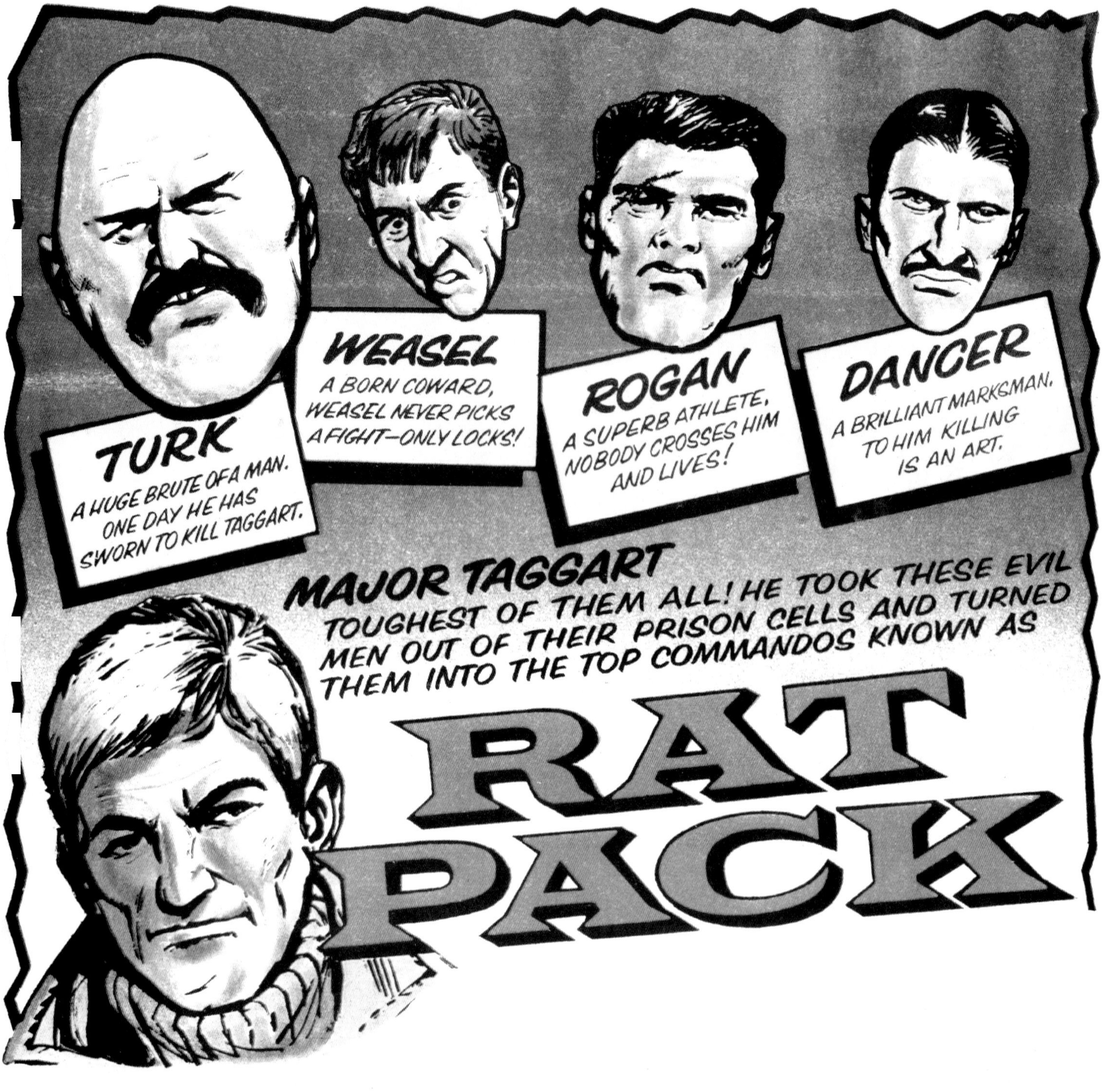
WEASEL
A BORN COWARD, WEASEL NEVER PICKS A FIGHT—ONLY LOCKS!
TURK
A HUGE BRUTE OF A MAN. ONE DAY HE HAS SWORN TO KILL TAGGART.
ROGAN
A SUPERB ATHLETE, NOBODY CROSSES HIM AND LIVES!
DANCER
A BRILLIANT MARKSMAN. TO HIM KILLING IS AN ART.
MAJOR TAGGART
TOUGHEST OF THEM ALL! HE TOOK THESE EVIL MEN OUT OF THEIR PRISON CELLS AND TURNED THEM INTO THE TOP COMMANDOS KNOWN AS
RAT PACK

AN INTERVIEW WITH WRITER PAT MILLS

Pat Mills is considered by many fans to be the "Godfather of British Comics" after helping launch controversial but commercially successful titles *Action* and *2000AD* at IPC in the 1970s. His contributions to the latter included the ongoing series *Nemesis the Warlock*, *ABC Warriors* and *Sláine*. He developed *Battle Picture Weekly* with fellow writer John Wagner in the mid-1970s and went on to co-create the milestone series *Charley's War* with artist Joe Colquhoun, currently reprinted by Titan Books.

How did you begin your editorial career in comics and when did you join IPC as an editor?

I started at DC Thomson in Scotland, went freelance and worked on boys', girls' and humour comics for the publisher IPC. Male comics were going down the toilet, whereas girls' comics were flourishing with huge sales figures. So the publisher asked John Wagner and myself to create a boys' comic with girls' comic thinking, and also to rival DC Thomson's *Warlord*, which had been a

Rat Pack appeared in the first issue of *Battle Picture Weekly* on 8th March 1975 and ran until 5th July 1980.

Carlos Ezquerra, who drew the first strip, went on to co-create *Major Eazy* (right) with writer Alan Hebden.

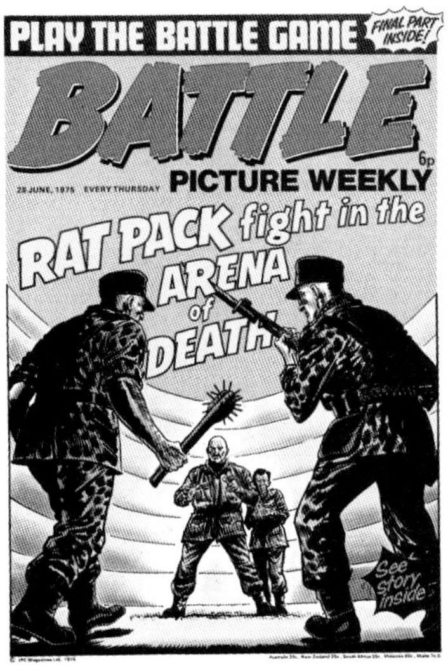

PLAY THE BATTLE GAME
FINAL PART INSIDE!
BATTLE
6p
PICTURE WEEKLY
RAT PACK fight in the ARENA of DEATH!
See story inside

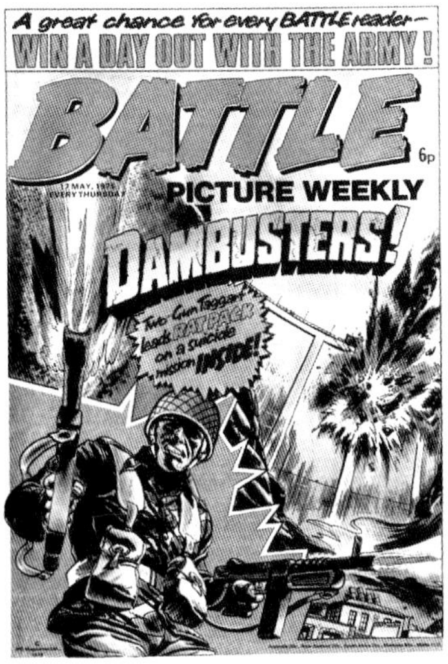

A great chance for every BATTLE reader—
WIN A DAY OUT WITH THE ARMY!
BATTLE
6p
PICTURE WEEKLY
DAMBUSTERS!

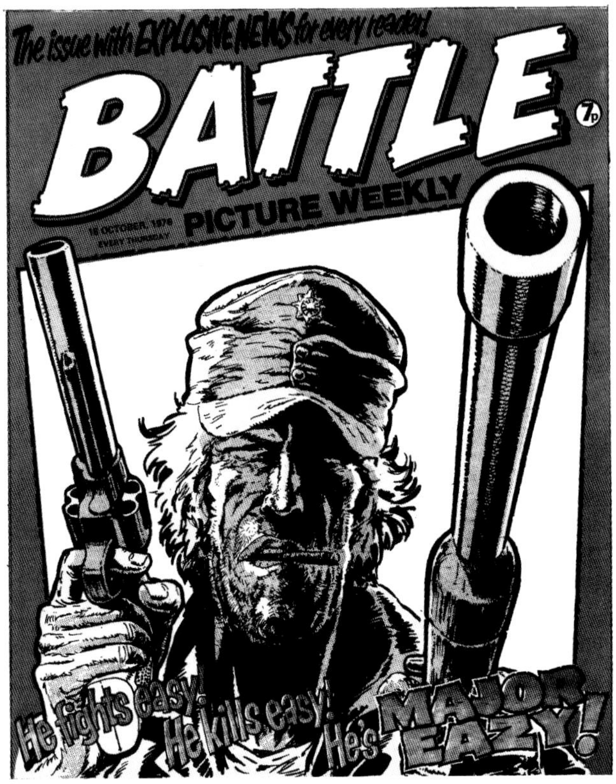

The issue with EXPLOSIVE NEWS for every reader!
BATTLE
7p
PICTURE WEEKLY
He fights easy! He kills easy! He's MAJOR EAZY!

huge success. The existing IPC staff were not to be told. We produced the end result, *Battle Picture Weekly*, in secret from a locked office and it was a big hit.

What was the inspiration for the *Rat Pack* series?

At IPC, we looked at what was popular at the time and in particular what were being called "new wave" movies: spaghetti westerns, *Dirty Harry* and in the case of *Rat Pack*, *The Dirty Dozen*. And look how topical it is even now, where you've got Quentin Tarantino remaking *Inglorious Basterds* [which is based on an Italian exploitation movie from the 70s]. It's an archetype that's never going to go away.

John and I decided we wanted a *Dirty Dozen*-type series and commissioned Gerry Finley-Day to create it. He came up with an excellent pitch which we fine-tuned and then Carlos Ezquerra went on to create it visually. He did a great job. It was very different, and very cool. I remember John and me endlessly rewriting and editing *Rat Pack* stories so they'd have the feeling we were looking for.

We all love these kinds of stories and there are so many variations on it… *The League of Gentlemen* and so on. I'm also delighted to hear there was a team-up between the Rat Pack and Major Eazy [another popular character from *Battle Picture Weekly*]. It's excellent and inspired bringing these groups of characters together.

Would you have liked to have seen further team-ups with the Rat Pack crew and other characters from *Battle*?

In an ideal world, what would have been fun, but would have taken some serious choreography between the creators and careful editorial arrangement, would have been to have a story with another character appearing in the background, like the Eagle just walking by on his way to kill Hitler.

Did you have a favourite Rat Packer?

Gerry's characters were all very well defined: Rogan, Weasel, Turk and Dancer. I thought he came up with some nice ideas. We had to be careful in those early days because there was a lot of resistance – even a guy who was trying to assassinate Hitler was seen as immoral. In other words, the idea of making a killer seem like a hero… in this day and age no one would think twice about it.

How did artist Massimo Belardinelli take over on *Rat Pack*?

I think what happened was we were looking desperately around for new artists, because Carlos couldn't draw the strip all the time. You're talking about six pages a week or something like that, and Carlos could only produce three or four. Then out of the blue came this artist – Massimo Belardinelli – who did a fantastic job on *Rat Pack*; it was

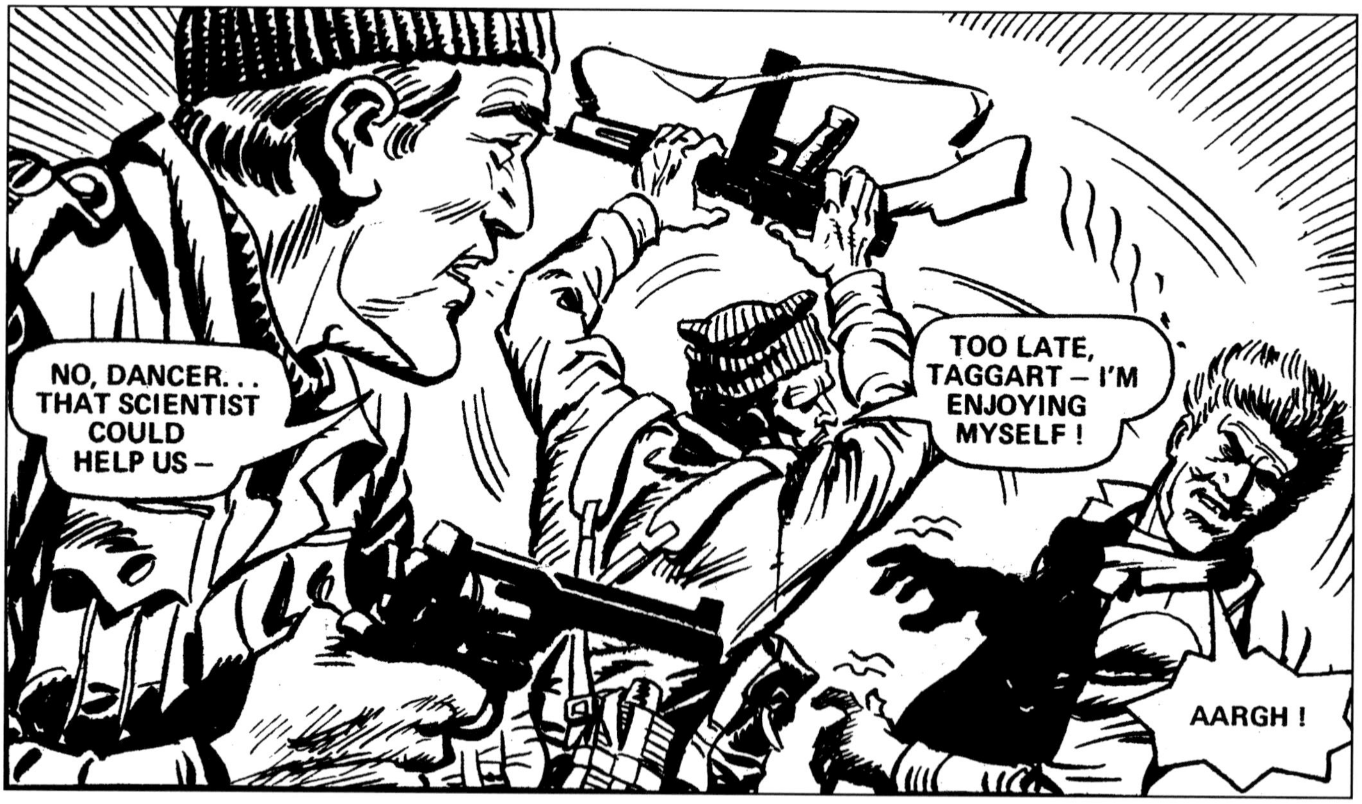
NO, DANCER... THAT SCIENTIST COULD HELP US –
TOO LATE, TAGGART – I'M ENJOYING MYSELF !
AARGH !

absolutely perfect! He was like a machine that you had to constantly keep feeding. I was very fond of Belardinelli's *Rat Pack* – I thought he really captured them visually, and just as well as Carlos did. Other artists? Hmm – no one comes to mind.

How important was Gerry Finley-Day's contribution to *Rat Pack*, and comics in general?

I'm often credited with starting the British comics revolution, but I didn't. Gerry started it with *Tammy*, I just took it to new levels. I didn't have a blank sheet of paper, I had what Gerry had done before as guide. Gerry started with nothing and that's what's so impressive about what he did. He was editor of *Tammy* at the time but freelancing for us. Actually, he was really our facilitator because he had said to John Sanders [the publisher at the time]: "Look, there's these two guys who could sort out the boys' comics, why don't you bring them in and get them to do it?"

So, he was very much there as an integral part of what John Wagner and I did on *Battle*. We would talk to him and say, "What about doing a story about this and that?" So he, if you like, became the slightly less visible third editor. Officially he was a co-creator but unofficially he had a comparable role. He certainly was very important in the creation of *Battle*. He was such a great writer.

Did you ever have the urge to give the series a more serious approach, like *Charley's War*?

We saw *Rat Pack* as a direct rival to the lead story in *Warlord* – also called *Warlord* – about an aristocrat who went on secret missions. Doubtless readers will see my influence here on *Rat Pack* – instead of aristocrats, we had a bunch of scum! The stories needed to be self-contained because cliffhangers had been abused as a dramatic device. This meant the characters couldn't develop and as the Rat Pack was a house "character", with a number of writers, there was no way we could turn it into a *Charley's War*.

Which writers do you think nailed the essence of the Pack?

Gerry created it, so his influence was paramount. As his achievements often get ignored I need to stress this. I was very into giving *Rat Pack* a movie flavour so you'll see my influence on the opening spreads, often taken from films; for example the underground image from *The Taking of Pelham 123*. I also was keen on using Flashman as a role model, hence there's an episode where they have to throw someone out to hold onto the gold.

I remember on one occasion John and I facilitated a story which was very well researched and put-together. We loved it. I think it's the one drawn by Carlos where Taggart looks down at a beautifully constructed scale model of the target. It didn't register with the readers in the slightest. We were dismayed! Then one week we ran out of time and John and I wrote an episode featuring an old-fashioned Gestapo torture chamber with iron maidens and so on.

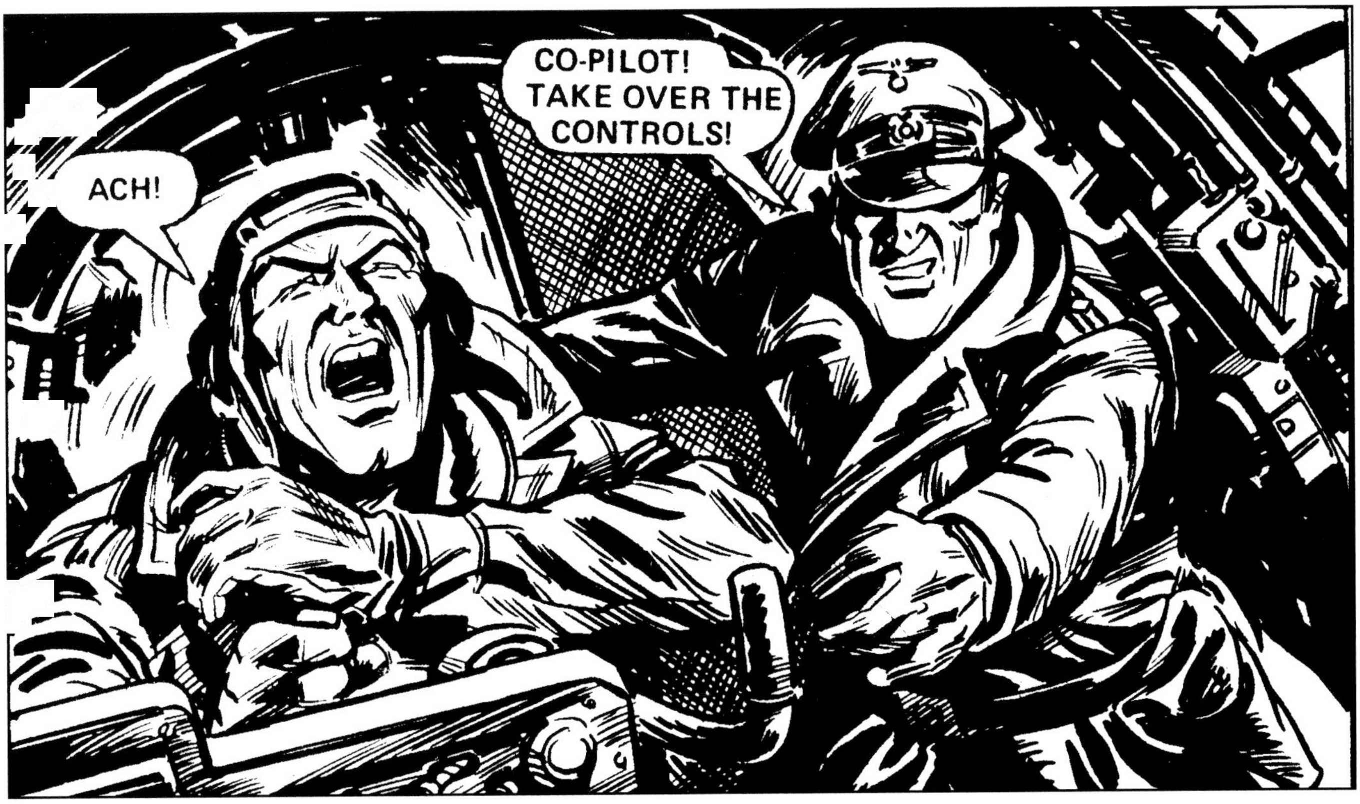
ACH!
CO-PILOT! TAKE OVER THE CONTROLS!

It was a quickly written filler and was crudely drawn. To our surprise, this relatively trashy *Rat Pack* story was *hugely* popular. So it's important to ignore adult assessments of such stories, which would rightly be the other way around. Kids could sometimes be scarily downmarket in their tastes.

In short, nailing the essence of the Pack was a moving target and I think that's why it didn't last longer. Significantly *D-Day Dawson* was the lead story in *Battle*, not *Rat Pack* – it was way ahead of anything else, a fact that's possibly a little unpalatable today because it hasn't aged as well as *Rat Pack*. John and I kept trying to kill the series off, but the readers loved it so we were over-ruled.

Coming back to *Rat Pack*, it was also extremely hard work. We were asking for novel-style stories from writers in six or eight pages. That's tough. And we didn't want old-style war stories, no matter how good they were (e.g. *War Picture Library*). We wanted camp, cool, modern-thinking stories. So we regularly made the lives of writers – with expert knowledge of war, but maybe lacking a certain cool – a misery and I'm sure we're not so fondly remembered by them. But our approach worked and *Battle* was very successful. It was the first boys' comic to break out of the Slough of Despond that existed at the time. Much of that was also down to the excellent editor we were given – Dave Hunt. A great, great editor and extremely rare in boys' comics during this era. I can't think of another in his league.

How was the UK comics market in the 1970s different from the 1980s and beyond? Were there any particular pitfalls or frustrations that you had to overcome?

Today, fandom rules. Back then it was "the kid in the street", so we're talking huge circulations, especially on the girls' comics, where *Tammy* sold 250,000 copies a week. Huge pitfalls and frustrations. The comics establishment didn't want to change, so John and I had to do our own thing. We felt some hostility and obstruction from the old guard, on *Battle*, and later when I created *Action* and *2000AD*. Hence why *Battle* was created in secret.

Why don't we still have a weekly British war comic?

We should. There's no reason why it shouldn't have survived like *2000AD* did. If it had been around long enough for Garth Ennis and others to submit scripts, it would still be published today. It might even be ahead of *2000AD*. In my final *Charley's War* collection, I'm going to give an indication of some of the stories that could have appeared in *Battle* had it survived. Better still, why doesn't someone bring it back?

Interview conducted by David Leach and JP Rutter

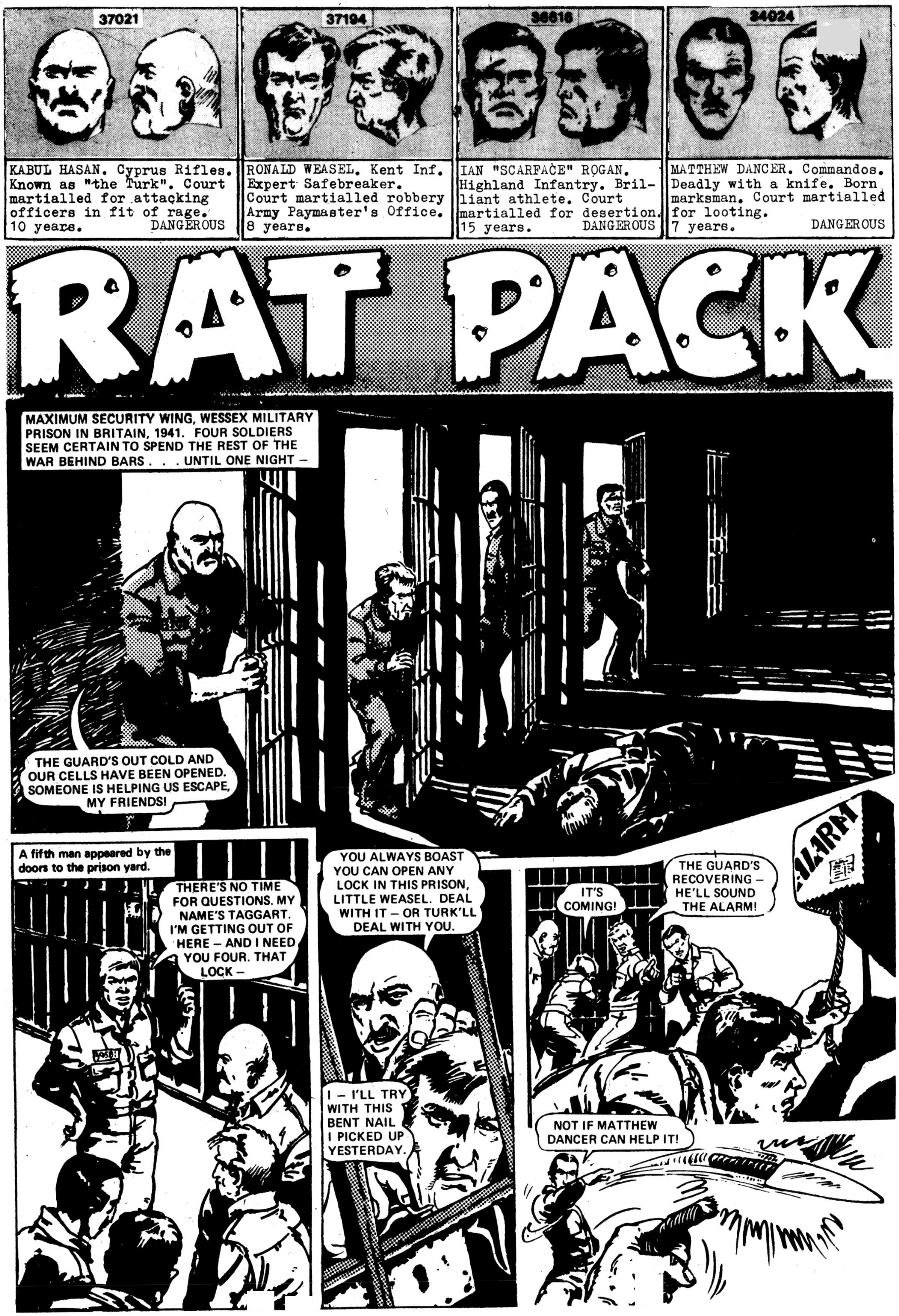
37021
37194
KABUL HASAN. Cyprus Rifles. Known as "the Turk". Court martialled for attacking officers in fit of rage. 10 years. DANGEROUS
RONALD WEASEL. Kent Inf. Expert Safebreaker. Court martialled robbery Army Paymaster's Office. 8 years.
IAN "SCARFACE" ROGAN. Highland Infantry. Brilliant athlete. Court martialled for desertion. 15 years. DANGEROUS
MATTHEW DANCER. Commandos. Deadly with a knife. Born marksman. Court martialled for looting. 7 years. DANGEROUS
RAT PACK
MAXIMUM SECURITY WING, WESSEX MILITARY PRISON IN BRITAIN, 1941. FOUR SOLDIERS SEEM CERTAIN TO SPEND THE REST OF THE WAR BEHIND BARS . . . UNTIL ONE NIGHT –
THE GUARD'S OUT COLD AND OUR CELLS HAVE BEEN OPENED. SOMEONE IS HELPING US ESCAPE, MY FRIENDS!
A fifth man appeared by the doors to the prison yard.
THERE'S NO TIME FOR QUESTIONS. MY NAME'S TAGGART. I'M GETTING OUT OF HERE – AND I NEED YOU FOUR. THAT LOCK –
YOU ALWAYS BOAST YOU CAN OPEN ANY LOCK IN THIS PRISON, LITTLE WEASEL. DEAL WITH IT – OR TURK'LL DEAL WITH YOU.
I – I'LL TRY WITH THIS BENT NAIL I PICKED UP YESTERDAY.
IT'S COMING!
THE GUARD'S RECOVERING – HE'LL SOUND THE ALARM!
ALARM
NOT IF MATTHEW DANCER CAN HELP IT!

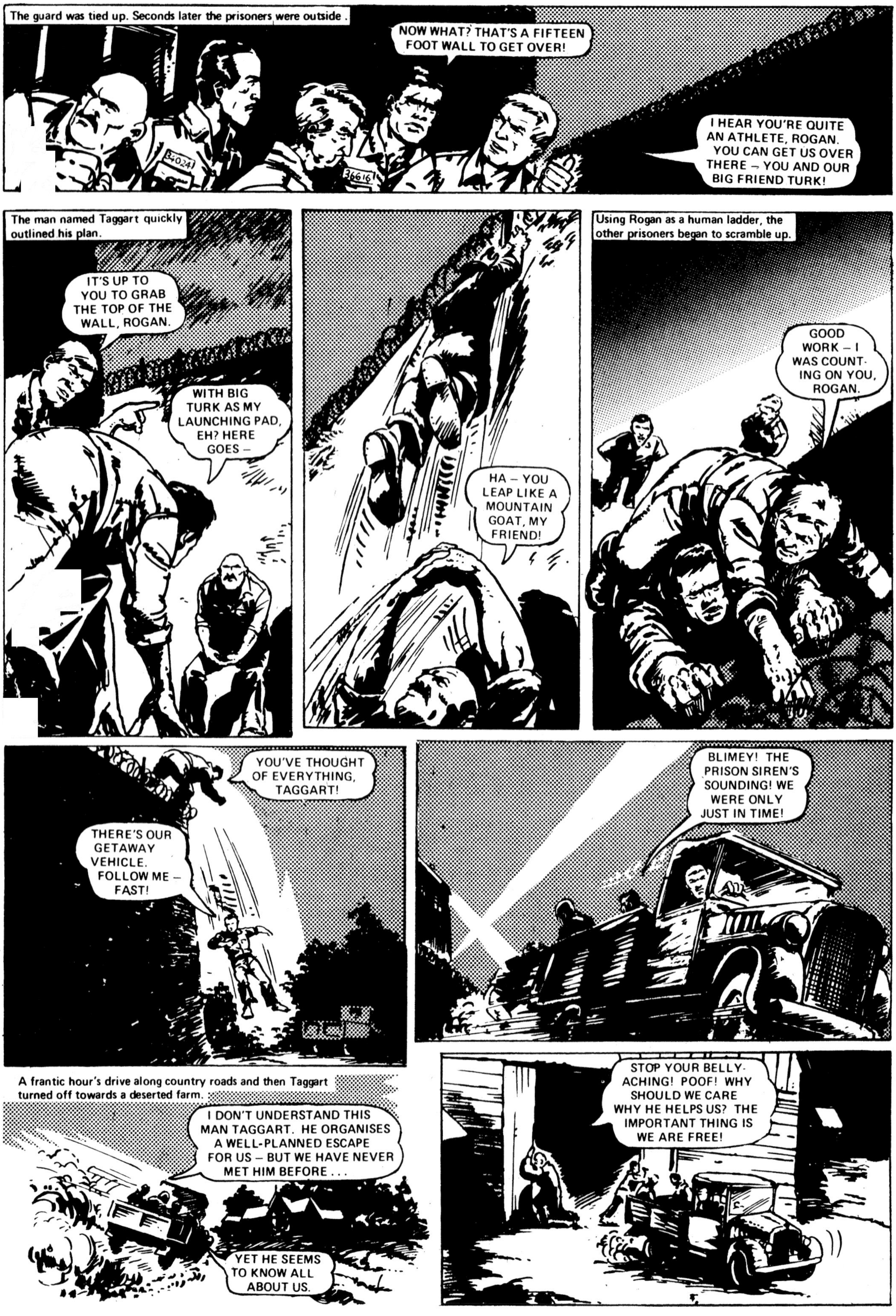
The guard was tied up. Seconds later the prisoners were outside .
NOW WHAT? THAT'S A FIFTEEN FOOT WALL TO GET OVER!
I HEAR YOU'RE QUITE AN ATHLETE, ROGAN. YOU CAN GET US OVER THERE – YOU AND OUR BIG FRIEND TURK!
The man named Taggart quickly outlined his plan.
IT'S UP TO YOU TO GRAB THE TOP OF THE WALL, ROGAN.
WITH BIG TURK AS MY LAUNCHING PAD, EH? HERE GOES –
HA – YOU LEAP LIKE A MOUNTAIN GOAT, MY FRIEND!
Using Rogan as a human ladder, the other prisoners began to scramble up.
GOOD WORK – I WAS COUNTING ON YOU, ROGAN.
YOU'VE THOUGHT OF EVERYTHING, TAGGART!
THERE'S OUR GETAWAY VEHICLE. FOLLOW ME – FAST!
BLIMEY! THE PRISON SIREN'S SOUNDING! WE WERE ONLY JUST IN TIME!
A frantic hour's drive along country roads and then Taggart turned off towards a deserted farm.
I DON'T UNDERSTAND THIS MAN TAGGART. HE ORGANISES A WELL-PLANNED ESCAPE FOR US – BUT WE HAVE NEVER MET HIM BEFORE . . .
YET HE SEEMS TO KNOW ALL ABOUT US.
STOP YOUR BELLY-ACHING! POOF! WHY SHOULD WE CARE WHY HE HELPS US? THE IMPORTANT THING IS WE ARE FREE!

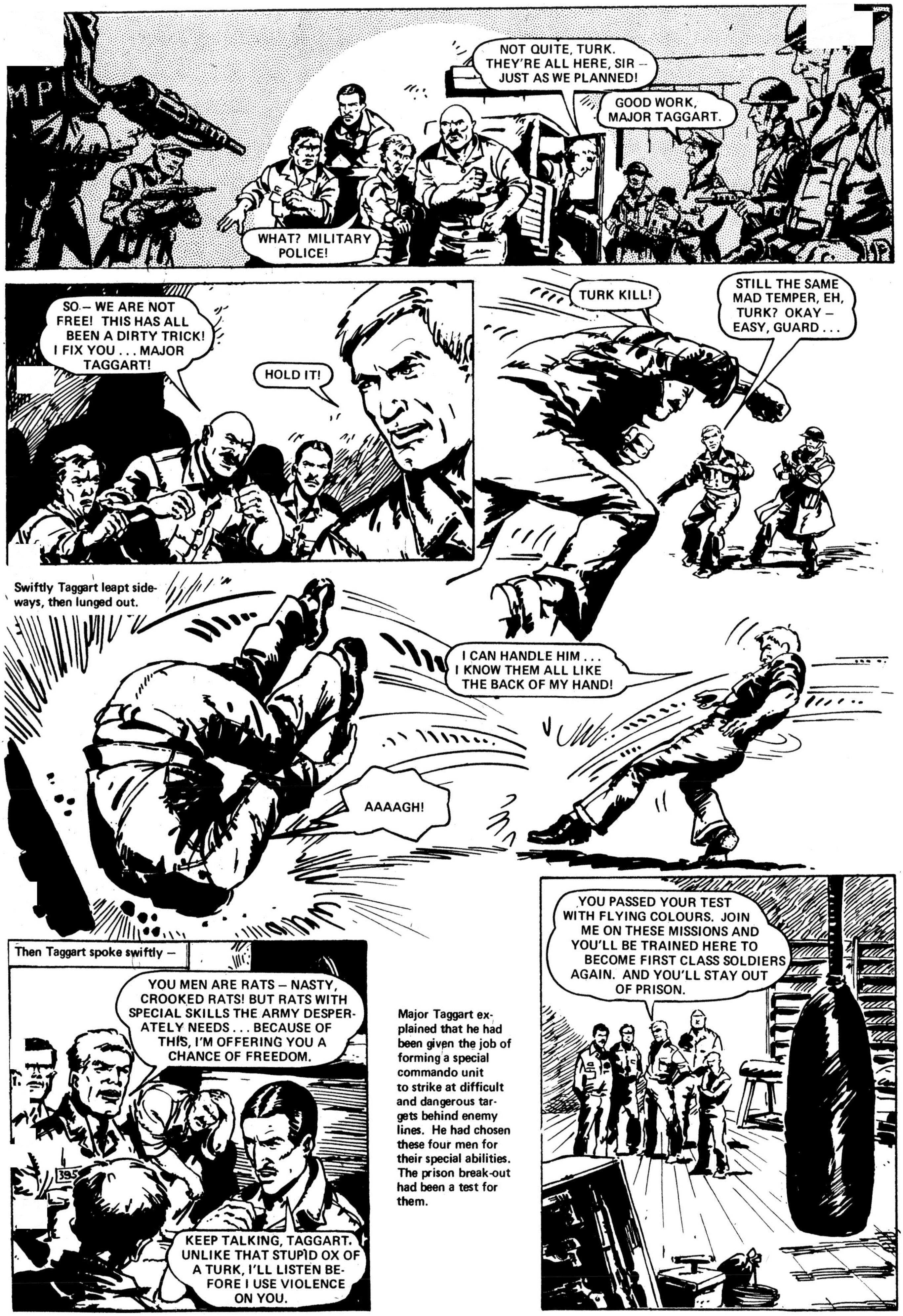
NOT QUITE, TURK. THEY'RE ALL HERE, SIR — JUST AS WE PLANNED!
GOOD WORK, MAJOR TAGGART.
WHAT? MILITARY POLICE!
SO — WE ARE NOT FREE! THIS HAS ALL BEEN A DIRTY TRICK! I FIX YOU . . . MAJOR TAGGART!
HOLD IT!
TURK KILL!
STILL THE SAME MAD TEMPER, EH, TURK? OKAY — EASY, GUARD . . .
Swiftly Taggart leapt sideways, then lunged out.
I CAN HANDLE HIM . . . I KNOW THEM ALL LIKE THE BACK OF MY HAND!
AAAAGH!
Then Taggart spoke swiftly —
YOU MEN ARE RATS — NASTY, CROOKED RATS! BUT RATS WITH SPECIAL SKILLS THE ARMY DESPERATELY NEEDS . . . BECAUSE OF THIS, I'M OFFERING YOU A CHANCE OF FREEDOM.
KEEP TALKING, TAGGART. UNLIKE THAT STUPID OX OF A TURK, I'LL LISTEN BEFORE I USE VIOLENCE ON YOU.
Major Taggart explained that he had been given the job of forming a special commando unit to strike at difficult and dangerous targets behind enemy lines. He had chosen these four men for their special abilities. The prison break-out had been a test for them.
YOU PASSED YOUR TEST WITH FLYING COLOURS. JOIN ME ON THESE MISSIONS AND YOU'LL BE TRAINED HERE TO BECOME FIRST CLASS SOLDIERS AGAIN. AND YOU'LL STAY OUT OF PRISON.

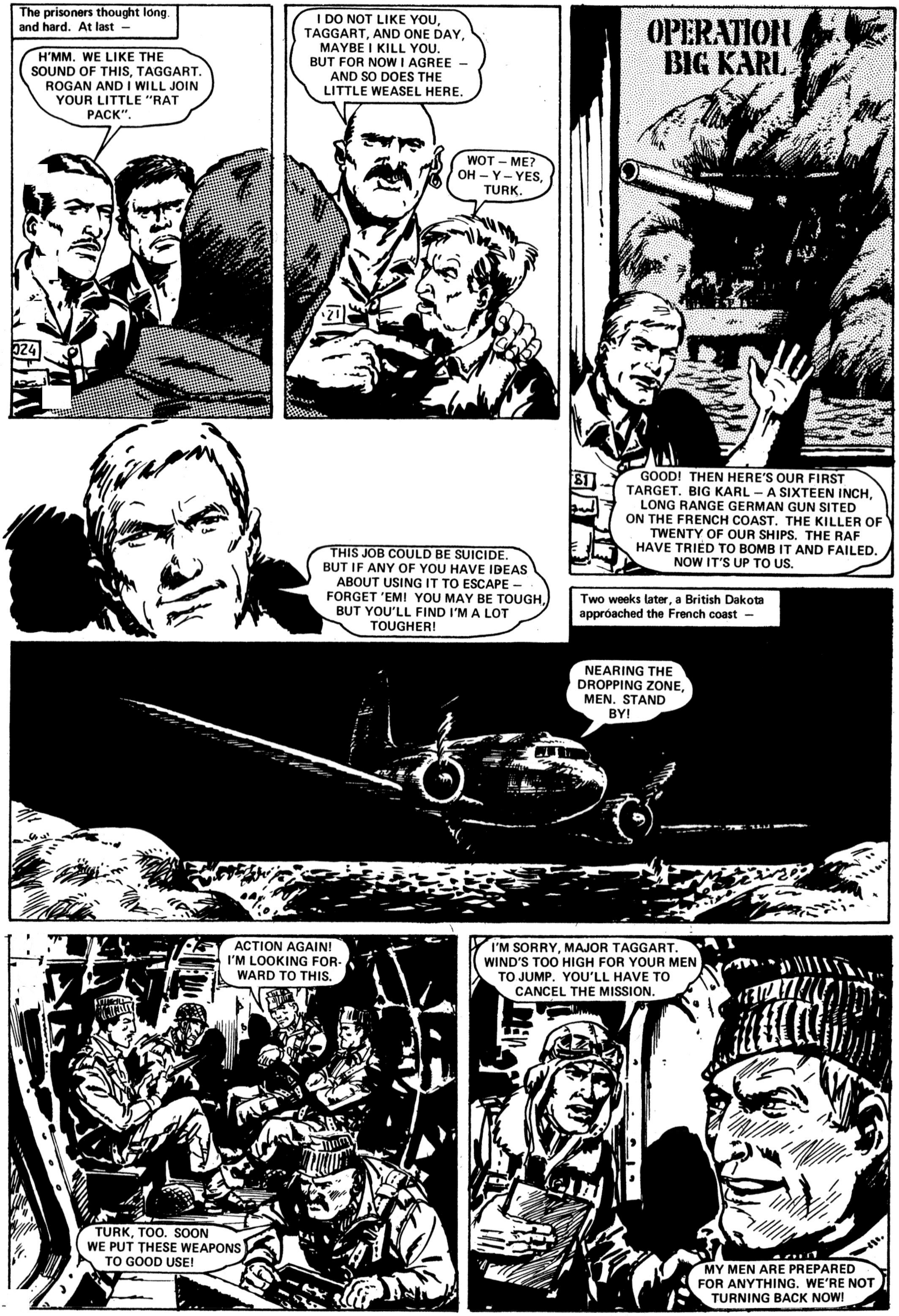
The prisoners thought long and hard. At last –
H'MM. WE LIKE THE SOUND OF THIS, TAGGART. ROGAN AND I WILL JOIN YOUR LITTLE "RAT PACK".
I DO NOT LIKE YOU, TAGGART, AND ONE DAY, MAYBE I KILL YOU. BUT FOR NOW I AGREE – AND SO DOES THE LITTLE WEASEL HERE.
WOT – ME? OH – Y – YES, TURK.
OPERATION BIG KARL
GOOD! THEN HERE'S OUR FIRST TARGET. BIG KARL – A SIXTEEN INCH, LONG RANGE GERMAN GUN SITED ON THE FRENCH COAST. THE KILLER OF TWENTY OF OUR SHIPS. THE RAF HAVE TRIED TO BOMB IT AND FAILED. NOW IT'S UP TO US.
THIS JOB COULD BE SUICIDE. BUT IF ANY OF YOU HAVE IDEAS ABOUT USING IT TO ESCAPE – FORGET 'EM! YOU MAY BE TOUGH, BUT YOU'LL FIND I'M A LOT TOUGHER!
Two weeks later, a British Dakota approached the French coast –
NEARING THE DROPPING ZONE, MEN. STAND BY!
ACTION AGAIN! I'M LOOKING FORWARD TO THIS.
TURK, TOO. SOON WE PUT THESE WEAPONS TO GOOD USE!
I'M SORRY, MAJOR TAGGART. WIND'S TOO HIGH FOR YOUR MEN TO JUMP. YOU'LL HAVE TO CANCEL THE MISSION.
MY MEN ARE PREPARED FOR ANYTHING. WE'RE NOT TURNING BACK NOW!

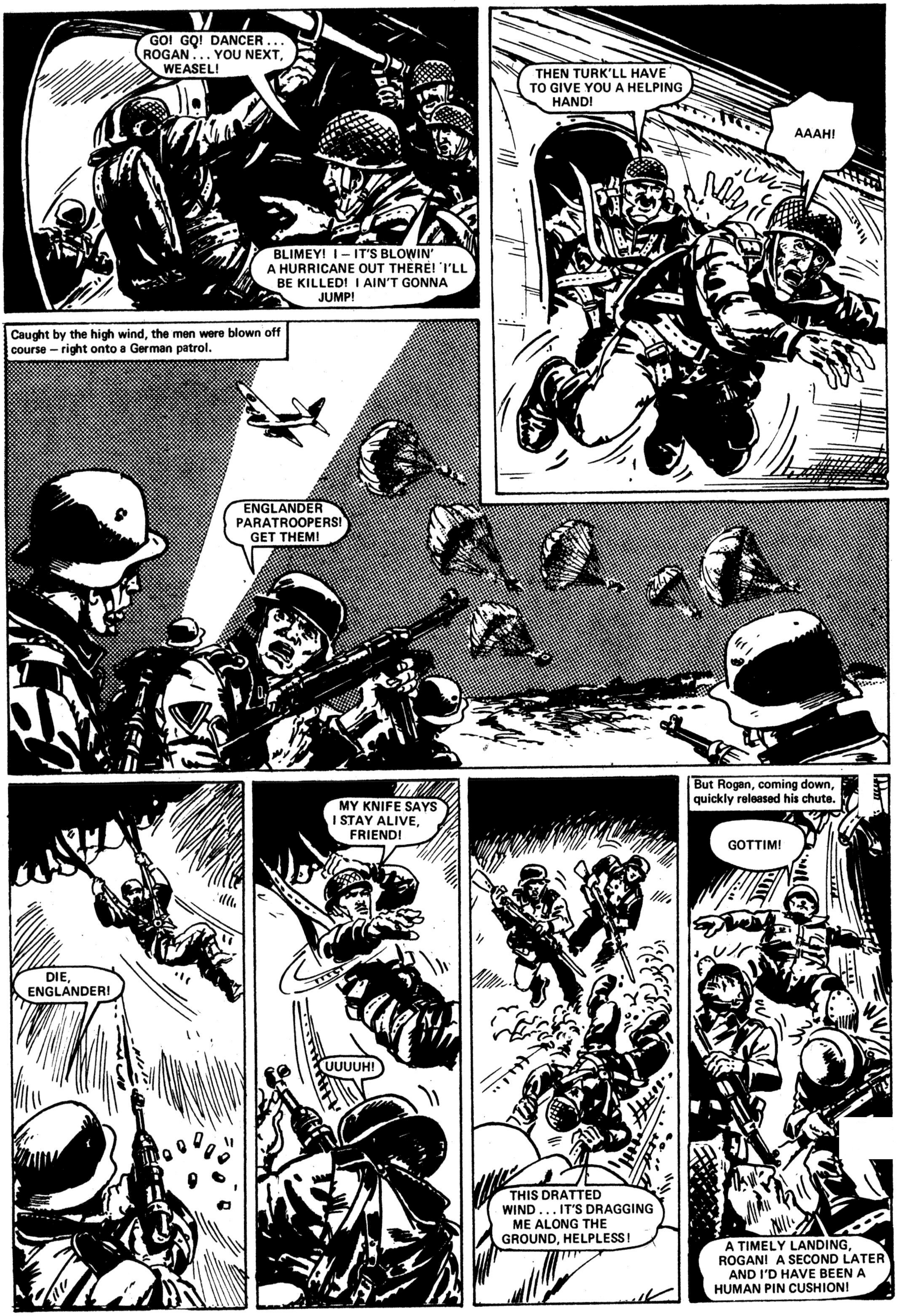
GO! GO! DANCER . . . ROGAN . . . YOU NEXT, WEASEL!
BLIMEY! I – IT'S BLOWIN' A HURRICANE OUT THERE! I'LL BE KILLED! I AIN'T GONNA JUMP!
THEN TURK'LL HAVE TO GIVE YOU A HELPING HAND!
AAAH!
Caught by the high wind, the men were blown off course – right onto a German patrol.
ENGLANDER PARATROOPERS! GET THEM!
DIE, ENGLANDER!
MY KNIFE SAYS I STAY ALIVE, FRIEND!
UUUUH!
THIS DRATTED WIND . . . IT'S DRAGGING ME ALONG THE GROUND, HELPLESS!
But Rogan, coming down, quickly released his chute.
GOTTIM!
A TIMELY LANDING, ROGAN! A SECOND LATER AND I'D HAVE BEEN A HUMAN PIN CUSHION!

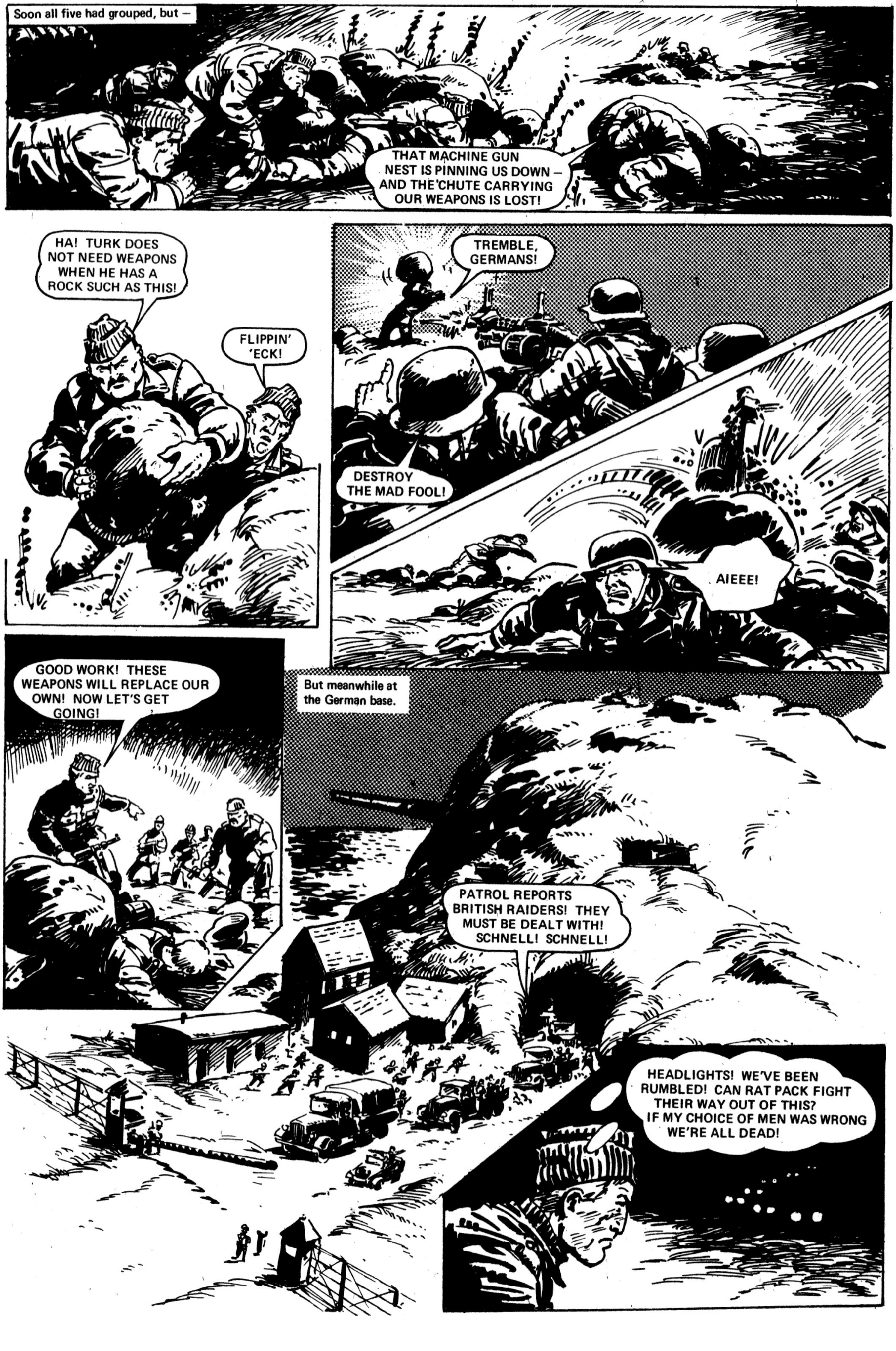
Soon all five had grouped, but —
THAT MACHINE GUN NEST IS PINNING US DOWN — AND THE 'CHUTE CARRYING OUR WEAPONS IS LOST!
HA! TURK DOES NOT NEED WEAPONS WHEN HE HAS A ROCK SUCH AS THIS!
FLIPPIN' 'ECK!
TREMBLE, GERMANS!
DESTROY THE MAD FOOL!
AIEEE!
GOOD WORK! THESE WEAPONS WILL REPLACE OUR OWN! NOW LET'S GET GOING!
But meanwhile at the German base.
PATROL REPORTS BRITISH RAIDERS! THEY MUST BE DEALT WITH! SCHNELL! SCHNELL!
HEADLIGHTS! WE'VE BEEN RUMBLED! CAN RAT PACK FIGHT THEIR WAY OUT OF THIS? IF MY CHOICE OF MEN WAS WRONG WE'RE ALL DEAD!

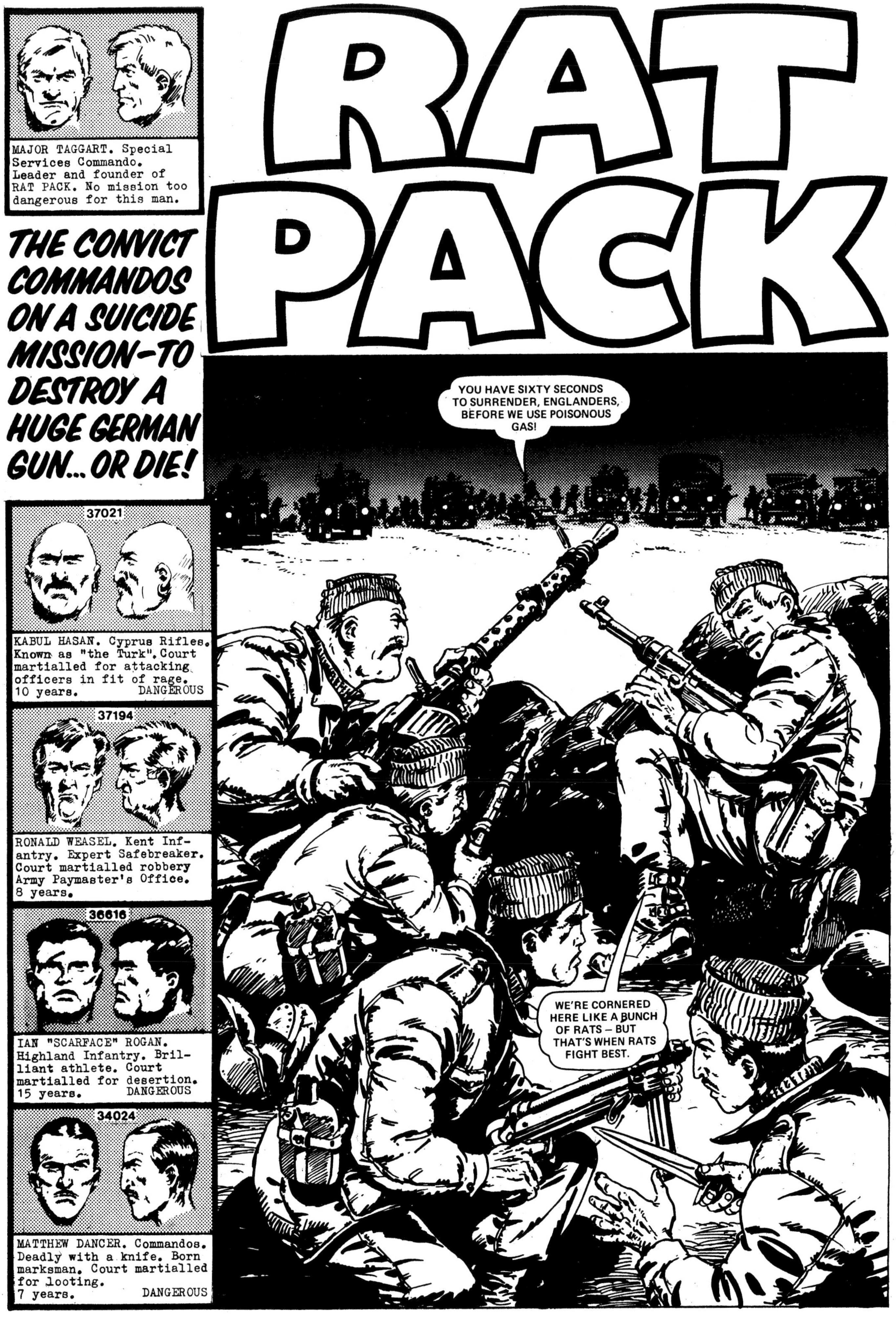
RAT PACK
MAJOR TAGGART. Special Services Commando. Leader and founder of RAT PACK. No mission too dangerous for this man.
THE CONVICT COMMANDOS ON A SUICIDE MISSION–TO DESTROY A HUGE GERMAN GUN... OR DIE!
37021
KABUL HASAN. Cyprus Rifles. Known as "the Turk". Court martialled for attacking officers in fit of rage. 10 years. DANGEROUS
37194
RONALD WEASEL. Kent Infantry. Expert Safebreaker. Court martialled robbery Army Paymaster's Office. 8 years.
36616
IAN "SCARFACE" ROGAN. Highland Infantry. Brilliant athlete. Court martialled for desertion. 15 years. DANGEROUS
34024
MATTHEW DANCER. Commandos. Deadly with a knife. Born marksman. Court martialled for looting. 7 years. DANGEROUS
YOU HAVE SIXTY SECONDS TO SURRENDER, ENGLANDERS, BEFORE WE USE POISONOUS GAS!
WE'RE CORNERED HERE LIKE A BUNCH OF RATS – BUT THAT'S WHEN RATS FIGHT BEST.

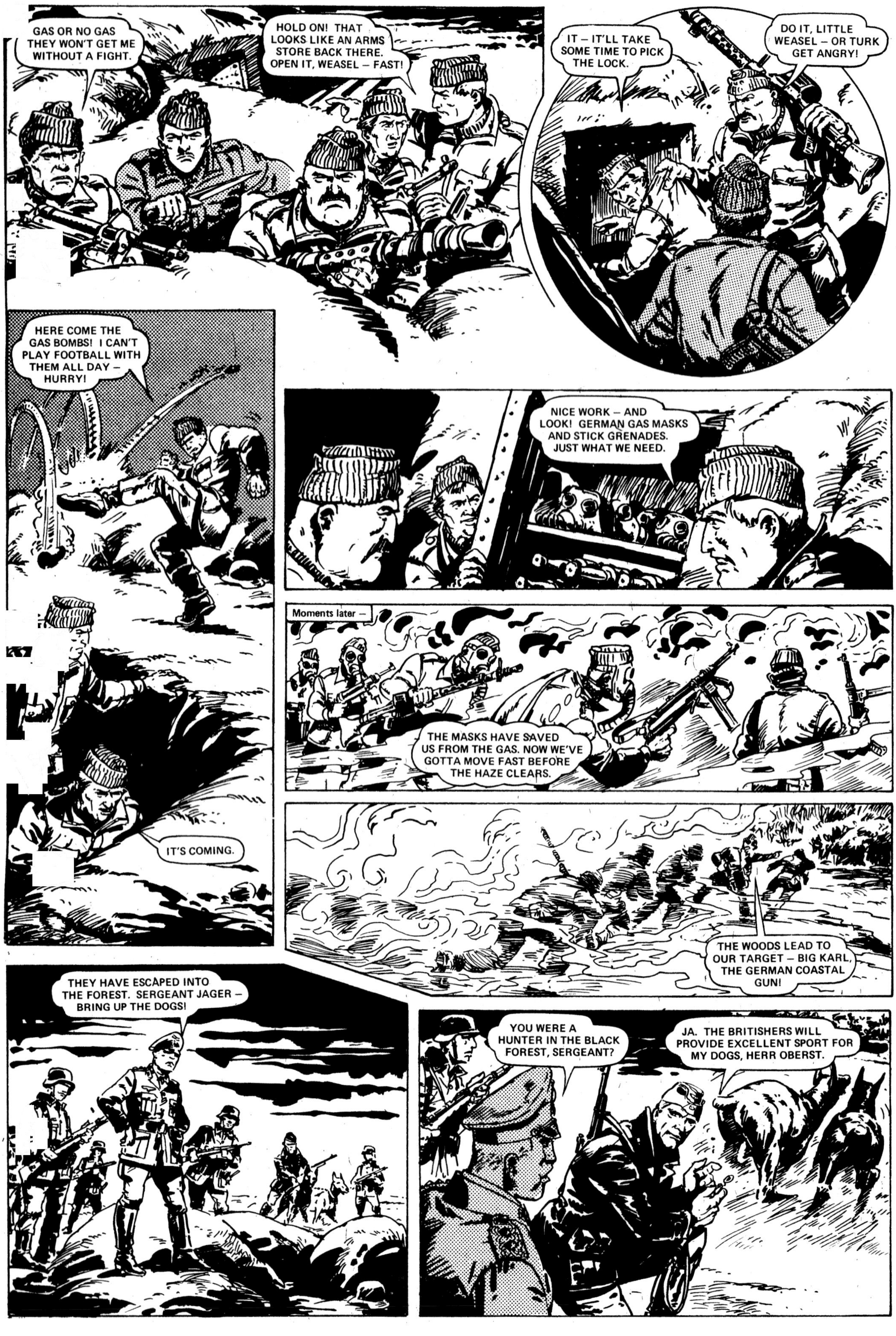
GAS OR NO GAS THEY WON'T GET ME WITHOUT A FIGHT.
HOLD ON! THAT LOOKS LIKE AN ARMS STORE BACK THERE. OPEN IT, WEASEL – FAST!
IT – IT'LL TAKE SOME TIME TO PICK THE LOCK.
DO IT, LITTLE WEASEL – OR TURK GET ANGRY!
HERE COME THE GAS BOMBS! I CAN'T PLAY FOOTBALL WITH THEM ALL DAY – HURRY!
NICE WORK – AND LOOK! GERMAN GAS MASKS AND STICK GRENADES. JUST WHAT WE NEED.
IT'S COMING.
Moments later –
THE MASKS HAVE SAVED US FROM THE GAS. NOW WE'VE GOTTA MOVE FAST BEFORE THE HAZE CLEARS.
THE WOODS LEAD TO OUR TARGET – BIG KARL, THE GERMAN COASTAL GUN!
THEY HAVE ESCAPED INTO THE FOREST. SERGEANT JAGER – BRING UP THE DOGS!
YOU WERE A HUNTER IN THE BLACK FOREST, SERGEANT?
JA. THE BRITISHERS WILL PROVIDE EXCELLENT SPORT FOR MY DOGS, HERR OBERST.

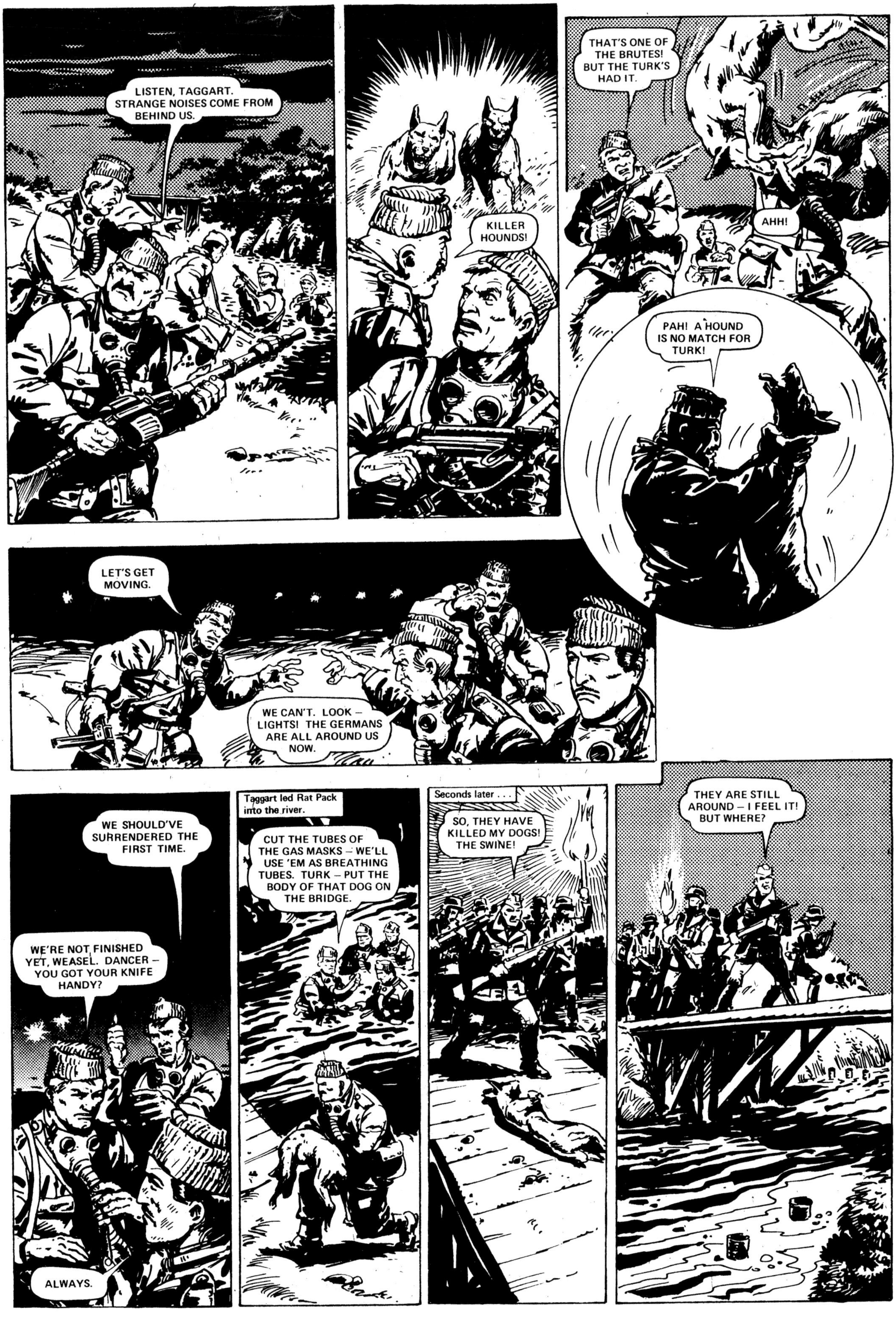

LISTEN, TAGGART. STRANGE NOISES COME FROM BEHIND US.
KILLER HOUNDS!
THAT'S ONE OF THE BRUTES! BUT THE TURK'S HAD IT.
AHH!
PAH! A HOUND IS NO MATCH FOR TURK!
LET'S GET MOVING.
WE CAN'T. LOOK – LIGHTS! THE GERMANS ARE ALL AROUND US NOW.
WE SHOULD'VE SURRENDERED THE FIRST TIME.
WE'RE NOT FINISHED YET, WEASEL. DANCER – YOU GOT YOUR KNIFE HANDY?
ALWAYS.
Taggart led Rat Pack into the river.
CUT THE TUBES OF THE GAS MASKS – WE'LL USE 'EM AS BREATHING TUBES. TURK – PUT THE BODY OF THAT DOG ON THE BRIDGE.
Seconds later . . .
SO, THEY HAVE KILLED MY DOGS! THE SWINE!
THEY ARE STILL AROUND – I FEEL IT! BUT WHERE?

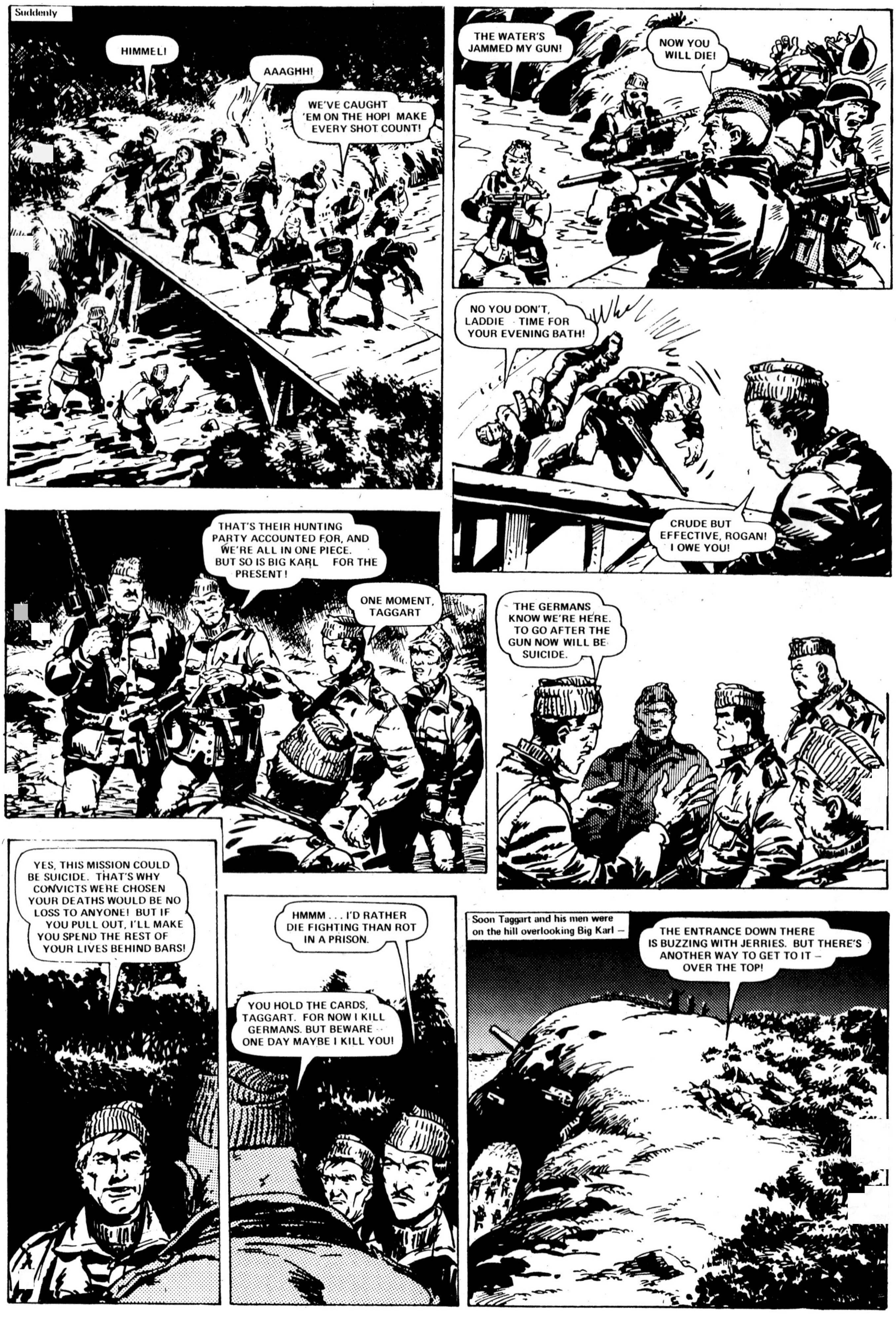
Suddenly
HIMMEL!
AAAGHH!
WE'VE CAUGHT 'EM ON THE HOP! MAKE EVERY SHOT COUNT!
THE WATER'S JAMMED MY GUN!
NOW YOU WILL DIE!
NO YOU DON'T, LADDIE - TIME FOR YOUR EVENING BATH!
CRUDE BUT EFFECTIVE, ROGAN! I OWE YOU!
THAT'S THEIR HUNTING PARTY ACCOUNTED FOR, AND WE'RE ALL IN ONE PIECE. BUT SO IS BIG KARL - FOR THE PRESENT!
ONE MOMENT, TAGGART
THE GERMANS KNOW WE'RE HERE. TO GO AFTER THE GUN NOW WILL BE SUICIDE.
YES, THIS MISSION COULD BE SUICIDE. THAT'S WHY CONVICTS WERE CHOSEN - YOUR DEATHS WOULD BE NO LOSS TO ANYONE! BUT IF YOU PULL OUT, I'LL MAKE YOU SPEND THE REST OF YOUR LIVES BEHIND BARS!
HMMM . . . I'D RATHER DIE FIGHTING THAN ROT IN A PRISON.
YOU HOLD THE CARDS, TAGGART. FOR NOW I KILL GERMANS. BUT BEWARE - ONE DAY MAYBE I KILL YOU!
Soon Taggart and his men were on the hill overlooking Big Karl —
THE ENTRANCE DOWN THERE IS BUZZING WITH JERRIES. BUT THERE'S ANOTHER WAY TO GET TO IT — OVER THE TOP!

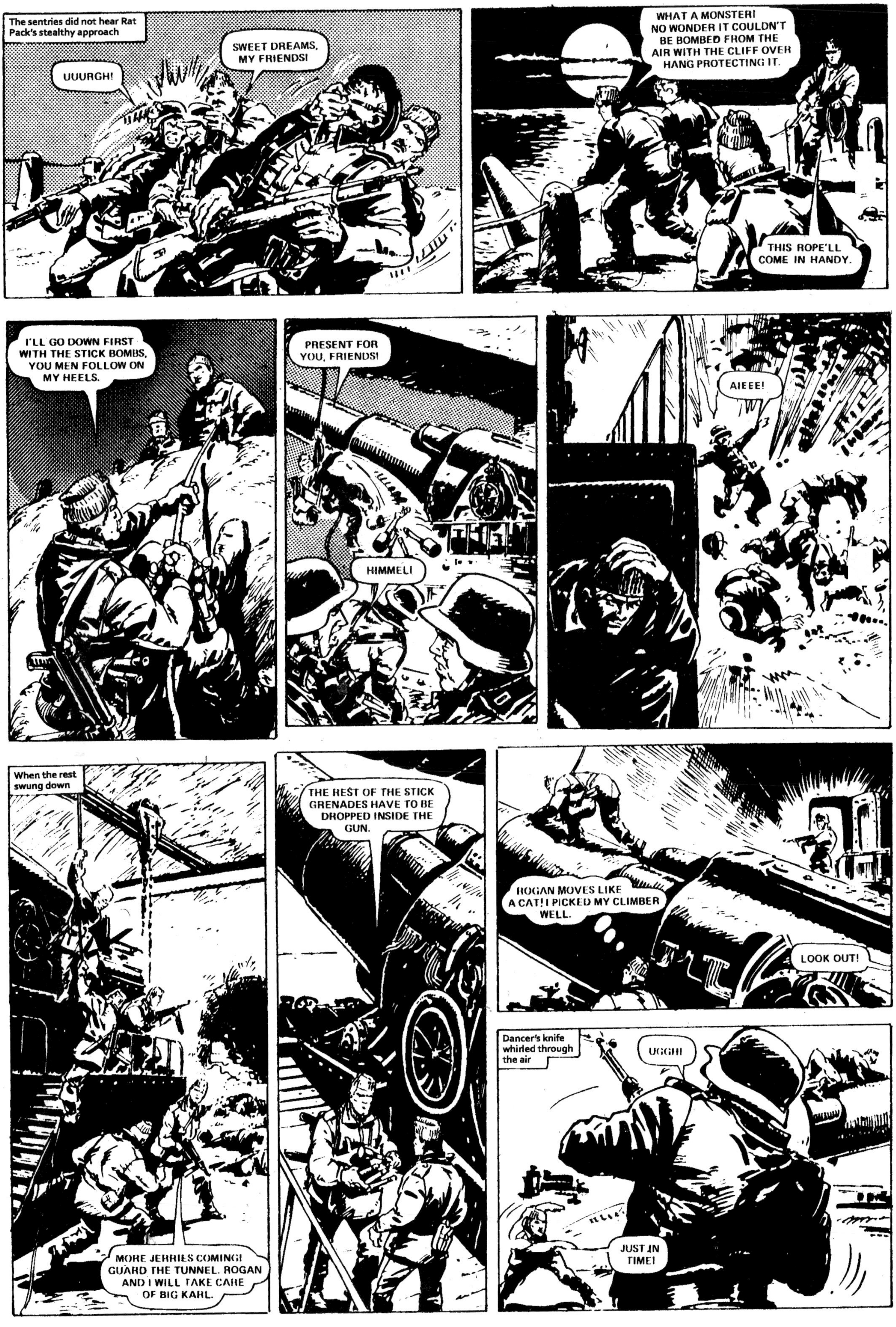
The sentries did not hear Rat Pack's stealthy approach
UUURGH!
SWEET DREAMS, MY FRIENDS!
WHAT A MONSTER! NO WONDER IT COULDN'T BE BOMBED FROM THE AIR WITH THE CLIFF OVER HANG PROTECTING IT.
THIS ROPE'LL COME IN HANDY.
I'LL GO DOWN FIRST WITH THE STICK BOMBS, YOU MEN FOLLOW ON MY HEELS.
PRESENT FOR YOU, FRIENDS!
HIMMEL!
AIEEE!
When the rest swung down
MORE JERRIES COMING! GUARD THE TUNNEL. ROGAN AND I WILL TAKE CARE OF BIG KARL.
THE REST OF THE STICK GRENADES HAVE TO BE DROPPED INSIDE THE GUN.
ROGAN MOVES LIKE A CAT! I PICKED MY CLIMBER WELL.
LOOK OUT!
Dancer's knife whirled through the air
UGGH!
JUST IN TIME!

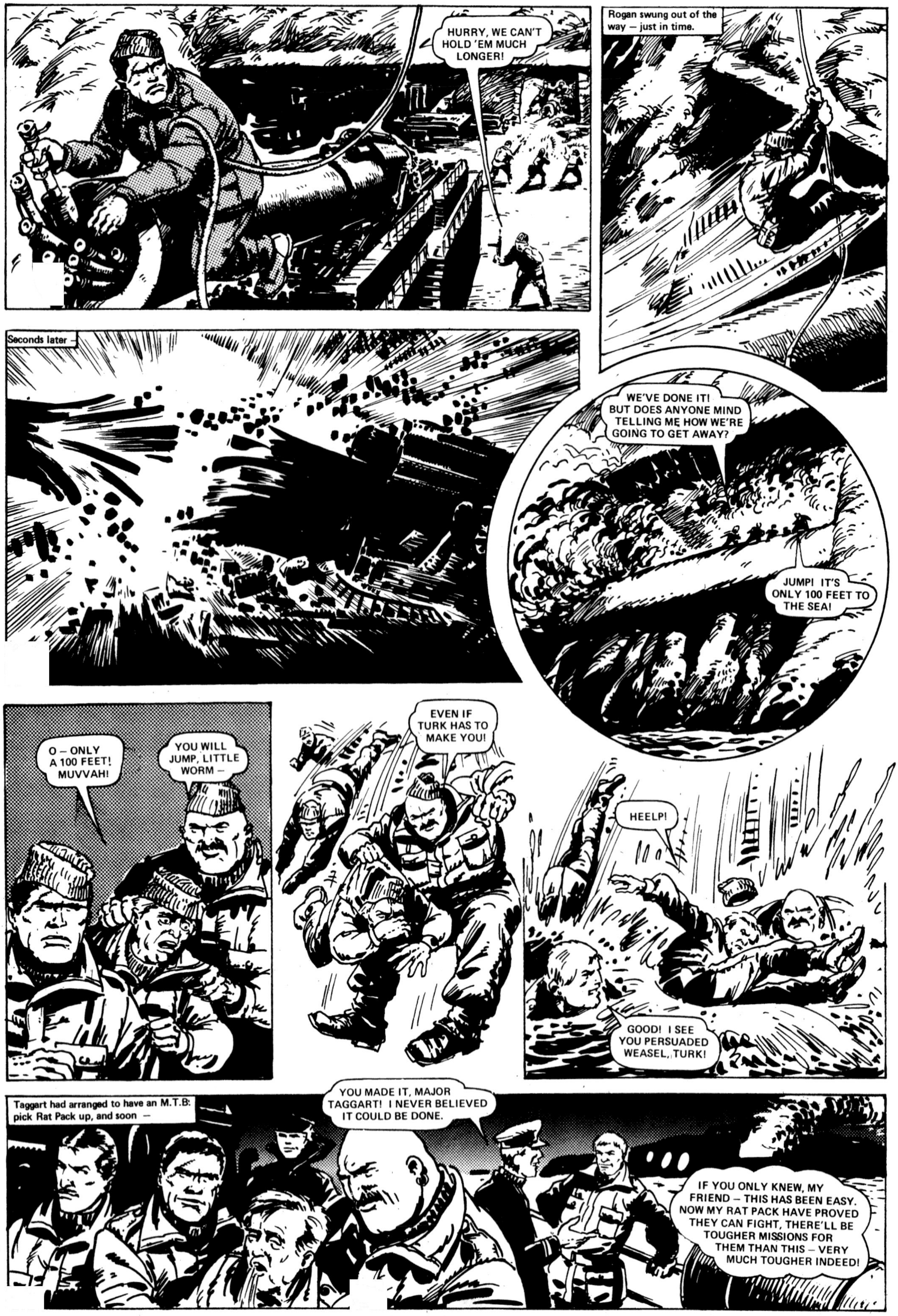
HURRY, WE CAN'T HOLD 'EM MUCH LONGER!
Rogan swung out of the way – just in time.
Seconds later –
WE'VE DONE IT! BUT DOES ANYONE MIND TELLING ME HOW WE'RE GOING TO GET AWAY?
JUMP! IT'S ONLY 100 FEET TO THE SEA!
O – ONLY A 100 FEET! MUVVAH!
YOU WILL JUMP, LITTLE WORM –
EVEN IF TURK HAS TO MAKE YOU!
HEELP!
GOOD! I SEE YOU PERSUADED WEASEL, TURK!
Taggart had arranged to have an M.T.B. pick Rat Pack up, and soon –
YOU MADE IT, MAJOR TAGGART! I NEVER BELIEVED IT COULD BE DONE.
IF YOU ONLY KNEW, MY FRIEND – THIS HAS BEEN EASY. NOW MY RAT PACK HAVE PROVED THEY CAN FIGHT, THERE'LL BE TOUGHER MISSIONS FOR THEM THAN THIS – VERY MUCH TOUGHER INDEED!

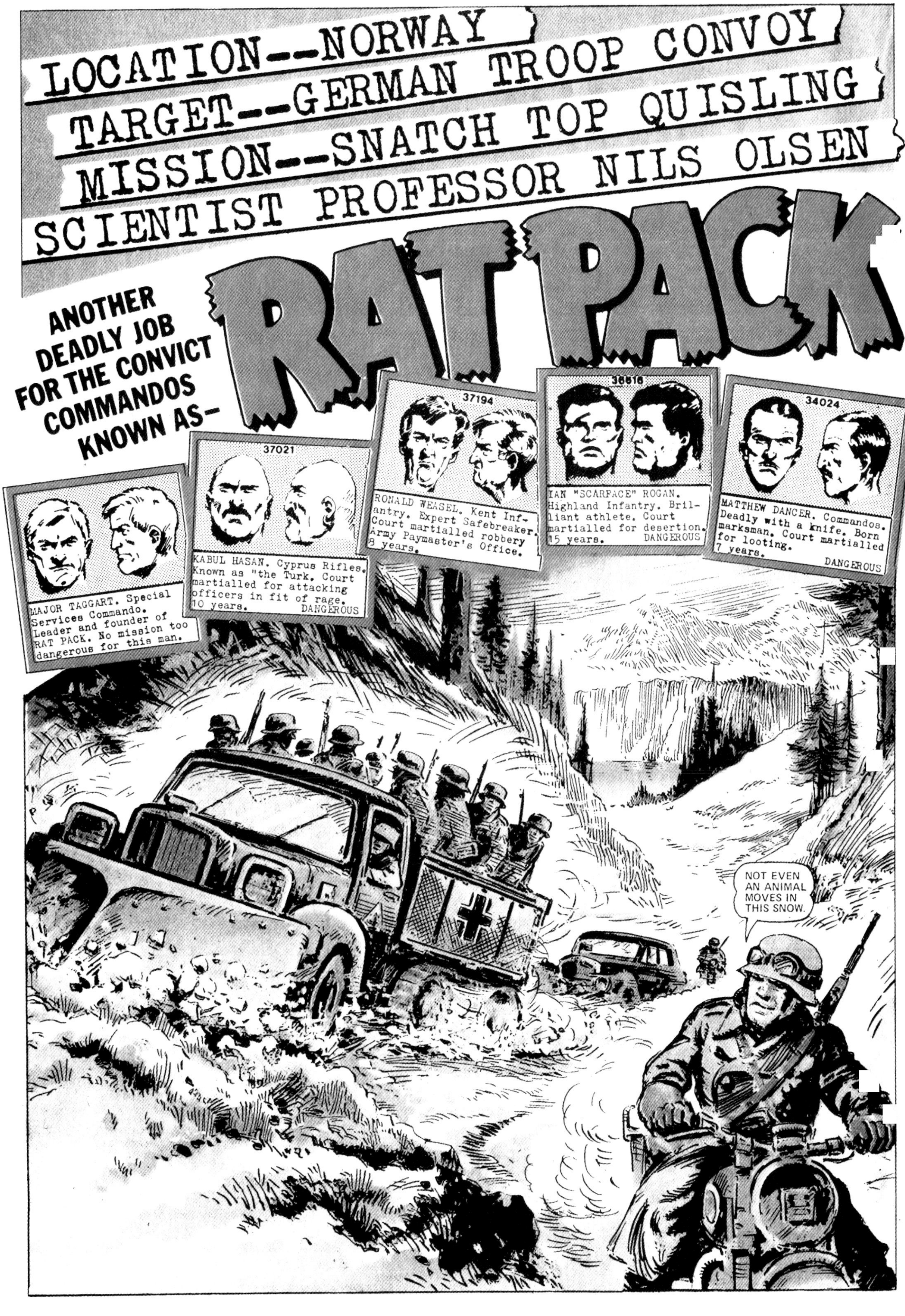

LOCATION--NORWAY
TARGET--GERMAN TROOP CONVOY
MISSION--SNATCH TOP QUISLING
SCIENTIST PROFESSOR NILS OLSEN
ANOTHER DEADLY JOB FOR THE CONVICT COMMANDOS KNOWN AS-
RAT PACK
MAJOR TAGGART. Special Services Commando. Leader and founder of RAT PACK. No mission too dangerous for this man.
37021
KABUL HASAN. Cyprus Rifles. Known as "the Turk. Court martialled for attacking officers in fit of rage. 10 years. DANGEROUS
37194
RONALD WEASEL. Kent Infantry. Expert Safebreaker. Court martialled robbery Army Paymaster's Office. 8 years.
36616
IAN "SCARFACE" ROGAN. Highland Infantry. Brilliant athlete. Court martialled for desertion. 15 years. DANGEROUS
34024
MATTHEW DANCER. Commandos. Deadly with a knife. Born marksman. Court martialled for looting. 7 years. DANGEROUS
NOT EVEN AN ANIMAL MOVES IN THIS SNOW.

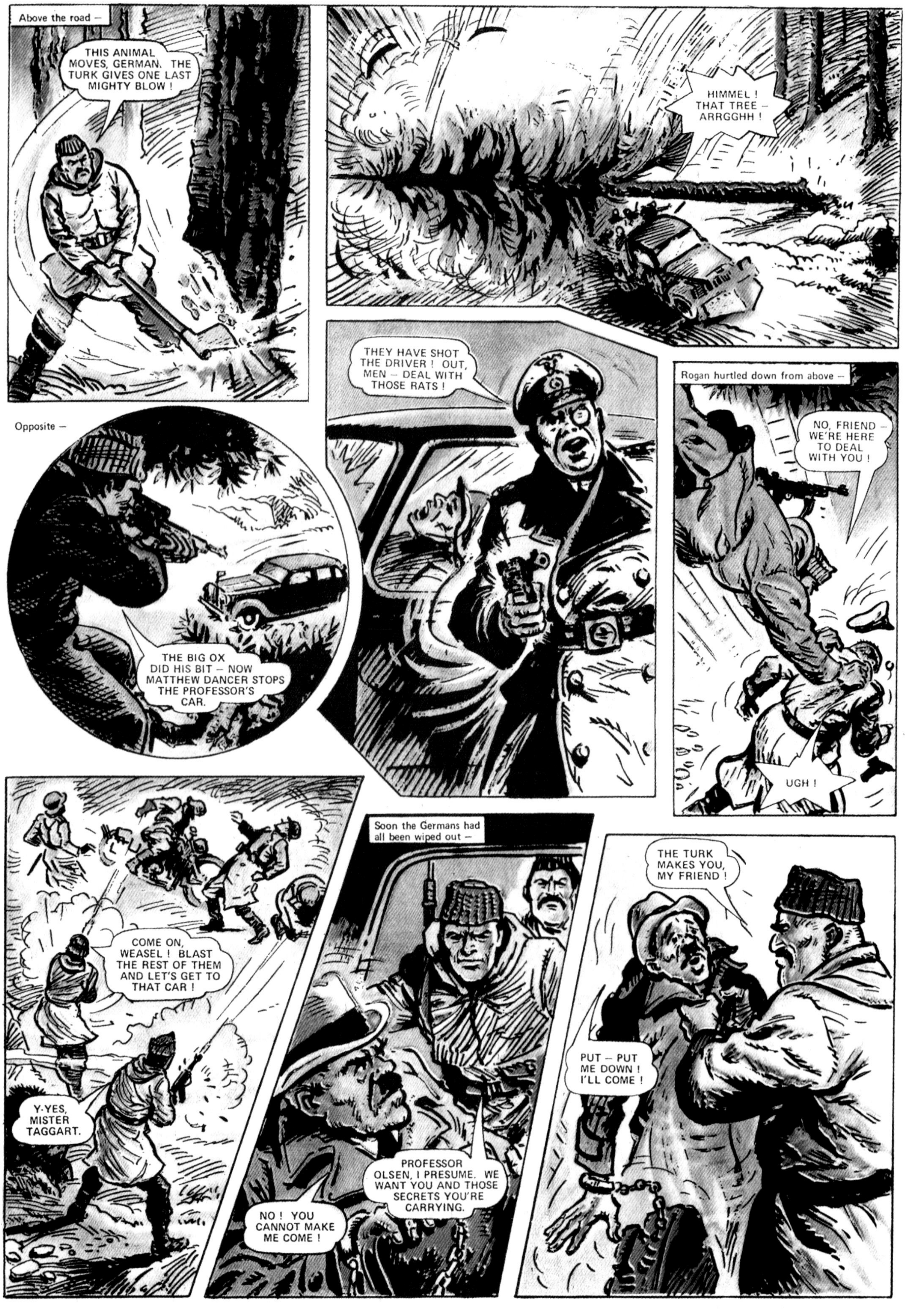
Above the road –
THIS ANIMAL MOVES, GERMAN. THE TURK GIVES ONE LAST MIGHTY BLOW !
HIMMEL ! THAT TREE – ARRGGHH !
Opposite –
THE BIG OX DID HIS BIT – NOW MATTHEW DANCER STOPS THE PROFESSOR'S CAR.
THEY HAVE SHOT THE DRIVER ! OUT, MEN – DEAL WITH THOSE RATS !
Rogan hurtled down from above –
NO, FRIEND – WE'RE HERE TO DEAL WITH YOU !
UGH !
COME ON, WEASEL ! BLAST THE REST OF THEM AND LET'S GET TO THAT CAR !
Y-YES, MISTER TAGGART.
Soon the Germans had all been wiped out –
PROFESSOR OLSEN, I PRESUME. WE WANT YOU AND THOSE SECRETS YOU'RE CARRYING.
NO ! YOU CANNOT MAKE ME COME !
THE TURK MAKES YOU, MY FRIEND !
PUT – PUT ME DOWN ! I'LL COME !

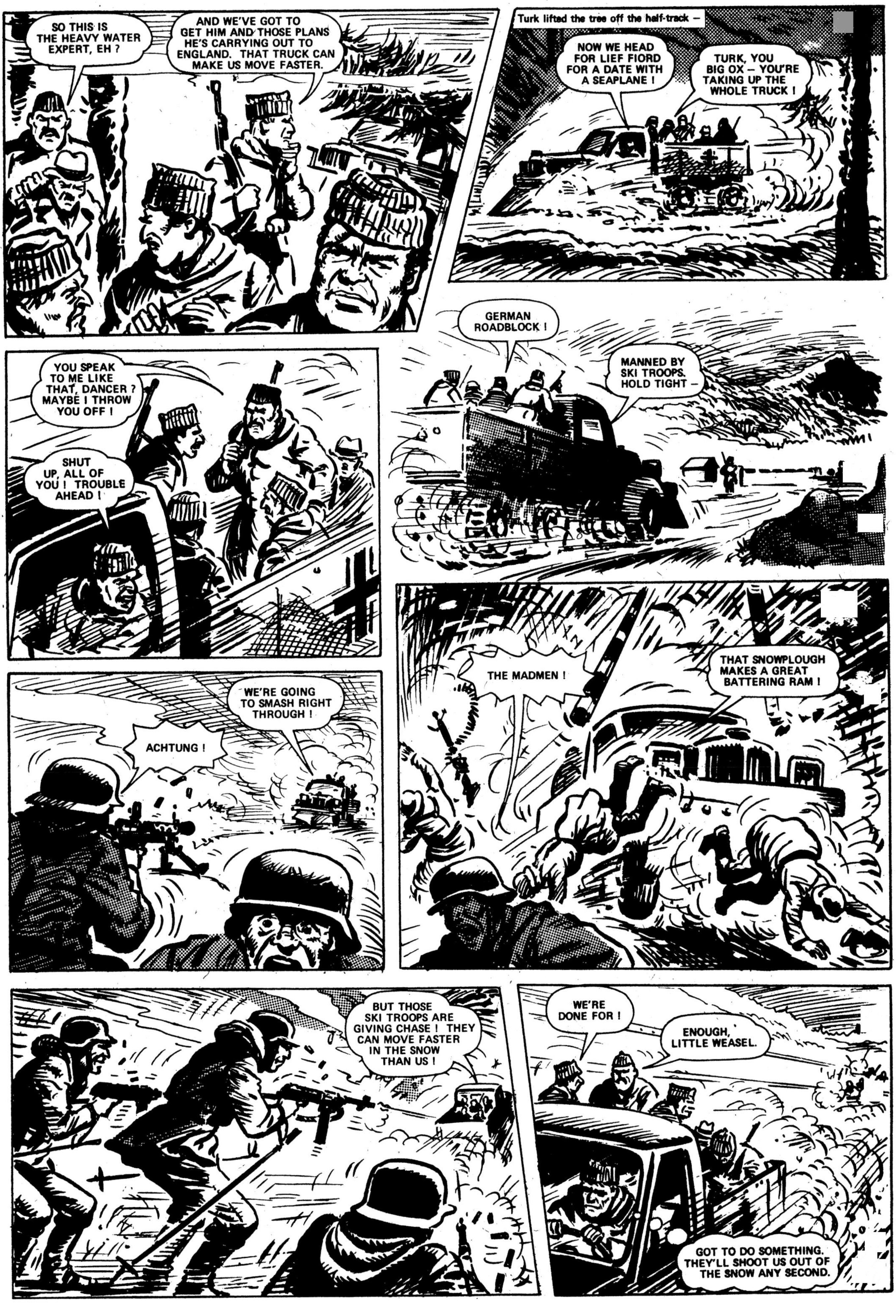
SO THIS IS THE HEAVY WATER EXPERT, EH ?
AND WE'VE GOT TO GET HIM AND THOSE PLANS HE'S CARRYING OUT TO ENGLAND. THAT TRUCK CAN MAKE US MOVE FASTER.
Turk lifted the tree off the half-track –
NOW WE HEAD FOR LIEF FIORD FOR A DATE WITH A SEAPLANE !
TURK, YOU BIG OX – YOU'RE TAKING UP THE WHOLE TRUCK !
YOU SPEAK TO ME LIKE THAT, DANCER ? MAYBE I THROW YOU OFF !
SHUT UP, ALL OF YOU ! TROUBLE AHEAD !
GERMAN ROADBLOCK !
MANNED BY SKI TROOPS. HOLD TIGHT –
WE'RE GOING TO SMASH RIGHT THROUGH !
ACHTUNG !
THE MADMEN !
THAT SNOWPLOUGH MAKES A GREAT BATTERING RAM !
BUT THOSE SKI TROOPS ARE GIVING CHASE ! THEY CAN MOVE FASTER IN THE SNOW THAN US !
WE'RE DONE FOR !
ENOUGH, LITTLE WEASEL.
GOT TO DO SOMETHING. THEY'LL SHOOT US OUT OF THE SNOW ANY SECOND.

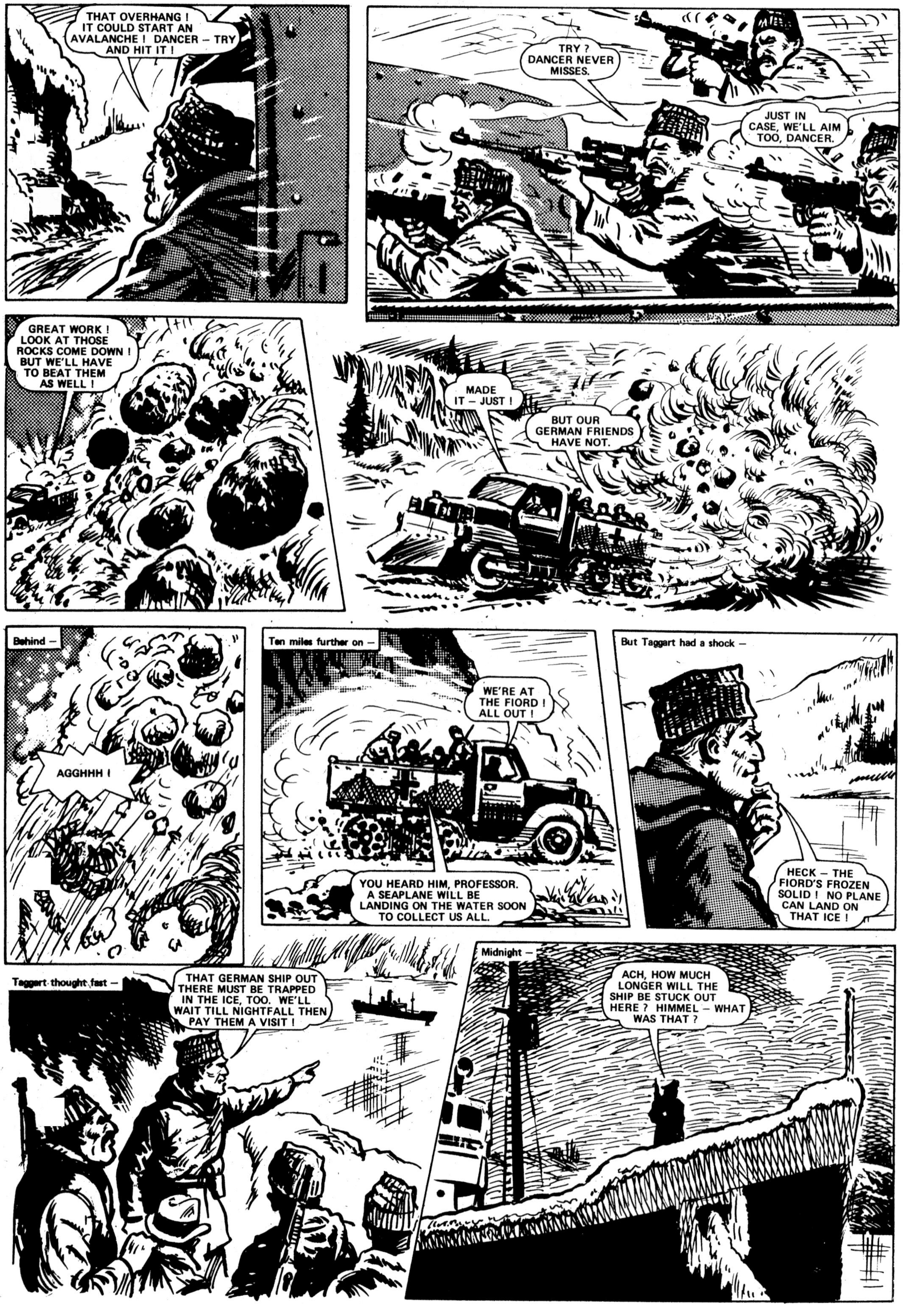
THAT OVERHANG ! IT COULD START AN AVALANCHE ! DANCER – TRY AND HIT IT !
TRY ? DANCER NEVER MISSES.
JUST IN CASE, WE'LL AIM TOO, DANCER.
GREAT WORK ! LOOK AT THOSE ROCKS COME DOWN ! BUT WE'LL HAVE TO BEAT THEM AS WELL !
MADE IT – JUST !
BUT OUR GERMAN FRIENDS HAVE NOT.
Behind –
AGGHHH !
Ten miles further on –
WE'RE AT THE FIORD ! ALL OUT !
YOU HEARD HIM, PROFESSOR. A SEAPLANE WILL BE LANDING ON THE WATER SOON TO COLLECT US ALL.
But Taggart had a shock –
HECK – THE FIORD'S FROZEN SOLID ! NO PLANE CAN LAND ON THAT ICE !
Taggart thought fast –
THAT GERMAN SHIP OUT THERE MUST BE TRAPPED IN THE ICE, TOO. WE'LL WAIT TILL NIGHTFALL THEN PAY THEM A VISIT !
Midnight –
ACH, HOW MUCH LONGER WILL THE SHIP BE STUCK OUT HERE ? HIMMEL – WHAT WAS THAT ?

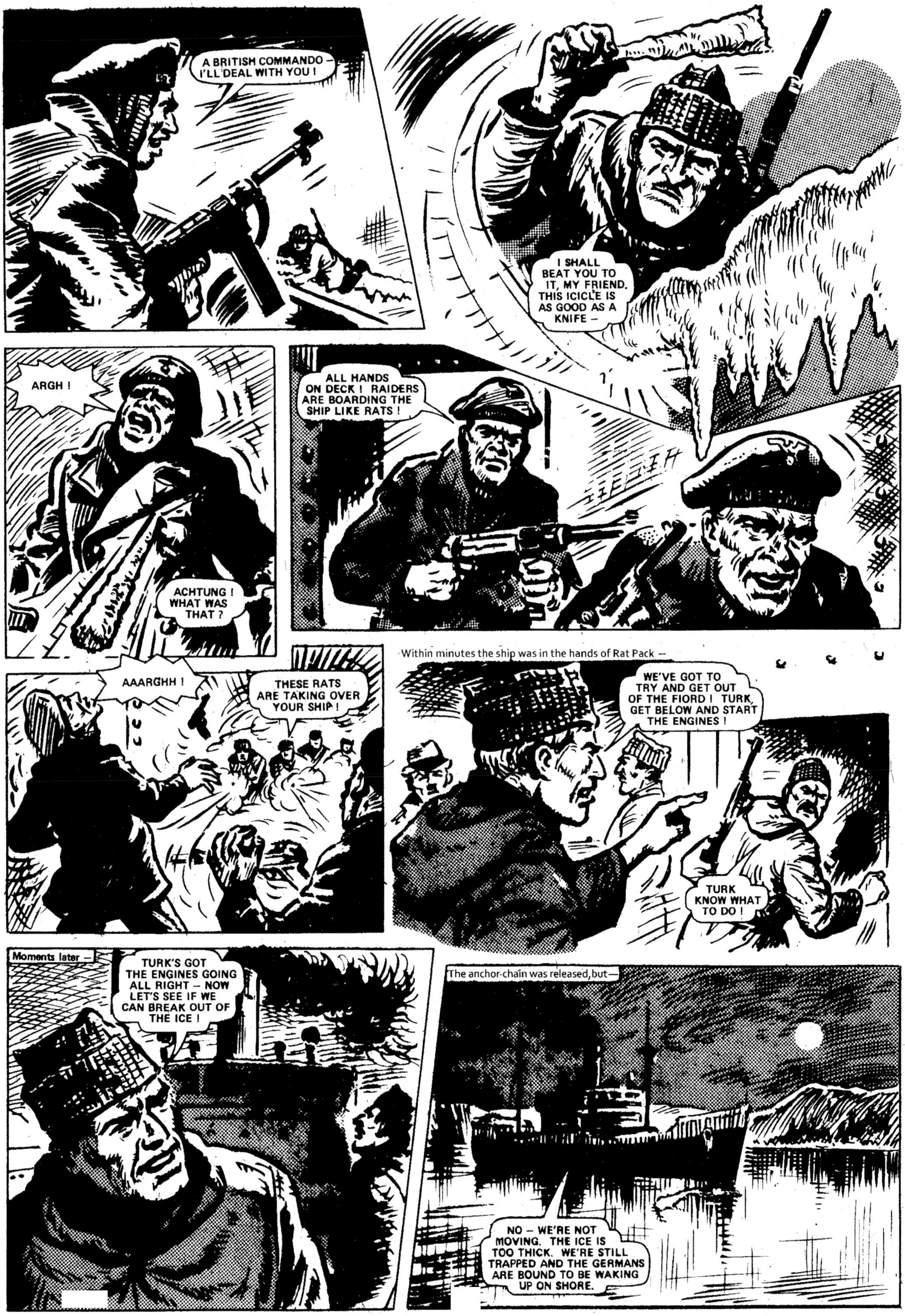
A BRITISH COMMANDO – I'LL DEAL WITH YOU !
I SHALL BEAT YOU TO IT, MY FRIEND. THIS ICICLE IS AS GOOD AS A KNIFE –
ARGH !
ACHTUNG ! WHAT WAS THAT ?
ALL HANDS ON DECK ! RAIDERS ARE BOARDING THE SHIP LIKE RATS !
AAARGHH !
THESE RATS ARE TAKING OVER YOUR SHIP !
Within minutes the ship was in the hands of Rat Pack –
WE'VE GOT TO TRY AND GET OUT OF THE FIORD ! TURK, GET BELOW AND START THE ENGINES !
TURK KNOW WHAT TO DO !
Moments later –
TURK'S GOT THE ENGINES GOING ALL RIGHT – NOW LET'S SEE IF WE CAN BREAK OUT OF THE ICE !
The anchor-chain was released, but–
NO – WE'RE NOT MOVING. THE ICE IS TOO THICK. WE'RE STILL TRAPPED AND THE GERMANS ARE BOUND TO BE WAKING UP ON SHORE.

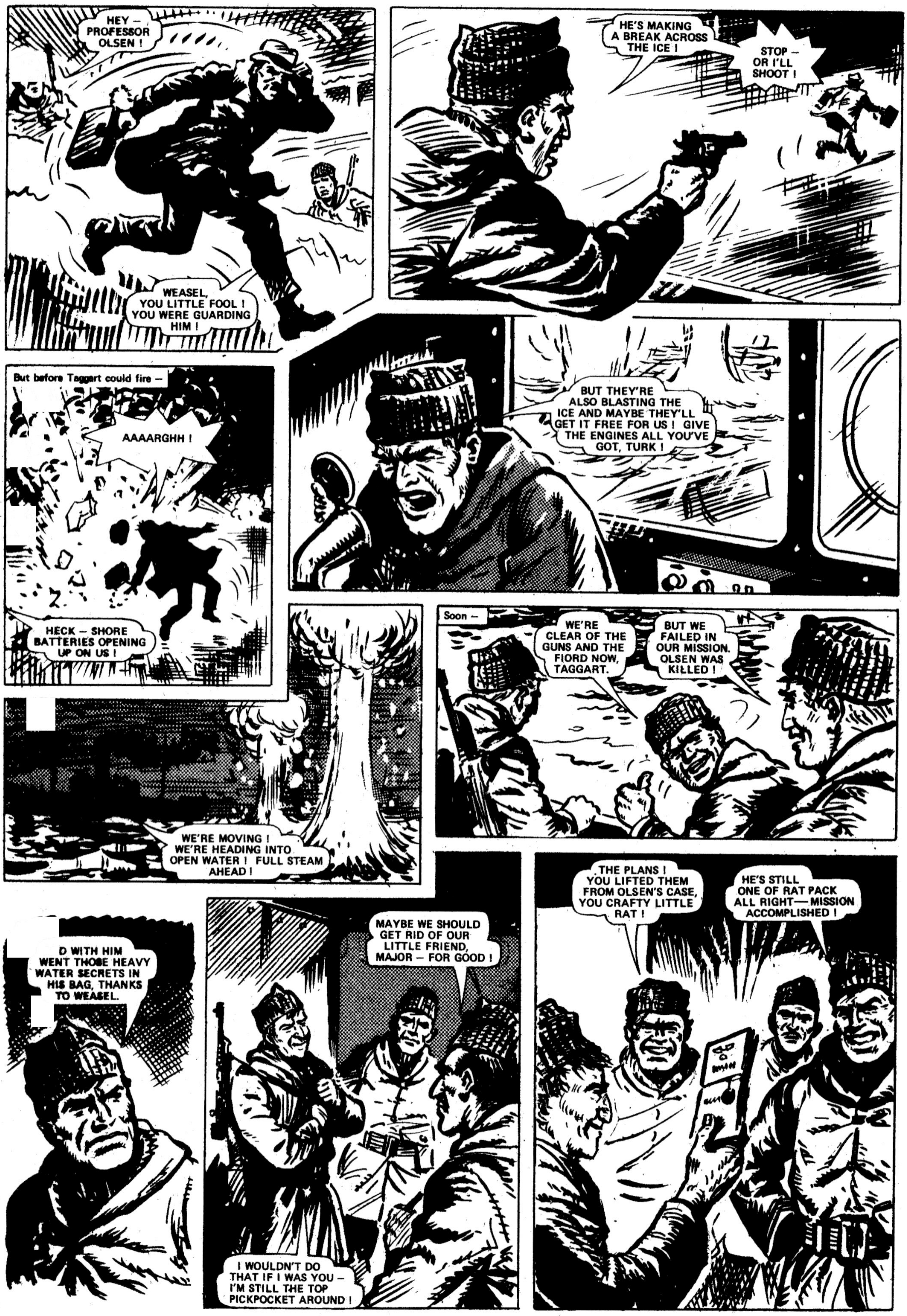
HEY – PROFESSOR OLSEN !
WEASEL, YOU LITTLE FOOL ! YOU WERE GUARDING HIM !
HE'S MAKING A BREAK ACROSS THE ICE !
STOP – OR I'LL SHOOT !
But before Taggart could fire –
AAAARGHH !
HECK – SHORE BATTERIES OPENING UP ON US !
BUT THEY'RE ALSO BLASTING THE ICE AND MAYBE THEY'LL GET IT FREE FOR US ! GIVE THE ENGINES ALL YOU'VE GOT, TURK !
WE'RE MOVING ! WE'RE HEADING INTO OPEN WATER ! FULL STEAM AHEAD !
Soon –
WE'RE CLEAR OF THE GUNS AND THE FIORD NOW, TAGGART.
BUT WE FAILED IN OUR MISSION. OLSEN WAS KILLED !
D WITH HIM WENT THOSE HEAVY WATER SECRETS IN HIS BAG, THANKS TO WEASEL.
MAYBE WE SHOULD GET RID OF OUR LITTLE FRIEND, MAJOR – FOR GOOD !
I WOULDN'T DO THAT IF I WAS YOU – I'M STILL THE TOP PICKPOCKET AROUND !
THE PLANS ! YOU LIFTED THEM FROM OLSEN'S CASE, YOU CRAFTY LITTLE RAT !
HE'S STILL ONE OF RAT PACK ALL RIGHT — MISSION ACCOMPLISHED !

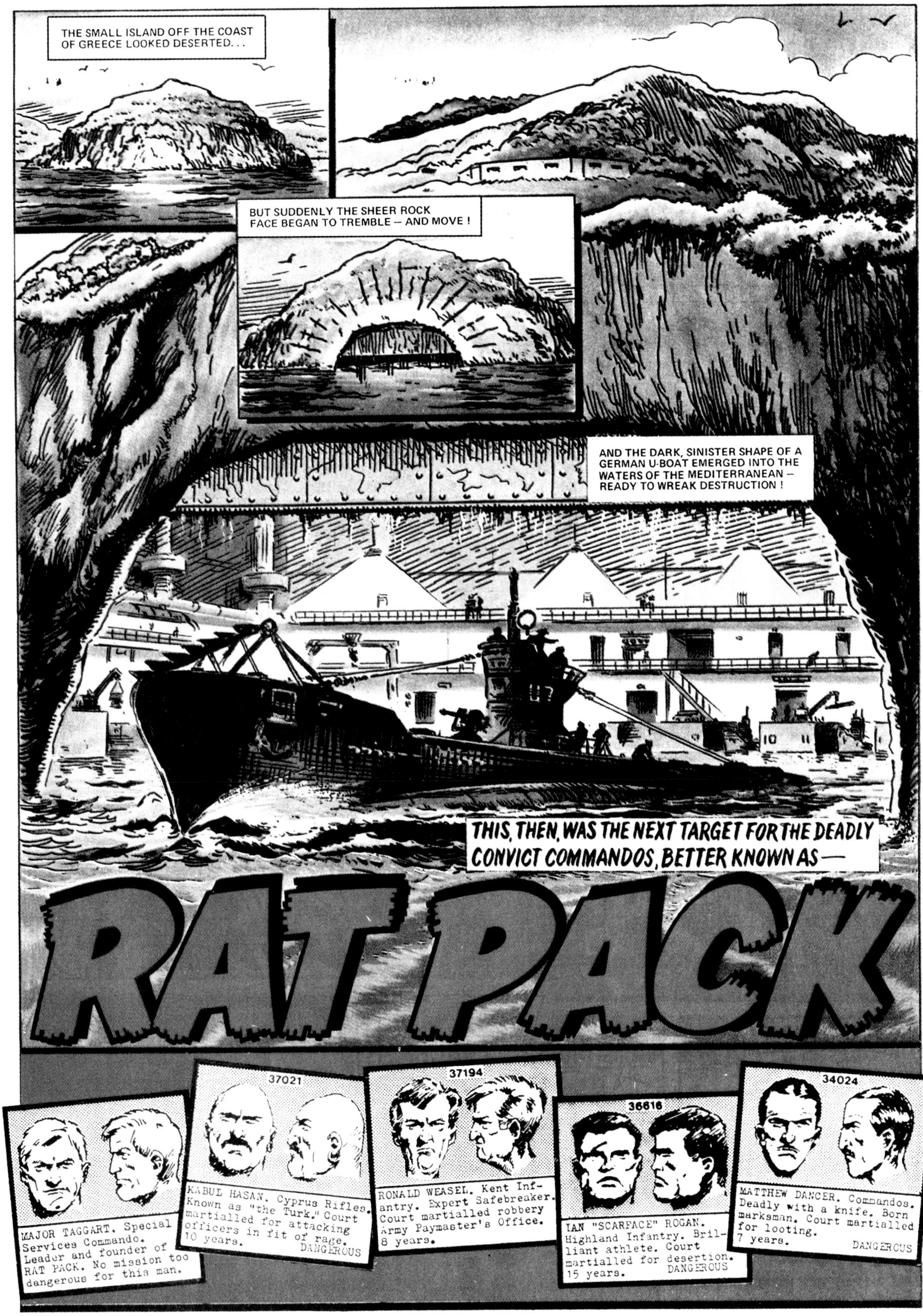

THE SMALL ISLAND OFF THE COAST OF GREECE LOOKED DESERTED...
BUT SUDDENLY THE SHEER ROCK FACE BEGAN TO TREMBLE – AND MOVE !
AND THE DARK, SINISTER SHAPE OF A GERMAN U-BOAT EMERGED INTO THE WATERS OF THE MEDITERRANEAN – READY TO WREAK DESTRUCTION !
THIS, THEN, WAS THE NEXT TARGET FOR THE DEADLY CONVICT COMMANDOS, BETTER KNOWN AS –
RAT PACK
MAJOR TAGGART. Special Services Commando. Leader and founder of RAT PACK. No mission too dangerous for this man.
37021
KABUL HASAN. Cyprus Rifles. Known as "the Turk." Court martialled for attacking officers in fit of rage. 10 years. DANGEROUS
37194
RONALD WEASEL. Kent Infantry. Expert Safebreaker. Court martialled robbery Army Paymaster's Office. 8 years.
36616
IAN "SCARFACE" ROGAN. Highland Infantry. Brilliant athlete. Court martialled for desertion. 15 years. DANGEROUS
34024
MATTHEW DANCER. Commandos. Deadly with a knife. Born marksman. Court martialled for looting. 7 years. DANGEROUS

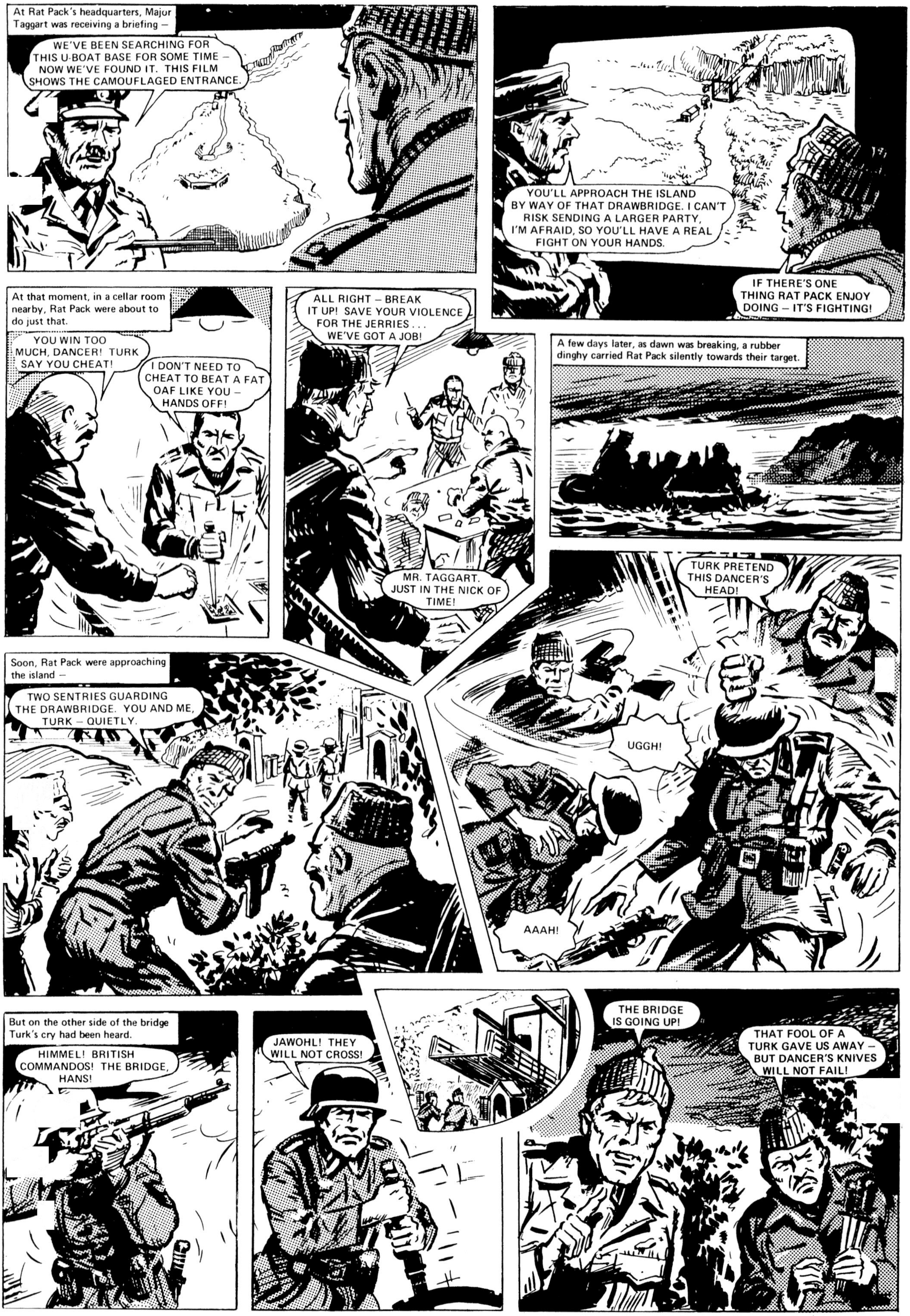

At Rat Pack's headquarters, Major Taggart was receiving a briefing –
WE'VE BEEN SEARCHING FOR THIS U-BOAT BASE FOR SOME TIME – NOW WE'VE FOUND IT. THIS FILM SHOWS THE CAMOUFLAGED ENTRANCE.
YOU'LL APPROACH THE ISLAND BY WAY OF THAT DRAWBRIDGE. I CAN'T RISK SENDING A LARGER PARTY, I'M AFRAID, SO YOU'LL HAVE A REAL FIGHT ON YOUR HANDS.
IF THERE'S ONE THING RAT PACK ENJOY DOING – IT'S FIGHTING!
At that moment, in a cellar room nearby, Rat Pack were about to do just that.
YOU WIN TOO MUCH, DANCER! TURK SAY YOU CHEAT!
I DON'T NEED TO CHEAT TO BEAT A FAT OAF LIKE YOU – HANDS OFF!
ALL RIGHT – BREAK IT UP! SAVE YOUR VIOLENCE FOR THE JERRIES . . . WE'VE GOT A JOB!
MR. TAGGART. JUST IN THE NICK OF TIME!
A few days later, as dawn was breaking, a rubber dinghy carried Rat Pack silently towards their target.
Soon, Rat Pack were approaching the island –
TWO SENTRIES GUARDING THE DRAWBRIDGE. YOU AND ME, TURK – QUIETLY.
TURK PRETEND THIS DANCER'S HEAD!
UGGH!
AAAH!
But on the other side of the bridge Turk's cry had been heard.
HIMMEL! BRITISH COMMANDOS! THE BRIDGE, HANS!
JAWOHL! THEY WILL NOT CROSS!
THE BRIDGE IS GOING UP!
THAT FOOL OF A TURK GAVE US AWAY – BUT DANCER'S KNIVES WILL NOT FAIL!

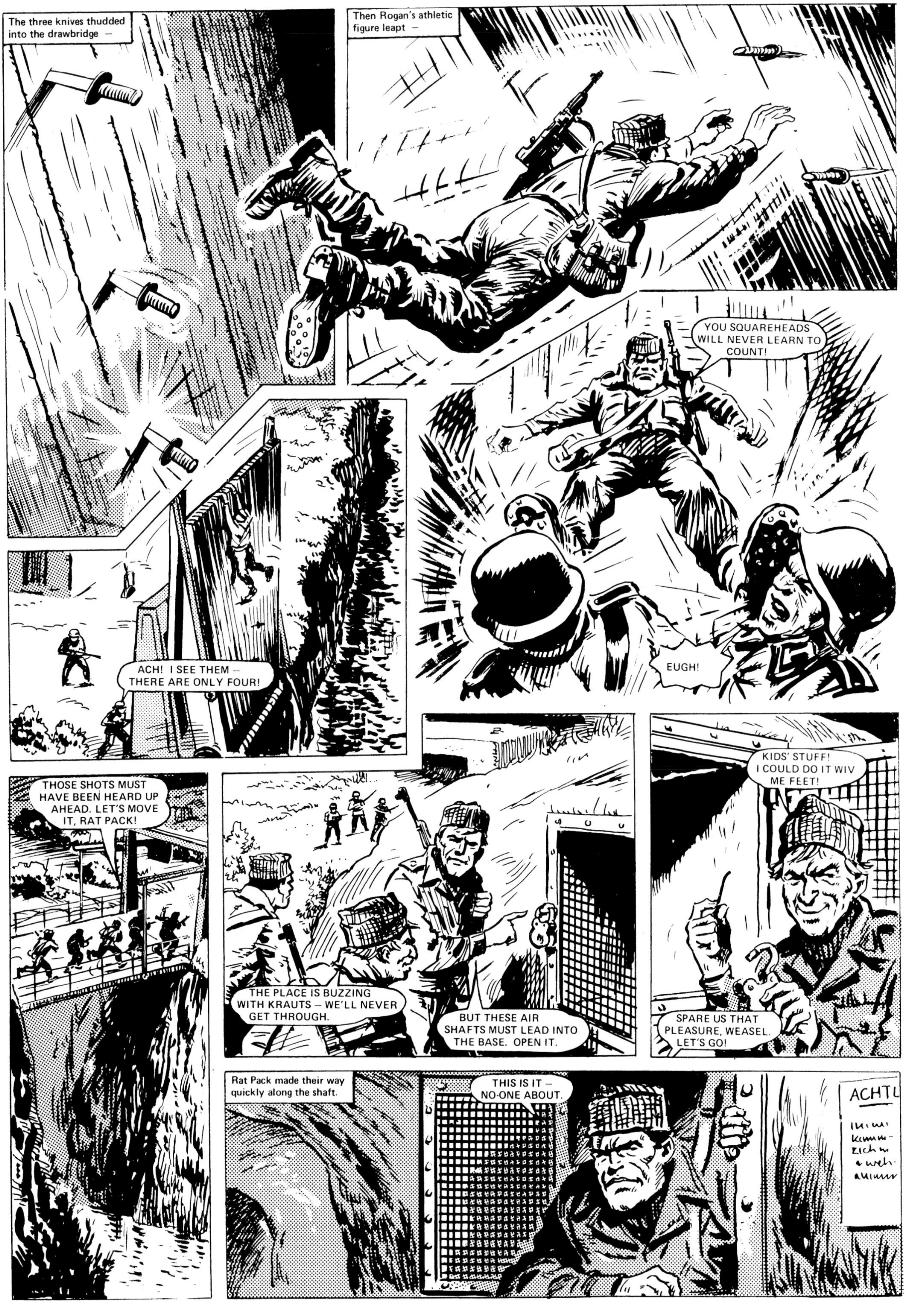

The three knives thudded into the drawbridge —
Then Rogan's athletic figure leapt —
YOU SQUAREHEADS WILL NEVER LEARN TO COUNT!
ACH! I SEE THEM — THERE ARE ONLY FOUR!
EUGH!
THOSE SHOTS MUST HAVE BEEN HEARD UP AHEAD. LET'S MOVE IT, RAT PACK!
THE PLACE IS BUZZING WITH KRAUTS — WE'LL NEVER GET THROUGH.
BUT THESE AIR SHAFTS MUST LEAD INTO THE BASE. OPEN IT.
KIDS' STUFF! I COULD DO IT WIV ME FEET!
SPARE US THAT PLEASURE, WEASEL. LET'S GO!
Rat Pack made their way quickly along the shaft.
THIS IS IT — NO-ONE ABOUT.
ACHTU

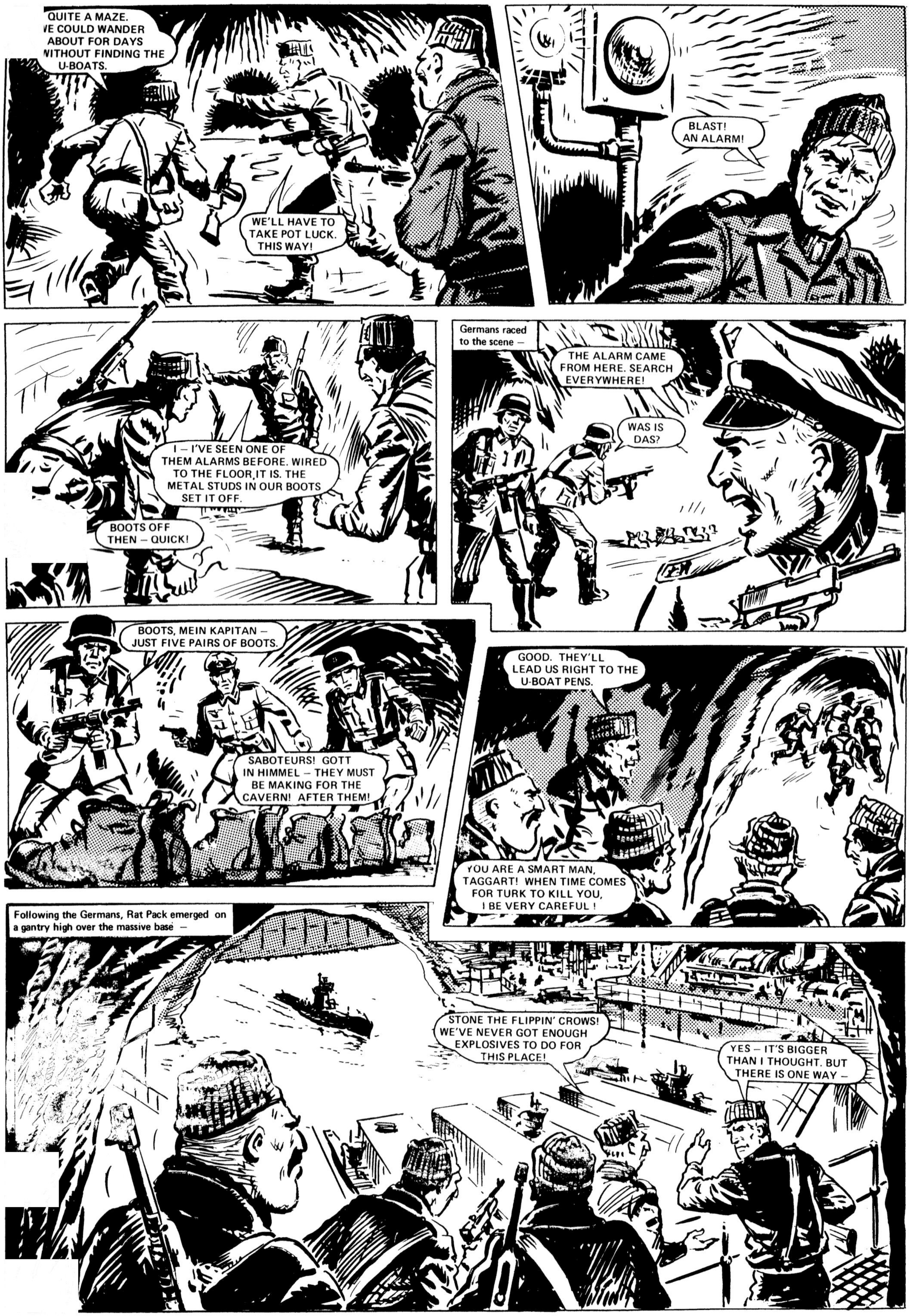
QUITE A MAZE. WE COULD WANDER ABOUT FOR DAYS WITHOUT FINDING THE U-BOATS.
WE'LL HAVE TO TAKE POT LUCK. THIS WAY!
BLAST! AN ALARM!
I – I'VE SEEN ONE OF THEM ALARMS BEFORE. WIRED TO THE FLOOR, IT IS. THE METAL STUDS IN OUR BOOTS SET IT OFF.
BOOTS OFF THEN – QUICK!
Germans raced to the scene –
THE ALARM CAME FROM HERE. SEARCH EVERYWHERE!
WAS IS DAS?
BOOTS, MEIN KAPITAN – JUST FIVE PAIRS OF BOOTS.
SABOTEURS! GOTT IN HIMMEL – THEY MUST BE MAKING FOR THE CAVERN! AFTER THEM!
GOOD. THEY'LL LEAD US RIGHT TO THE U-BOAT PENS.
YOU ARE A SMART MAN, TAGGART! WHEN TIME COMES FOR TURK TO KILL YOU, I BE VERY CAREFUL!
Following the Germans, Rat Pack emerged on a gantry high over the massive base –
STONE THE FLIPPIN' CROWS! WE'VE NEVER GOT ENOUGH EXPLOSIVES TO DO FOR THIS PLACE!
YES – IT'S BIGGER THAN I THOUGHT. BUT THERE IS ONE WAY –

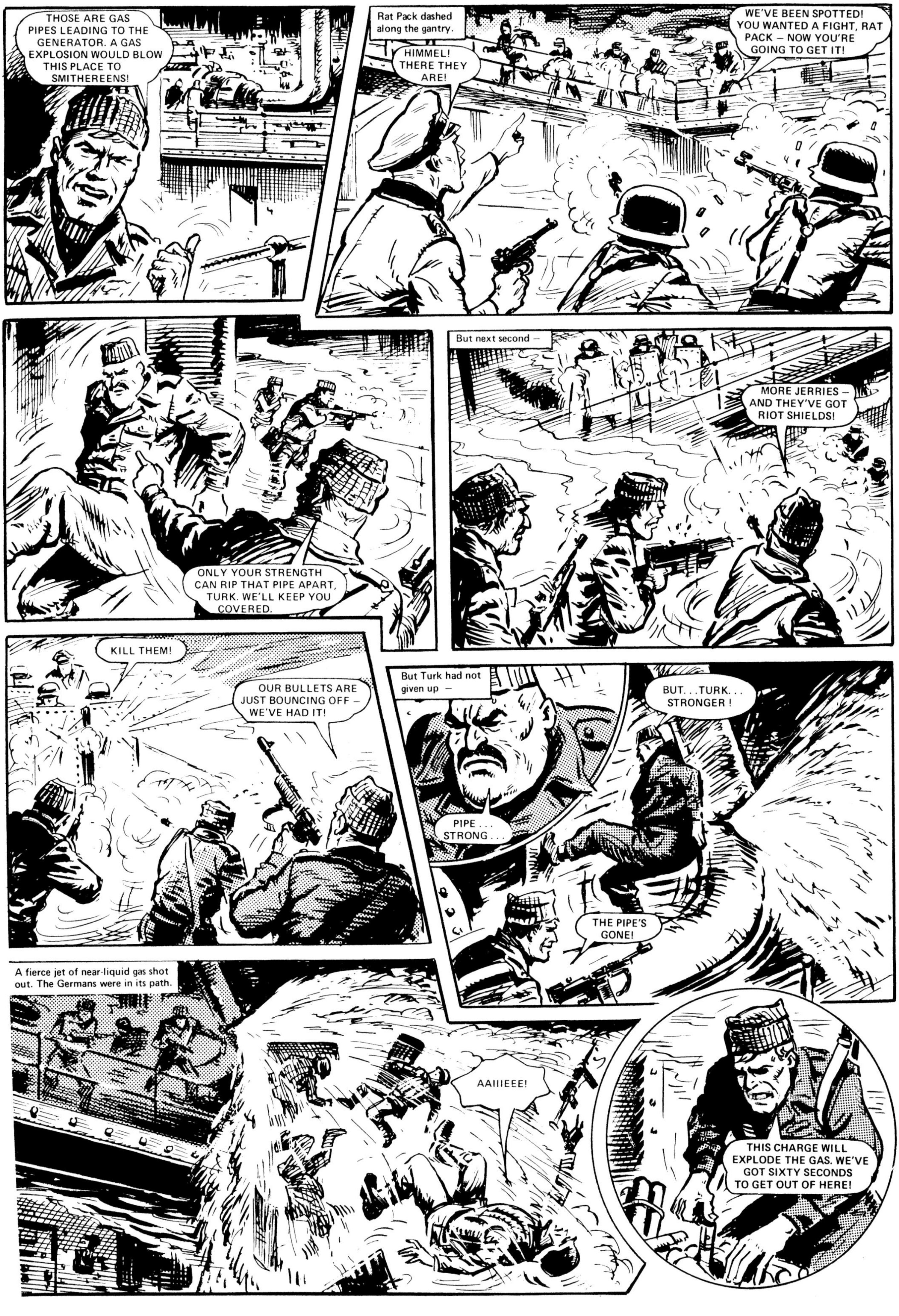
THOSE ARE GAS PIPES LEADING TO THE GENERATOR. A GAS EXPLOSION WOULD BLOW THIS PLACE TO SMITHEREENS!
Rat Pack dashed along the gantry.
HIMMEL! THERE THEY ARE!
WE'VE BEEN SPOTTED! YOU WANTED A FIGHT, RAT PACK – NOW YOU'RE GOING TO GET IT!
ONLY YOUR STRENGTH CAN RIP THAT PIPE APART, TURK. WE'LL KEEP YOU COVERED.
But next second –
MORE JERRIES – AND THEY'VE GOT RIOT SHIELDS!
KILL THEM!
OUR BULLETS ARE JUST BOUNCING OFF – WE'VE HAD IT!
But Turk had not given up –
PIPE . . . STRONG . . .
BUT. . .TURK. . . STRONGER !
THE PIPE'S GONE!
A fierce jet of near-liquid gas shot out. The Germans were in its path.
AAIIIEEE!
THIS CHARGE WILL EXPLODE THE GAS. WE'VE GOT SIXTY SECONDS TO GET OUT OF HERE!

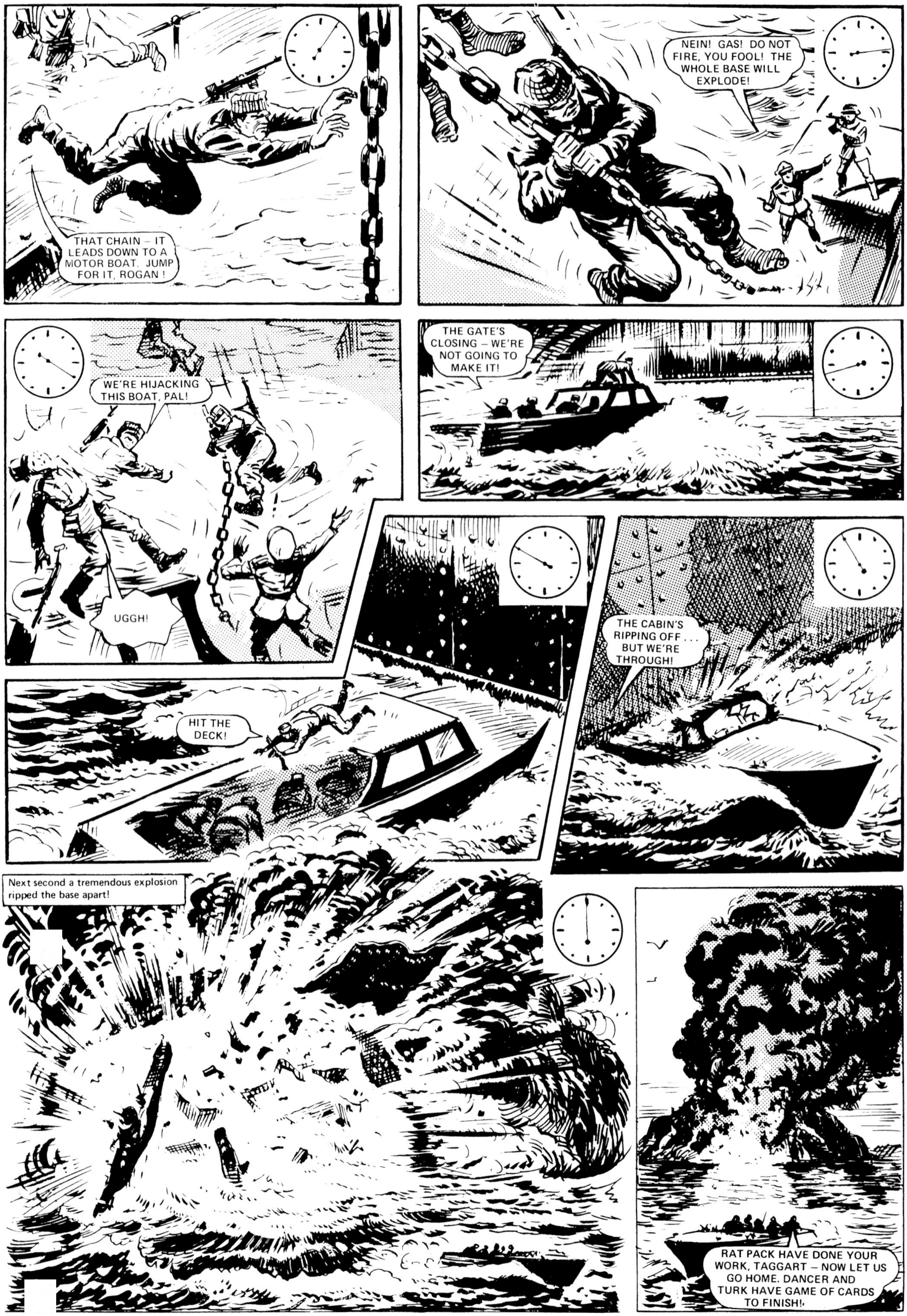
THAT CHAIN – IT LEADS DOWN TO A MOTOR BOAT. JUMP FOR IT, ROGAN !
NEIN! GAS! DO NOT FIRE, YOU FOOL! THE WHOLE BASE WILL EXPLODE!
WE'RE HIJACKING THIS BOAT, PAL!
UGGH!
THE GATE'S CLOSING – WE'RE NOT GOING TO MAKE IT!
HIT THE DECK!
THE CABIN'S RIPPING OFF . . . BUT WE'RE THROUGH!
Next second a tremendous explosion ripped the base apart!
RAT PACK HAVE DONE YOUR WORK, TAGGART – NOW LET US GO HOME. DANCER AND TURK HAVE GAME OF CARDS TO FINISH!

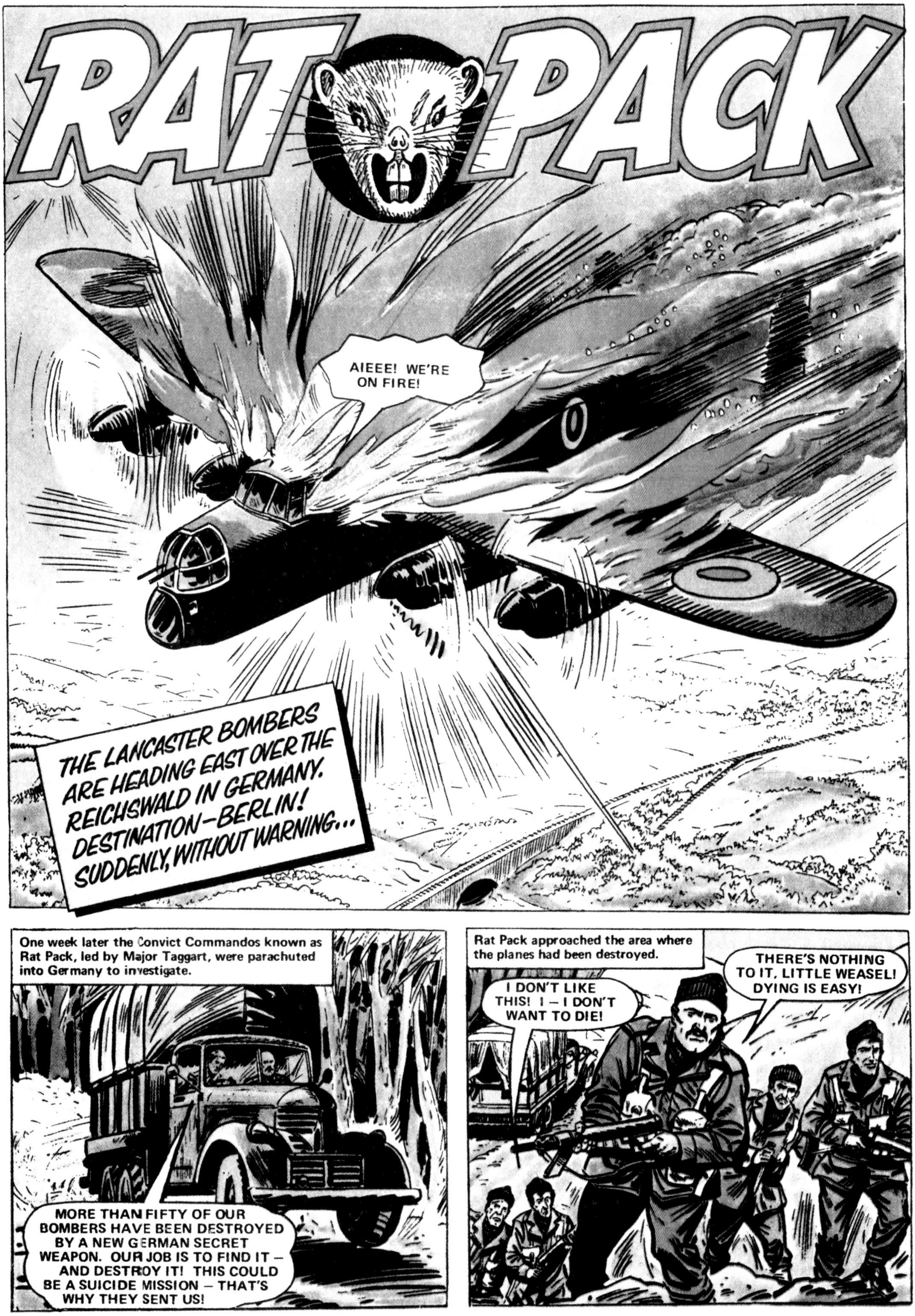
RAT PACK
AIEEE! WE'RE ON FIRE!
THE LANCASTER BOMBERS ARE HEADING EAST OVER THE REICHSWALD IN GERMANY. DESTINATION–BERLIN! SUDDENLY, WITHOUT WARNING...
One week later the Convict Commandos known as Rat Pack, led by Major Taggart, were parachuted into Germany to investigate.
MORE THAN FIFTY OF OUR BOMBERS HAVE BEEN DESTROYED BY A NEW GERMAN SECRET WEAPON. OUR JOB IS TO FIND IT – AND DESTROY IT! THIS COULD BE A SUICIDE MISSION – THAT'S WHY THEY SENT US!
Rat Pack approached the area where the planes had been destroyed.
I DON'T LIKE THIS! I – I DON'T WANT TO DIE!
THERE'S NOTHING TO IT, LITTLE WEASEL! DYING IS EASY!

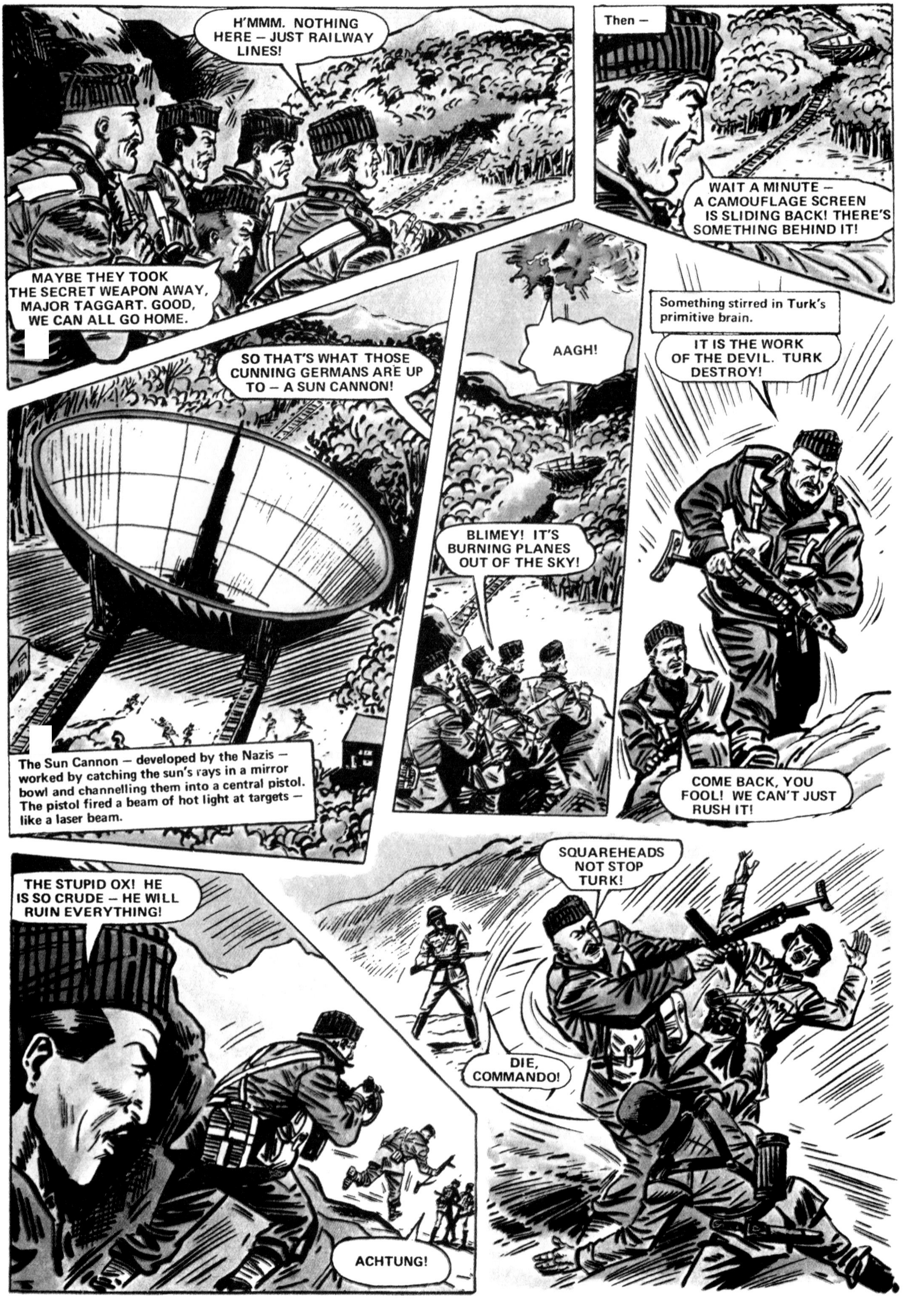
H'MMM. NOTHING HERE – JUST RAILWAY LINES!
MAYBE THEY TOOK THE SECRET WEAPON AWAY, MAJOR TAGGART. GOOD, WE CAN ALL GO HOME.
Then –
WAIT A MINUTE – A CAMOUFLAGE SCREEN IS SLIDING BACK! THERE'S SOMETHING BEHIND IT!
SO THAT'S WHAT THOSE CUNNING GERMANS ARE UP TO – A SUN CANNON!
The Sun Cannon – developed by the Nazis – worked by catching the sun's rays in a mirror bowl and channelling them into a central pistol. The pistol fired a beam of hot light at targets – like a laser beam.
AAGH!
BLIMEY! IT'S BURNING PLANES OUT OF THE SKY!
Something stirred in Turk's primitive brain.
IT IS THE WORK OF THE DEVIL. TURK DESTROY!
COME BACK, YOU FOOL! WE CAN'T JUST RUSH IT!
THE STUPID OX! HE IS SO CRUDE – HE WILL RUIN EVERYTHING!
ACHTUNG!
SQUAREHEADS NOT STOP TURK!
DIE, COMMANDO!

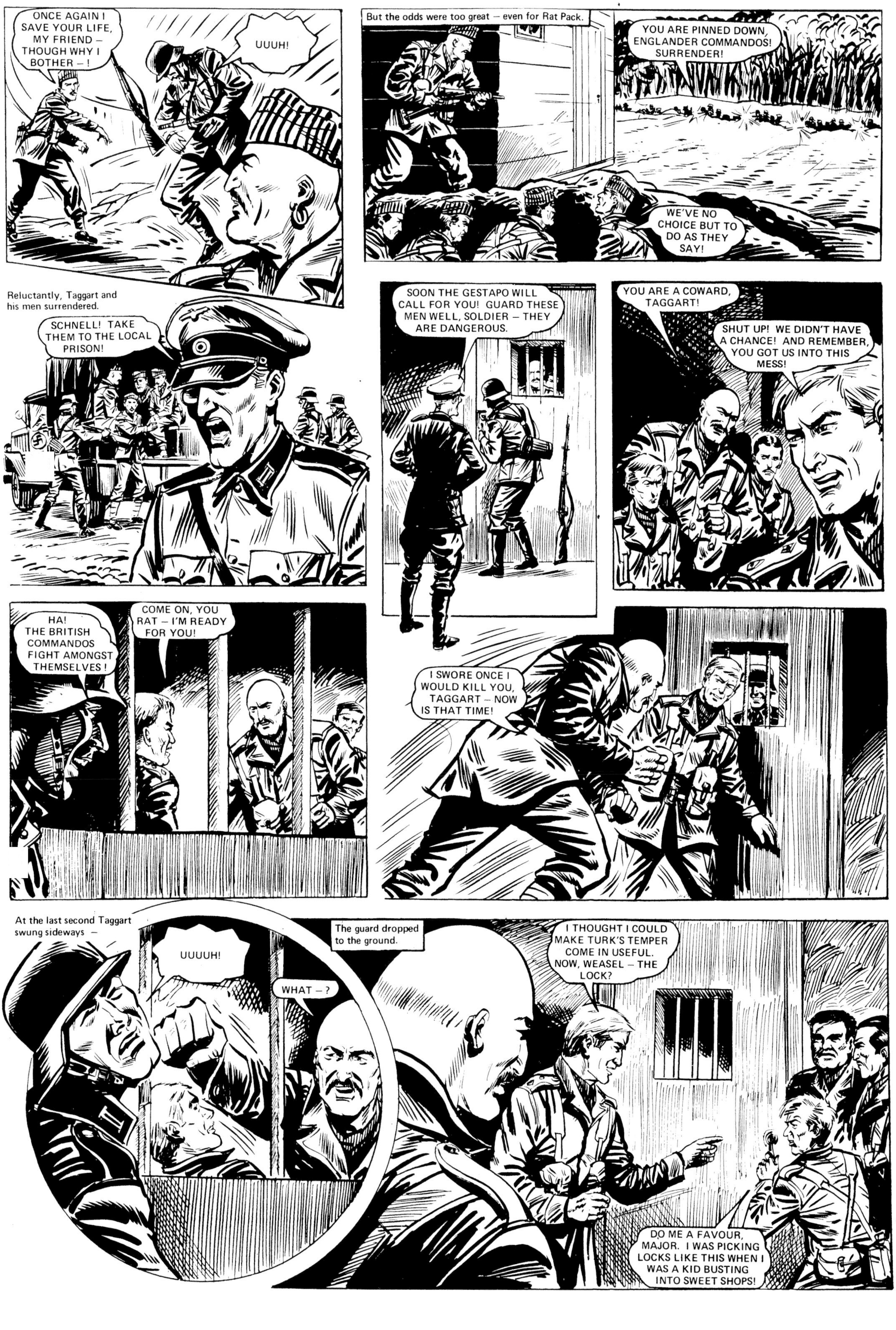

ONCE AGAIN I SAVE YOUR LIFE, MY FRIEND – THOUGH WHY I BOTHER – !
UUUH!
But the odds were too great – even for Rat Pack.
YOU ARE PINNED DOWN, ENGLANDER COMMANDOS! SURRENDER!
WE'VE NO CHOICE BUT TO DO AS THEY SAY!
Reluctantly, Taggart and his men surrendered.
SCHNELL! TAKE THEM TO THE LOCAL PRISON!
SOON THE GESTAPO WILL CALL FOR YOU! GUARD THESE MEN WELL, SOLDIER – THEY ARE DANGEROUS.
YOU ARE A COWARD, TAGGART!
SHUT UP! WE DIDN'T HAVE A CHANCE! AND REMEMBER, YOU GOT US INTO THIS MESS!
HA! THE BRITISH COMMANDOS FIGHT AMONGST THEMSELVES!
COME ON, YOU RAT – I'M READY FOR YOU!
I SWORE ONCE I WOULD KILL YOU, TAGGART – NOW IS THAT TIME!
At the last second Taggart swung sideways –
UUUUH!
WHAT – ?
The guard dropped to the ground.
I THOUGHT I COULD MAKE TURK'S TEMPER COME IN USEFUL. NOW, WEASEL – THE LOCK?
DO ME A FAVOUR, MAJOR. I WAS PICKING LOCKS LIKE THIS WHEN I WAS A KID BUSTING INTO SWEET SHOPS!

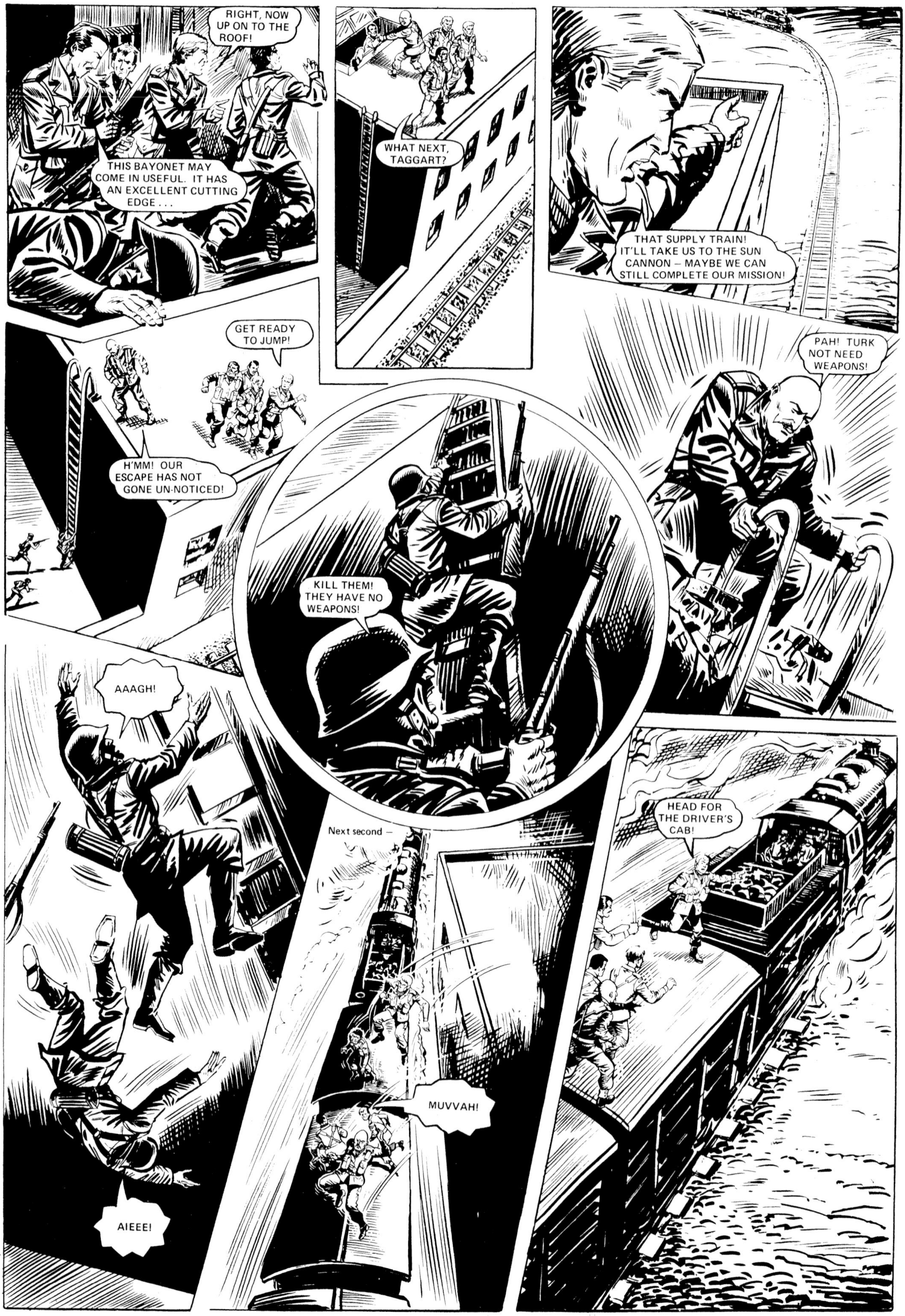
RIGHT, NOW UP ON TO THE ROOF!
THIS BAYONET MAY COME IN USEFUL. IT HAS AN EXCELLENT CUTTING EDGE . . .
WHAT NEXT, TAGGART?
THAT SUPPLY TRAIN! IT'LL TAKE US TO THE SUN CANNON – MAYBE WE CAN STILL COMPLETE OUR MISSION!
GET READY TO JUMP!
H'MM! OUR ESCAPE HAS NOT GONE UN-NOTICED!
KILL THEM! THEY HAVE NO WEAPONS!
PAH! TURK NOT NEED WEAPONS!
AAAGH!
AIEEE!
Next second –
MUVVAH!
HEAD FOR THE DRIVER'S CAB!

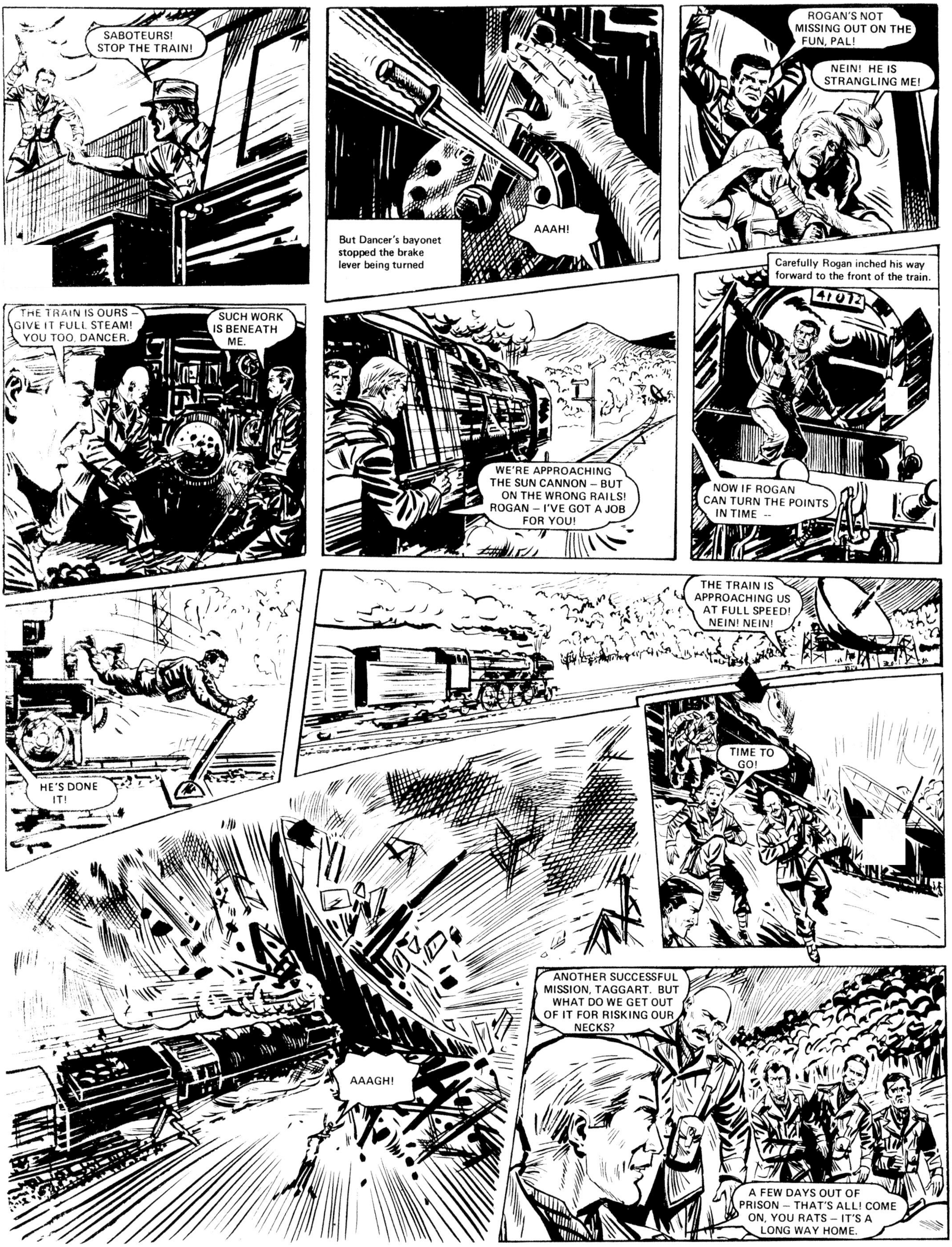
SABOTEURS! STOP THE TRAIN!
But Dancer's bayonet stopped the brake lever being turned
AAAH!
ROGAN'S NOT MISSING OUT ON THE FUN, PAL!
NEIN! HE IS STRANGLING ME!
THE TRAIN IS OURS – GIVE IT FULL STEAM! YOU TOO, DANCER.
SUCH WORK IS BENEATH ME.
WE'RE APPROACHING THE SUN CANNON – BUT ON THE WRONG RAILS! ROGAN – I'VE GOT A JOB FOR YOU!
Carefully Rogan inched his way forward to the front of the train.
NOW IF ROGAN CAN TURN THE POINTS IN TIME --
HE'S DONE IT!
THE TRAIN IS APPROACHING US AT FULL SPEED! NEIN! NEIN!
TIME TO GO!
AAAGH!
ANOTHER SUCCESSFUL MISSION, TAGGART. BUT WHAT DO WE GET OUT OF IT FOR RISKING OUR NECKS?
A FEW DAYS OUT OF PRISON – THAT'S ALL! COME ON, YOU RATS – IT'S A LONG WAY HOME.

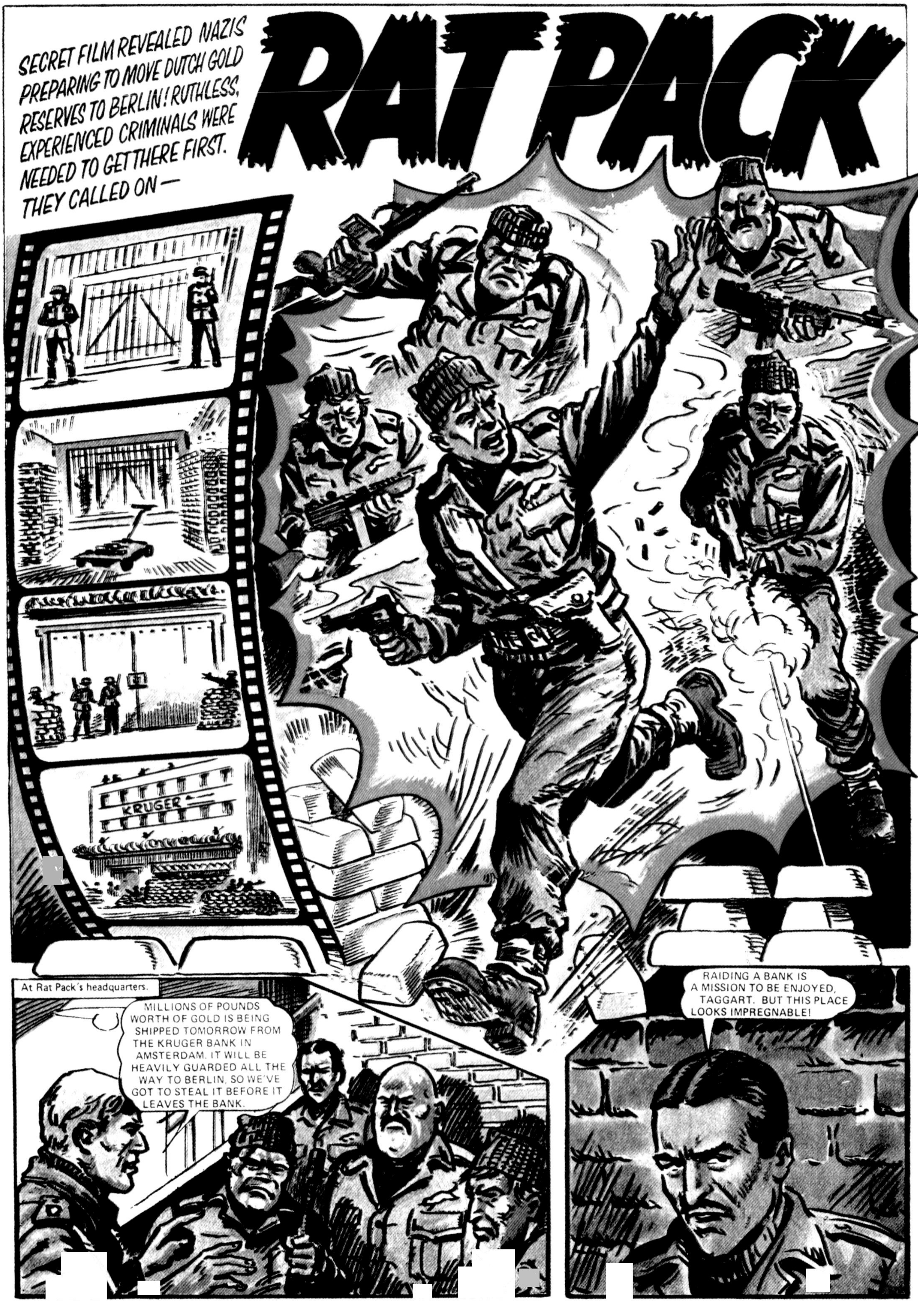
SECRET FILM REVEALED NAZIS PREPARING TO MOVE DUTCH GOLD RESERVES TO BERLIN! RUTHLESS, EXPERIENCED CRIMINALS WERE NEEDED TO GET THERE FIRST. THEY CALLED ON—
RAT PACK
KRUGER
At Rat Pack's headquarters.
MILLIONS OF POUNDS WORTH OF GOLD IS BEING SHIPPED TOMORROW FROM THE KRUGER BANK IN AMSTERDAM. IT WILL BE HEAVILY GUARDED ALL THE WAY TO BERLIN, SO WE'VE GOT TO STEAL IT BEFORE IT LEAVES THE BANK.
RAIDING A BANK IS A MISSION TO BE ENJOYED, TAGGART. BUT THIS PLACE LOOKS IMPREGNABLE!

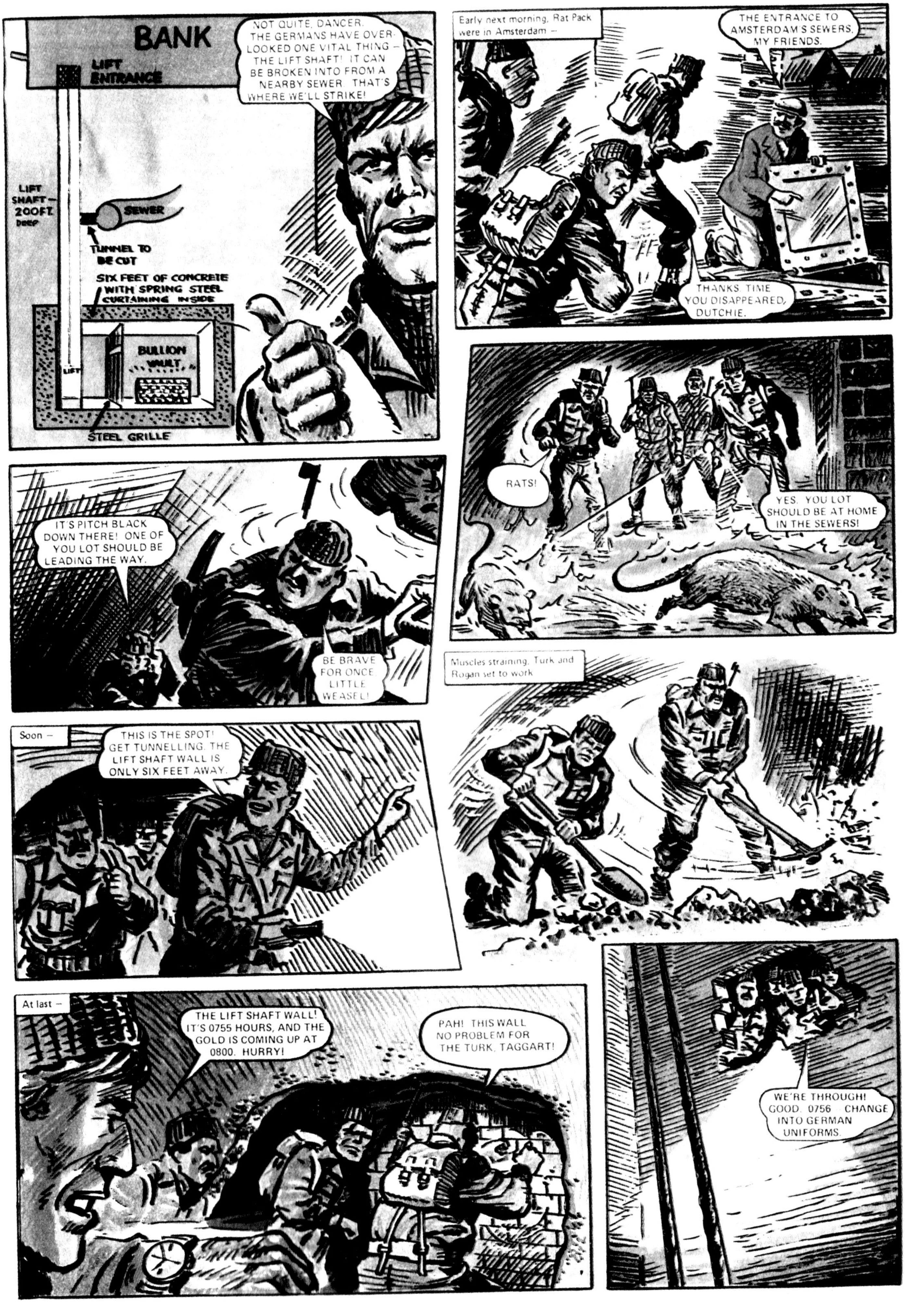
BANK
LIFT ENTRANCE
LIFT SHAFT—200FT. DEEP
SEWER
TUNNEL TO BE CUT
SIX FEET OF CONCRETE WITH SPRING STEEL CURTAINING INSIDE
BULLION VAULT
LIFT
STEEL GRILLE
NOT QUITE, DANCER. THE GERMANS HAVE OVERLOOKED ONE VITAL THING — THE LIFT SHAFT! IT CAN BE BROKEN INTO FROM A NEARBY SEWER. THAT'S WHERE WE'LL STRIKE!
Early next morning, Rat Pack were in Amsterdam —
THE ENTRANCE TO AMSTERDAM'S SEWERS, MY FRIENDS.
THANKS. TIME YOU DISAPPEARED, DUTCHIE.
IT'S PITCH BLACK DOWN THERE! ONE OF YOU LOT SHOULD BE LEADING THE WAY.
BE BRAVE FOR ONCE, LITTLE WEASEL!
RATS!
YES. YOU LOT SHOULD BE AT HOME IN THE SEWERS!
Soon —
THIS IS THE SPOT! GET TUNNELLING. THE LIFT SHAFT WALL IS ONLY SIX FEET AWAY.
Muscles straining, Turk and Rogan set to work
At last —
THE LIFT SHAFT WALL! IT'S 0755 HOURS, AND THE GOLD IS COMING UP AT 0800. HURRY!
PAH! THIS WALL NO PROBLEM FOR THE TURK, TAGGART!
WE'RE THROUGH! GOOD. 0756. CHANGE INTO GERMAN UNIFORMS.

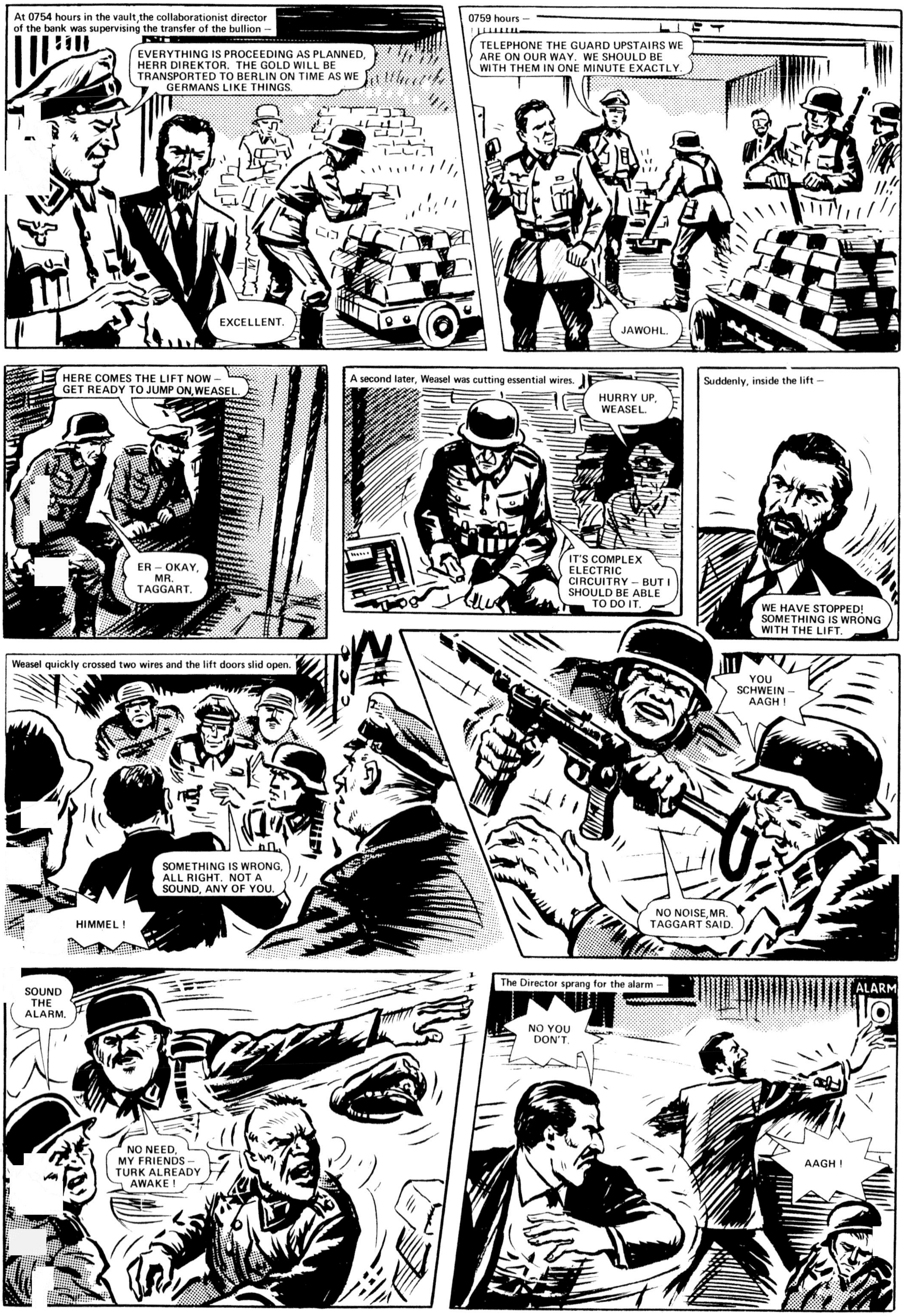
At 0754 hours in the vault, the collaborationist director of the bank was supervising the transfer of the bullion –
EVERYTHING IS PROCEEDING AS PLANNED, HERR DIREKTOR. THE GOLD WILL BE TRANSPORTED TO BERLIN ON TIME AS WE GERMANS LIKE THINGS.
EXCELLENT.
0759 hours –
TELEPHONE THE GUARD UPSTAIRS WE ARE ON OUR WAY. WE SHOULD BE WITH THEM IN ONE MINUTE EXACTLY.
JAWOHL.
HERE COMES THE LIFT NOW – GET READY TO JUMP ON, WEASEL.
ER – OKAY, MR. TAGGART.
A second later, Weasel was cutting essential wires.
HURRY UP, WEASEL.
IT'S COMPLEX ELECTRIC CIRCUITRY – BUT I SHOULD BE ABLE TO DO IT.
Suddenly, inside the lift –
WE HAVE STOPPED! SOMETHING IS WRONG WITH THE LIFT.
Weasel quickly crossed two wires and the lift doors slid open.
SOMETHING IS WRONG, ALL RIGHT. NOT A SOUND, ANY OF YOU.
HIMMEL !
YOU SCHWEIN – AAGH !
NO NOISE, MR. TAGGART SAID.
SOUND THE ALARM.
NO NEED, MY FRIENDS – TURK ALREADY AWAKE !
The Director sprang for the alarm –
ALARM
NO YOU DON'T.
AAGH !

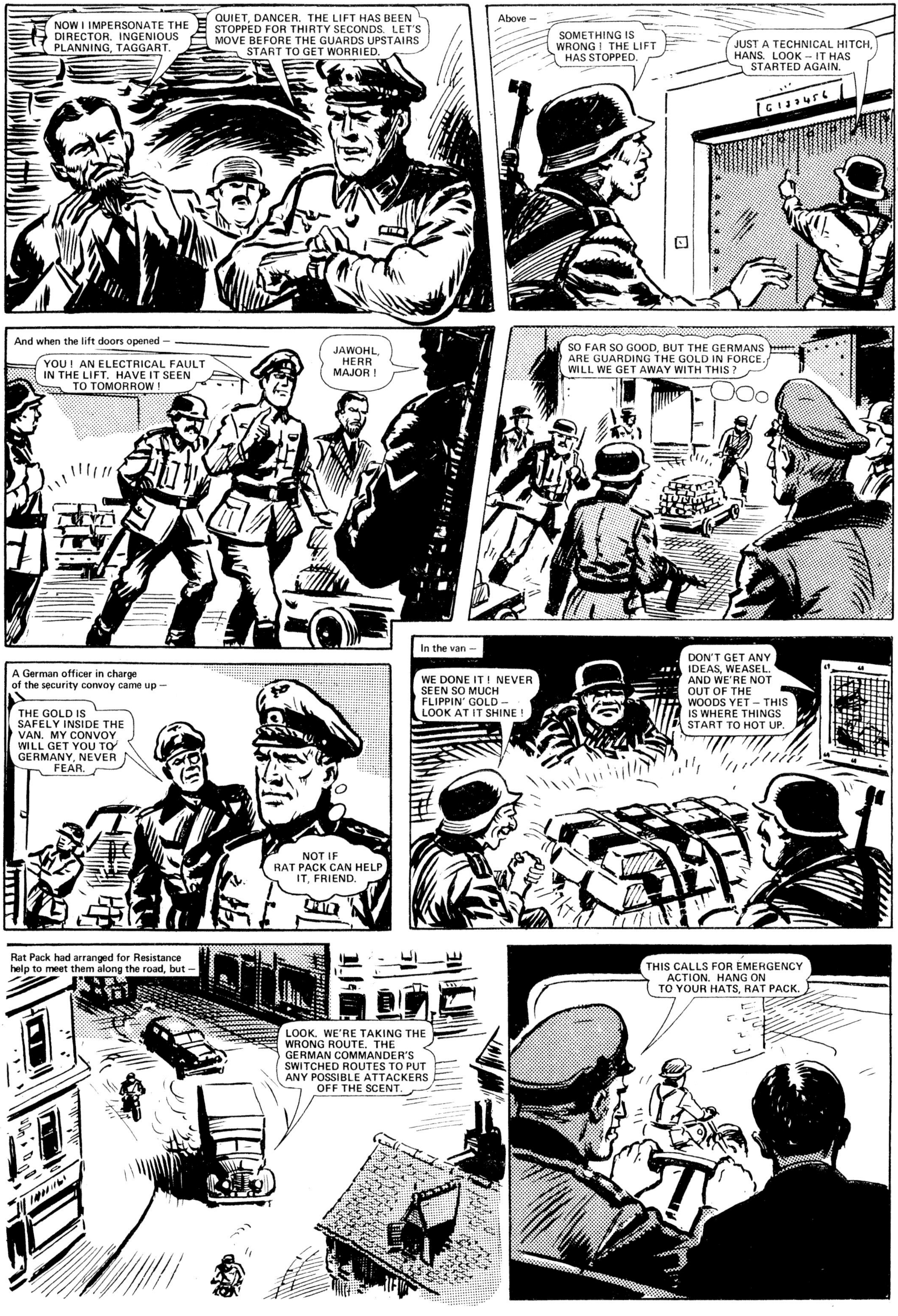
NOW I IMPERSONATE THE DIRECTOR. INGENIOUS PLANNING, TAGGART.
QUIET, DANCER. THE LIFT HAS BEEN STOPPED FOR THIRTY SECONDS. LET'S MOVE BEFORE THE GUARDS UPSTAIRS START TO GET WORRIED.
Above –
SOMETHING IS WRONG ! THE LIFT HAS STOPPED.
JUST A TECHNICAL HITCH, HANS. LOOK – IT HAS STARTED AGAIN.
And when the lift doors opened –
YOU ! AN ELECTRICAL FAULT IN THE LIFT. HAVE IT SEEN TO TOMORROW !
JAWOHL, HERR MAJOR !
SO FAR SO GOOD, BUT THE GERMANS ARE GUARDING THE GOLD IN FORCE. WILL WE GET AWAY WITH THIS ?
A German officer in charge of the security convoy came up –
THE GOLD IS SAFELY INSIDE THE VAN. MY CONVOY WILL GET YOU TO GERMANY, NEVER FEAR.
NOT IF RAT PACK CAN HELP IT, FRIEND.
In the van –
WE DONE IT ! NEVER SEEN SO MUCH FLIPPIN' GOLD – LOOK AT IT SHINE !
DON'T GET ANY IDEAS, WEASEL. AND WE'RE NOT OUT OF THE WOODS YET – THIS IS WHERE THINGS START TO HOT UP.
Rat Pack had arranged for Resistance help to meet them along the road, but –
LOOK. WE'RE TAKING THE WRONG ROUTE. THE GERMAN COMMANDER'S SWITCHED ROUTES TO PUT ANY POSSIBLE ATTACKERS OFF THE SCENT.
THIS CALLS FOR EMERGENCY ACTION. HANG ON TO YOUR HATS, RAT PACK.

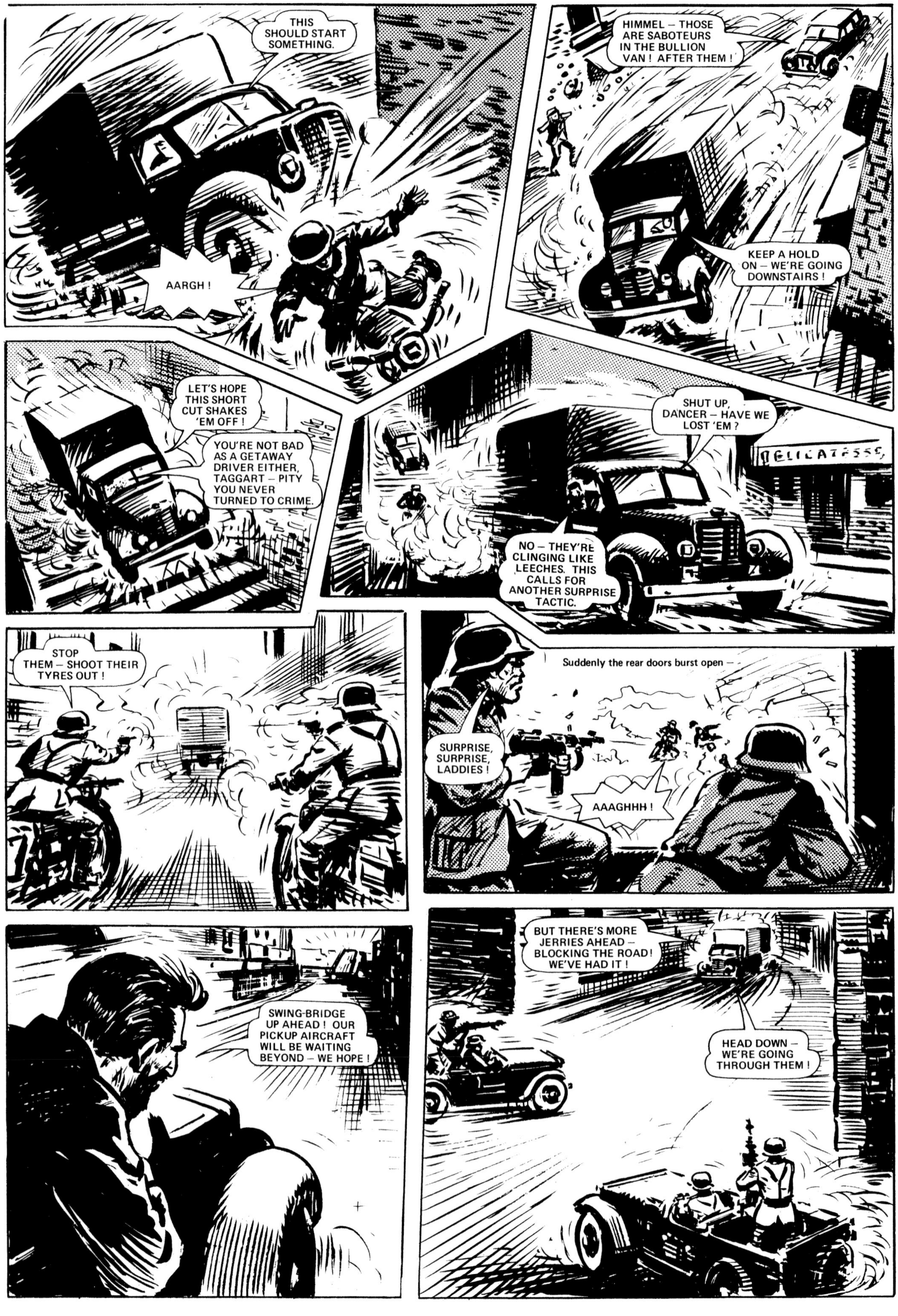
THIS SHOULD START SOMETHING.
AARGH !
HIMMEL – THOSE ARE SABOTEURS IN THE BULLION VAN ! AFTER THEM !
KEEP A HOLD ON – WE'RE GOING DOWNSTAIRS !
LET'S HOPE THIS SHORT CUT SHAKES 'EM OFF !
YOU'RE NOT BAD AS A GETAWAY DRIVER EITHER, TAGGART – PITY YOU NEVER TURNED TO CRIME.
SHUT UP, DANCER – HAVE WE LOST 'EM ?
NO – THEY'RE CLINGING LIKE LEECHES. THIS CALLS FOR ANOTHER SURPRISE TACTIC.
STOP THEM – SHOOT THEIR TYRES OUT !
Suddenly the rear doors burst open –
SURPRISE, SURPRISE, LADDIES !
AAAGHHH !
SWING-BRIDGE UP AHEAD ! OUR PICKUP AIRCRAFT WILL BE WAITING BEYOND – WE HOPE !
BUT THERE'S MORE JERRIES AHEAD – BLOCKING THE ROAD ! WE'VE HAD IT !
HEAD DOWN – WE'RE GOING THROUGH THEM !

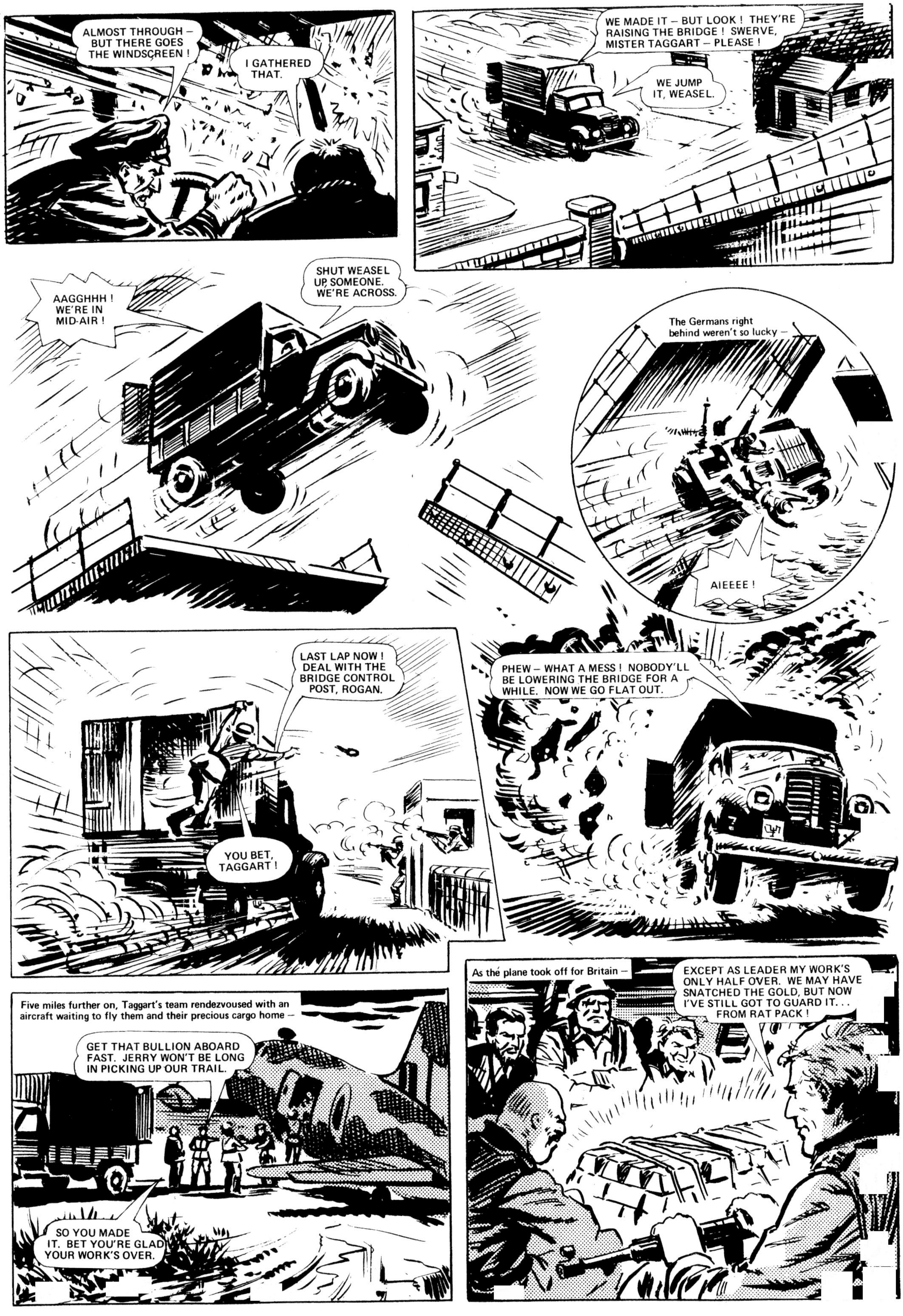

ALMOST THROUGH – BUT THERE GOES THE WINDSCREEN !
I GATHERED THAT.
WE MADE IT – BUT LOOK ! THEY'RE RAISING THE BRIDGE ! SWERVE, MISTER TAGGART – PLEASE !
WE JUMP IT, WEASEL.
AAGGHHH ! WE'RE IN MID-AIR !
SHUT WEASEL UP, SOMEONE. WE'RE ACROSS.
The Germans right behind weren't so lucky –
AIEEEE !
LAST LAP NOW ! DEAL WITH THE BRIDGE CONTROL POST, ROGAN.
YOU BET, TAGGART !
PHEW – WHAT A MESS ! NOBODY'LL BE LOWERING THE BRIDGE FOR A WHILE. NOW WE GO FLAT OUT.
Five miles further on, Taggart's team rendezvoused with an aircraft waiting to fly them and their precious cargo home –
GET THAT BULLION ABOARD FAST. JERRY WON'T BE LONG IN PICKING UP OUR TRAIL.
SO YOU MADE IT. BET YOU'RE GLAD YOUR WORK'S OVER.
As the plane took off for Britain –
EXCEPT AS LEADER MY WORK'S ONLY HALF OVER. WE MAY HAVE SNATCHED THE GOLD, BUT NOW I'VE STILL GOT TO GUARD IT. . . FROM RAT PACK !

RAT

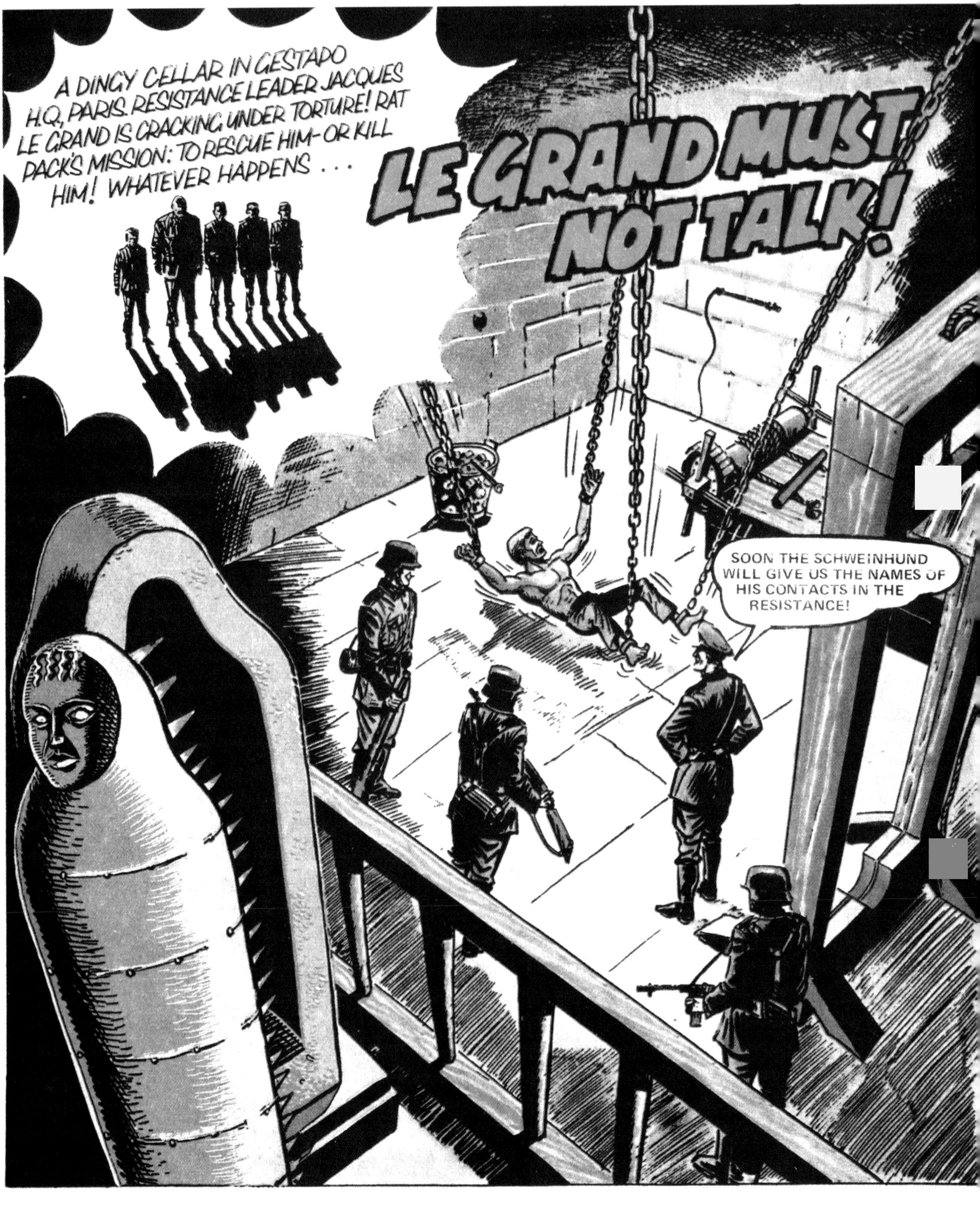
A DINGY CELLAR IN GESTAPO H.Q., PARIS. RESISTANCE LEADER JACQUES LE GRAND IS CRACKING UNDER TORTURE! RAT PACK'S MISSION: TO RESCUE HIM- OR KILL HIM! WHATEVER HAPPENS . . .
LE GRAND MUST NOT TALK!
SOON THE SCHWEINHUND WILL GIVE US THE NAMES OF HIS CONTACTS IN THE RESISTANCE!

PACK

In Britain Major Taggart briefed his convict Commandos.

IT'S A RACE AGAINST TIME, MEN. WE'VE GOT TO BREAK INTO THAT GESTAPO PRISON.

FORGET IT, TAGGART. I SPENT TWO YEARS ROTTING IN PRISON — I'M NOT BREAKING INTO ONE!

COUNT TURK OUT, TOO.

YOU'LL DO AS I SAY — NOW GET ABOARD THE PLANE!

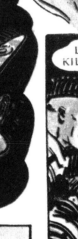

JUST REMEMBER THE DEAL I MADE WITH YOU RATS — YOUR FREEDOM PROVIDED YOU CARRY OUT TOUGH JOBS FOR BRITISH INTELLIGENCE. THIS'LL BE ONE OF THE TOUGHEST!

Later in an alley way near Gestapo H.Q.

LET TURK KILL GUARDS.

NO. I DON'T WANT ANY UNNECESSARY VIOLENCE. ROGAN WILL GET US IN — QUIETLY!

YEAH! FOLLOW ME!

MUVVAH! YOU KNOW I AIN'T GOT A HEAD FOR HEIGHTS.

On the roof opposite the H.Q.

APART FROM SPROUTING WINGS, I DON'T SEE HOW WE'LL MAKE IT ACROSS, ROGAN.

USING THE FLAGPOLE — THAT'S HOW!

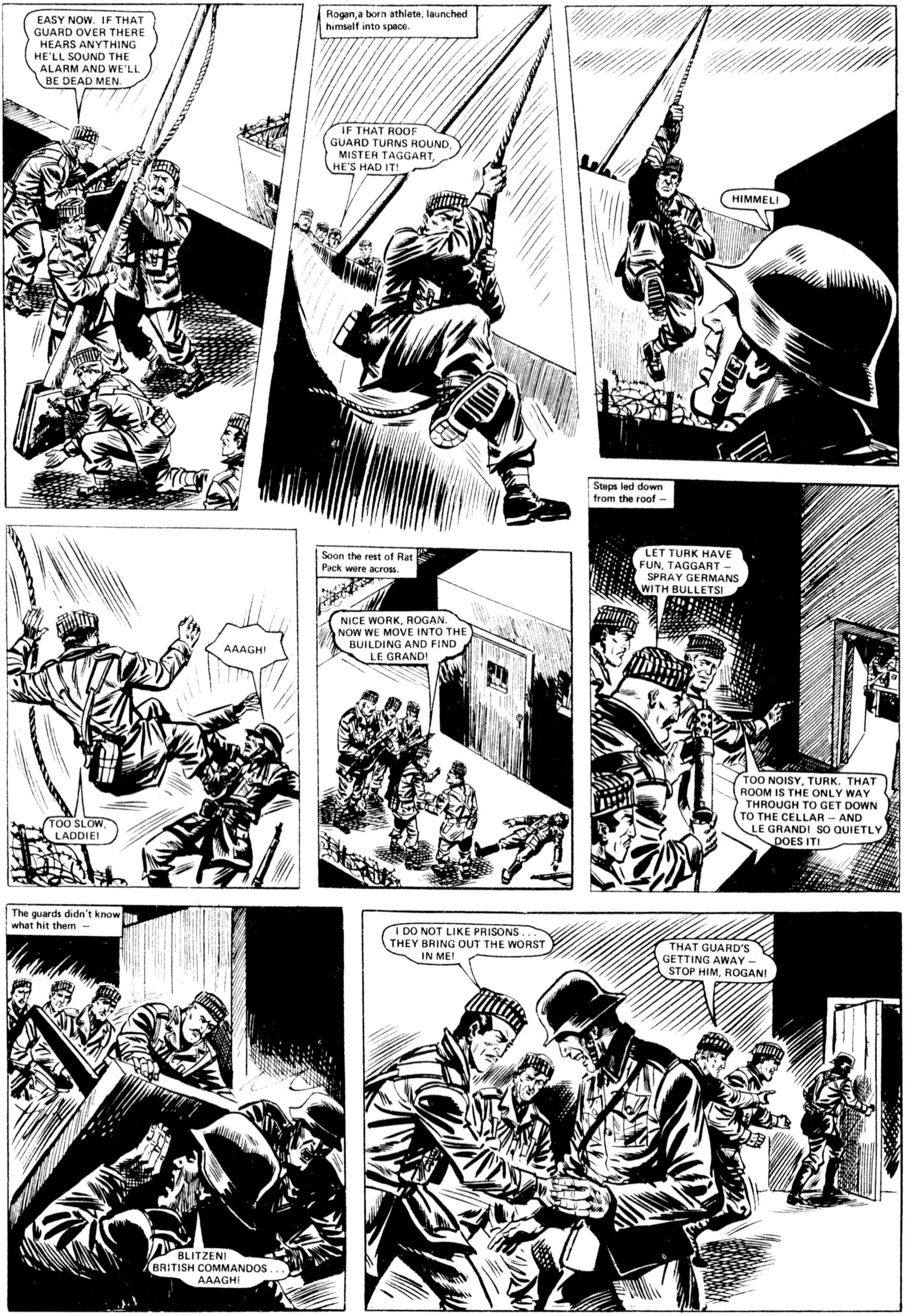
EASY NOW. IF THAT GUARD OVER THERE HEARS ANYTHING HE'LL SOUND THE ALARM AND WE'LL BE DEAD MEN.
Rogan, a born athlete, launched himself into space.
IF THAT ROOF GUARD TURNS ROUND, MISTER TAGGART, HE'S HAD IT!
HIMMEL!
AAAGH!
TOO SLOW, LADDIE!
Soon the rest of Rat Pack were across.
NICE WORK, ROGAN. NOW WE MOVE INTO THE BUILDING AND FIND LE GRAND!
Steps led down from the roof —
LET TURK HAVE FUN, TAGGART — SPRAY GERMANS WITH BULLETS!
TOO NOISY, TURK. THAT ROOM IS THE ONLY WAY THROUGH TO GET DOWN TO THE CELLAR — AND LE GRAND! SO QUIETLY DOES IT!
The guards didn't know what hit them —
BLITZEN! BRITISH COMMANDOS . . . AAAGH!
I DO NOT LIKE PRISONS . . . THEY BRING OUT THE WORST IN ME!
THAT GUARD'S GETTING AWAY — STOP HIM, ROGAN!

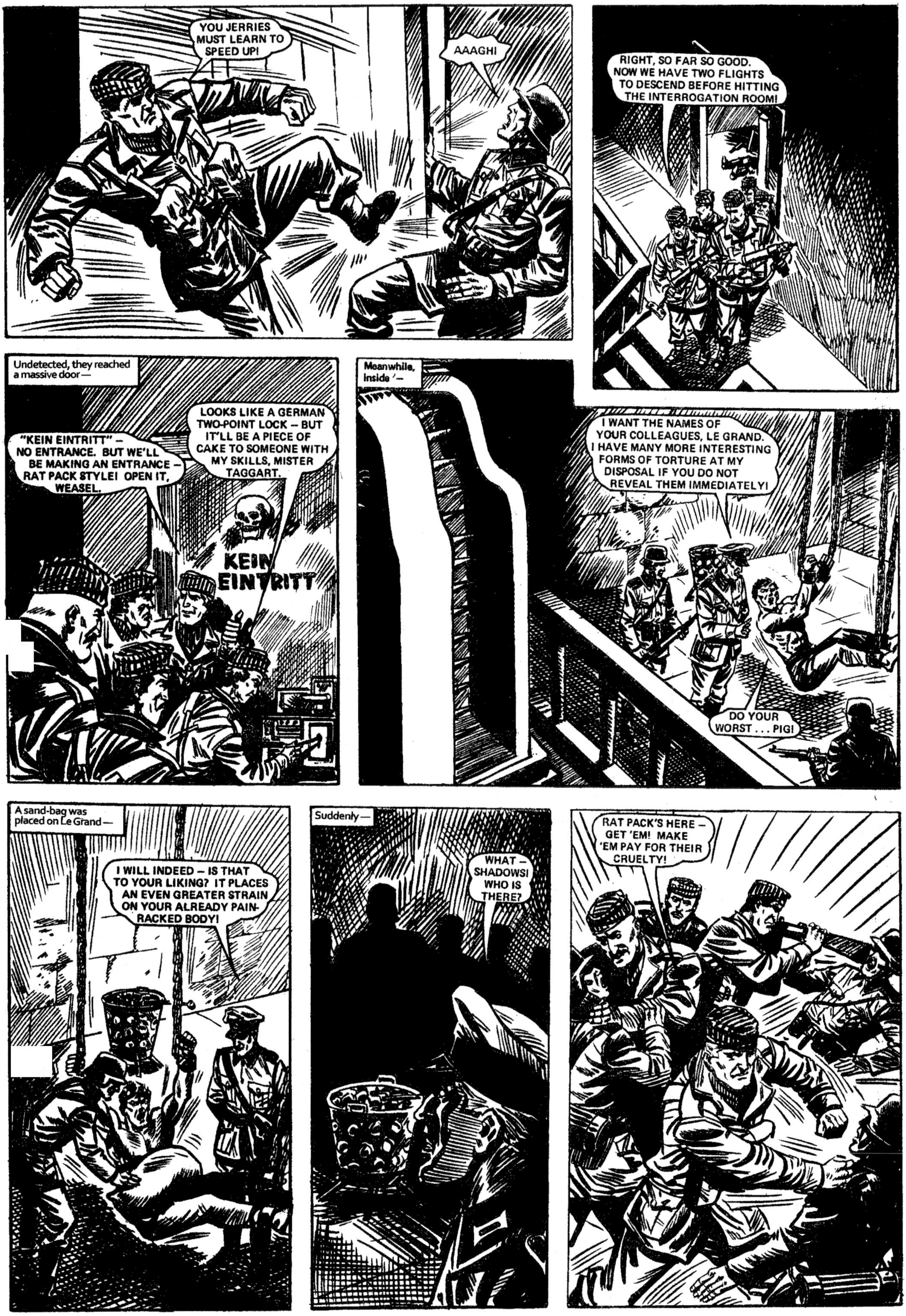
YOU JERRIES MUST LEARN TO SPEED UP!
AAAGH!
RIGHT, SO FAR SO GOOD. NOW WE HAVE TWO FLIGHTS TO DESCEND BEFORE HITTING THE INTERROGATION ROOM!
Undetected, they reached a massive door —
"KEIN EINTRITT" — NO ENTRANCE. BUT WE'LL BE MAKING AN ENTRANCE — RAT PACK STYLE! OPEN IT, WEASEL.
LOOKS LIKE A GERMAN TWO-POINT LOCK — BUT IT'LL BE A PIECE OF CAKE TO SOMEONE WITH MY SKILLS, MISTER TAGGART.
KEIN EINTRITT
Meanwhile, inside —
I WANT THE NAMES OF YOUR COLLEAGUES, LE GRAND. I HAVE MANY MORE INTERESTING FORMS OF TORTURE AT MY DISPOSAL IF YOU DO NOT REVEAL THEM IMMEDIATELY!
DO YOUR WORST . . . PIG!
A sand-bag was placed on Le Grand —
I WILL INDEED — IS THAT TO YOUR LIKING? IT PLACES AN EVEN GREATER STRAIN ON YOUR ALREADY PAIN-RACKED BODY!
Suddenly —
WHAT — SHADOWS! WHO IS THERE?
RAT PACK'S HERE — GET 'EM! MAKE 'EM PAY FOR THEIR CRUELTY!

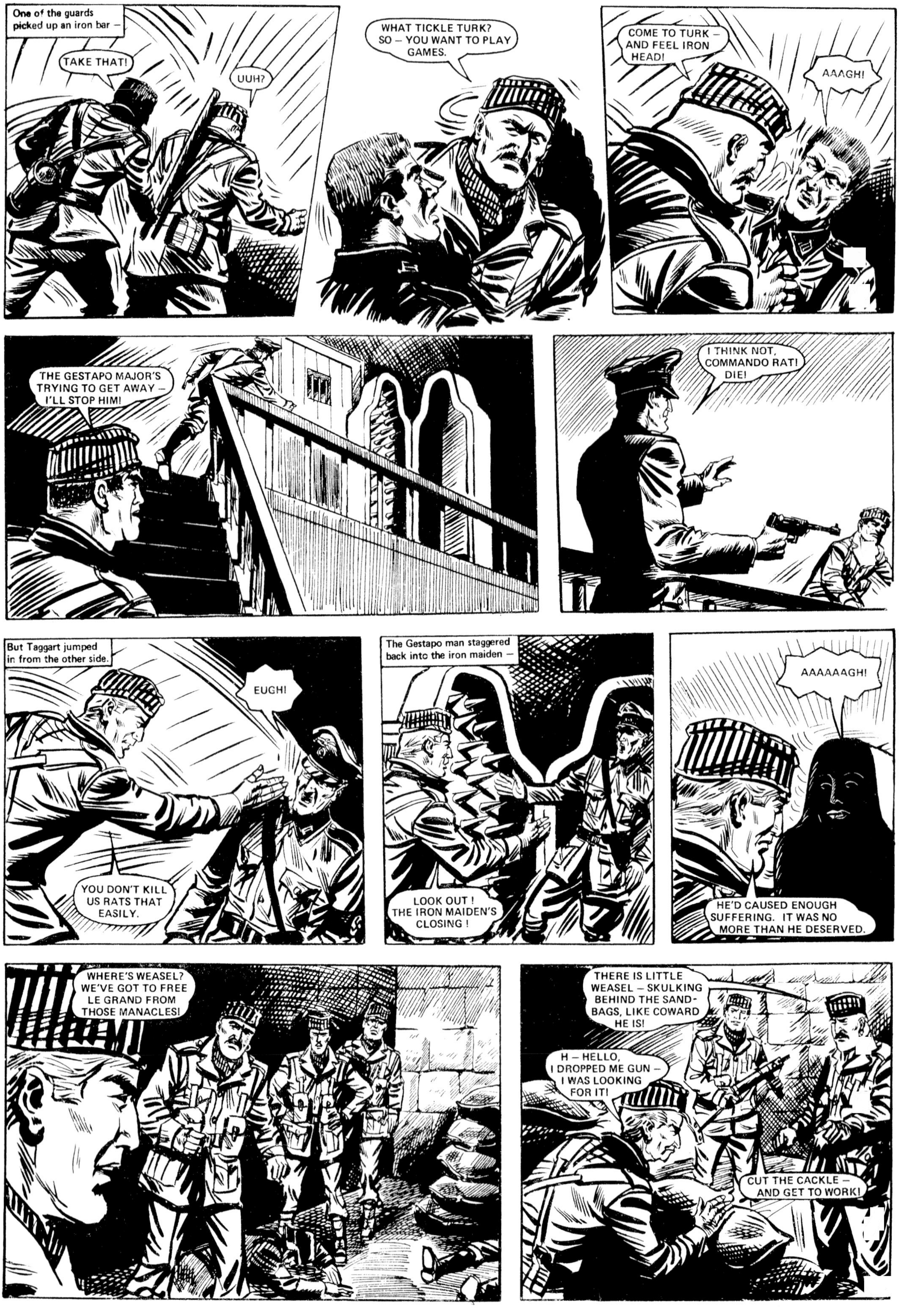
One of the guards picked up an iron bar –
TAKE THAT!
UUH?
WHAT TICKLE TURK? SO – YOU WANT TO PLAY GAMES.
COME TO TURK – AND FEEL IRON HEAD!
AAAGH!
THE GESTAPO MAJOR'S TRYING TO GET AWAY – I'LL STOP HIM!
I THINK NOT, COMMANDO RAT! DIE!
But Taggart jumped in from the other side.
EUGH!
YOU DON'T KILL US RATS THAT EASILY.
The Gestapo man staggered back into the iron maiden –
LOOK OUT ! THE IRON MAIDEN'S CLOSING !
AAAAAAGH!
HE'D CAUSED ENOUGH SUFFERING. IT WAS NO MORE THAN HE DESERVED.
WHERE'S WEASEL? WE'VE GOT TO FREE LE GRAND FROM THOSE MANACLES!
THERE IS LITTLE WEASEL – SKULKING BEHIND THE SAND-BAGS, LIKE COWARD HE IS!
H – HELLO, I DROPPED ME GUN – I WAS LOOKING FOR IT!
CUT THE CACKLE – AND GET TO WORK!

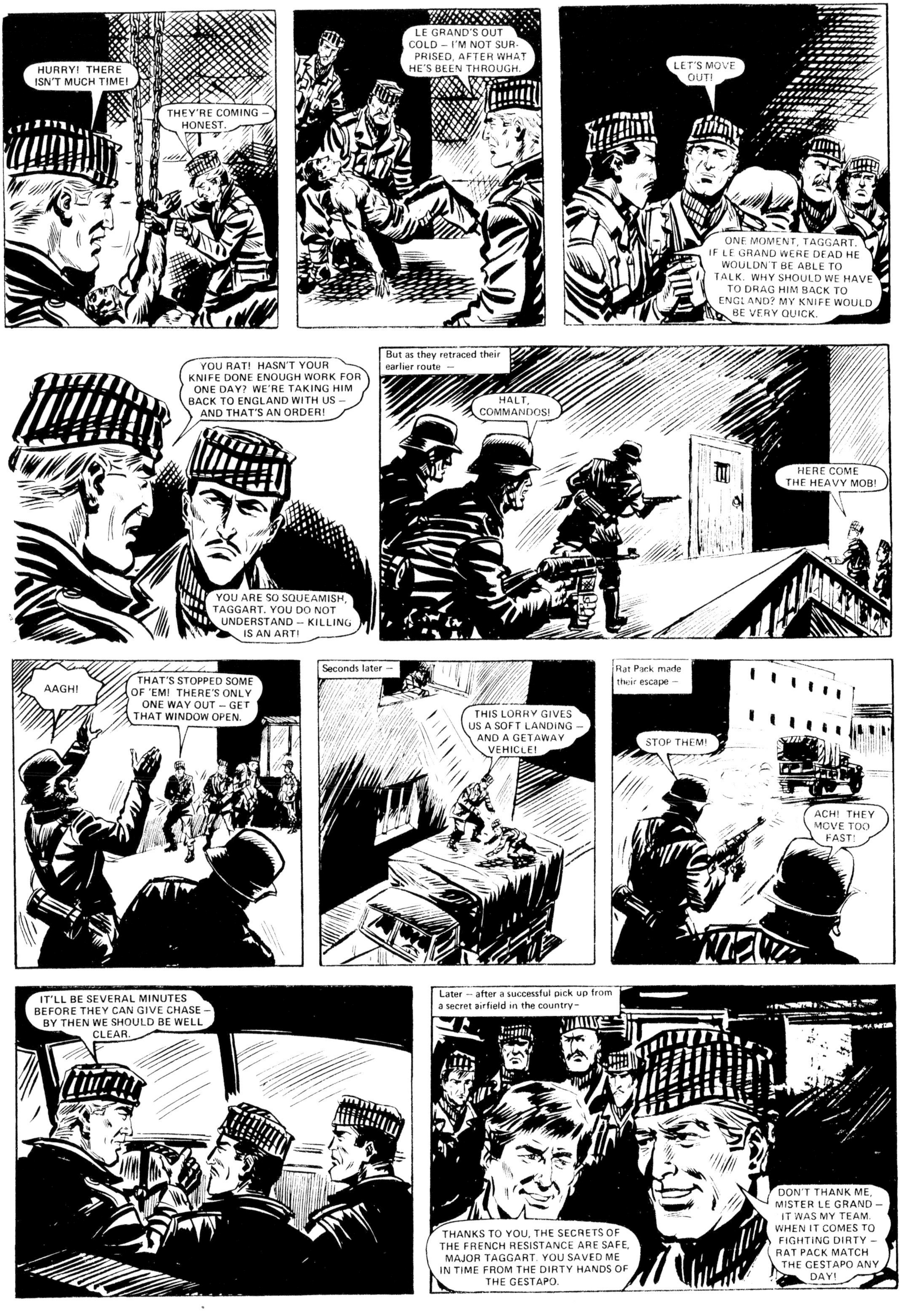
HURRY! THERE ISN'T MUCH TIME!
THEY'RE COMING — HONEST.
LE GRAND'S OUT COLD — I'M NOT SURPRISED, AFTER WHAT HE'S BEEN THROUGH.
LET'S MOVE OUT!
ONE MOMENT, TAGGART. IF LE GRAND WERE DEAD HE WOULDN'T BE ABLE TO TALK. WHY SHOULD WE HAVE TO DRAG HIM BACK TO ENGLAND? MY KNIFE WOULD BE VERY QUICK.
YOU RAT! HASN'T YOUR KNIFE DONE ENOUGH WORK FOR ONE DAY? WE'RE TAKING HIM BACK TO ENGLAND WITH US — AND THAT'S AN ORDER!
YOU ARE SO SQUEAMISH, TAGGART. YOU DO NOT UNDERSTAND — KILLING IS AN ART!
But as they retraced their earlier route —
HALT, COMMANDOS!
HERE COME THE HEAVY MOB!
AAGH!
THAT'S STOPPED SOME OF 'EM! THERE'S ONLY ONE WAY OUT — GET THAT WINDOW OPEN.
Seconds later —
THIS LORRY GIVES US A SOFT LANDING — AND A GETAWAY VEHICLE!
Rat Pack made their escape —
STOP THEM!
ACH! THEY MOVE TOO FAST!
IT'LL BE SEVERAL MINUTES BEFORE THEY CAN GIVE CHASE — BY THEN WE SHOULD BE WELL CLEAR.
Later — after a successful pick up from a secret airfield in the country—
THANKS TO YOU, THE SECRETS OF THE FRENCH RESISTANCE ARE SAFE, MAJOR TAGGART. YOU SAVED ME IN TIME FROM THE DIRTY HANDS OF THE GESTAPO.
DON'T THANK ME, MISTER LE GRAND — IT WAS MY TEAM. WHEN IT COMES TO FIGHTING DIRTY — RAT PACK MATCH THE GESTAPO ANY DAY!

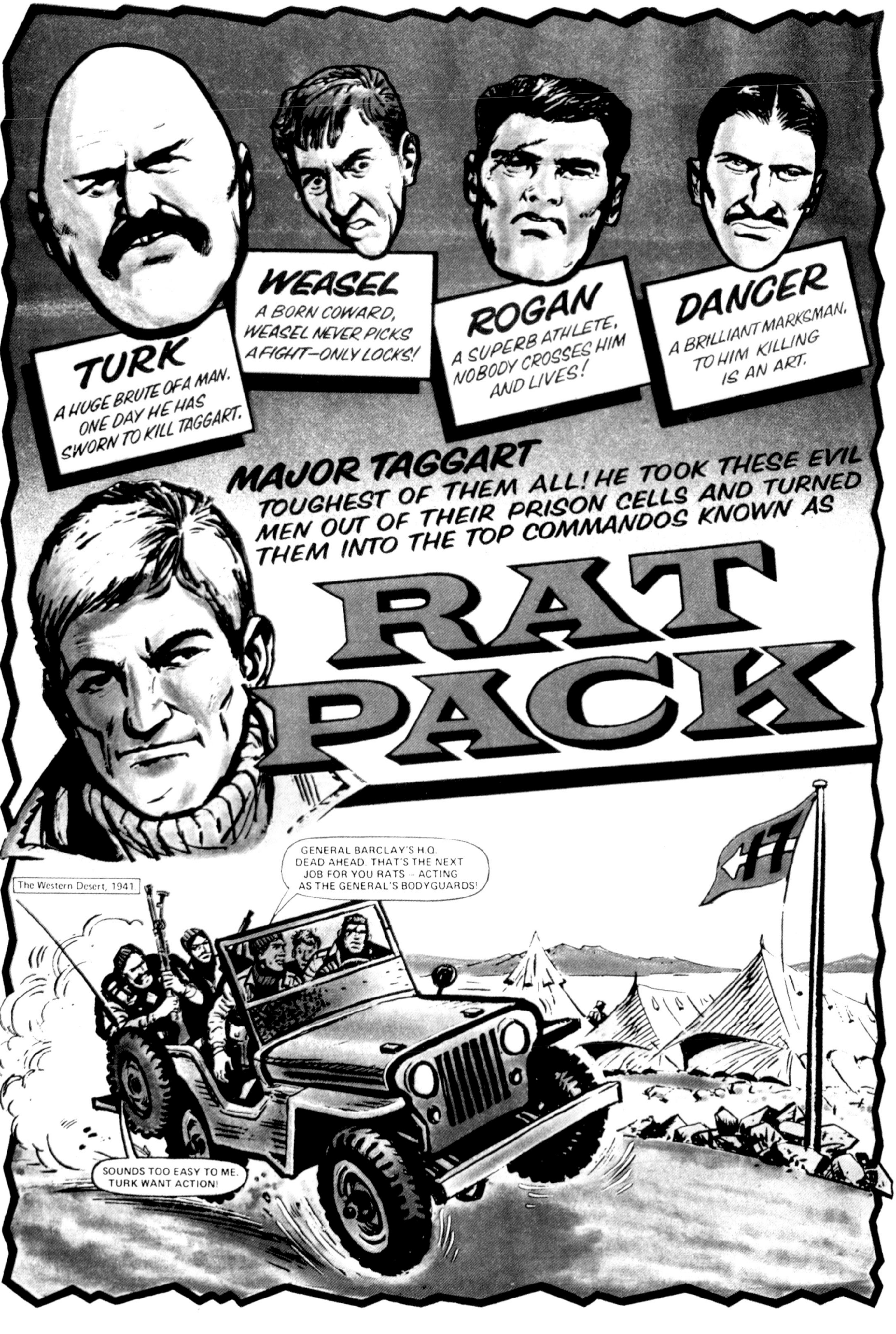
TURK
A HUGE BRUTE OF A MAN. ONE DAY HE HAS SWORN TO KILL TAGGART.
WEASEL
A BORN COWARD, WEASEL NEVER PICKS A FIGHT—ONLY LOCKS!
ROGAN
A SUPERB ATHLETE, NOBODY CROSSES HIM AND LIVES!
DANCER
A BRILLIANT MARKSMAN, TO HIM KILLING IS AN ART.
MAJOR TAGGART
TOUGHEST OF THEM ALL! HE TOOK THESE EVIL MEN OUT OF THEIR PRISON CELLS AND TURNED THEM INTO THE TOP COMMANDOS KNOWN AS
RAT PACK
The Western Desert, 1941.
GENERAL BARCLAY'S H.Q. DEAD AHEAD. THAT'S THE NEXT JOB FOR YOU RATS – ACTING AS THE GENERAL'S BODYGUARDS!
SOUNDS TOO EASY TO ME. TURK WANT ACTION!

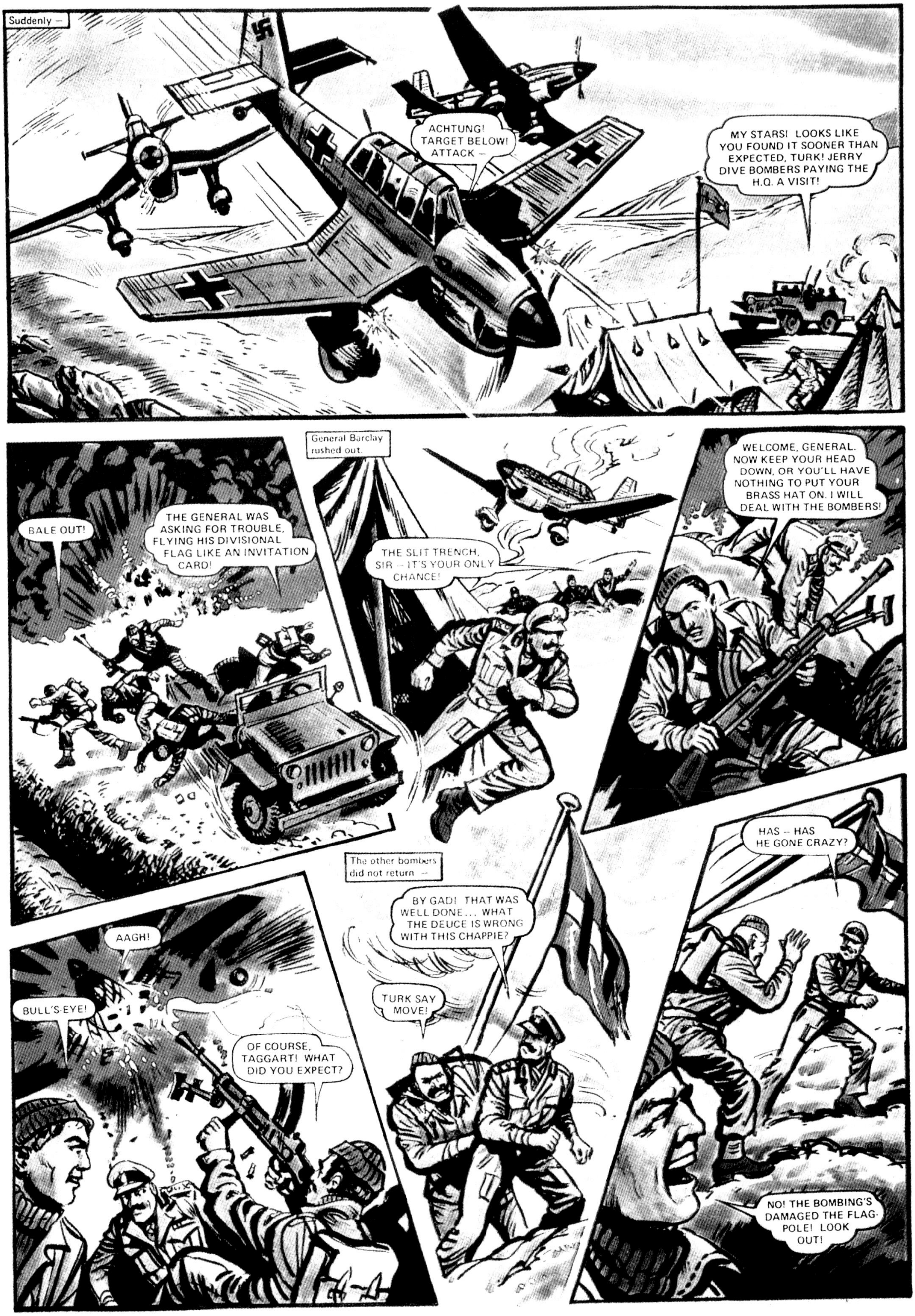
Suddenly —
ACHTUNG! TARGET BELOW! ATTACK —
MY STARS! LOOKS LIKE YOU FOUND IT SOONER THAN EXPECTED, TURK! JERRY DIVE BOMBERS PAYING THE H.Q. A VISIT!
BALE OUT!
THE GENERAL WAS ASKING FOR TROUBLE, FLYING HIS DIVISIONAL FLAG LIKE AN INVITATION CARD!
General Barclay rushed out.
THE SLIT TRENCH, SIR — IT'S YOUR ONLY CHANCE!
WELCOME, GENERAL. NOW KEEP YOUR HEAD DOWN, OR YOU'LL HAVE NOTHING TO PUT YOUR BRASS HAT ON. I WILL DEAL WITH THE BOMBERS!
AAGH!
BULL'S-EYE!
OF COURSE, TAGGART! WHAT DID YOU EXPECT?
The other bombers did not return —
BY GAD! THAT WAS WELL DONE... WHAT THE DEUCE IS WRONG WITH THIS CHAPPIE?
TURK SAY MOVE!
HAS — HAS HE GONE CRAZY?
NO! THE BOMBING'S DAMAGED THE FLAG-POLE! LOOK OUT!

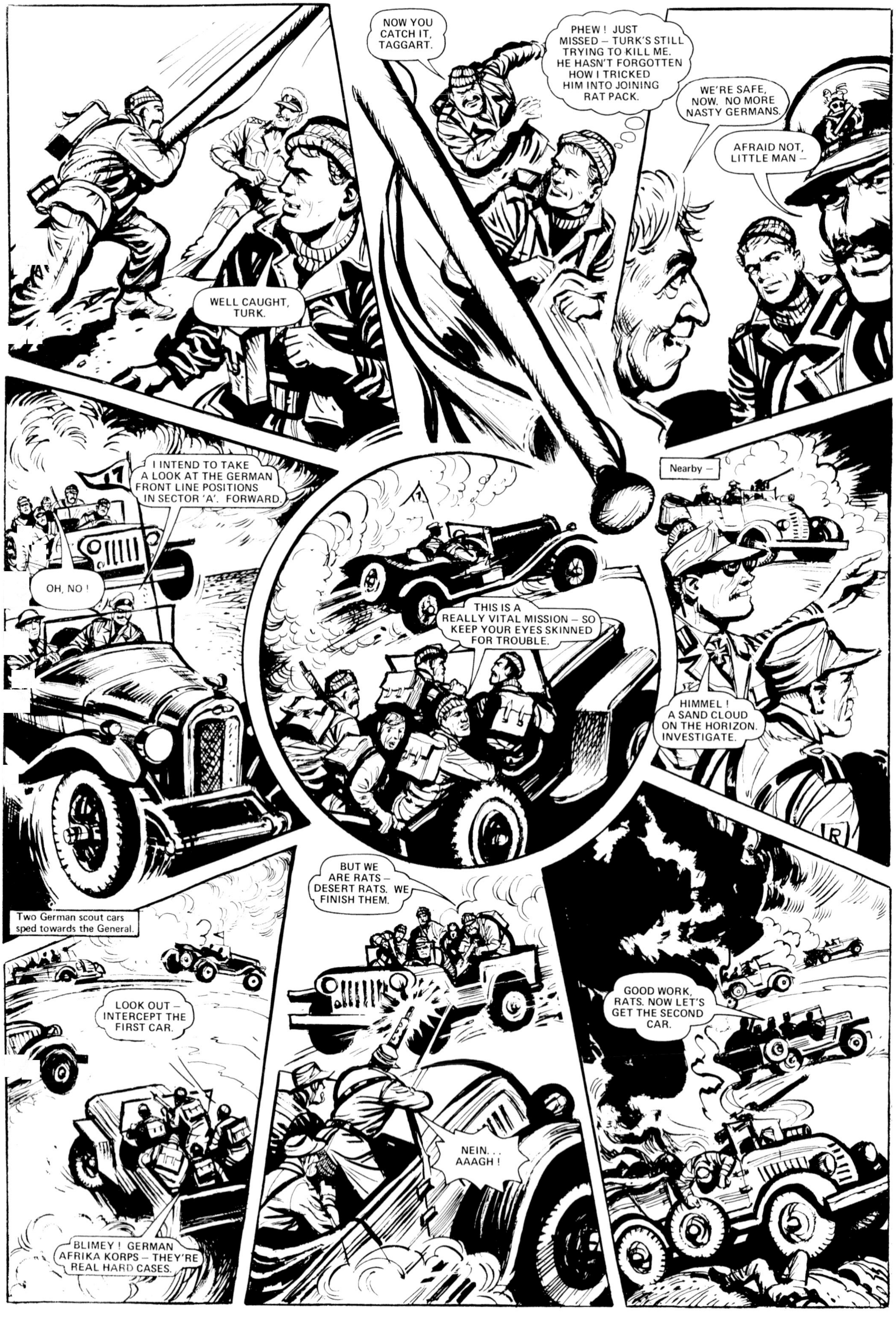
WELL CAUGHT, TURK.
NOW YOU CATCH IT, TAGGART.
PHEW ! JUST MISSED – TURK'S STILL TRYING TO KILL ME. HE HASN'T FORGOTTEN HOW I TRICKED HIM INTO JOINING RAT PACK.
WE'RE SAFE, NOW. NO MORE NASTY GERMANS.
AFRAID NOT, LITTLE MAN –
I INTEND TO TAKE A LOOK AT THE GERMAN FRONT LINE POSITIONS IN SECTOR 'A'. FORWARD.
OH, NO !
THIS IS A REALLY VITAL MISSION – SO KEEP YOUR EYES SKINNED FOR TROUBLE.
Nearby –
HIMMEL ! A SAND CLOUD ON THE HORIZON. INVESTIGATE.
Two German scout cars sped towards the General.
LOOK OUT – INTERCEPT THE FIRST CAR.
BLIMEY ! GERMAN AFRIKA KORPS – THEY'RE REAL HARD CASES.
BUT WE ARE RATS – DESERT RATS. WE FINISH THEM.
NEIN. . . AAAGH !
GOOD WORK, RATS. NOW LET'S GET THE SECOND CAR.

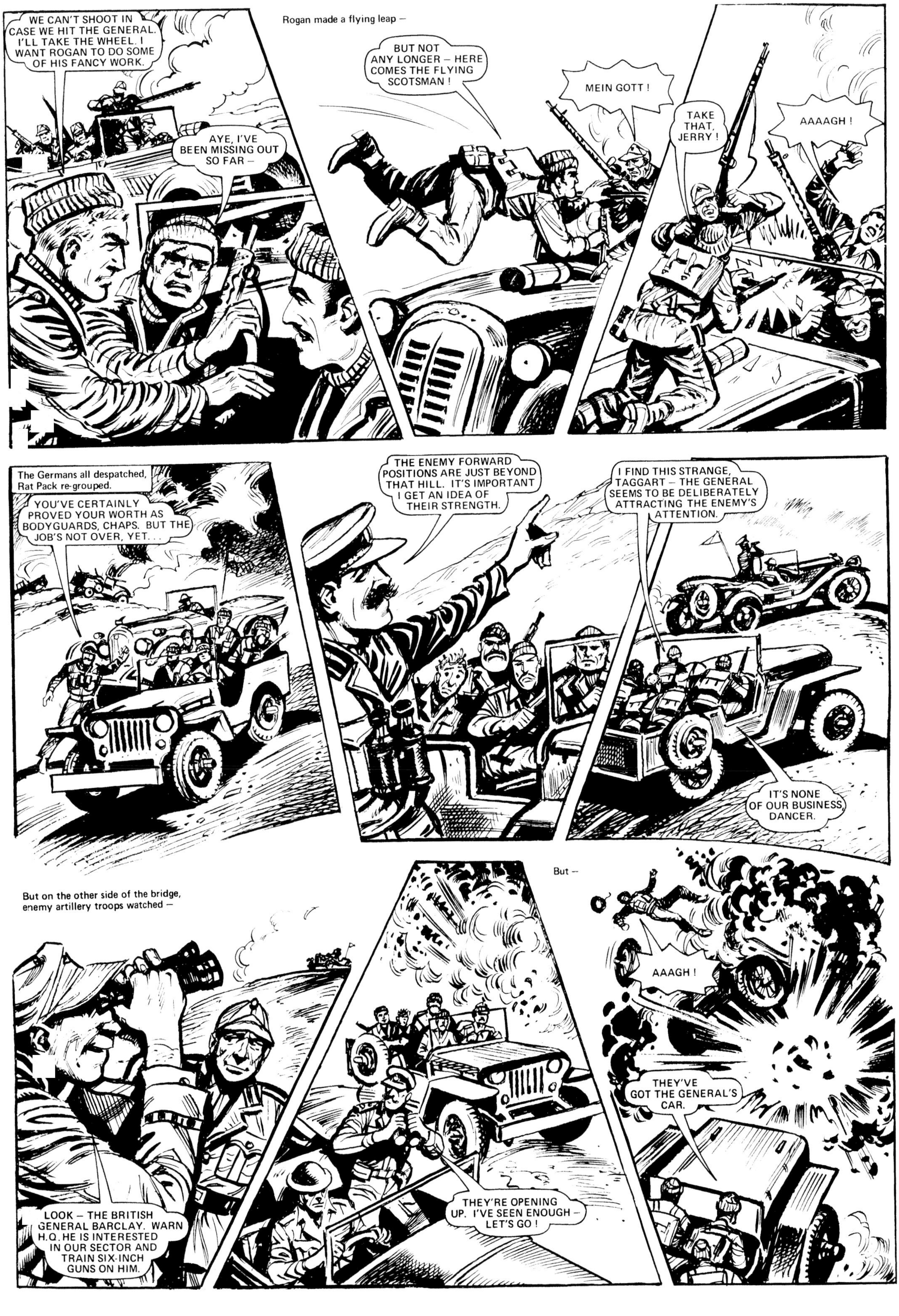
WE CAN'T SHOOT IN CASE WE HIT THE GENERAL. I'LL TAKE THE WHEEL. I WANT ROGAN TO DO SOME OF HIS FANCY WORK.
AYE, I'VE BEEN MISSING OUT SO FAR –
Rogan made a flying leap –
BUT NOT ANY LONGER – HERE COMES THE FLYING SCOTSMAN!
MEIN GOTT!
TAKE THAT, JERRY!
AAAAGH!
The Germans all despatched, Rat Pack re-grouped.
YOU'VE CERTAINLY PROVED YOUR WORTH AS BODYGUARDS, CHAPS. BUT THE JOB'S NOT OVER, YET...
THE ENEMY FORWARD POSITIONS ARE JUST BEYOND THAT HILL. IT'S IMPORTANT I GET AN IDEA OF THEIR STRENGTH.
I FIND THIS STRANGE, TAGGART – THE GENERAL SEEMS TO BE DELIBERATELY ATTRACTING THE ENEMY'S ATTENTION.
IT'S NONE OF OUR BUSINESS, DANCER.
But on the other side of the bridge, enemy artillery troops watched –
LOOK – THE BRITISH GENERAL BARCLAY. WARN H.Q. HE IS INTERESTED IN OUR SECTOR AND TRAIN SIX-INCH GUNS ON HIM.
THEY'RE OPENING UP. I'VE SEEN ENOUGH – LET'S GO!
But –
AAAGH!
THEY'VE GOT THE GENERAL'S CAR.

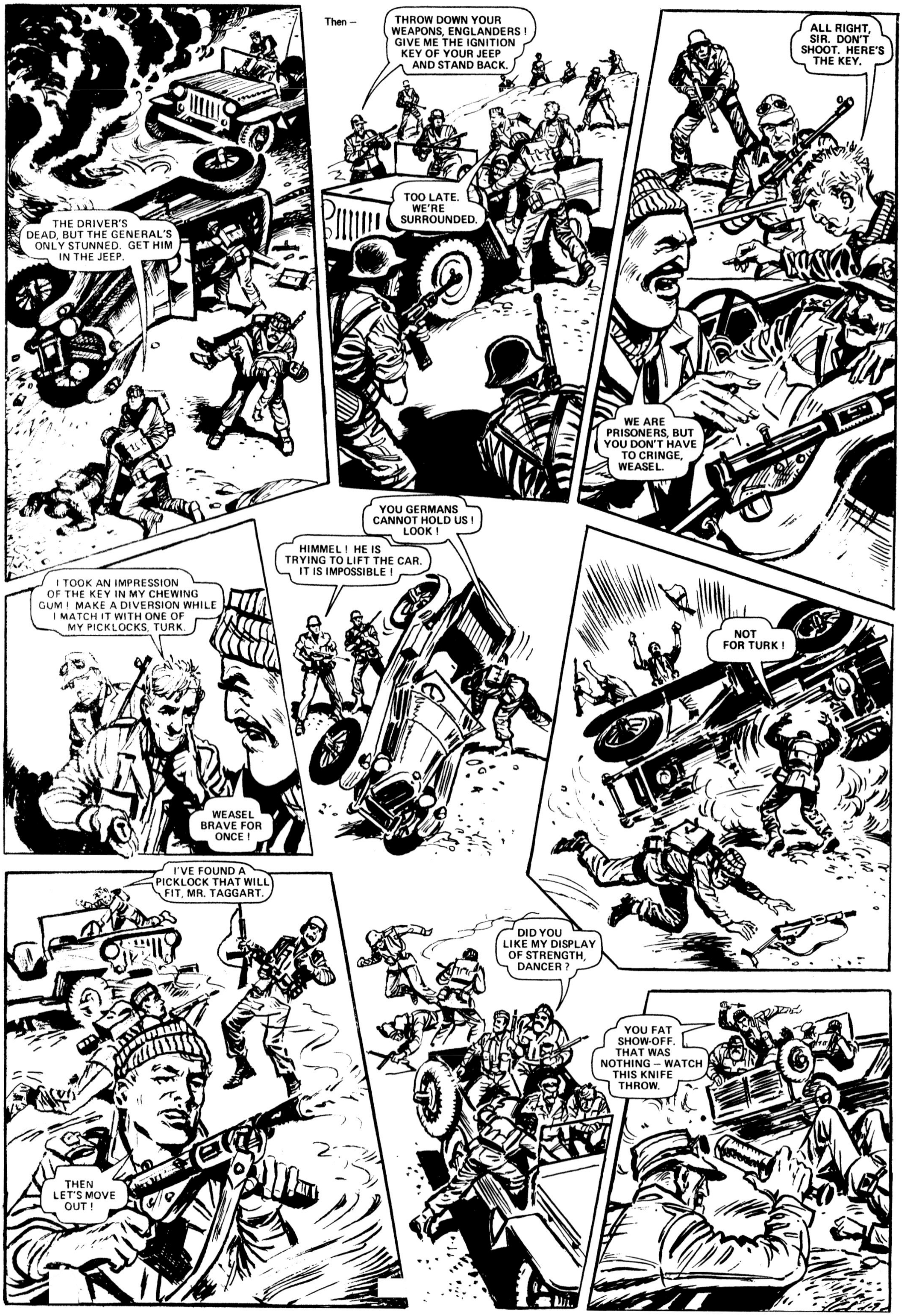
THE DRIVER'S DEAD, BUT THE GENERAL'S ONLY STUNNED. GET HIM IN THE JEEP.
Then –
THROW DOWN YOUR WEAPONS, ENGLANDERS ! GIVE ME THE IGNITION KEY OF YOUR JEEP AND STAND BACK.
TOO LATE. WE'RE SURROUNDED.
ALL RIGHT, SIR. DON'T SHOOT. HERE'S THE KEY.
WE ARE PRISONERS, BUT YOU DON'T HAVE TO CRINGE, WEASEL.
I TOOK AN IMPRESSION OF THE KEY IN MY CHEWING GUM ! MAKE A DIVERSION WHILE I MATCH IT WITH ONE OF MY PICKLOCKS, TURK.
WEASEL BRAVE FOR ONCE !
YOU GERMANS CANNOT HOLD US ! LOOK !
HIMMEL ! HE IS TRYING TO LIFT THE CAR. IT IS IMPOSSIBLE !
NOT FOR TURK !
I'VE FOUND A PICKLOCK THAT WILL FIT, MR. TAGGART.
THEN LET'S MOVE OUT !
DID YOU LIKE MY DISPLAY OF STRENGTH, DANCER ?
YOU FAT SHOW-OFF. THAT WAS NOTHING – WATCH THIS KNIFE THROW.

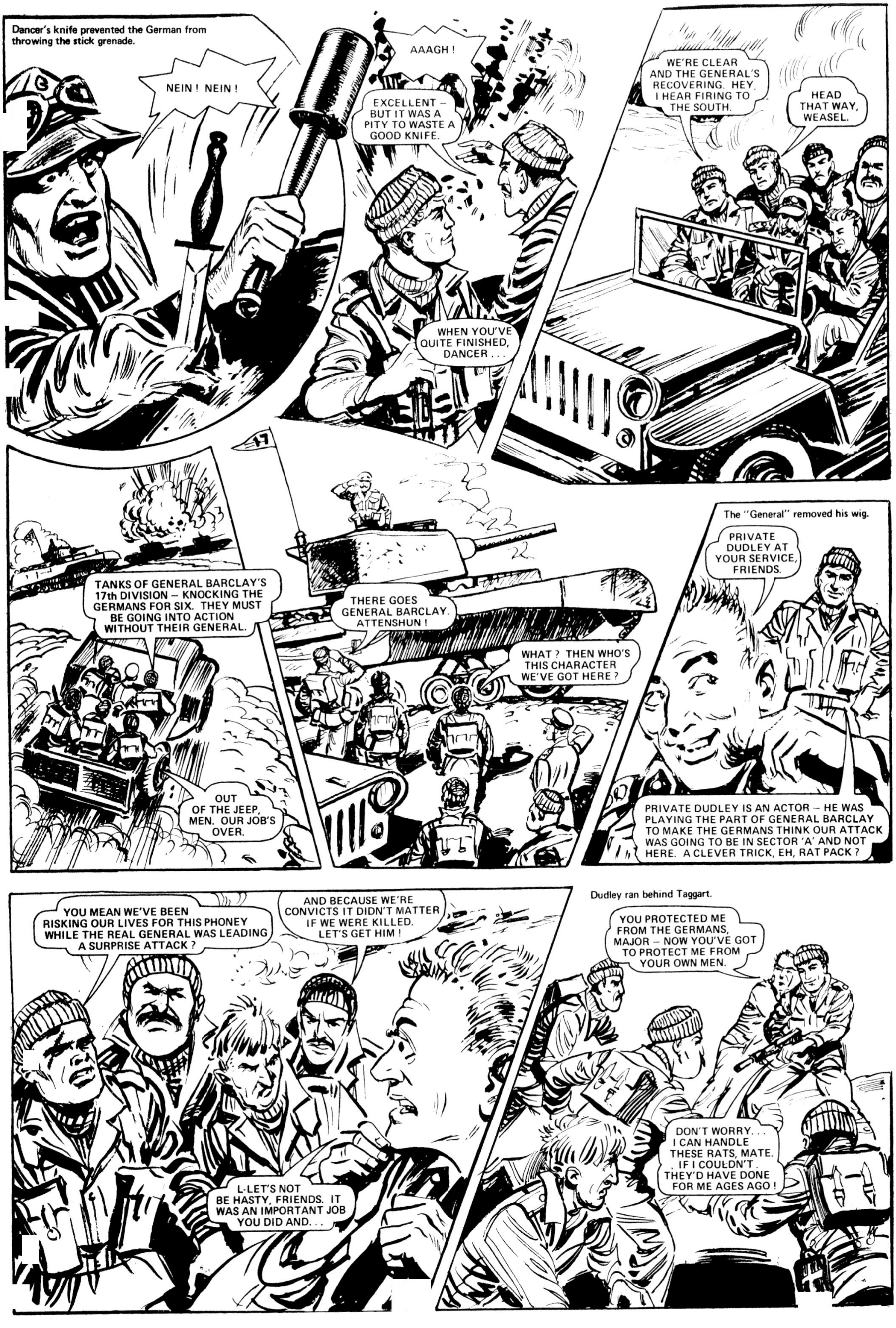
Dancer's knife prevented the German from throwing the stick grenade.
NEIN ! NEIN !
AAAGH !
EXCELLENT – BUT IT WAS A PITY TO WASTE A GOOD KNIFE.
WHEN YOU'VE QUITE FINISHED, DANCER . . .
WE'RE CLEAR AND THE GENERAL'S RECOVERING. HEY, I HEAR FIRING TO THE SOUTH.
HEAD THAT WAY, WEASEL.
TANKS OF GENERAL BARCLAY'S 17th DIVISION – KNOCKING THE GERMANS FOR SIX. THEY MUST BE GOING INTO ACTION WITHOUT THEIR GENERAL.
OUT OF THE JEEP, MEN. OUR JOB'S OVER.
THERE GOES GENERAL BARCLAY. ATTENSHUN !
WHAT ? THEN WHO'S THIS CHARACTER WE'VE GOT HERE ?
The "General" removed his wig.
PRIVATE DUDLEY AT YOUR SERVICE, FRIENDS.
PRIVATE DUDLEY IS AN ACTOR – HE WAS PLAYING THE PART OF GENERAL BARCLAY TO MAKE THE GERMANS THINK OUR ATTACK WAS GOING TO BE IN SECTOR 'A' AND NOT HERE. A CLEVER TRICK, EH, RAT PACK ?
YOU MEAN WE'VE BEEN RISKING OUR LIVES FOR THIS PHONEY WHILE THE REAL GENERAL WAS LEADING A SURPRISE ATTACK ?
AND BECAUSE WE'RE CONVICTS IT DIDN'T MATTER IF WE WERE KILLED. LET'S GET HIM !
L-LET'S NOT BE HASTY, FRIENDS. IT WAS AN IMPORTANT JOB YOU DID AND. . .
Dudley ran behind Taggart.
YOU PROTECTED ME FROM THE GERMANS, MAJOR – NOW YOU'VE GOT TO PROTECT ME FROM YOUR OWN MEN.
DON'T WORRY. . . I CAN HANDLE THESE RATS, MATE. IF I COULDN'T, THEY'D HAVE DONE FOR ME AGES AGO !

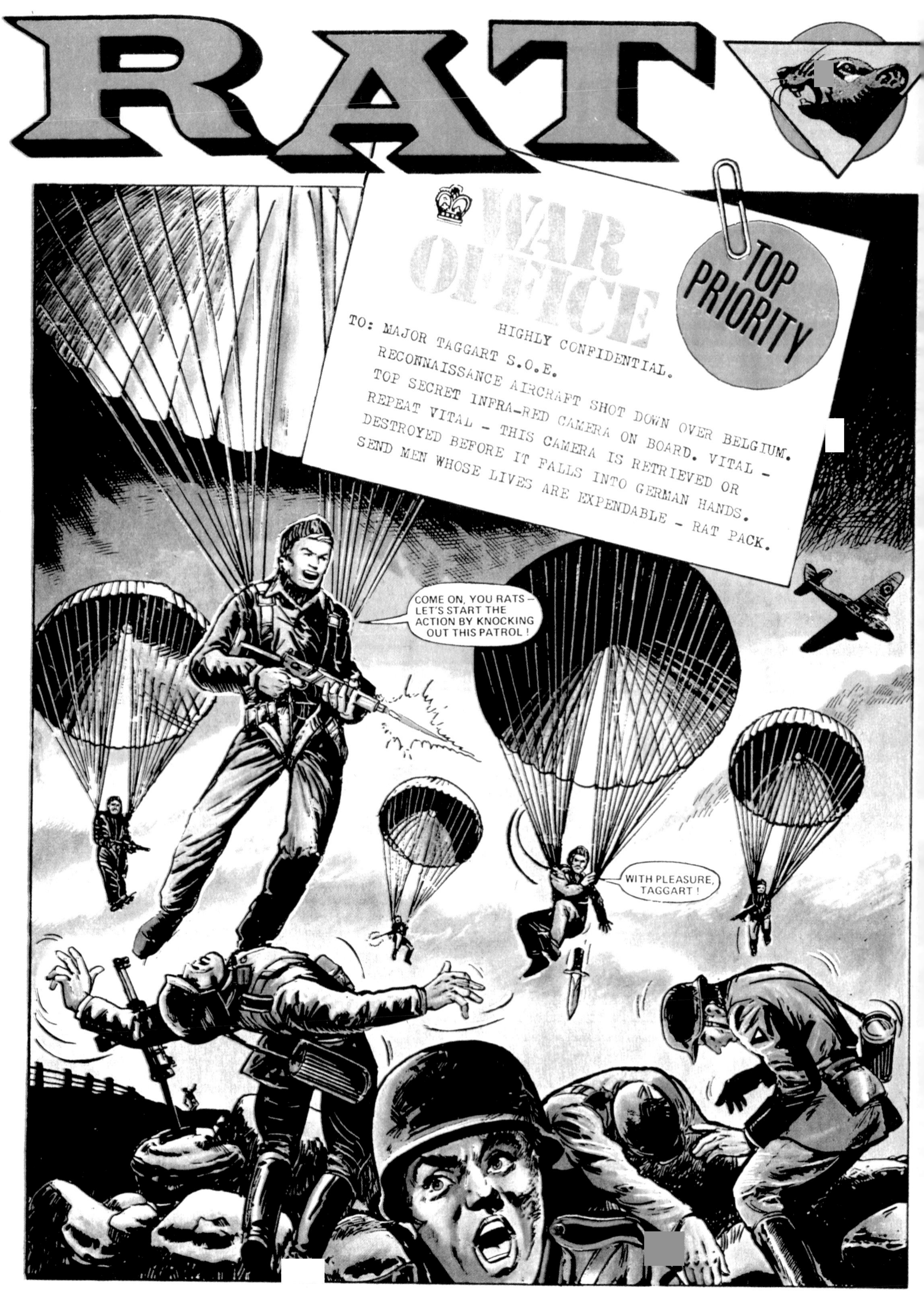
RAT PACK
WAR OFFICE
TOP PRIORITY
HIGHLY CONFIDENTIAL.
TO: MAJOR TAGGART S.O.E.
RECONNAISSANCE AIRCRAFT SHOT DOWN OVER BELGIUM.
TOP SECRET INFRA-RED CAMERA ON BOARD. VITAL -
REPEAT VITAL - THIS CAMERA IS RETRIEVED OR
DESTROYED BEFORE IT FALLS INTO GERMAN HANDS.
SEND MEN WHOSE LIVES ARE EXPENDABLE - RAT PACK.
COME ON, YOU RATS - LET'S START THE ACTION BY KNOCKING OUT THIS PATROL !
WITH PLEASURE, TAGGART !

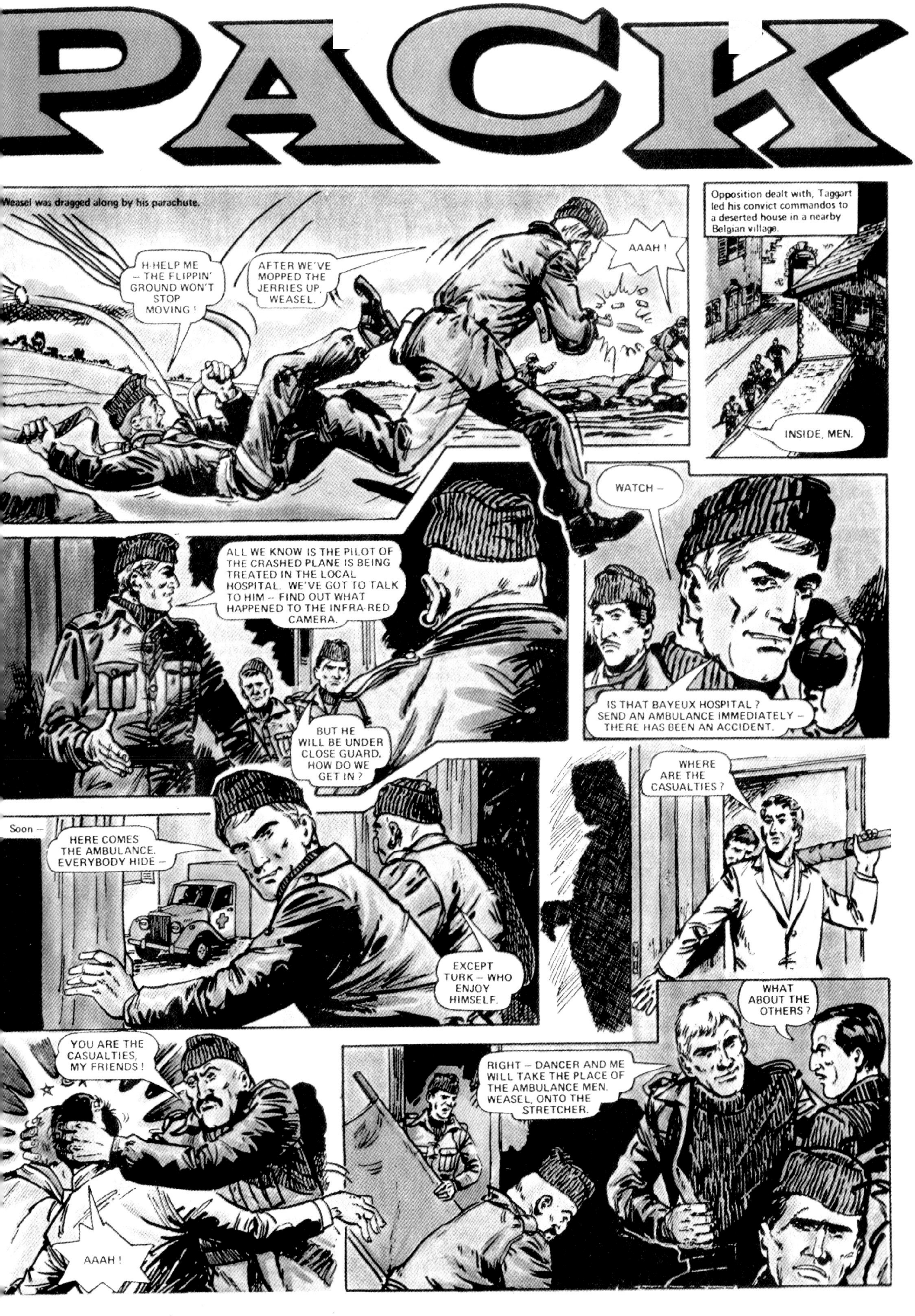
PACK
Weasel was dragged along by his parachute.
H-HELP ME – THE FLIPPIN' GROUND WON'T STOP MOVING!
AFTER WE'VE MOPPED THE JERRIES UP, WEASEL.
AAAH!
Opposition dealt with, Taggart led his convict commandos to a deserted house in a nearby Belgian village.
INSIDE, MEN.
ALL WE KNOW IS THE PILOT OF THE CRASHED PLANE IS BEING TREATED IN THE LOCAL HOSPITAL. WE'VE GOT TO TALK TO HIM – FIND OUT WHAT HAPPENED TO THE INFRA-RED CAMERA.
BUT HE WILL BE UNDER CLOSE GUARD, HOW DO WE GET IN?
WATCH –
IS THAT BAYEUX HOSPITAL? SEND AN AMBULANCE IMMEDIATELY – THERE HAS BEEN AN ACCIDENT.
Soon –
HERE COMES THE AMBULANCE. EVERYBODY HIDE –
EXCEPT TURK – WHO ENJOY HIMSELF.
WHERE ARE THE CASUALTIES?
YOU ARE THE CASUALTIES, MY FRIENDS!
AAAH!
WHAT ABOUT THE OTHERS?
RIGHT – DANCER AND ME WILL TAKE THE PLACE OF THE AMBULANCE MEN. WEASEL, ONTO THE STRETCHER.

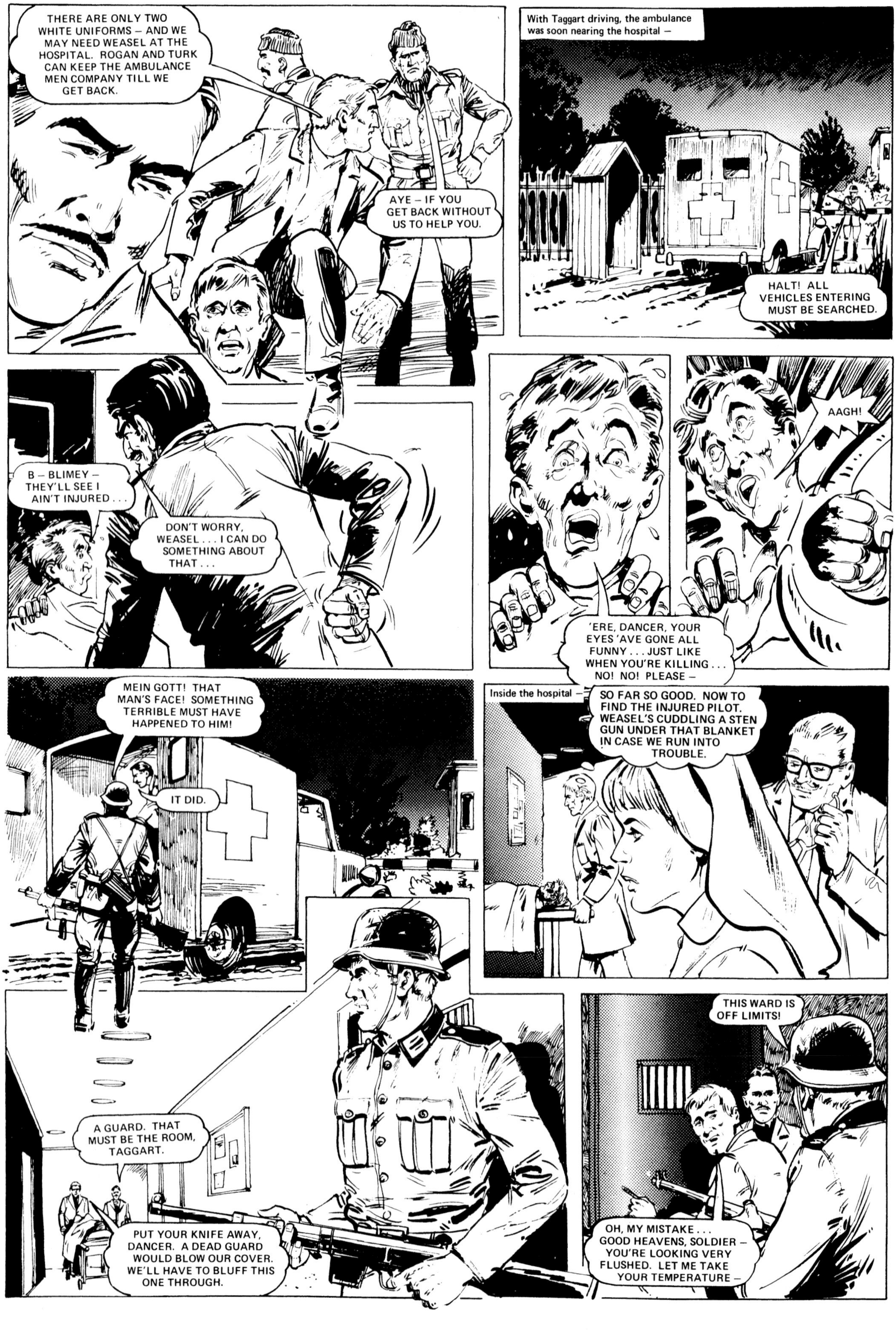
THERE ARE ONLY TWO WHITE UNIFORMS — AND WE MAY NEED WEASEL AT THE HOSPITAL. ROGAN AND TURK CAN KEEP THE AMBULANCE MEN COMPANY TILL WE GET BACK.
AYE — IF YOU GET BACK WITHOUT US TO HELP YOU.
With Taggart driving, the ambulance was soon nearing the hospital —
HALT! ALL VEHICLES ENTERING MUST BE SEARCHED.
B — BLIMEY — THEY'LL SEE I AIN'T INJURED . . .
DON'T WORRY, WEASEL . . . I CAN DO SOMETHING ABOUT THAT . . .
'ERE, DANCER, YOUR EYES 'AVE GONE ALL FUNNY . . . JUST LIKE WHEN YOU'RE KILLING . . . NO! NO! PLEASE —
AAGH!
MEIN GOTT! THAT MAN'S FACE! SOMETHING TERRIBLE MUST HAVE HAPPENED TO HIM!
IT DID.
Inside the hospital —
SO FAR SO GOOD. NOW TO FIND THE INJURED PILOT. WEASEL'S CUDDLING A STEN GUN UNDER THAT BLANKET IN CASE WE RUN INTO TROUBLE.
A GUARD. THAT MUST BE THE ROOM, TAGGART.
PUT YOUR KNIFE AWAY, DANCER. A DEAD GUARD WOULD BLOW OUR COVER. WE'LL HAVE TO BLUFF THIS ONE THROUGH.
THIS WARD IS OFF LIMITS!
OH, MY MISTAKE . . . GOOD HEAVENS, SOLDIER — YOU'RE LOOKING VERY FLUSHED. LET ME TAKE YOUR TEMPERATURE —

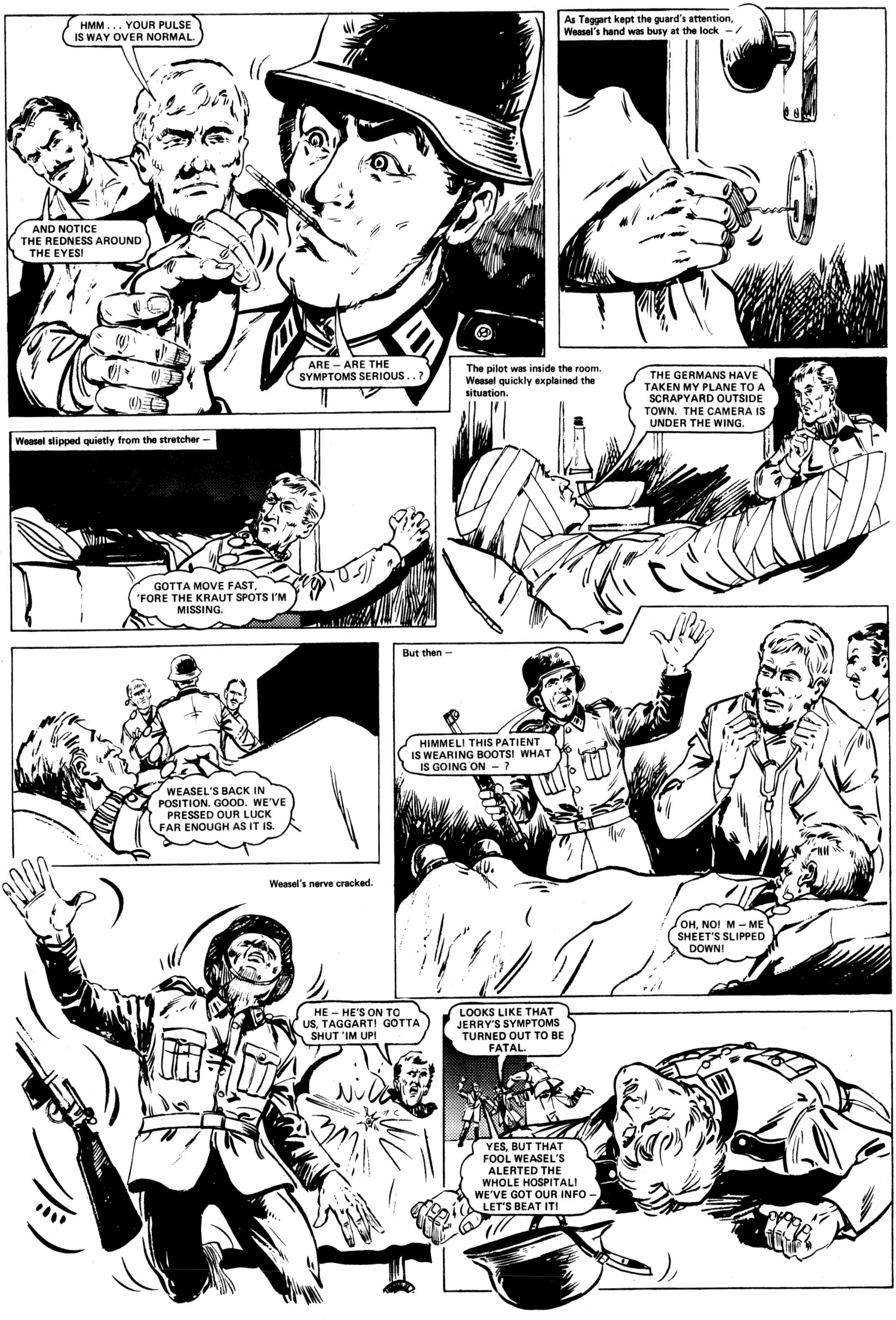
HMM . . . YOUR PULSE IS WAY OVER NORMAL.
AND NOTICE THE REDNESS AROUND THE EYES!
ARE – ARE THE SYMPTOMS SERIOUS . . ?
As Taggart kept the guard's attention, Weasel's hand was busy at the lock –
The pilot was inside the room. Weasel quickly explained the situation.
THE GERMANS HAVE TAKEN MY PLANE TO A SCRAPYARD OUTSIDE TOWN. THE CAMERA IS UNDER THE WING.
Weasel slipped quietly from the stretcher –
GOTTA MOVE FAST, 'FORE THE KRAUT SPOTS I'M MISSING.
WEASEL'S BACK IN POSITION. GOOD. WE'VE PRESSED OUR LUCK FAR ENOUGH AS IT IS.
But then –
HIMMEL! THIS PATIENT IS WEARING BOOTS! WHAT IS GOING ON – ?
OH, NO! M – ME SHEET'S SLIPPED DOWN!
Weasel's nerve cracked.
HE – HE'S ON TO US, TAGGART! GOTTA SHUT 'IM UP!
LOOKS LIKE THAT JERRY'S SYMPTOMS TURNED OUT TO BE FATAL.
YES, BUT THAT FOOL WEASEL'S ALERTED THE WHOLE HOSPITAL! WE'VE GOT OUR INFO – LET'S BEAT IT!

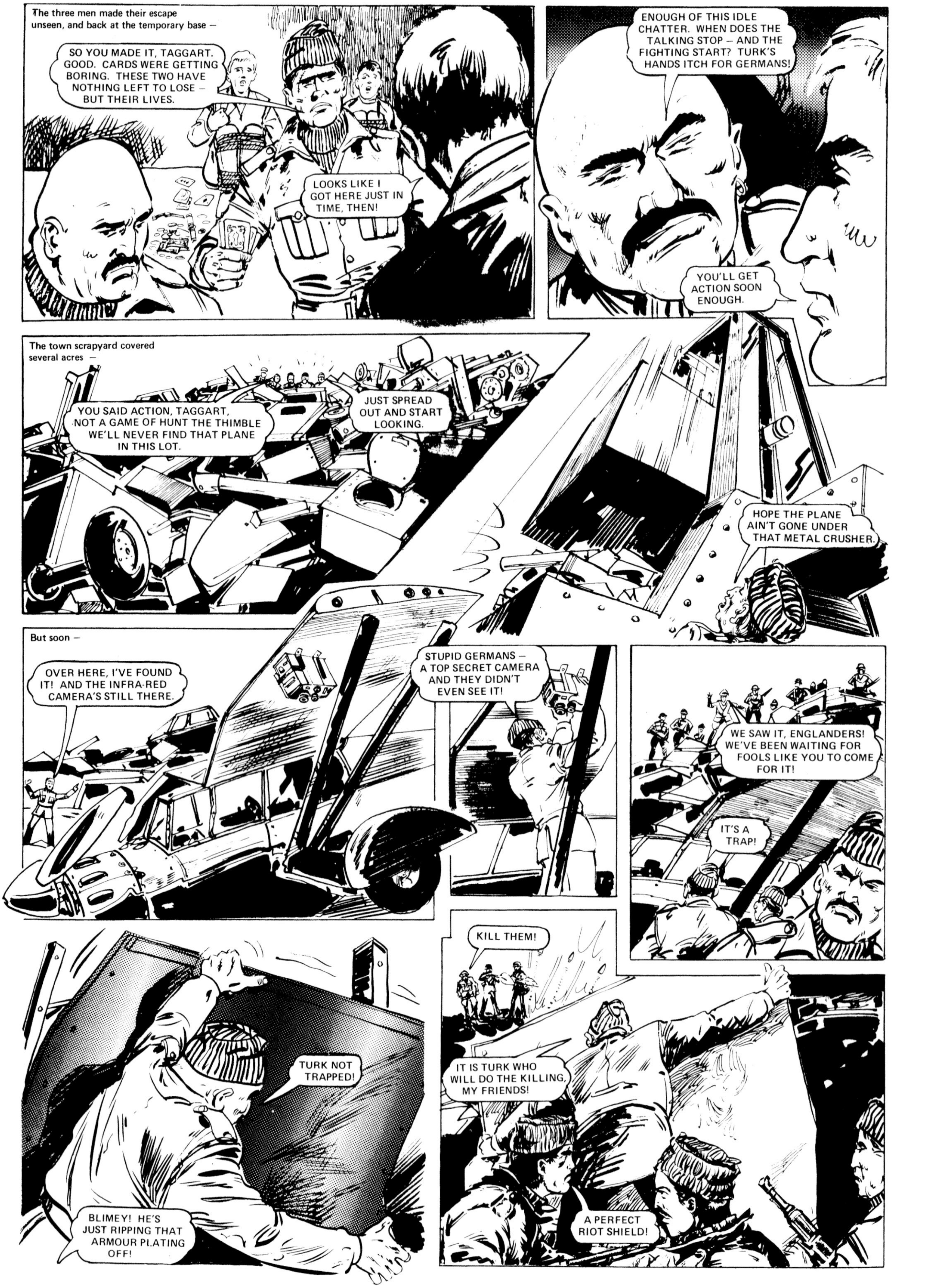
The three men made their escape unseen, and back at the temporary base —
SO YOU MADE IT, TAGGART. GOOD. CARDS WERE GETTING BORING. THESE TWO HAVE NOTHING LEFT TO LOSE — BUT THEIR LIVES.
LOOKS LIKE I GOT HERE JUST IN TIME, THEN!
ENOUGH OF THIS IDLE CHATTER. WHEN DOES THE TALKING STOP — AND THE FIGHTING START? TURK'S HANDS ITCH FOR GERMANS!
YOU'LL GET ACTION SOON ENOUGH.
The town scrapyard covered several acres —
YOU SAID ACTION, TAGGART, NOT A GAME OF HUNT THE THIMBLE. WE'LL NEVER FIND THAT PLANE IN THIS LOT.
JUST SPREAD OUT AND START LOOKING.
HOPE THE PLANE AIN'T GONE UNDER THAT METAL CRUSHER.
But soon —
OVER HERE, I'VE FOUND IT! AND THE INFRA-RED CAMERA'S STILL THERE.
STUPID GERMANS — A TOP SECRET CAMERA AND THEY DIDN'T EVEN SEE IT!
WE SAW IT, ENGLANDERS! WE'VE BEEN WAITING FOR FOOLS LIKE YOU TO COME FOR IT!
IT'S A TRAP!
TURK NOT TRAPPED!
BLIMEY! HE'S JUST RIPPING THAT ARMOUR PLATING OFF!
KILL THEM!
IT IS TURK WHO WILL DO THE KILLING, MY FRIENDS!
A PERFECT RIOT SHIELD!

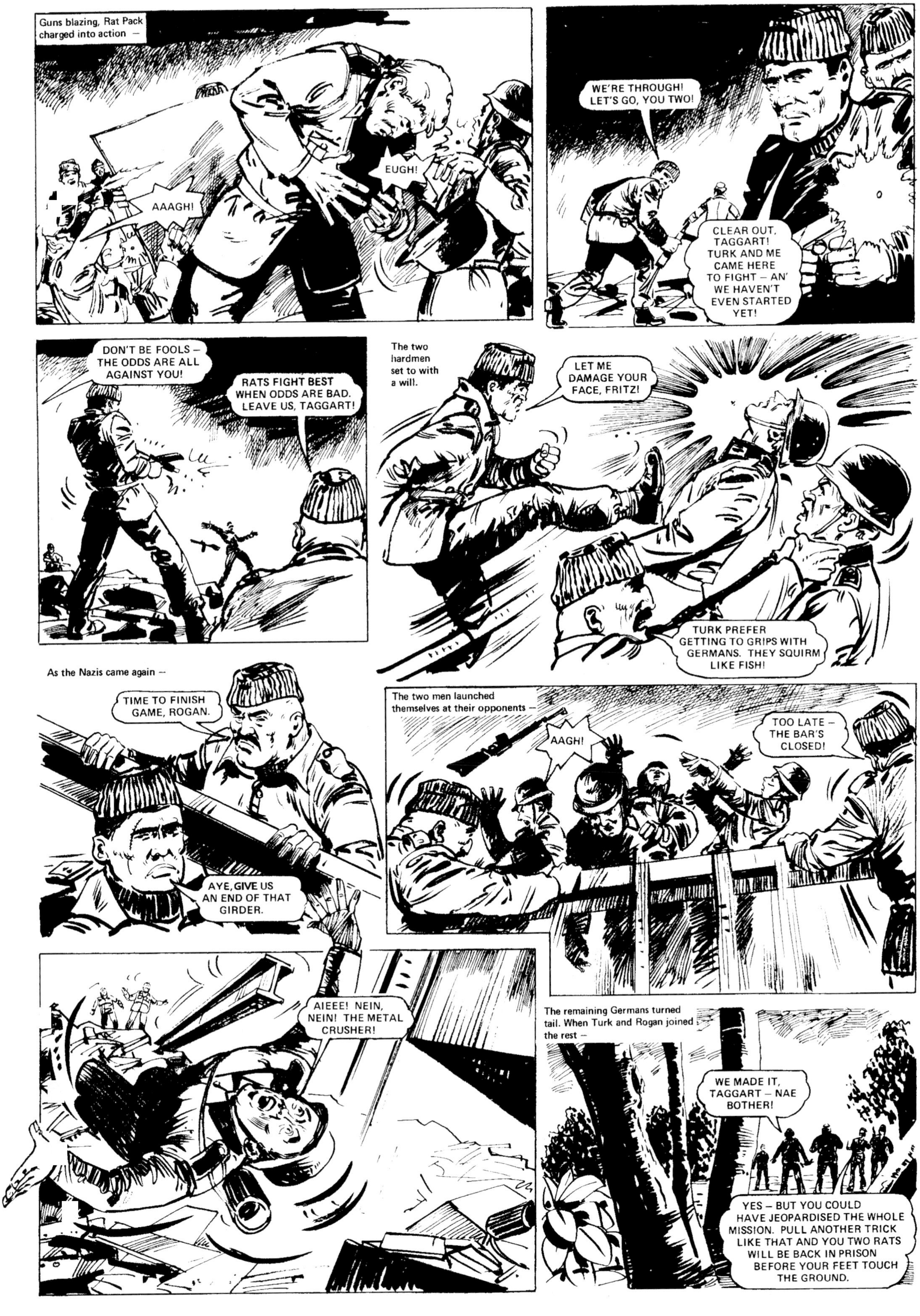
Guns blazing, Rat Pack charged into action –
AAAGH!
EUGH!
WE'RE THROUGH! LET'S GO, YOU TWO!
CLEAR OUT, TAGGART! TURK AND ME CAME HERE TO FIGHT – AN' WE HAVEN'T EVEN STARTED YET!
DON'T BE FOOLS – THE ODDS ARE ALL AGAINST YOU!
RATS FIGHT BEST WHEN ODDS ARE BAD. LEAVE US, TAGGART!
The two hardmen set to with a will.
LET ME DAMAGE YOUR FACE, FRITZ!
TURK PREFER GETTING TO GRIPS WITH GERMANS. THEY SQUIRM LIKE FISH!
As the Nazis came again –
TIME TO FINISH GAME, ROGAN.
AYE, GIVE US AN END OF THAT GIRDER.
The two men launched themselves at their opponents –
AAGH!
TOO LATE – THE BAR'S CLOSED!
AIEEE! NEIN, NEIN! THE METAL CRUSHER!
The remaining Germans turned tail. When Turk and Rogan joined the rest –
WE MADE IT, TAGGART – NAE BOTHER!
YES – BUT YOU COULD HAVE JEOPARDISED THE WHOLE MISSION. PULL ANOTHER TRICK LIKE THAT AND YOU TWO RATS WILL BE BACK IN PRISON BEFORE YOUR FEET TOUCH THE GROUND.

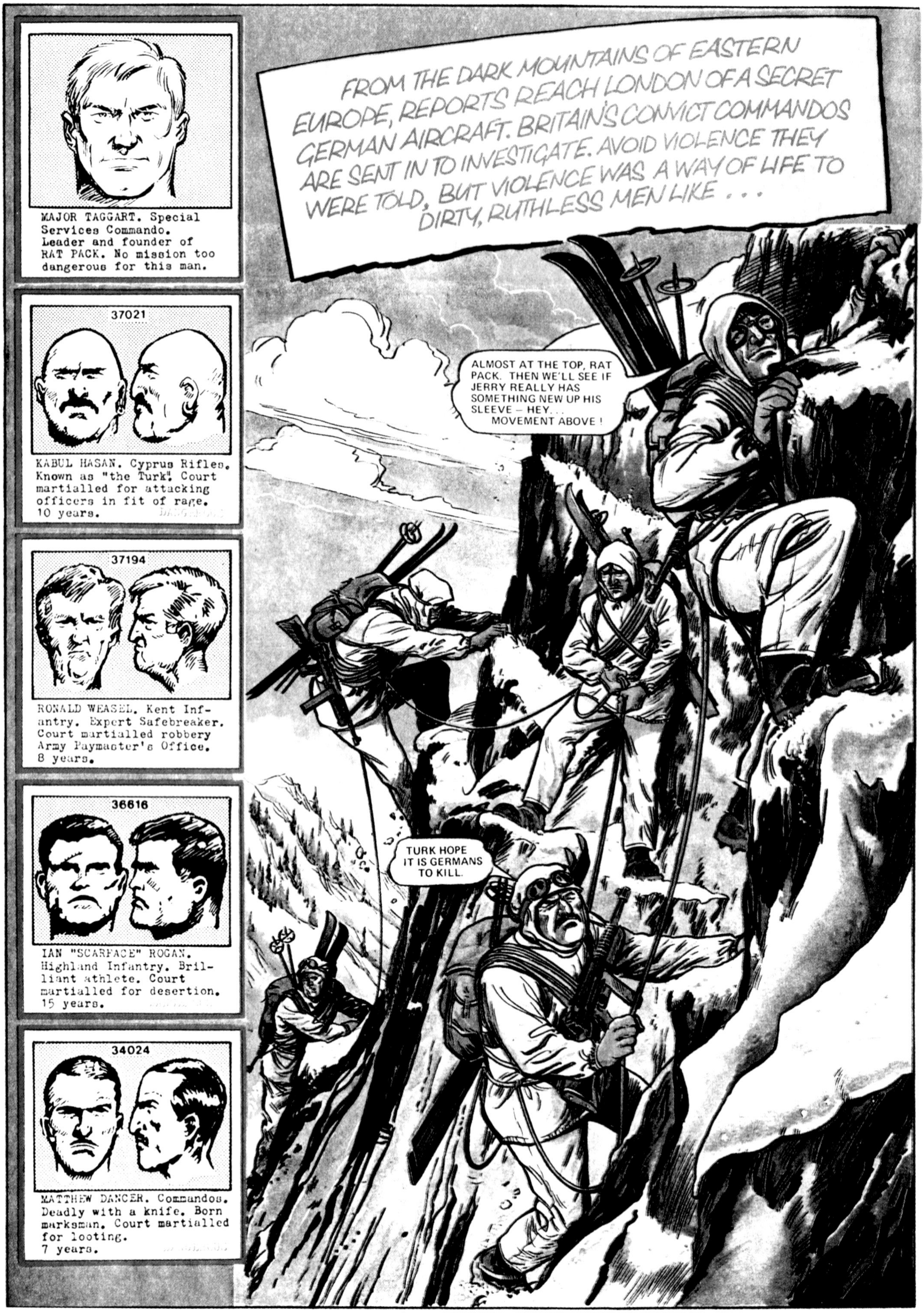
MAJOR TAGGART. Special Services Commando. Leader and founder of RAT PACK. No mission too dangerous for this man.
37021
KABUL HASAN. Cyprus Rifles. Known as "the Turk". Court martialled for attacking officers in fit of rage. 10 years.
37194
RONALD WEASEL. Kent Infantry. Expert Safebreaker. Court martialled robbery Army Paymaster's Office. 8 years.
36616
IAN "SCARFACE" ROGAN. Highland Infantry. Brilliant athlete. Court martialled for desertion. 15 years.
34024
MATTHEW DANCER. Commandos. Deadly with a knife. Born marksman. Court martialled for looting. 7 years.
FROM THE DARK MOUNTAINS OF EASTERN EUROPE, REPORTS REACH LONDON OF A SECRET GERMAN AIRCRAFT. BRITAIN'S CONVICT COMMANDOS ARE SENT IN TO INVESTIGATE. AVOID VIOLENCE THEY WERE TOLD, BUT VIOLENCE WAS A WAY OF LIFE TO DIRTY, RUTHLESS MEN LIKE . . .
ALMOST AT THE TOP, RAT PACK. THEN WE'LL SEE IF JERRY REALLY HAS SOMETHING NEW UP HIS SLEEVE – HEY... MOVEMENT ABOVE !
TURK HOPE IT IS GERMANS TO KILL.

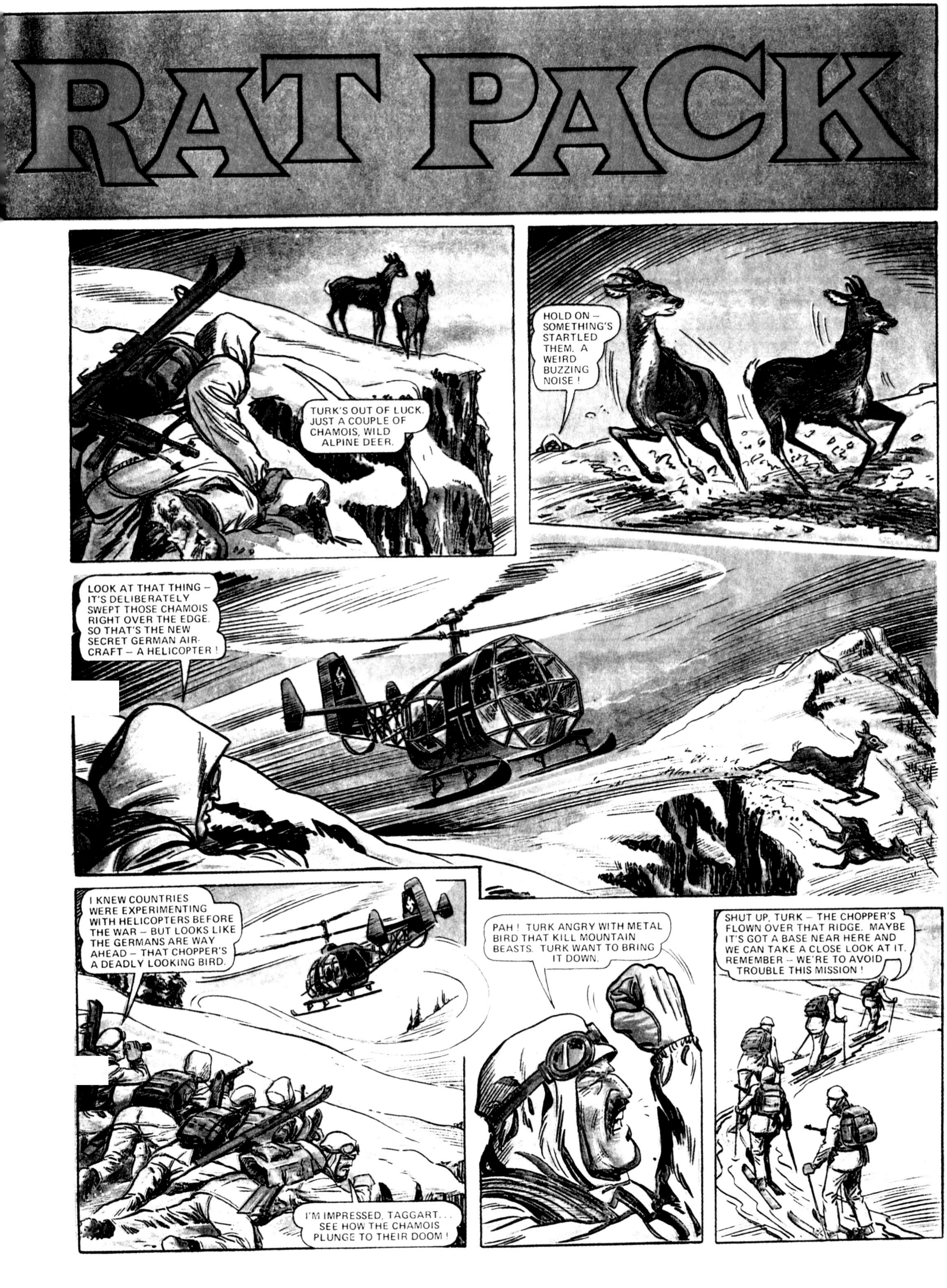
RAT PACK
TURK'S OUT OF LUCK. JUST A COUPLE OF CHAMOIS, WILD ALPINE DEER.
HOLD ON — SOMETHING'S STARTLED THEM. A WEIRD BUZZING NOISE !
LOOK AT THAT THING — IT'S DELIBERATELY SWEPT THOSE CHAMOIS RIGHT OVER THE EDGE. SO THAT'S THE NEW SECRET GERMAN AIR-CRAFT — A HELICOPTER !
I KNEW COUNTRIES WERE EXPERIMENTING WITH HELICOPTERS BEFORE THE WAR — BUT LOOKS LIKE THE GERMANS ARE WAY AHEAD — THAT CHOPPER'S A DEADLY LOOKING BIRD.
I'M IMPRESSED, TAGGART. . . SEE HOW THE CHAMOIS PLUNGE TO THEIR DOOM !
PAH ! TURK ANGRY WITH METAL BIRD THAT KILL MOUNTAIN BEASTS. TURK WANT TO BRING IT DOWN.
SHUT UP, TURK — THE CHOPPER'S FLOWN OVER THAT RIDGE. MAYBE IT'S GOT A BASE NEAR HERE AND WE CAN TAKE A CLOSE LOOK AT IT. REMEMBER — WE'RE TO AVOID TROUBLE THIS MISSION !

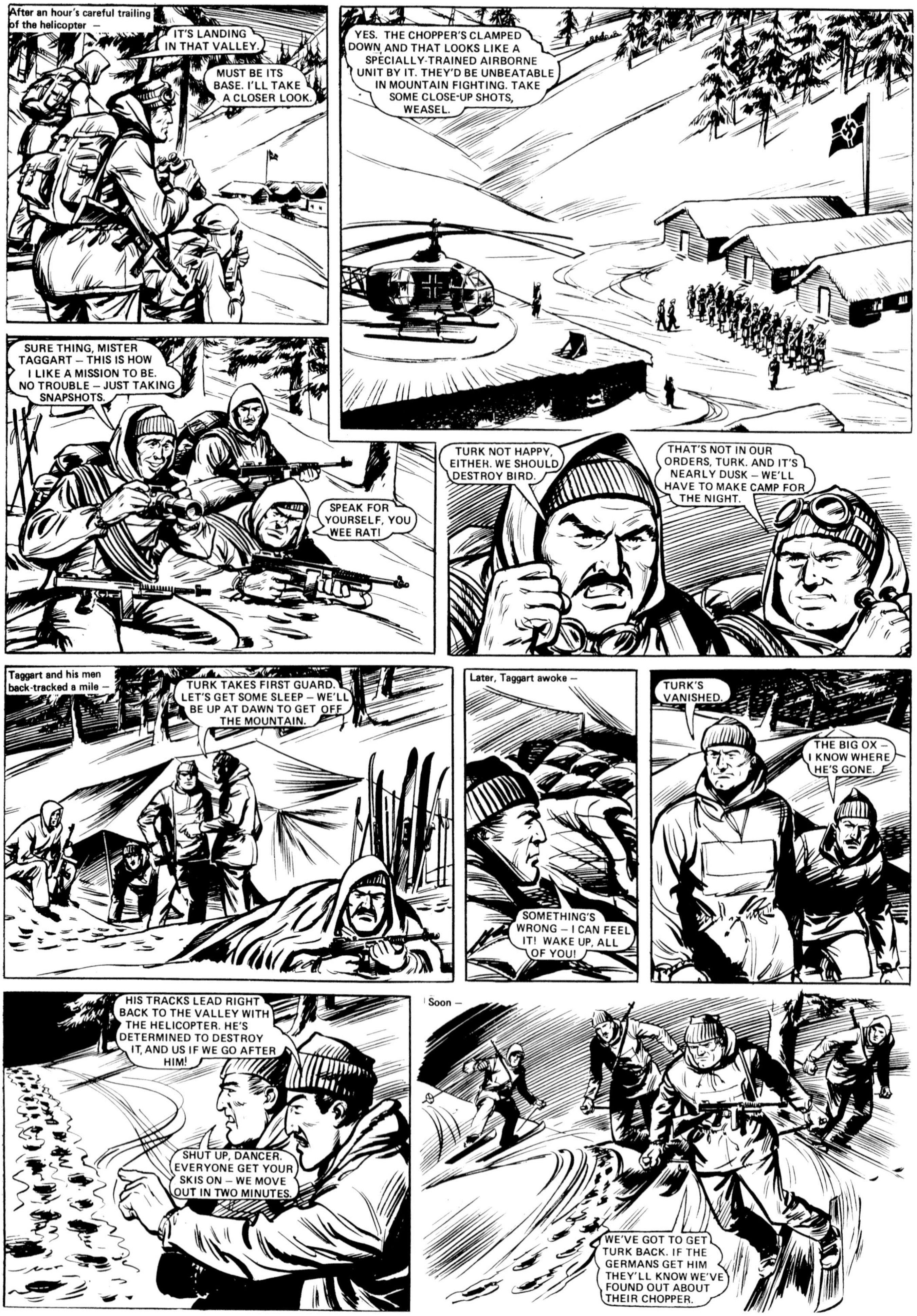

After an hour's careful trailing of the helicopter –
IT'S LANDING IN THAT VALLEY.
MUST BE ITS BASE. I'LL TAKE A CLOSER LOOK.
YES. THE CHOPPER'S CLAMPED DOWN AND THAT LOOKS LIKE A SPECIALLY-TRAINED AIRBORNE UNIT BY IT. THEY'D BE UNBEATABLE IN MOUNTAIN FIGHTING. TAKE SOME CLOSE-UP SHOTS, WEASEL.
SURE THING, MISTER TAGGART – THIS IS HOW I LIKE A MISSION TO BE. NO TROUBLE – JUST TAKING SNAPSHOTS.
SPEAK FOR YOURSELF, YOU WEE RAT!
TURK NOT HAPPY, EITHER. WE SHOULD DESTROY BIRD.
THAT'S NOT IN OUR ORDERS, TURK. AND IT'S NEARLY DUSK – WE'LL HAVE TO MAKE CAMP FOR THE NIGHT.
Taggart and his men back-tracked a mile –
TURK TAKES FIRST GUARD. LET'S GET SOME SLEEP – WE'LL BE UP AT DAWN TO GET OFF THE MOUNTAIN.
Later, Taggart awoke –
SOMETHING'S WRONG – I CAN FEEL IT! WAKE UP, ALL OF YOU!
TURK'S VANISHED.
THE BIG OX – I KNOW WHERE HE'S GONE.
HIS TRACKS LEAD RIGHT BACK TO THE VALLEY WITH THE HELICOPTER. HE'S DETERMINED TO DESTROY IT, AND US IF WE GO AFTER HIM!
SHUT UP, DANCER. EVERYONE GET YOUR SKIS ON – WE MOVE OUT IN TWO MINUTES.
Soon –
WE'VE GOT TO GET TURK BACK. IF THE GERMANS GET HIM THEY'LL KNOW WE'VE FOUND OUT ABOUT THEIR CHOPPER.

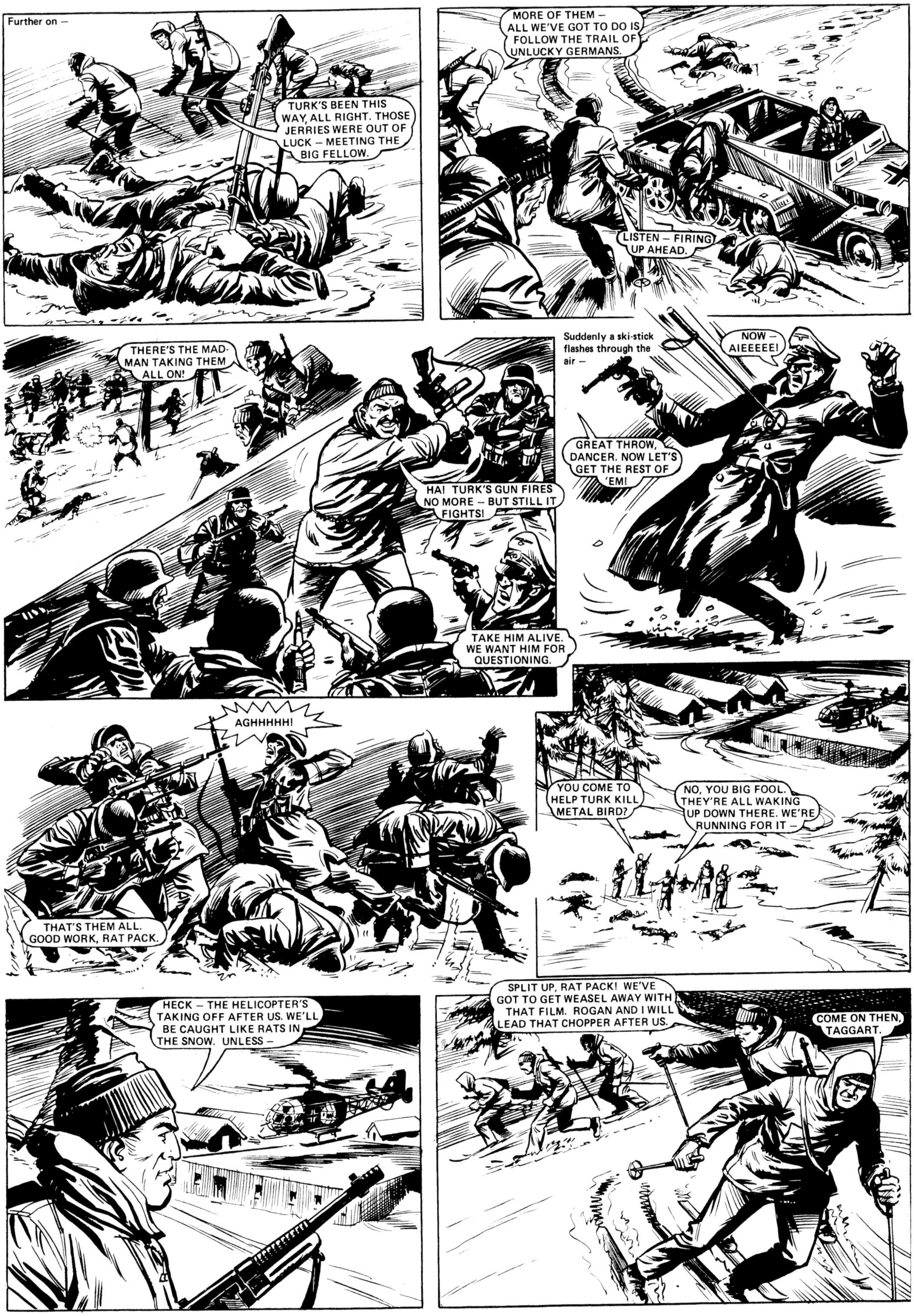

Further on –
TURK'S BEEN THIS WAY, ALL RIGHT. THOSE JERRIES WERE OUT OF LUCK – MEETING THE BIG FELLOW.
MORE OF THEM – ALL WE'VE GOT TO DO IS FOLLOW THE TRAIL OF UNLUCKY GERMANS.
LISTEN – FIRING UP AHEAD.
THERE'S THE MADMAN TAKING THEM ALL ON!
HA! TURK'S GUN FIRES NO MORE – BUT STILL IT FIGHTS!
TAKE HIM ALIVE. WE WANT HIM FOR QUESTIONING.
Suddenly a ski-stick flashes through the air –
NOW – AIEEEEE!
GREAT THROW, DANCER. NOW LET'S GET THE REST OF 'EM!
AGHHHHH!
THAT'S THEM ALL. GOOD WORK, RAT PACK.
YOU COME TO HELP TURK KILL METAL BIRD?
NO, YOU BIG FOOL. THEY'RE ALL WAKING UP DOWN THERE. WE'RE RUNNING FOR IT –
HECK – THE HELICOPTER'S TAKING OFF AFTER US. WE'LL BE CAUGHT LIKE RATS IN THE SNOW. UNLESS –
SPLIT UP, RAT PACK! WE'VE GOT TO GET WEASEL AWAY WITH THAT FILM. ROGAN AND I WILL LEAD THAT CHOPPER AFTER US.
COME ON THEN, TAGGART.

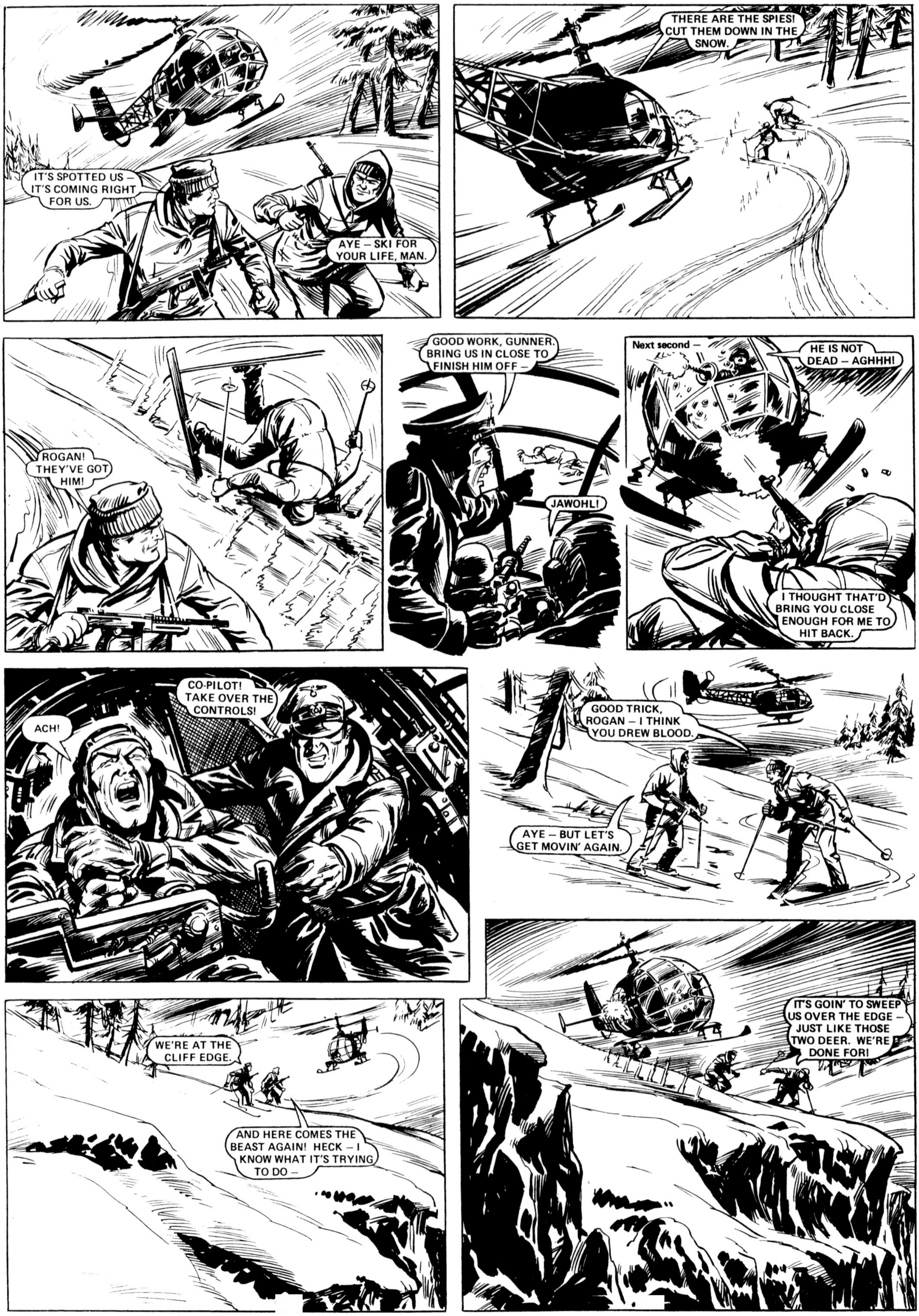
IT'S SPOTTED US – IT'S COMING RIGHT FOR US.
AYE – SKI FOR YOUR LIFE, MAN.
THERE ARE THE SPIES! CUT THEM DOWN IN THE SNOW.
ROGAN! THEY'VE GOT HIM!
GOOD WORK, GUNNER. BRING US IN CLOSE TO FINISH HIM OFF –
JAWOHL!
Next second –
HE IS NOT DEAD – AGHHH!
I THOUGHT THAT'D BRING YOU CLOSE ENOUGH FOR ME TO HIT BACK.
ACH!
CO-PILOT! TAKE OVER THE CONTROLS!
GOOD TRICK, ROGAN – I THINK YOU DREW BLOOD.
AYE – BUT LET'S GET MOVIN' AGAIN.
WE'RE AT THE CLIFF EDGE.
AND HERE COMES THE BEAST AGAIN! HECK – I KNOW WHAT IT'S TRYING TO DO –
IT'S GOIN' TO SWEEP US OVER THE EDGE – JUST LIKE THOSE TWO DEER. WE'RE DONE FOR!

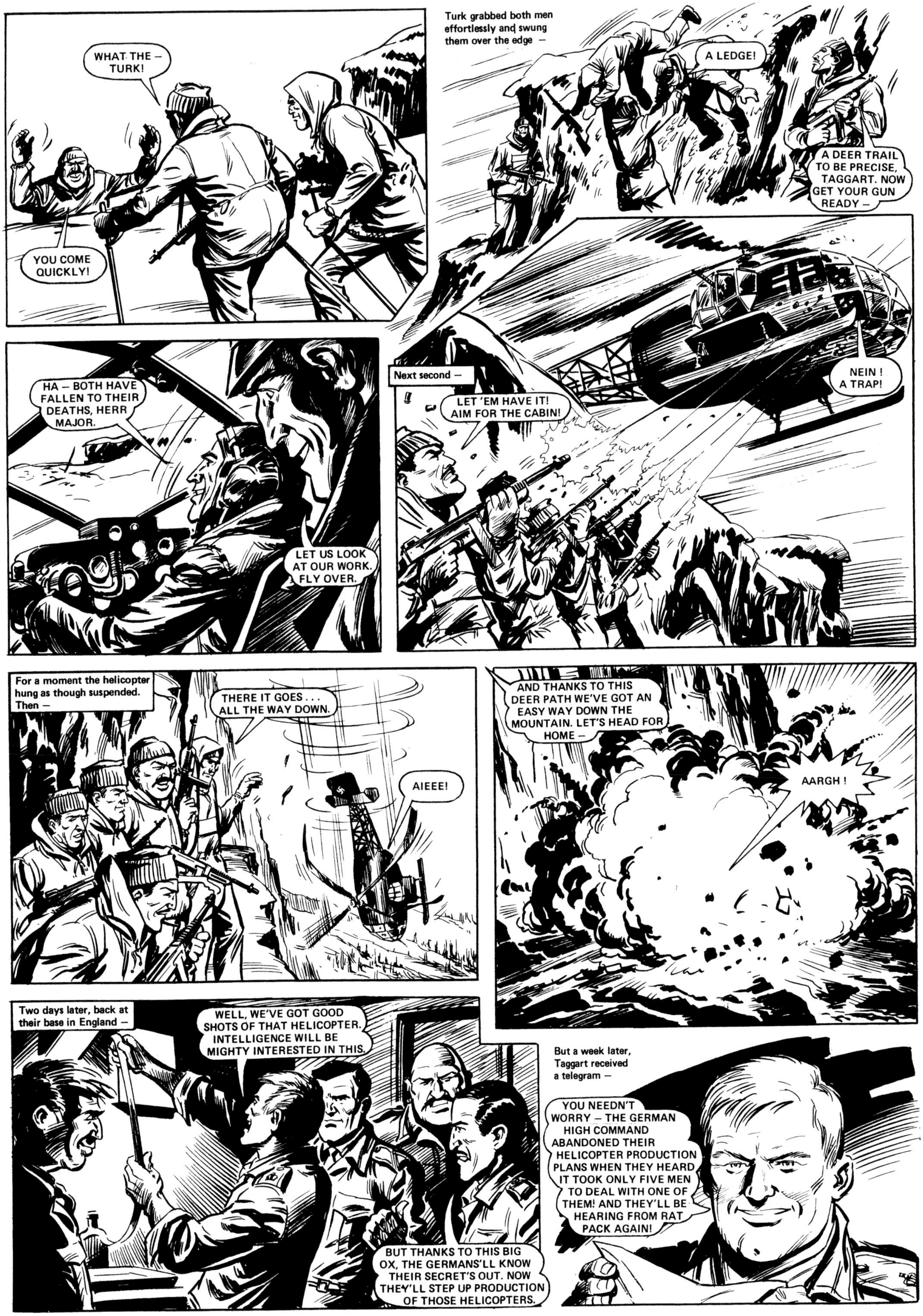

WHAT THE — TURK!
YOU COME QUICKLY!
Turk grabbed both men effortlessly and swung them over the edge —
A LEDGE!
A DEER TRAIL TO BE PRECISE, TAGGART. NOW GET YOUR GUN READY —
HA — BOTH HAVE FALLEN TO THEIR DEATHS, HERR MAJOR.
LET US LOOK AT OUR WORK. FLY OVER.
Next second —
LET 'EM HAVE IT! AIM FOR THE CABIN!
NEIN ! A TRAP!
For a moment the helicopter hung as though suspended. Then —
THERE IT GOES . . . ALL THE WAY DOWN.
AIEEE!
AND THANKS TO THIS DEER PATH WE'VE GOT AN EASY WAY DOWN THE MOUNTAIN. LET'S HEAD FOR HOME —
AARGH !
Two days later, back at their base in England —
WELL, WE'VE GOT GOOD SHOTS OF THAT HELICOPTER. INTELLIGENCE WILL BE MIGHTY INTERESTED IN THIS.
BUT THANKS TO THIS BIG OX, THE GERMANS'LL KNOW THEIR SECRET'S OUT. NOW THEY'LL STEP UP PRODUCTION OF THOSE HELICOPTERS.
But a week later, Taggart received a telegram —
YOU NEEDN'T WORRY — THE GERMAN HIGH COMMAND ABANDONED THEIR HELICOPTER PRODUCTION PLANS WHEN THEY HEARD IT TOOK ONLY FIVE MEN TO DEAL WITH ONE OF THEM! AND THEY'LL BE HEARING FROM RAT PACK AGAIN!

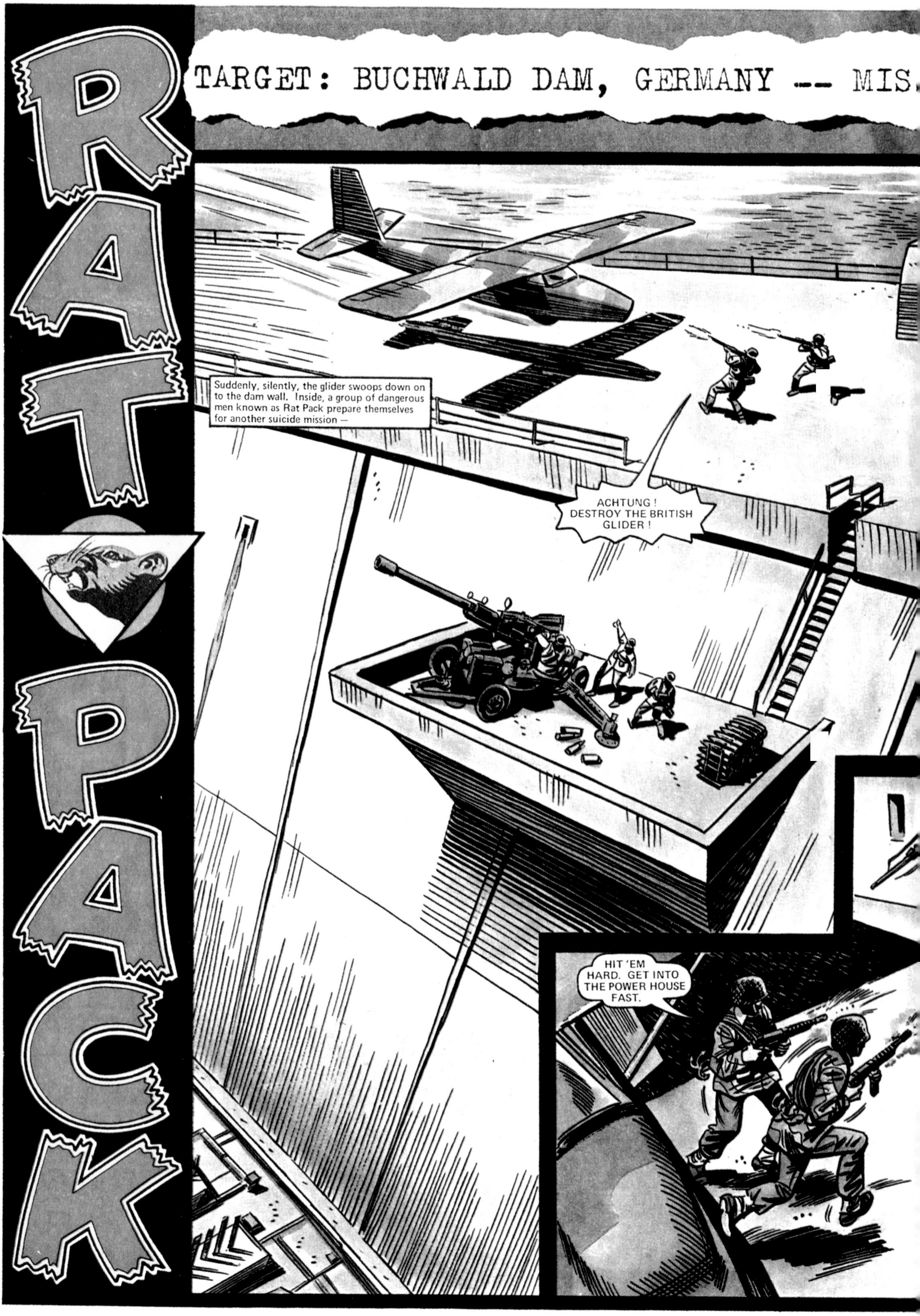
RAT PACK
TARGET: BUCHWALD DAM, GERMANY -- MIS
Suddenly, silently, the glider swoops down on to the dam wall. Inside, a group of dangerous men known as Rat Pack prepare themselves for another suicide mission –
ACHTUNG! DESTROY THE BRITISH GLIDER!
HIT 'EM HARD. GET INTO THE POWER HOUSE FAST.

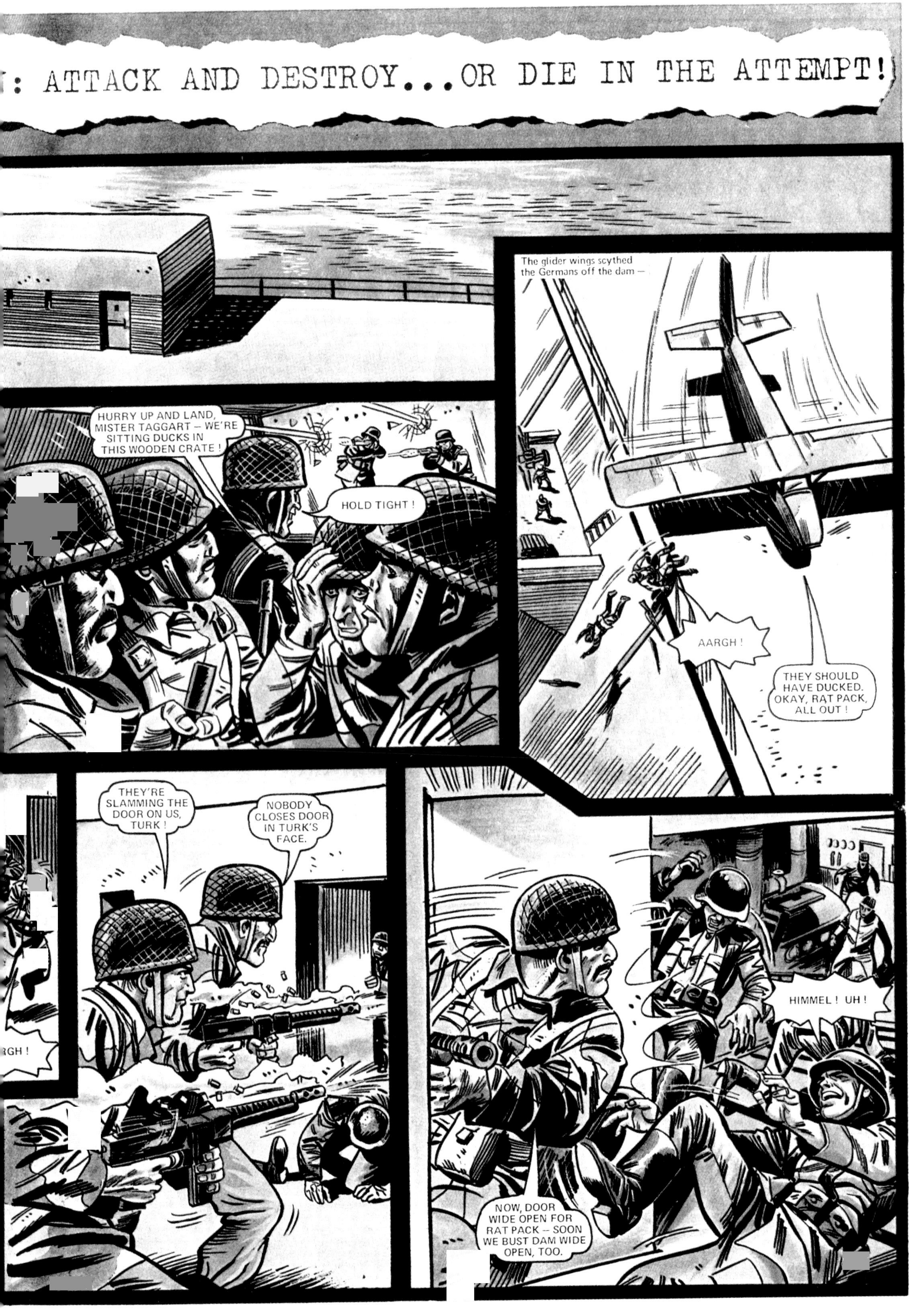
: ATTACK AND DESTROY...OR DIE IN THE ATTEMPT!
HURRY UP AND LAND, MISTER TAGGART – WE'RE SITTING DUCKS IN THIS WOODEN CRATE!
HOLD TIGHT!
The glider wings scythed the Germans off the dam –
AARGH!
THEY SHOULD HAVE DUCKED. OKAY, RAT PACK, ALL OUT!
THEY'RE SLAMMING THE DOOR ON US, TURK!
NOBODY CLOSES DOOR IN TURK'S FACE.
RGH!
HIMMEL! UH!
NOW, DOOR WIDE OPEN FOR RAT PACK – SOON WE BUST DAM WIDE OPEN, TOO.

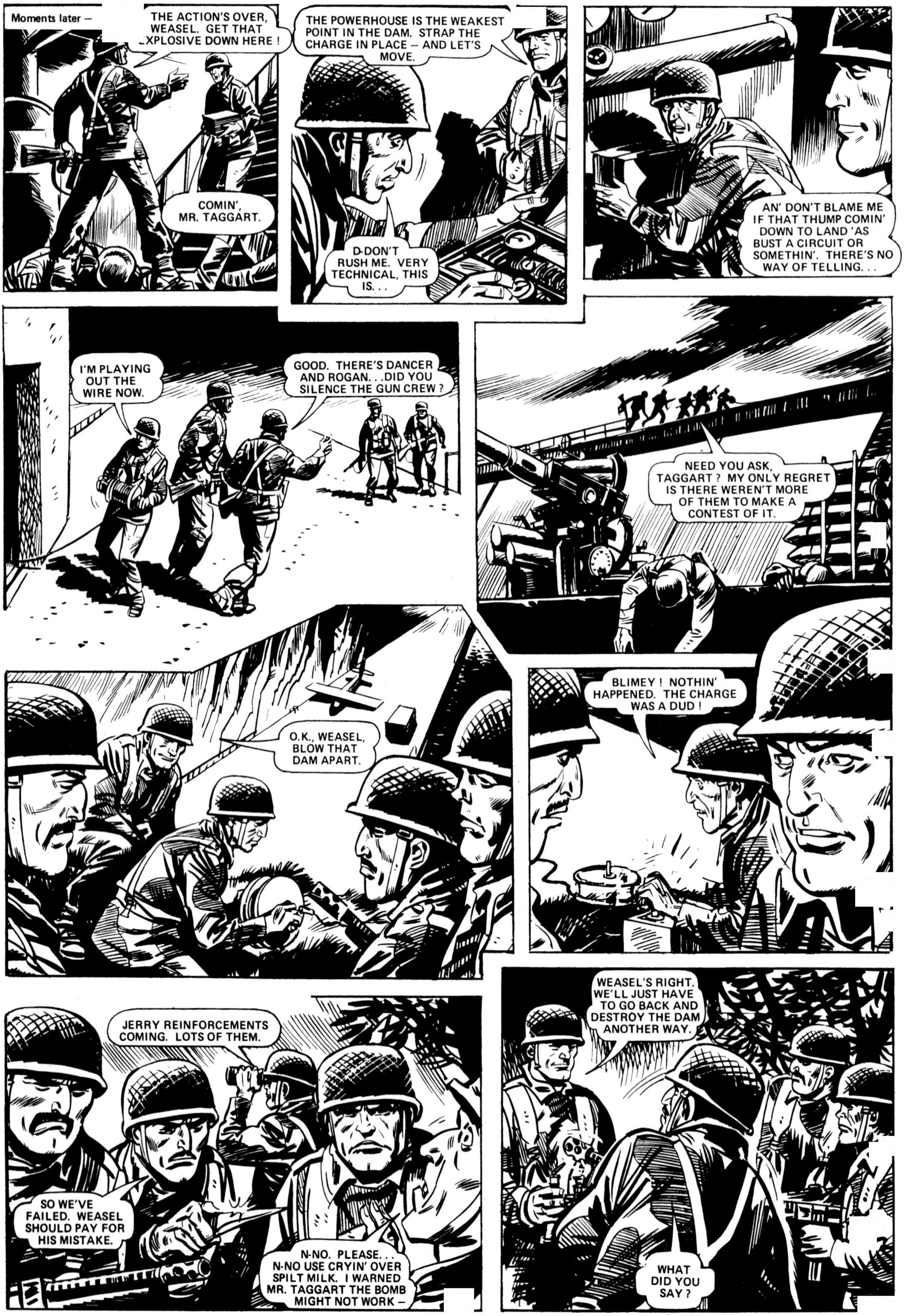
Moments later –
THE ACTION'S OVER, WEASEL. GET THAT EXPLOSIVE DOWN HERE !
COMIN', MR. TAGGART.
THE POWERHOUSE IS THE WEAKEST POINT IN THE DAM. STRAP THE CHARGE IN PLACE – AND LET'S MOVE.
D-DON'T RUSH ME. VERY TECHNICAL, THIS IS. . .
AN' DON'T BLAME ME IF THAT THUMP COMIN' DOWN TO LAND 'AS BUST A CIRCUIT OR SOMETHIN'. THERE'S NO WAY OF TELLING. . .
I'M PLAYING OUT THE WIRE NOW.
GOOD. THERE'S DANCER AND ROGAN. . .DID YOU SILENCE THE GUN CREW ?
NEED YOU ASK, TAGGART ? MY ONLY REGRET IS THERE WEREN'T MORE OF THEM TO MAKE A CONTEST OF IT.
O.K., WEASEL, BLOW THAT DAM APART.
BLIMEY ! NOTHIN' HAPPENED. THE CHARGE WAS A DUD !
JERRY REINFORCEMENTS COMING. LOTS OF THEM.
SO WE'VE FAILED. WEASEL SHOULD PAY FOR HIS MISTAKE.
N-NO. PLEASE. . . N-NO USE CRYIN' OVER SPILT MILK. I WARNED MR. TAGGART THE BOMB MIGHT NOT WORK –
WEASEL'S RIGHT. WE'LL JUST HAVE TO GO BACK AND DESTROY THE DAM ANOTHER WAY.
WHAT DID YOU SAY ?

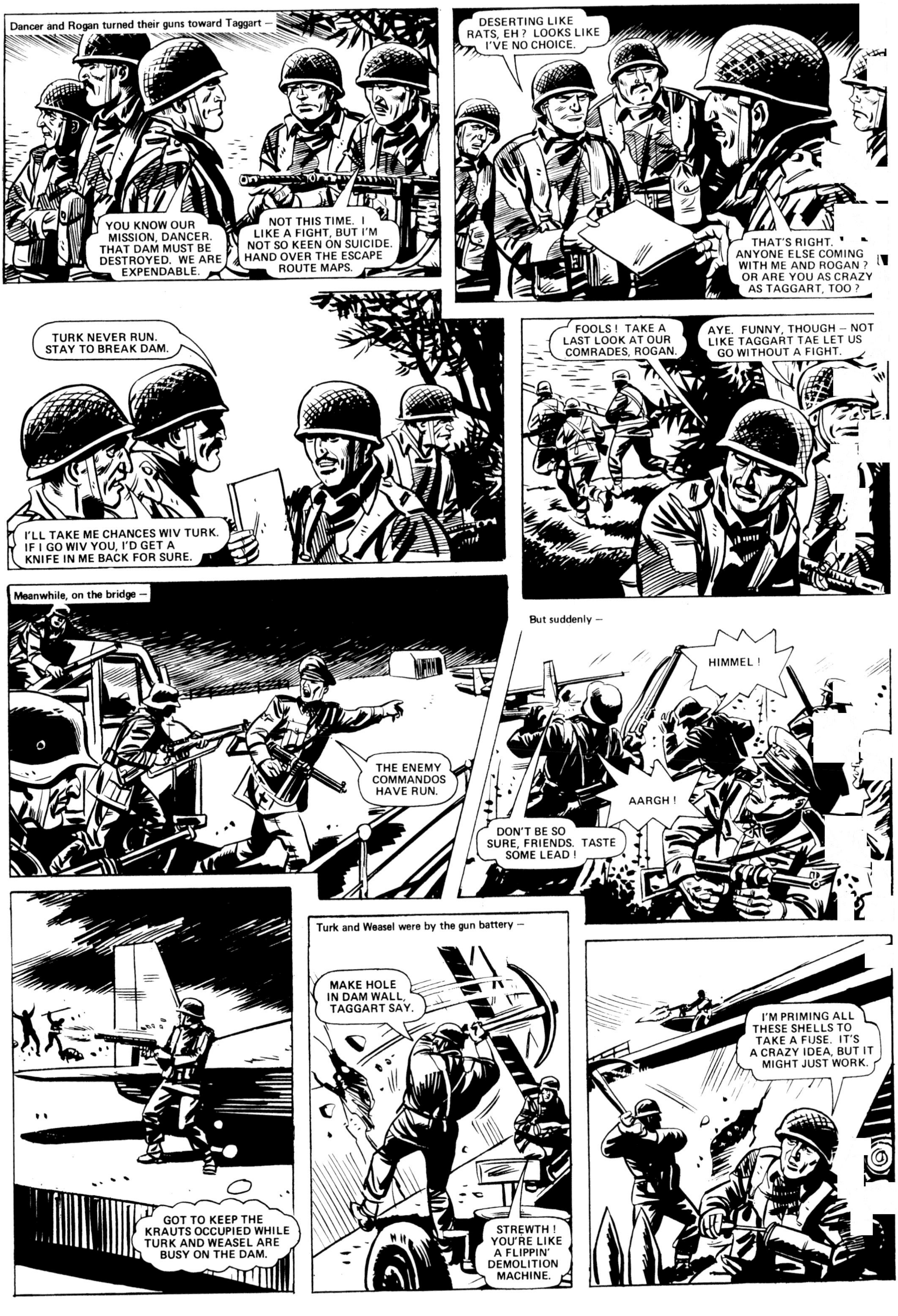
Dancer and Rogan turned their guns toward Taggart —
YOU KNOW OUR MISSION, DANCER. THAT DAM MUST BE DESTROYED. WE ARE EXPENDABLE.
NOT THIS TIME. I LIKE A FIGHT, BUT I'M NOT SO KEEN ON SUICIDE. HAND OVER THE ESCAPE ROUTE MAPS.
DESERTING LIKE RATS, EH? LOOKS LIKE I'VE NO CHOICE.
THAT'S RIGHT. ANYONE ELSE COMING WITH ME AND ROGAN? OR ARE YOU AS CRAZY AS TAGGART, TOO?
TURK NEVER RUN. STAY TO BREAK DAM.
I'LL TAKE ME CHANCES WIV TURK. IF I GO WIV YOU, I'D GET A KNIFE IN ME BACK FOR SURE.
FOOLS! TAKE A LAST LOOK AT OUR COMRADES, ROGAN.
AYE. FUNNY, THOUGH — NOT LIKE TAGGART TAE LET US GO WITHOUT A FIGHT.
Meanwhile, on the bridge —
THE ENEMY COMMANDOS HAVE RUN.
But suddenly —
HIMMEL!
AARGH!
DON'T BE SO SURE, FRIENDS. TASTE SOME LEAD!
GOT TO KEEP THE KRAUTS OCCUPIED WHILE TURK AND WEASEL ARE BUSY ON THE DAM.
Turk and Weasel were by the gun battery —
MAKE HOLE IN DAM WALL, TAGGART SAY.
STREWTH! YOU'RE LIKE A FLIPPIN' DEMOLITION MACHINE.
I'M PRIMING ALL THESE SHELLS TO TAKE A FUSE. IT'S A CRAZY IDEA, BUT IT MIGHT JUST WORK.

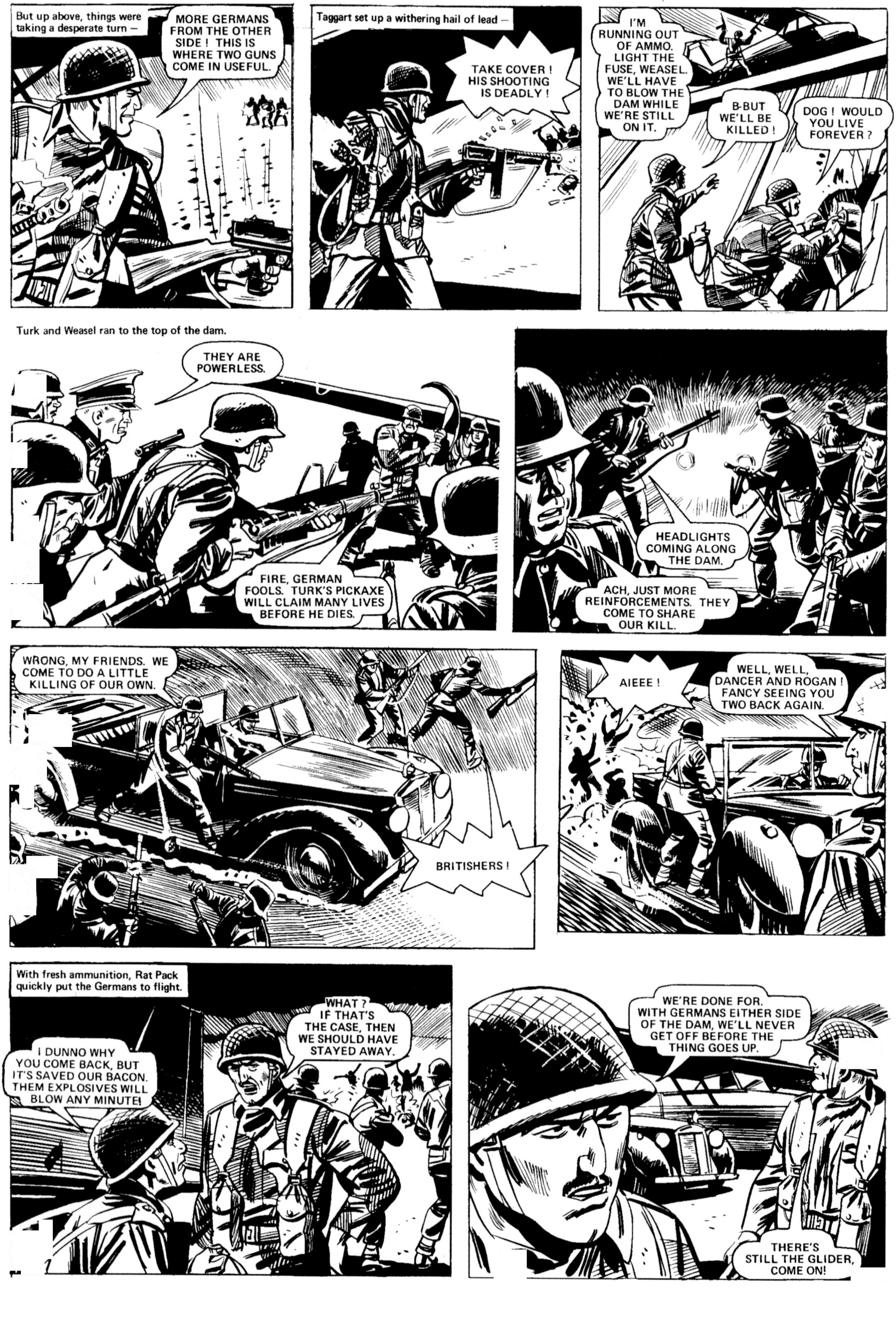
But up above, things were taking a desperate turn —
MORE GERMANS FROM THE OTHER SIDE ! THIS IS WHERE TWO GUNS COME IN USEFUL.
Taggart set up a withering hail of lead —
TAKE COVER ! HIS SHOOTING IS DEADLY !
I'M RUNNING OUT OF AMMO. LIGHT THE FUSE, WEASEL. WE'LL HAVE TO BLOW THE DAM WHILE WE'RE STILL ON IT.
B-BUT WE'LL BE KILLED !
DOG ! WOULD YOU LIVE FOREVER ?
Turk and Weasel ran to the top of the dam.
THEY ARE POWERLESS.
FIRE, GERMAN FOOLS. TURK'S PICKAXE WILL CLAIM MANY LIVES BEFORE HE DIES.
HEADLIGHTS COMING ALONG THE DAM.
ACH, JUST MORE REINFORCEMENTS. THEY COME TO SHARE OUR KILL.
WRONG, MY FRIENDS. WE COME TO DO A LITTLE KILLING OF OUR OWN.
BRITISHERS !
AIEEE !
WELL, WELL, DANCER AND ROGAN ! FANCY SEEING YOU TWO BACK AGAIN.
With fresh ammunition, Rat Pack quickly put the Germans to flight.
I DUNNO WHY YOU COME BACK, BUT IT'S SAVED OUR BACON. THEM EXPLOSIVES WILL BLOW ANY MINUTE!
WHAT ? IF THAT'S THE CASE, THEN WE SHOULD HAVE STAYED AWAY.
WE'RE DONE FOR. WITH GERMANS EITHER SIDE OF THE DAM, WE'LL NEVER GET OFF BEFORE THE THING GOES UP.
THERE'S STILL THE GLIDER, COME ON!

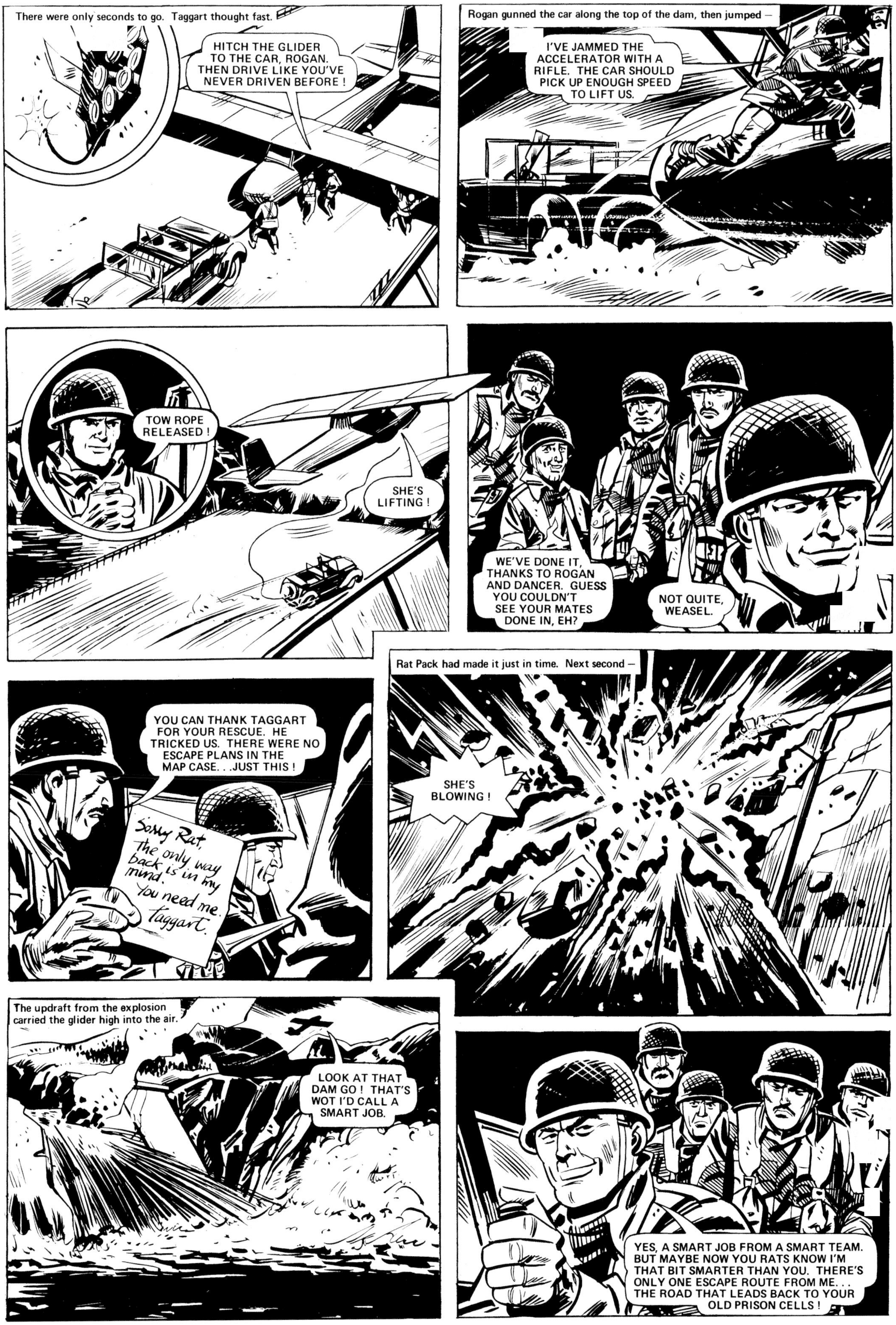
There were only seconds to go. Taggart thought fast.
HITCH THE GLIDER TO THE CAR, ROGAN. THEN DRIVE LIKE YOU'VE NEVER DRIVEN BEFORE !
Rogan gunned the car along the top of the dam, then jumped –
I'VE JAMMED THE ACCELERATOR WITH A RIFLE. THE CAR SHOULD PICK UP ENOUGH SPEED TO LIFT US.
TOW ROPE RELEASED !
SHE'S LIFTING !
WE'VE DONE IT, THANKS TO ROGAN AND DANCER. GUESS YOU COULDN'T SEE YOUR MATES DONE IN, EH?
NOT QUITE, WEASEL.
YOU CAN THANK TAGGART FOR YOUR RESCUE. HE TRICKED US. THERE WERE NO ESCAPE PLANS IN THE MAP CASE. . .JUST THIS !
Sorry Rat, The only way back is in my mind. You need me. Taggart.
Rat Pack had made it just in time. Next second –
SHE'S BLOWING !
The updraft from the explosion carried the glider high into the air.
LOOK AT THAT DAM GO ! THAT'S WOT I'D CALL A SMART JOB.
YES, A SMART JOB FROM A SMART TEAM. BUT MAYBE NOW YOU RATS KNOW I'M THAT BIT SMARTER THAN YOU. THERE'S ONLY ONE ESCAPE ROUTE FROM ME. . . THE ROAD THAT LEADS BACK TO YOUR OLD PRISON CELLS !

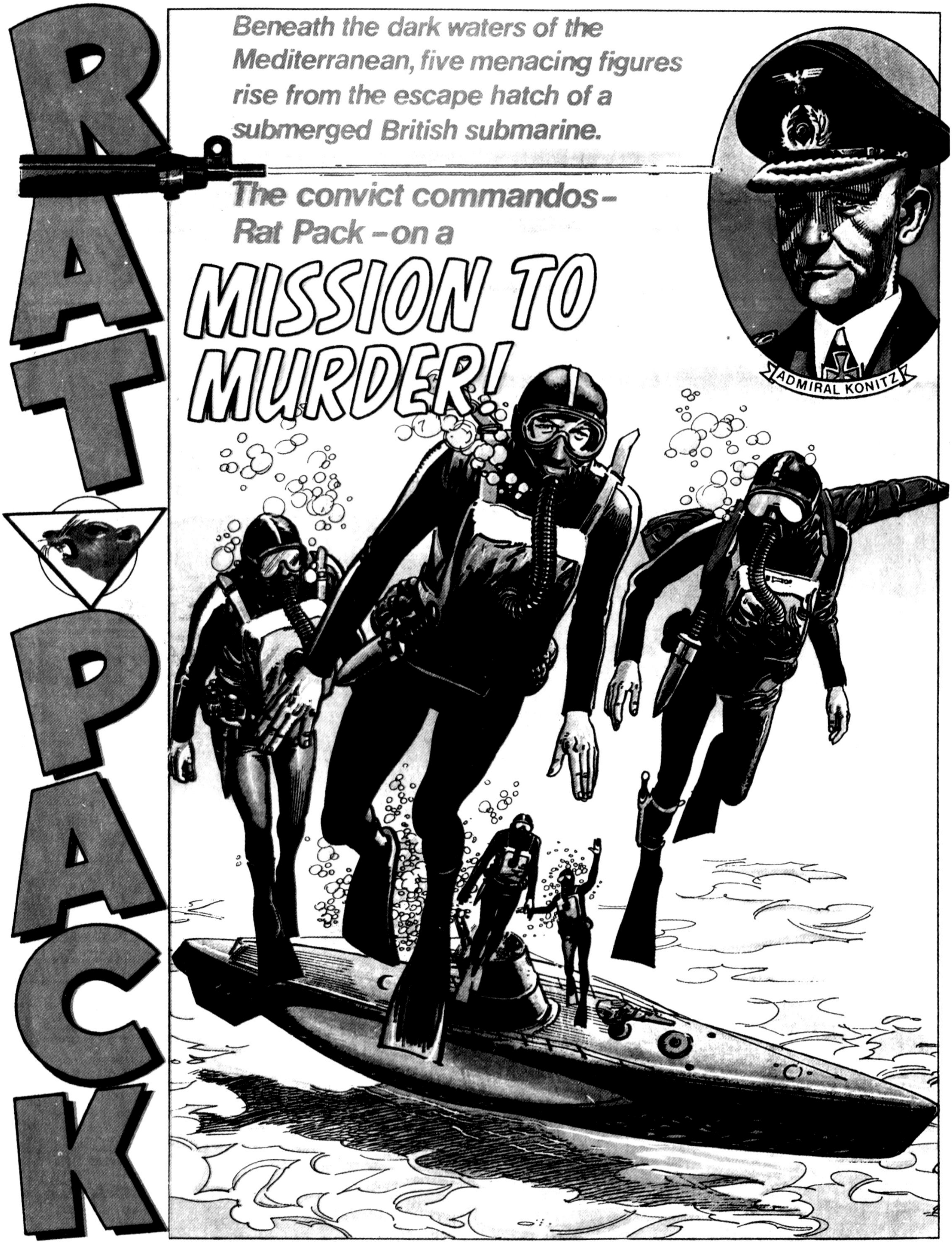
RAT PACK
Beneath the dark waters of the Mediterranean, five menacing figures rise from the escape hatch of a submerged British submarine.
The convict commandos - Rat Pack - on a
MISSION TO MURDER!
ADMIRAL KONITZ

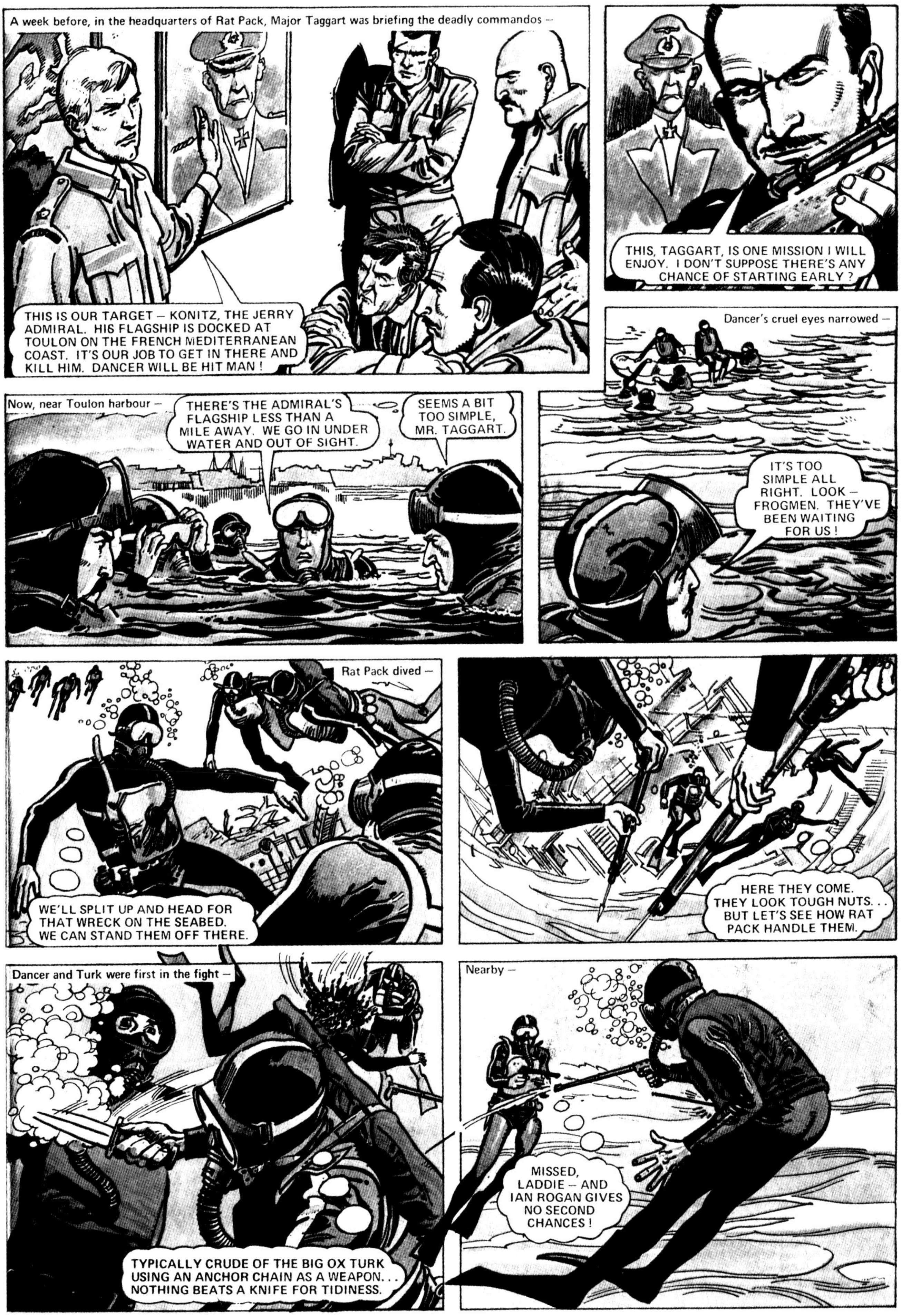

A week before, in the headquarters of Rat Pack, Major Taggart was briefing the deadly commandos –
THIS IS OUR TARGET – KONITZ, THE JERRY ADMIRAL. HIS FLAGSHIP IS DOCKED AT TOULON ON THE FRENCH MEDITERRANEAN COAST. IT'S OUR JOB TO GET IN THERE AND KILL HIM. DANCER WILL BE HIT MAN !
THIS, TAGGART, IS ONE MISSION I WILL ENJOY. I DON'T SUPPOSE THERE'S ANY CHANCE OF STARTING EARLY ?
Dancer's cruel eyes narrowed –
Now, near Toulon harbour –
THERE'S THE ADMIRAL'S FLAGSHIP LESS THAN A MILE AWAY. WE GO IN UNDER WATER AND OUT OF SIGHT.
SEEMS A BIT TOO SIMPLE, MR. TAGGART.
IT'S TOO SIMPLE ALL RIGHT. LOOK – FROGMEN. THEY'VE BEEN WAITING FOR US !
Rat Pack dived –
WE'LL SPLIT UP AND HEAD FOR THAT WRECK ON THE SEABED. WE CAN STAND THEM OFF THERE.
HERE THEY COME. THEY LOOK TOUGH NUTS. . . BUT LET'S SEE HOW RAT PACK HANDLE THEM.
Dancer and Turk were first in the fight –
TYPICALLY CRUDE OF THE BIG OX TURK USING AN ANCHOR CHAIN AS A WEAPON. . . NOTHING BEATS A KNIFE FOR TIDINESS.
Nearby –
MISSED, LADDIE – AND IAN ROGAN GIVES NO SECOND CHANCES !

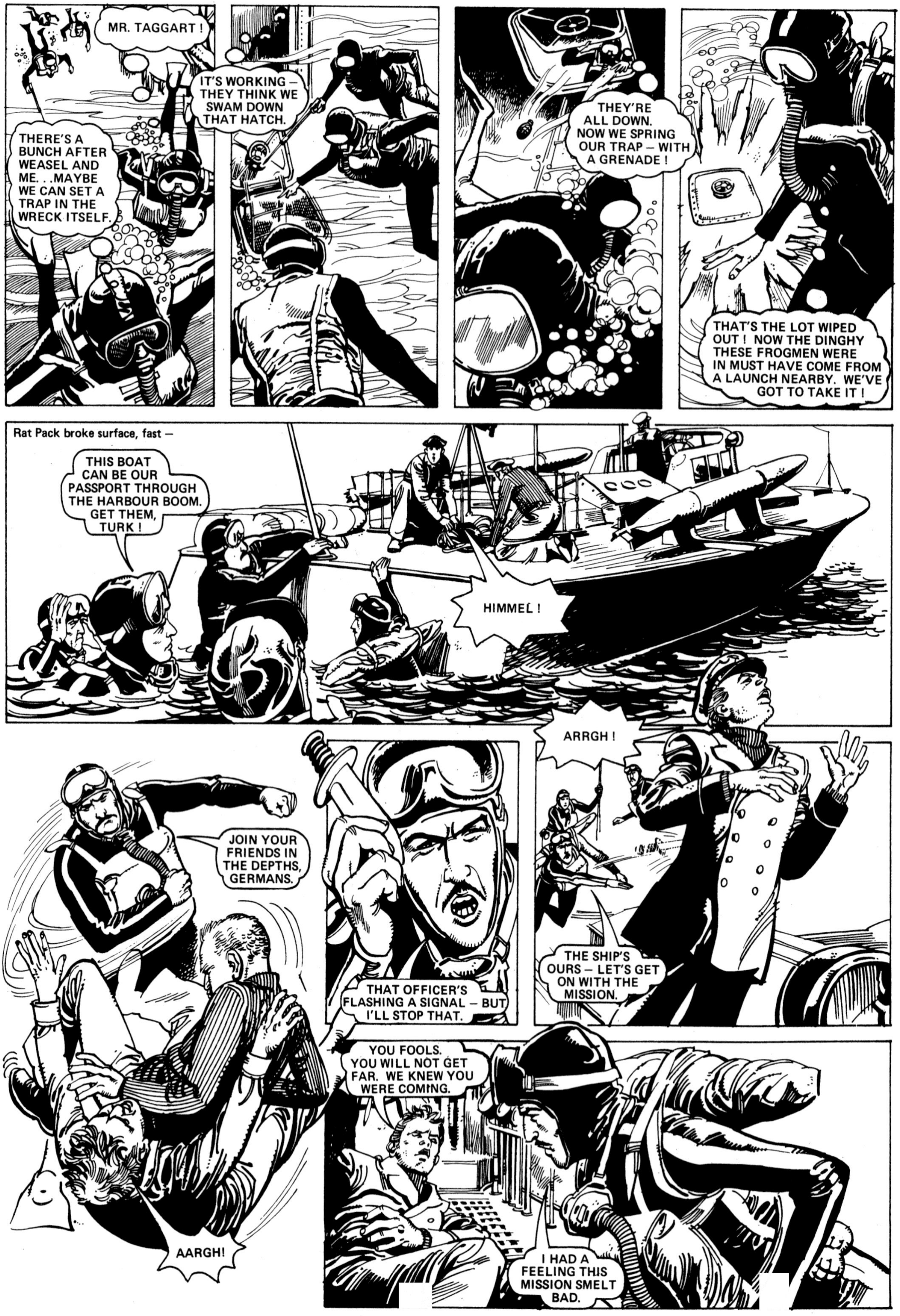
MR. TAGGART !
THERE'S A BUNCH AFTER WEASEL AND ME. . .MAYBE WE CAN SET A TRAP IN THE WRECK ITSELF.
IT'S WORKING – THEY THINK WE SWAM DOWN THAT HATCH.
THEY'RE ALL DOWN. NOW WE SPRING OUR TRAP – WITH A GRENADE !
THAT'S THE LOT WIPED OUT ! NOW THE DINGHY THESE FROGMEN WERE IN MUST HAVE COME FROM A LAUNCH NEARBY. WE'VE GOT TO TAKE IT !
Rat Pack broke surface, fast –
THIS BOAT CAN BE OUR PASSPORT THROUGH THE HARBOUR BOOM. GET THEM, TURK !
HIMMEL !
JOIN YOUR FRIENDS IN THE DEPTHS, GERMANS.
AARGH!
THAT OFFICER'S FLASHING A SIGNAL – BUT I'LL STOP THAT.
ARRGH !
THE SHIP'S OURS – LET'S GET ON WITH THE MISSION.
YOU FOOLS. YOU WILL NOT GET FAR. WE KNEW YOU WERE COMING.
I HAD A FEELING THIS MISSION SMELT BAD.

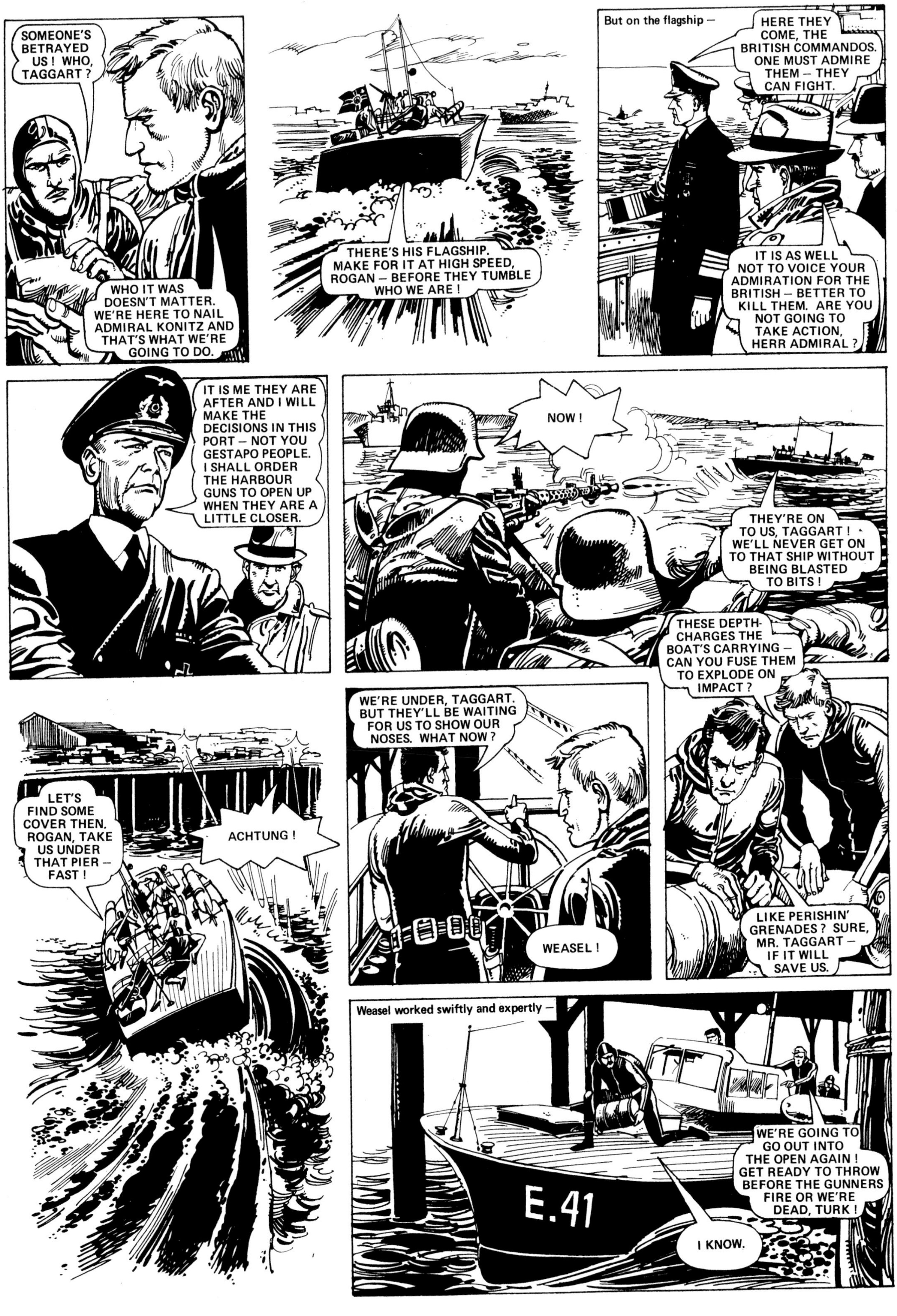
SOMEONE'S BETRAYED US ! WHO, TAGGART ?
WHO IT WAS DOESN'T MATTER. WE'RE HERE TO NAIL ADMIRAL KONITZ AND THAT'S WHAT WE'RE GOING TO DO.
THERE'S HIS FLAGSHIP. MAKE FOR IT AT HIGH SPEED, ROGAN — BEFORE THEY TUMBLE WHO WE ARE !
But on the flagship —
HERE THEY COME, THE BRITISH COMMANDOS. ONE MUST ADMIRE THEM — THEY CAN FIGHT.
IT IS AS WELL NOT TO VOICE YOUR ADMIRATION FOR THE BRITISH — BETTER TO KILL THEM. ARE YOU NOT GOING TO TAKE ACTION, HERR ADMIRAL ?
IT IS ME THEY ARE AFTER AND I WILL MAKE THE DECISIONS IN THIS PORT — NOT YOU GESTAPO PEOPLE. I SHALL ORDER THE HARBOUR GUNS TO OPEN UP WHEN THEY ARE A LITTLE CLOSER.
NOW !
THEY'RE ON TO US, TAGGART ! WE'LL NEVER GET ON TO THAT SHIP WITHOUT BEING BLASTED TO BITS !
LET'S FIND SOME COVER THEN. ROGAN, TAKE US UNDER THAT PIER — FAST !
ACHTUNG !
WE'RE UNDER, TAGGART. BUT THEY'LL BE WAITING FOR US TO SHOW OUR NOSES. WHAT NOW ?
WEASEL !
THESE DEPTH-CHARGES THE BOAT'S CARRYING — CAN YOU FUSE THEM TO EXPLODE ON IMPACT ?
LIKE PERISHIN' GRENADES ? SURE, MR. TAGGART — IF IT WILL SAVE US.
Weasel worked swiftly and expertly —
E.41
WE'RE GOING TO GO OUT INTO THE OPEN AGAIN ! GET READY TO THROW BEFORE THE GUNNERS FIRE OR WE'RE DEAD, TURK !
I KNOW.

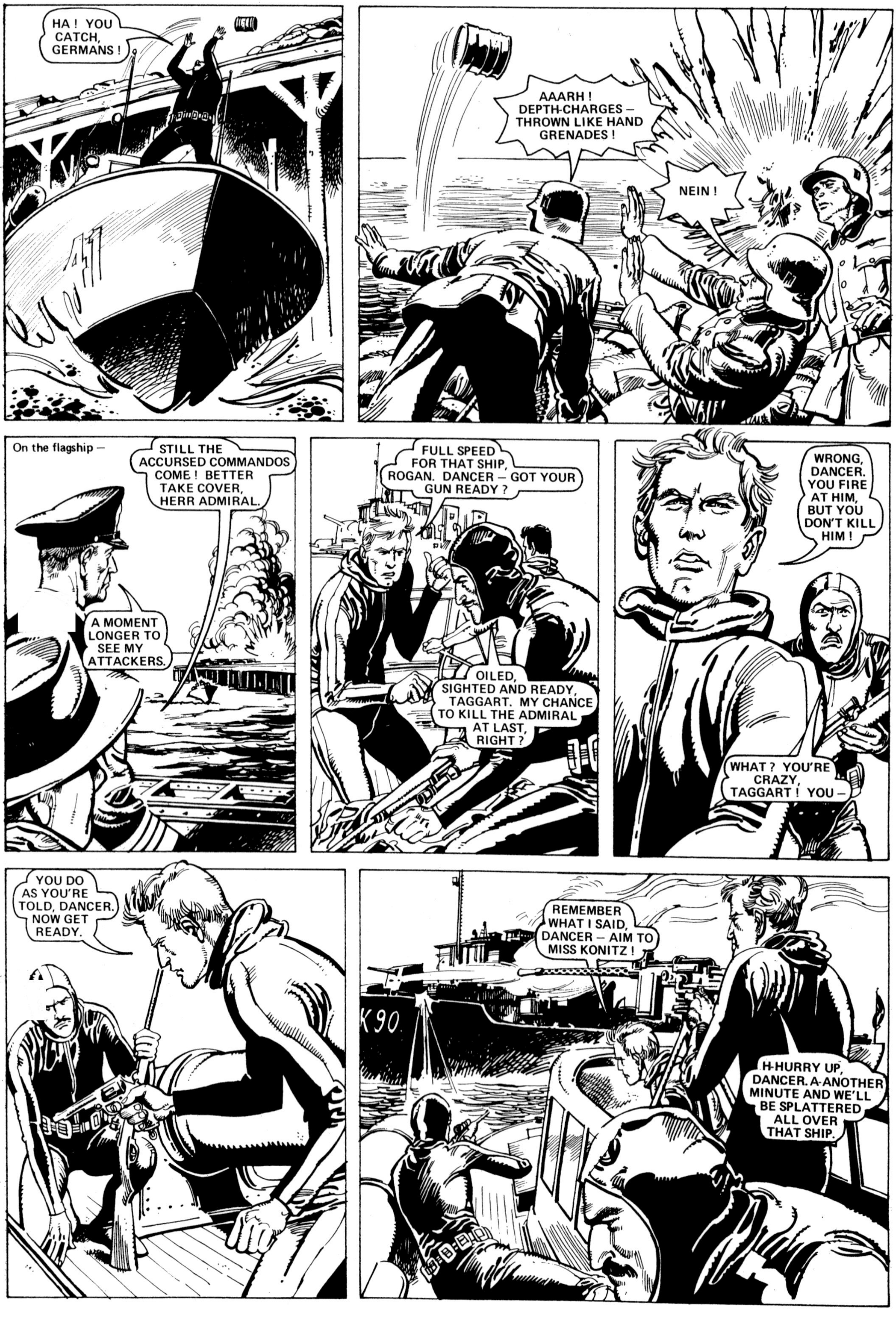

HA ! YOU CATCH, GERMANS !
AAARH ! DEPTH-CHARGES – THROWN LIKE HAND GRENADES !
NEIN !
On the flagship –
STILL THE ACCURSED COMMANDOS COME ! BETTER TAKE COVER, HERR ADMIRAL.
A MOMENT LONGER TO SEE MY ATTACKERS.
FULL SPEED FOR THAT SHIP, ROGAN. DANCER – GOT YOUR GUN READY ?
OILED, SIGHTED AND READY, TAGGART. MY CHANCE TO KILL THE ADMIRAL AT LAST, RIGHT ?
WRONG, DANCER. YOU FIRE AT HIM, BUT YOU DON'T KILL HIM !
WHAT ? YOU'RE CRAZY, TAGGART ! YOU –
YOU DO AS YOU'RE TOLD, DANCER. NOW GET READY.
REMEMBER WHAT I SAID, DANCER – AIM TO MISS KONITZ !
H-HURRY UP, DANCER. A-ANOTHER MINUTE AND WE'LL BE SPLATTERED ALL OVER THAT SHIP.

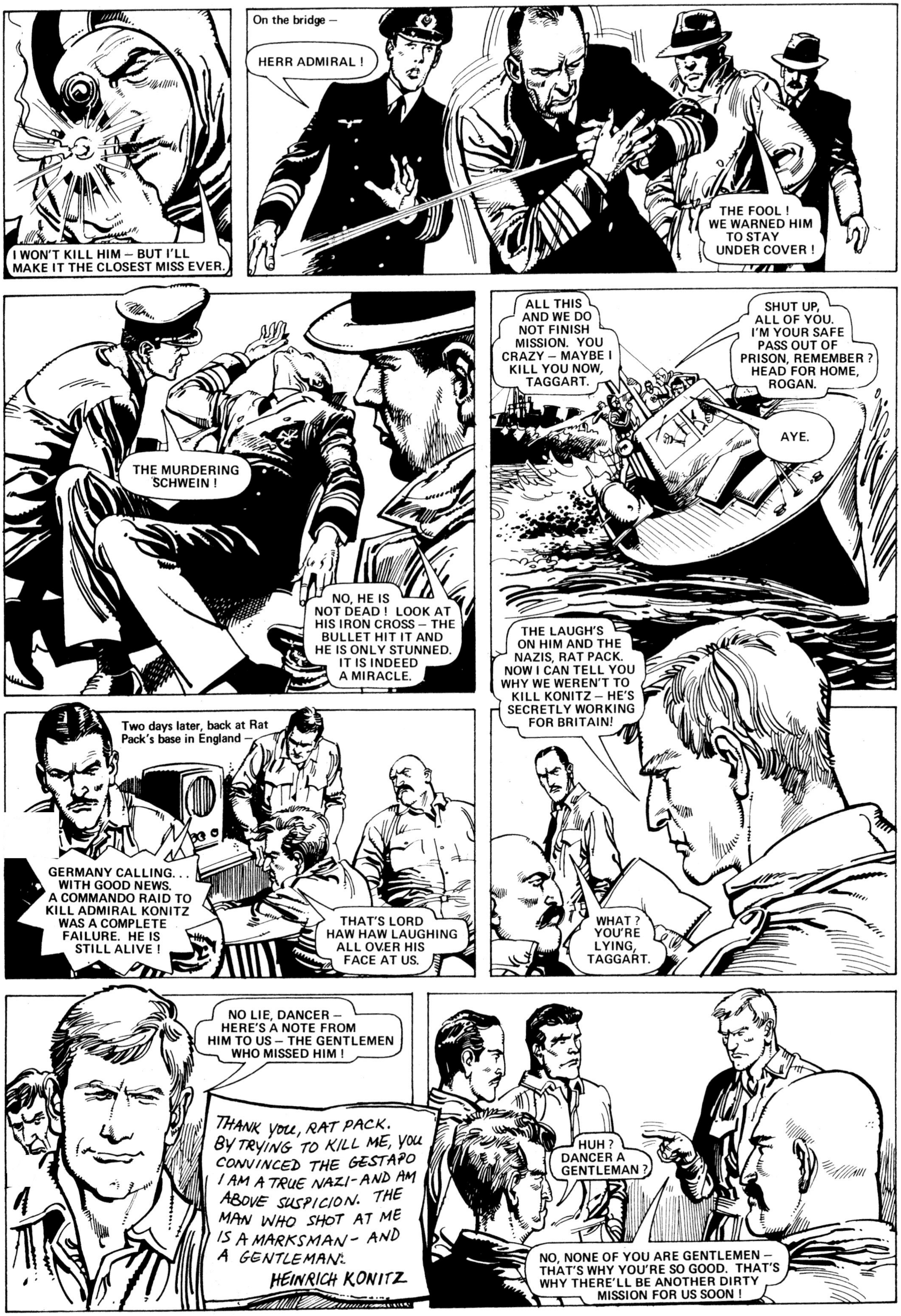
I WON'T KILL HIM – BUT I'LL MAKE IT THE CLOSEST MISS EVER.
On the bridge –
HERR ADMIRAL !
THE FOOL ! WE WARNED HIM TO STAY UNDER COVER !
THE MURDERING SCHWEIN !
NO, HE IS NOT DEAD ! LOOK AT HIS IRON CROSS – THE BULLET HIT IT AND HE IS ONLY STUNNED. IT IS INDEED A MIRACLE.
ALL THIS AND WE DO NOT FINISH MISSION. YOU CRAZY – MAYBE I KILL YOU NOW, TAGGART.
SHUT UP, ALL OF YOU. I'M YOUR SAFE PASS OUT OF PRISON, REMEMBER ? HEAD FOR HOME, ROGAN.
AYE.
Two days later, back at Rat Pack's base in England –
GERMANY CALLING. . . WITH GOOD NEWS. A COMMANDO RAID TO KILL ADMIRAL KONITZ WAS A COMPLETE FAILURE. HE IS STILL ALIVE !
THAT'S LORD HAW HAW LAUGHING ALL OVER HIS FACE AT US.
THE LAUGH'S ON HIM AND THE NAZIS, RAT PACK. NOW I CAN TELL YOU WHY WE WEREN'T TO KILL KONITZ – HE'S SECRETLY WORKING FOR BRITAIN!
WHAT ? YOU'RE LYING, TAGGART.
NO LIE, DANCER – HERE'S A NOTE FROM HIM TO US – THE GENTLEMEN WHO MISSED HIM !
THANK YOU, RAT PACK. BY TRYING TO KILL ME, YOU CONVINCED THE GESTAPO I AM A TRUE NAZI – AND AM ABOVE SUSPICION. THE MAN WHO SHOT AT ME IS A MARKSMAN – AND A GENTLEMAN. HEINRICH KONITZ
HUH ? DANCER A GENTLEMAN ?
NO, NONE OF YOU ARE GENTLEMEN – THAT'S WHY YOU'RE SO GOOD. THAT'S WHY THERE'LL BE ANOTHER DIRTY MISSION FOR US SOON !

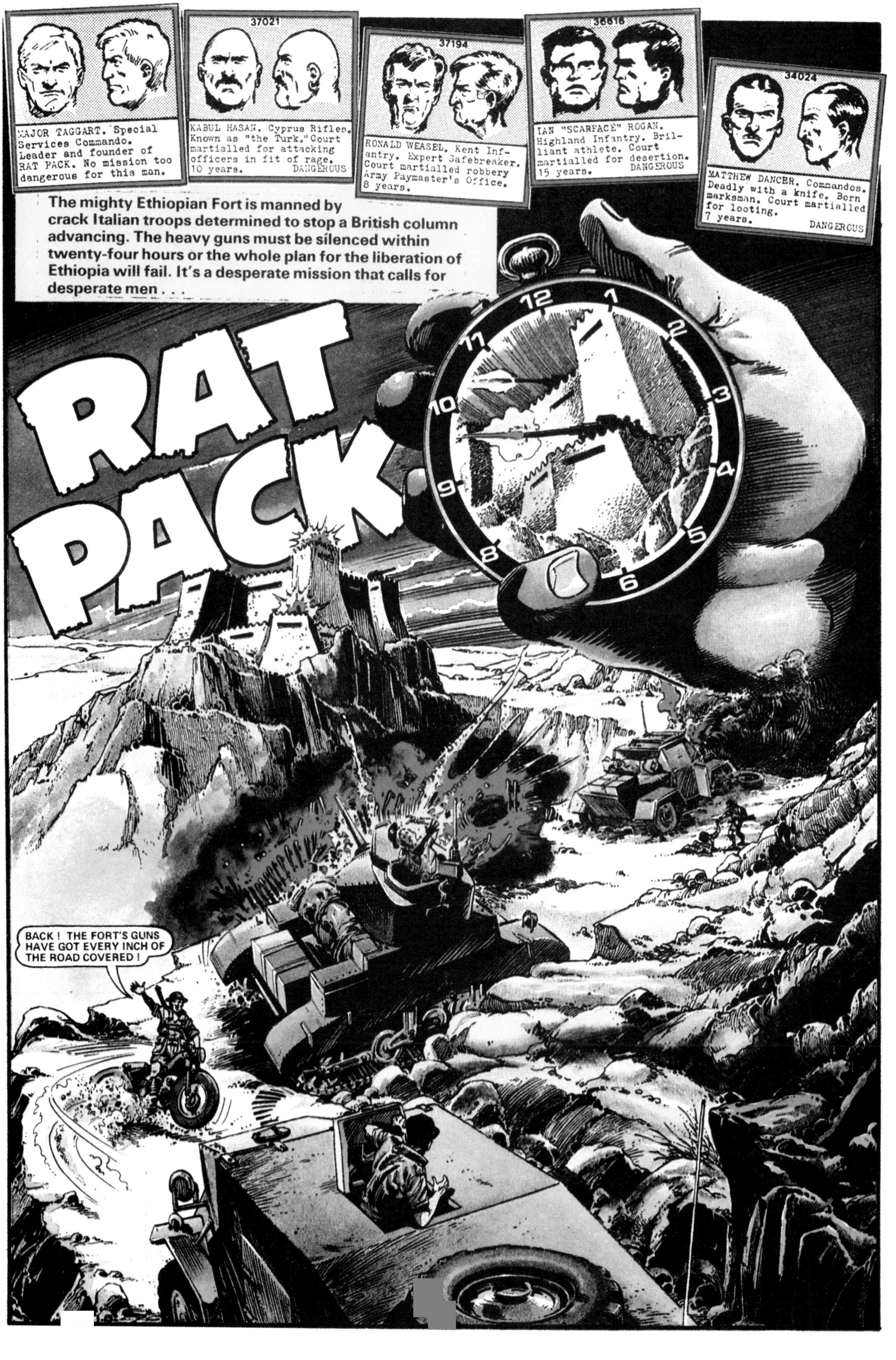
MAJOR TAGGART. Special Services Commando. Leader and founder of RAT PACK. No mission too dangerous for this man.
37021
KABUL HASAN. Cyprus Rifles. Known as "the Turk." Court martialled for attacking officers in fit of rage. 10 years. DANGEROUS
37194
RONALD WEASEL. Kent Infantry. Expert Safebreaker. Court martialled robbery Army Paymaster's Office. 8 years.
36616
IAN "SCARFACE" ROGAN. Highland Infantry. Brilliant athlete. Court martialled for desertion. 15 years. DANGEROUS
34024
MATTHEW DANCER. Commandos. Deadly with a knife. Born marksman. Court martialled for looting. 7 years. DANGEROUS
The mighty Ethiopian Fort is manned by crack Italian troops determined to stop a British column advancing. The heavy guns must be silenced within twenty-four hours or the whole plan for the liberation of Ethiopia will fail. It's a desperate mission that calls for desperate men . . .
RAT PACK
BACK ! THE FORT'S GUNS HAVE GOT EVERY INCH OF THE ROAD COVERED !

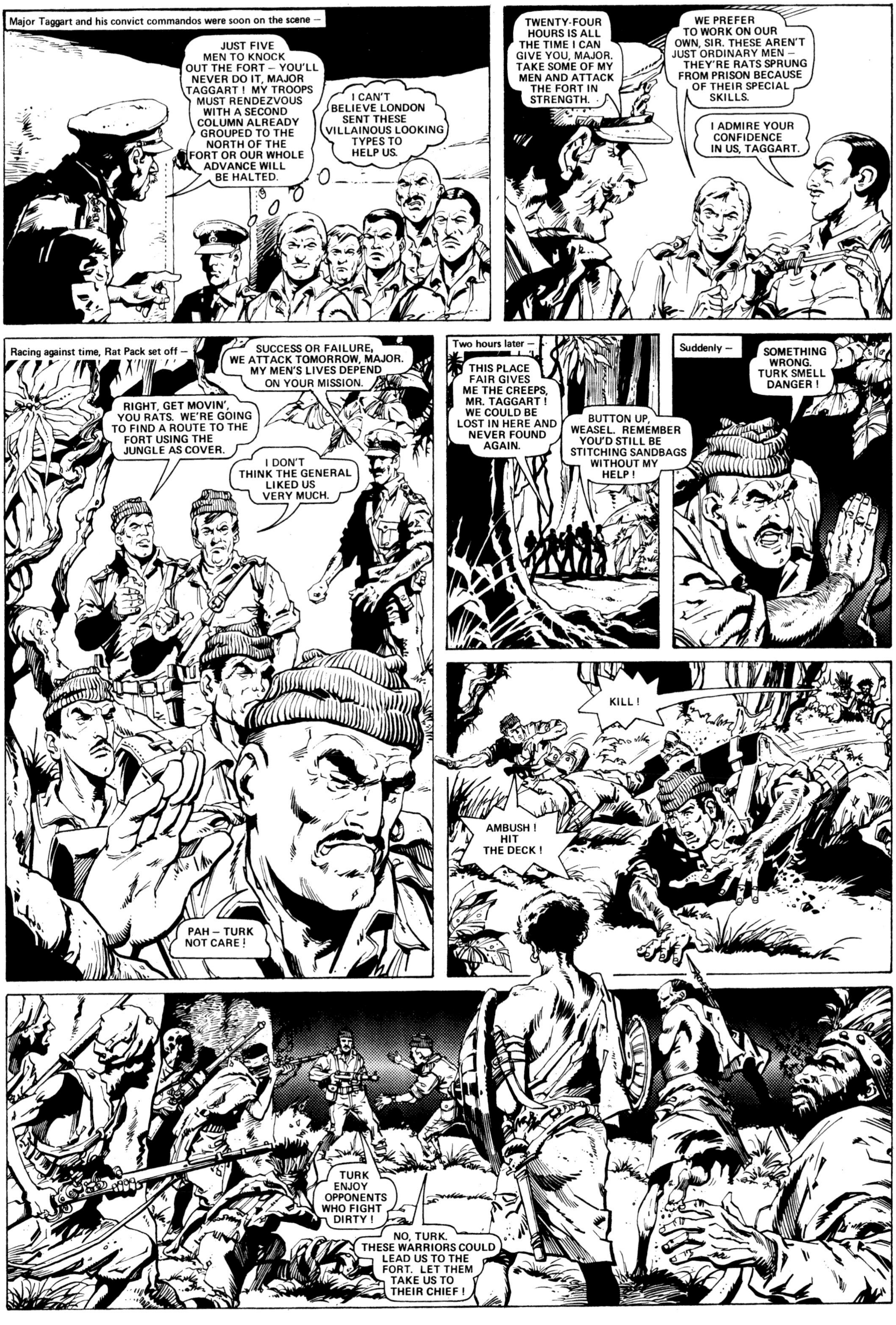
Major Taggart and his convict commandos were soon on the scene –
JUST FIVE MEN TO KNOCK OUT THE FORT – YOU'LL NEVER DO IT, MAJOR TAGGART ! MY TROOPS MUST RENDEZVOUS WITH A SECOND COLUMN ALREADY GROUPED TO THE NORTH OF THE FORT OR OUR WHOLE ADVANCE WILL BE HALTED.
I CAN'T BELIEVE LONDON SENT THESE VILLAINOUS LOOKING TYPES TO HELP US.
TWENTY-FOUR HOURS IS ALL THE TIME I CAN GIVE YOU, MAJOR. TAKE SOME OF MY MEN AND ATTACK THE FORT IN STRENGTH.
WE PREFER TO WORK ON OUR OWN, SIR. THESE AREN'T JUST ORDINARY MEN – THEY'RE RATS SPRUNG FROM PRISON BECAUSE OF THEIR SPECIAL SKILLS.
I ADMIRE YOUR CONFIDENCE IN US, TAGGART.
Racing against time, Rat Pack set off –
SUCCESS OR FAILURE, WE ATTACK TOMORROW, MAJOR. MY MEN'S LIVES DEPEND ON YOUR MISSION.
RIGHT, GET MOVIN', YOU RATS. WE'RE GOING TO FIND A ROUTE TO THE FORT USING THE JUNGLE AS COVER.
I DON'T THINK THE GENERAL LIKED US VERY MUCH.
PAH – TURK NOT CARE !
Two hours later –
THIS PLACE FAIR GIVES ME THE CREEPS, MR. TAGGART ! WE COULD BE LOST IN HERE AND NEVER FOUND AGAIN.
BUTTON UP, WEASEL. REMEMBER YOU'D STILL BE STITCHING SANDBAGS WITHOUT MY HELP !
Suddenly –
SOMETHING WRONG. TURK SMELL DANGER !
KILL !
AMBUSH ! HIT THE DECK !
TURK ENJOY OPPONENTS WHO FIGHT DIRTY !
NO, TURK. THESE WARRIORS COULD LEAD US TO THE FORT. LET THEM TAKE US TO THEIR CHIEF !

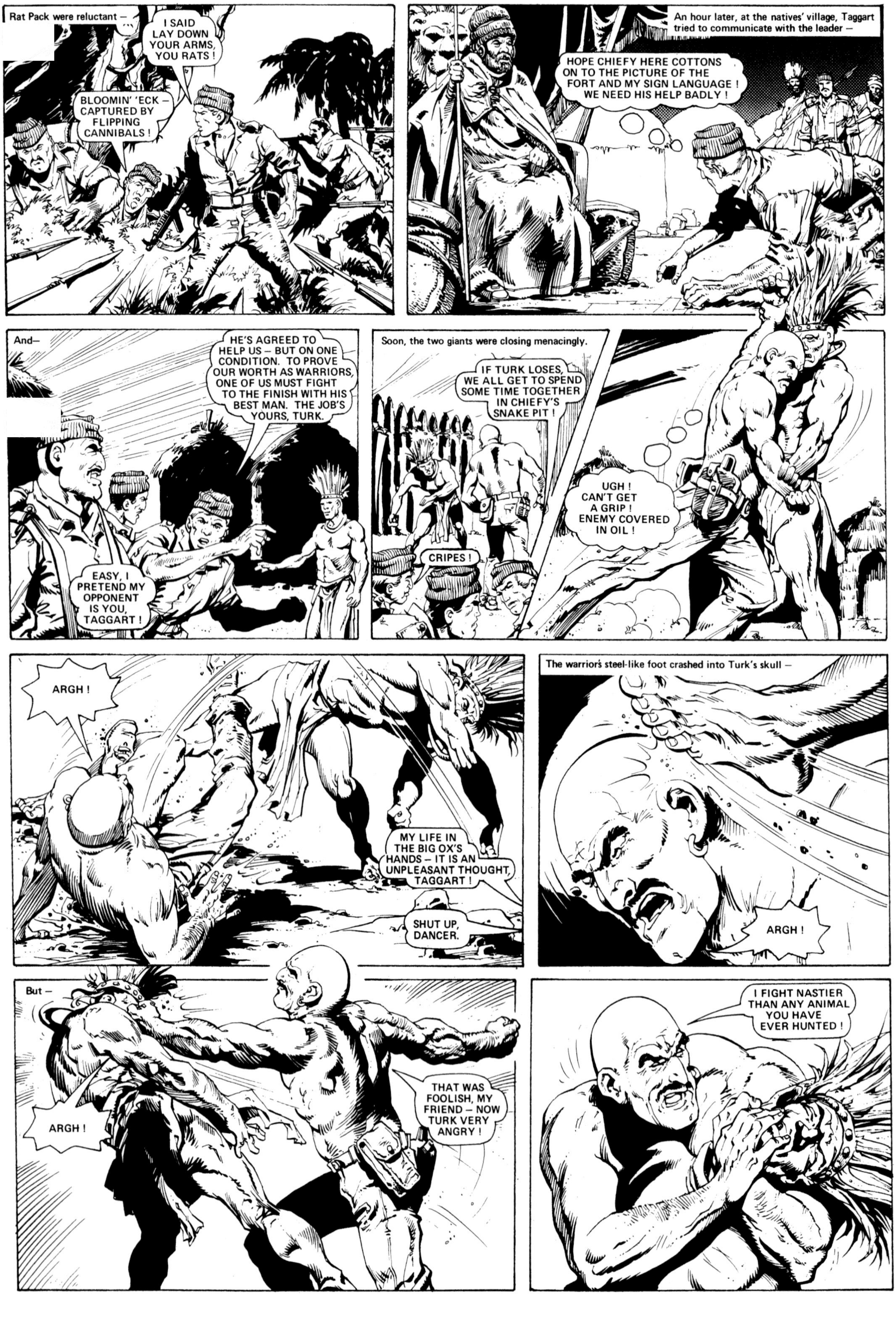
Rat Pack were reluctant –
I SAID LAY DOWN YOUR ARMS, YOU RATS !
BLOOMIN' 'ECK – CAPTURED BY FLIPPING CANNIBALS !
An hour later, at the natives' village, Taggart tried to communicate with the leader –
HOPE CHIEFY HERE COTTONS ON TO THE PICTURE OF THE FORT AND MY SIGN LANGUAGE ! WE NEED HIS HELP BADLY !
And–
HE'S AGREED TO HELP US – BUT ON ONE CONDITION. TO PROVE OUR WORTH AS WARRIORS, ONE OF US MUST FIGHT TO THE FINISH WITH HIS BEST MAN. THE JOB'S YOURS, TURK.
EASY, I PRETEND MY OPPONENT IS YOU, TAGGART !
Soon, the two giants were closing menacingly.
IF TURK LOSES, WE ALL GET TO SPEND SOME TIME TOGETHER IN CHIEFY'S SNAKE PIT !
CRIPES !
UGH ! CAN'T GET A GRIP ! ENEMY COVERED IN OIL !
ARGH !
MY LIFE IN THE BIG OX'S HANDS – IT IS AN UNPLEASANT THOUGHT, TAGGART !
SHUT UP, DANCER.
The warrior's steel-like foot crashed into Turk's skull –
ARGH !
But –
ARGH !
THAT WAS FOOLISH, MY FRIEND – NOW TURK VERY ANGRY !
I FIGHT NASTIER THAN ANY ANIMAL YOU HAVE EVER HUNTED !

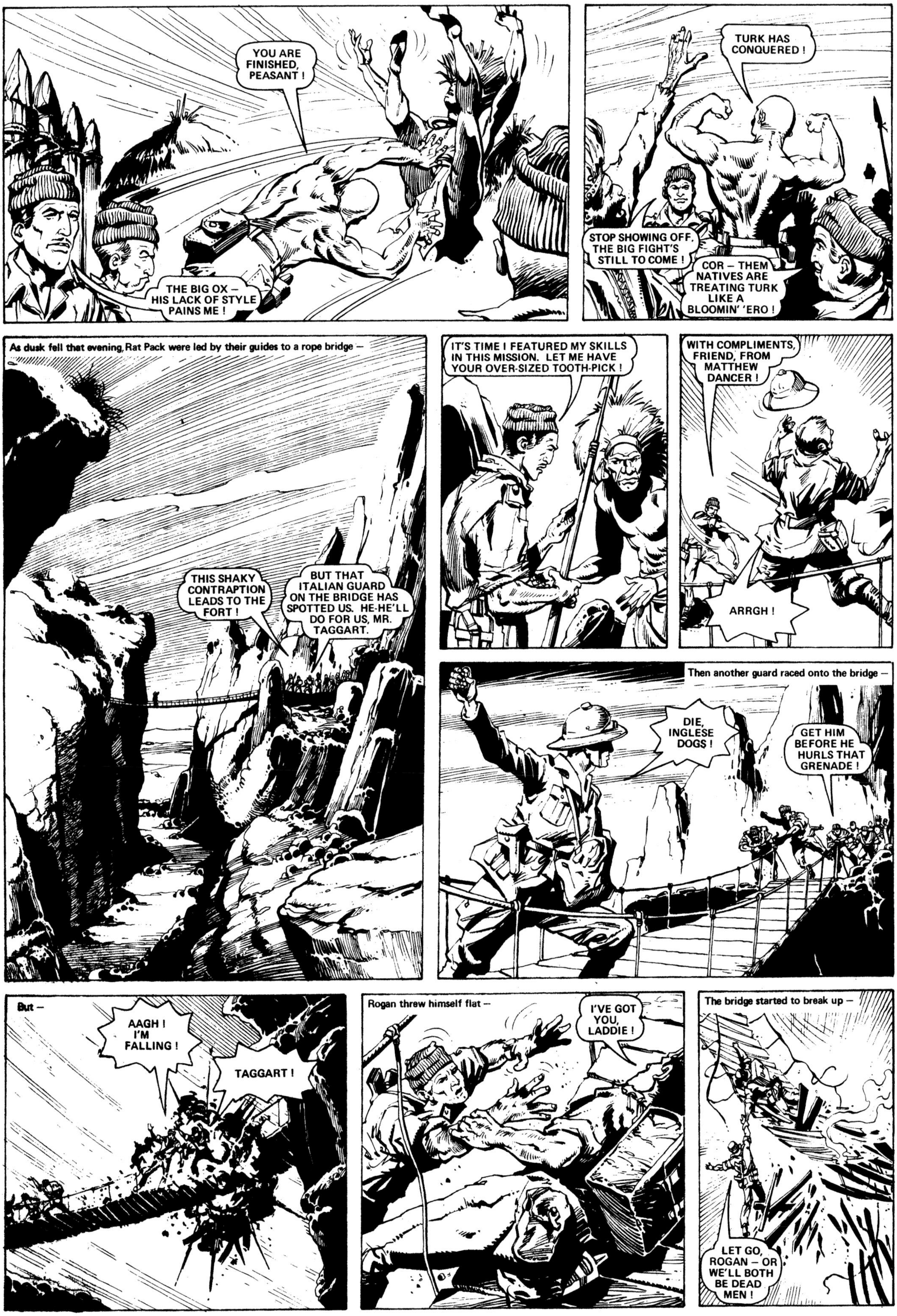
YOU ARE FINISHED, PEASANT !
THE BIG OX — HIS LACK OF STYLE PAINS ME !
TURK HAS CONQUERED !
STOP SHOWING OFF. THE BIG FIGHT'S STILL TO COME !
COR — THEM NATIVES ARE TREATING TURK LIKE A BLOOMIN' 'ERO !
As dusk fell that evening, Rat Pack were led by their guides to a rope bridge —
THIS SHAKY CONTRAPTION LEADS TO THE FORT !
BUT THAT ITALIAN GUARD ON THE BRIDGE HAS SPOTTED US. HE-HE'LL DO FOR US, MR. TAGGART.
IT'S TIME I FEATURED MY SKILLS IN THIS MISSION. LET ME HAVE YOUR OVER-SIZED TOOTH-PICK !
WITH COMPLIMENTS, FRIEND, FROM MATTHEW DANCER !
ARRGH !
Then another guard raced onto the bridge —
DIE, INGLESE DOGS !
GET HIM BEFORE HE HURLS THAT GRENADE !
But —
AAGH ! I'M FALLING !
TAGGART !
Rogan threw himself flat —
I'VE GOT YOU, LADDIE !
The bridge started to break up —
LET GO, ROGAN — OR WE'LL BOTH BE DEAD MEN !

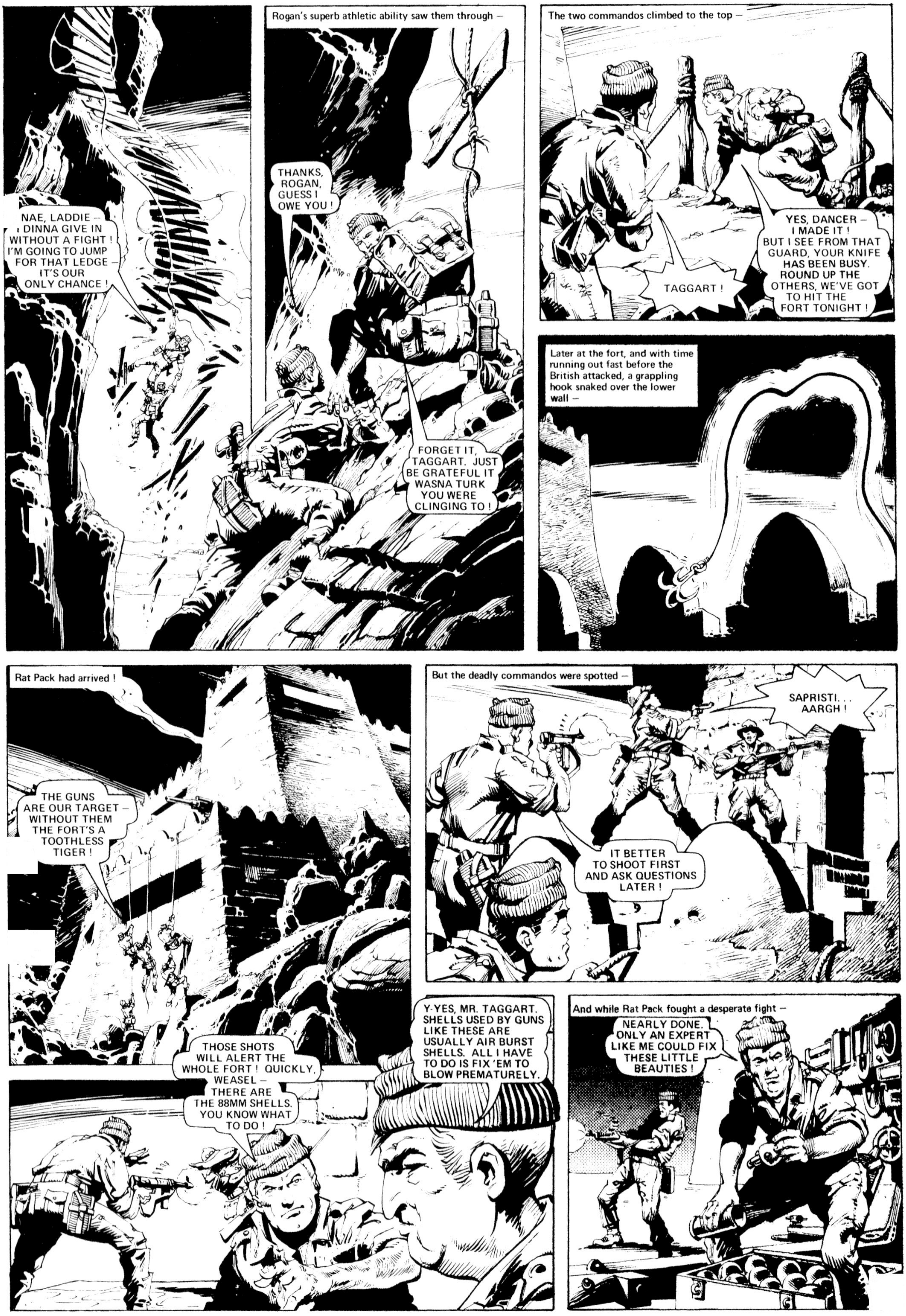
NAE, LADDIE – I DINNA GIVE IN WITHOUT A FIGHT! I'M GOING TO JUMP FOR THAT LEDGE – IT'S OUR ONLY CHANCE!
Rogan's superb athletic ability saw them through –
THANKS, ROGAN, GUESS I OWE YOU!
FORGET IT, TAGGART. JUST BE GRATEFUL IT WASNA TURK YOU WERE CLINGING TO!
The two commandos climbed to the top –
TAGGART!
YES, DANCER – I MADE IT! BUT I SEE FROM THAT GUARD, YOUR KNIFE HAS BEEN BUSY. ROUND UP THE OTHERS, WE'VE GOT TO HIT THE FORT TONIGHT!
Later at the fort, and with time running out fast before the British attacked, a grappling hook snaked over the lower wall –
Rat Pack had arrived!
THE GUNS ARE OUR TARGET – WITHOUT THEM THE FORT'S A TOOTHLESS TIGER!
But the deadly commandos were spotted –
SAPRISTI. . . AARGH!
IT BETTER TO SHOOT FIRST AND ASK QUESTIONS LATER!
THOSE SHOTS WILL ALERT THE WHOLE FORT! QUICKLY, WEASEL – THERE ARE THE 88MM SHELLS. YOU KNOW WHAT TO DO!
Y-YES, MR. TAGGART. SHELLS USED BY GUNS LIKE THESE ARE USUALLY AIR BURST SHELLS. ALL I HAVE TO DO IS FIX 'EM TO BLOW PREMATURELY.
And while Rat Pack fought a desperate fight –
NEARLY DONE. ONLY AN EXPERT LIKE ME COULD FIX THESE LITTLE BEAUTIES!

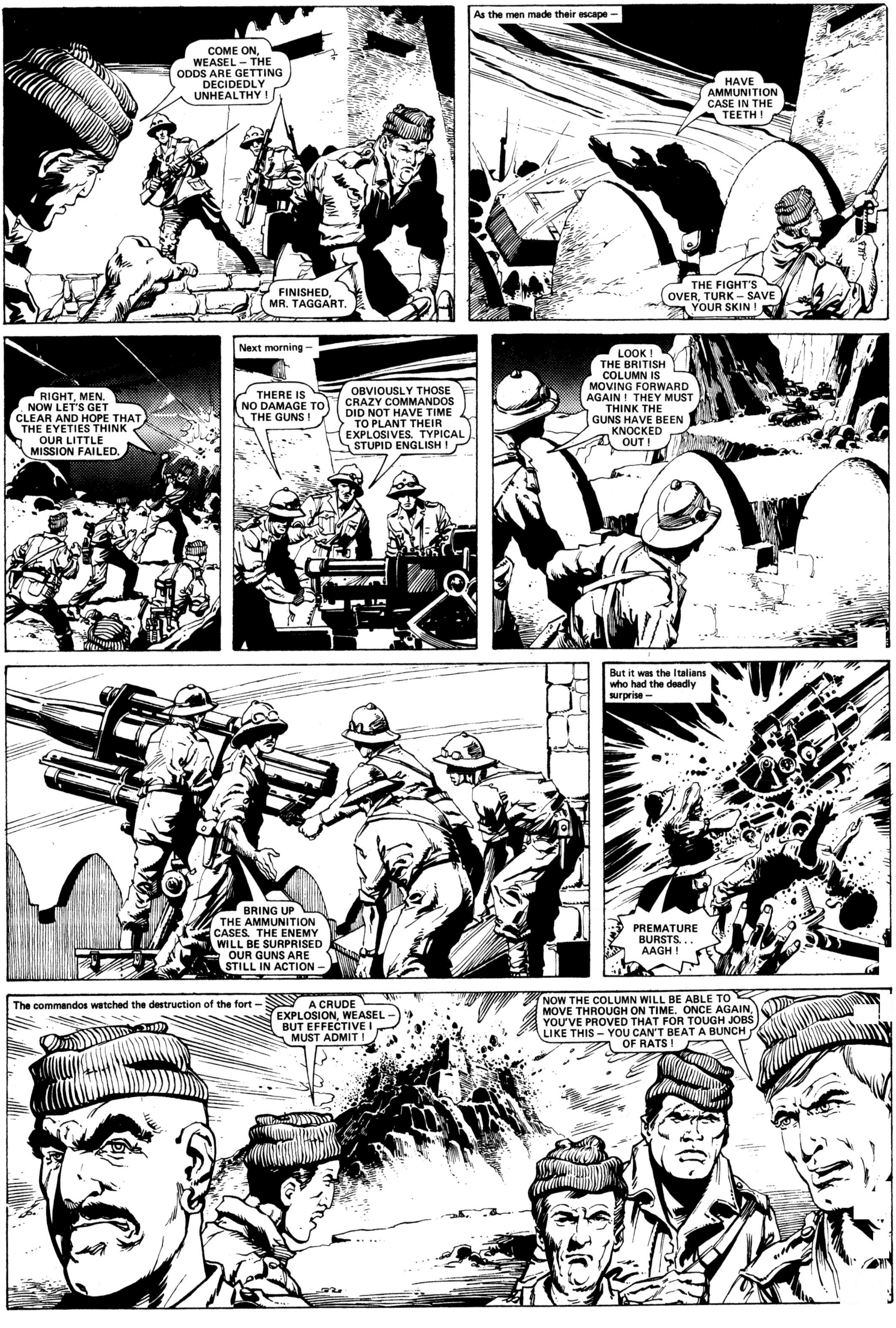
COME ON, WEASEL – THE ODDS ARE GETTING DECIDEDLY UNHEALTHY !
FINISHED, MR. TAGGART.
As the men made their escape –
HAVE AMMUNITION CASE IN THE TEETH !
THE FIGHT'S OVER, TURK – SAVE YOUR SKIN !
RIGHT, MEN. NOW LET'S GET CLEAR AND HOPE THAT THE EYETIES THINK OUR LITTLE MISSION FAILED.
Next morning –
THERE IS NO DAMAGE TO THE GUNS !
OBVIOUSLY THOSE CRAZY COMMANDOS DID NOT HAVE TIME TO PLANT THEIR EXPLOSIVES. TYPICAL STUPID ENGLISH !
LOOK ! THE BRITISH COLUMN IS MOVING FORWARD AGAIN ! THEY MUST THINK THE GUNS HAVE BEEN KNOCKED OUT !
BRING UP THE AMMUNITION CASES. THE ENEMY WILL BE SURPRISED OUR GUNS ARE STILL IN ACTION –
But it was the Italians who had the deadly surprise –
PREMATURE BURSTS. . . AAGH !
The commandos watched the destruction of the fort –
A CRUDE EXPLOSION, WEASEL – BUT EFFECTIVE I MUST ADMIT !
NOW THE COLUMN WILL BE ABLE TO MOVE THROUGH ON TIME. ONCE AGAIN, YOU'VE PROVED THAT FOR TOUGH JOBS LIKE THIS – YOU CAN'T BEAT A BUNCH OF RATS !

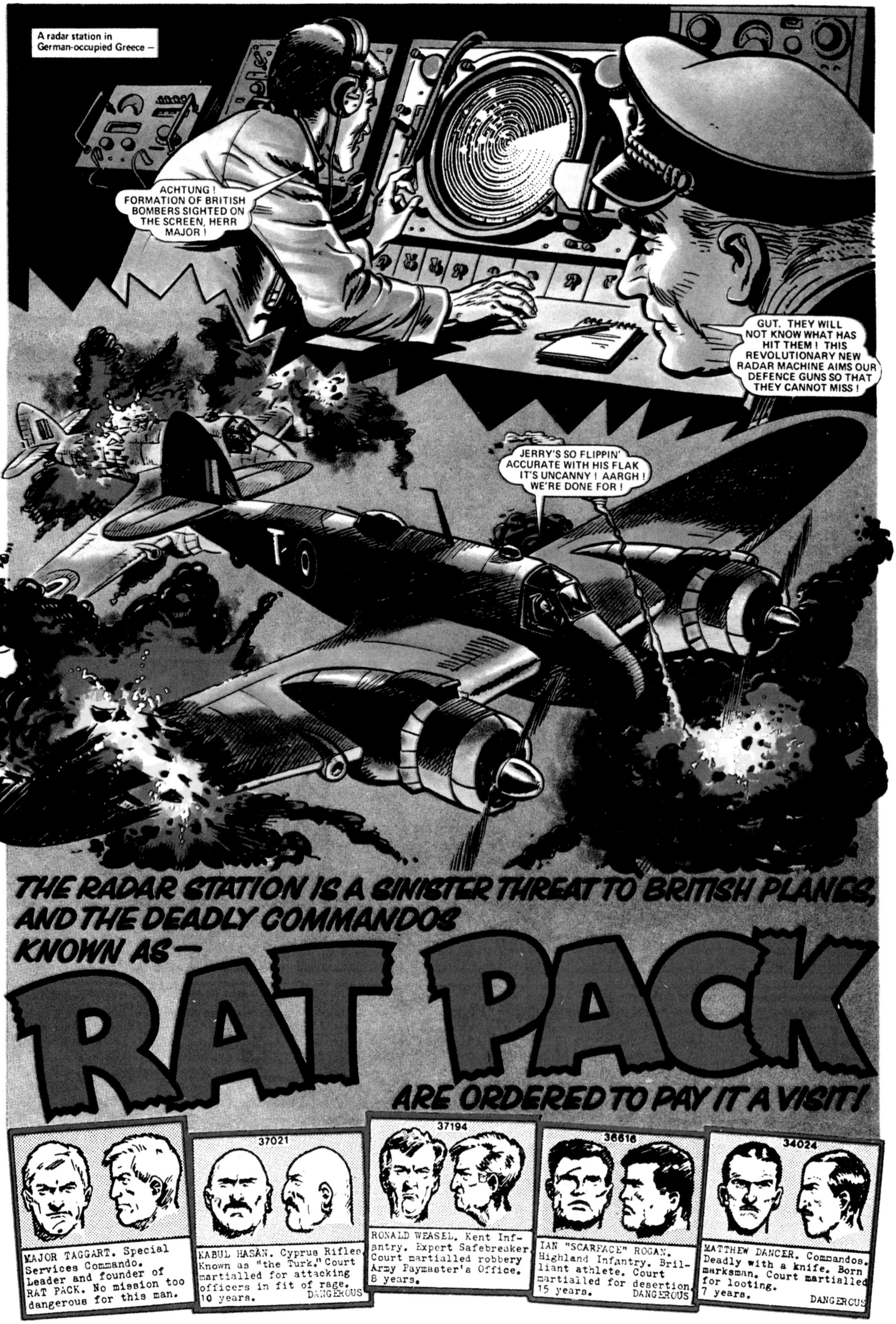

A radar station in German-occupied Greece –
ACHTUNG ! FORMATION OF BRITISH BOMBERS SIGHTED ON THE SCREEN, HERR MAJOR !
GUT. THEY WILL NOT KNOW WHAT HAS HIT THEM ! THIS REVOLUTIONARY NEW RADAR MACHINE AIMS OUR DEFENCE GUNS SO THAT THEY CANNOT MISS !
JERRY'S SO FLIPPIN' ACCURATE WITH HIS FLAK IT'S UNCANNY ! AARGH ! WE'RE DONE FOR !
THE RADAR STATION IS A SINISTER THREAT TO BRITISH PLANES, AND THE DEADLY COMMANDOS KNOWN AS—
RAT PACK
ARE ORDERED TO PAY IT A VISIT!
MAJOR TAGGART. Special Services Commando. Leader and founder of RAT PACK. No mission too dangerous for this man.
37021
KABUL HASAN. Cyprus Rifles. Known as "the Turk." Court martialled for attacking officers in fit of rage. 10 years. DANGEROUS
37194
RONALD WEASEL. Kent Infantry. Expert Safebreaker. Court martialled robbery Army Paymaster's Office. 8 years.
36616
IAN "SCARFACE" ROGAN. Highland Infantry. Brilliant athlete. Court martialled for desertion. 15 years. DANGEROUS
34024
MATTHEW DANCER. Commandos. Deadly with a knife. Born marksman. Court martialled for looting. 7 years. DANGEROUS

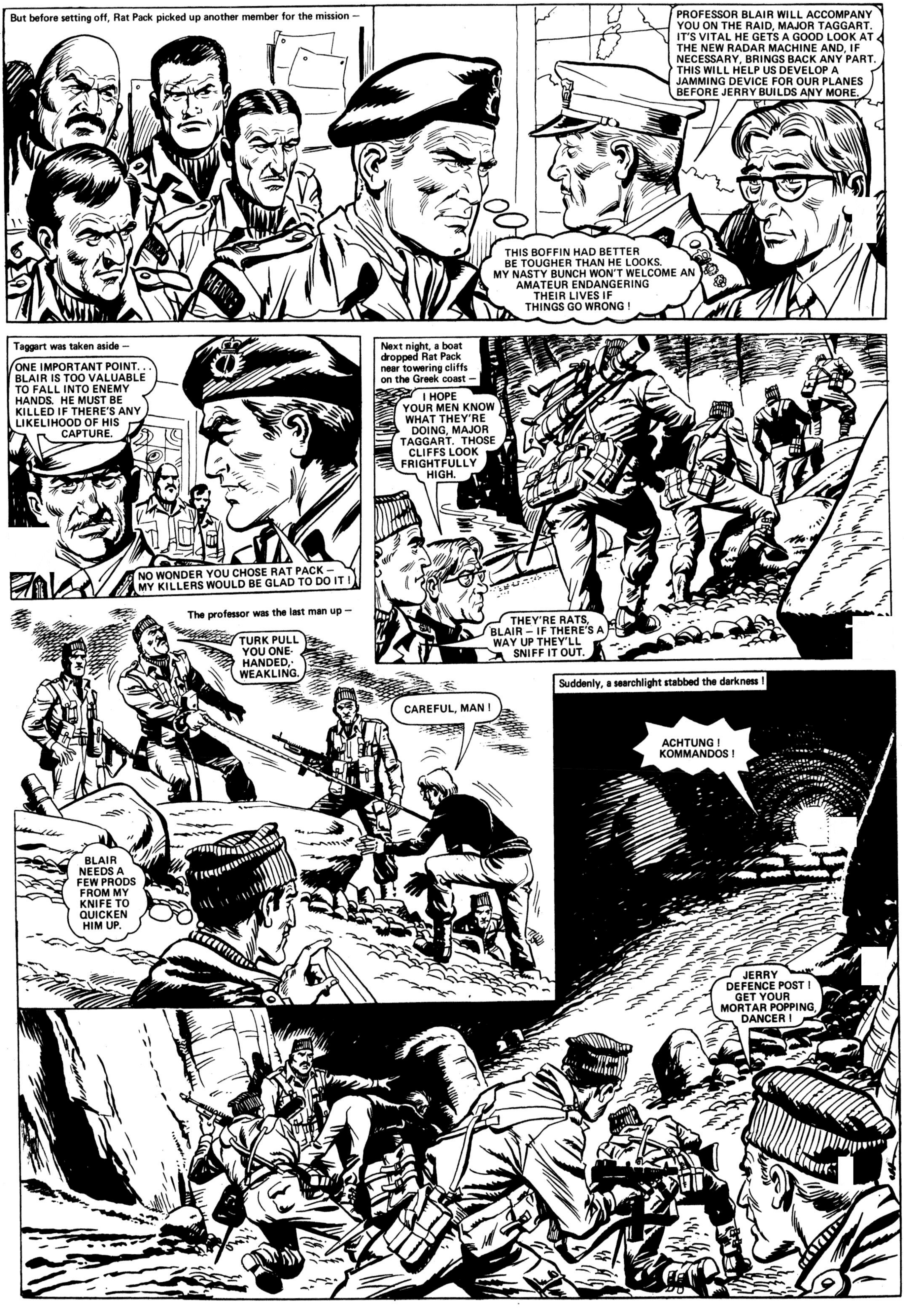
But before setting off, Rat Pack picked up another member for the mission –
PROFESSOR BLAIR WILL ACCOMPANY YOU ON THE RAID, MAJOR TAGGART. IT'S VITAL HE GETS A GOOD LOOK AT THE NEW RADAR MACHINE AND, IF NECESSARY, BRINGS BACK ANY PART. THIS WILL HELP US DEVELOP A JAMMING DEVICE FOR OUR PLANES BEFORE JERRY BUILDS ANY MORE.
THIS BOFFIN HAD BETTER BE TOUGHER THAN HE LOOKS. MY NASTY BUNCH WON'T WELCOME AN AMATEUR ENDANGERING THEIR LIVES IF THINGS GO WRONG !
Taggart was taken aside –
ONE IMPORTANT POINT. . . BLAIR IS TOO VALUABLE TO FALL INTO ENEMY HANDS. HE MUST BE KILLED IF THERE'S ANY LIKELIHOOD OF HIS CAPTURE.
NO WONDER YOU CHOSE RAT PACK – MY KILLERS WOULD BE GLAD TO DO IT !
Next night, a boat dropped Rat Pack near towering cliffs on the Greek coast –
I HOPE YOUR MEN KNOW WHAT THEY'RE DOING, MAJOR TAGGART. THOSE CLIFFS LOOK FRIGHTFULLY HIGH.
THEY'RE RATS, BLAIR – IF THERE'S A WAY UP THEY'LL SNIFF IT OUT.
The professor was the last man up –
TURK PULL YOU ONE-HANDED, WEAKLING.
CAREFUL, MAN !
BLAIR NEEDS A FEW PRODS FROM MY KNIFE TO QUICKEN HIM UP.
Suddenly, a searchlight stabbed the darkness !
ACHTUNG ! KOMMANDOS !
JERRY DEFENCE POST ! GET YOUR MORTAR POPPING, DANCER !

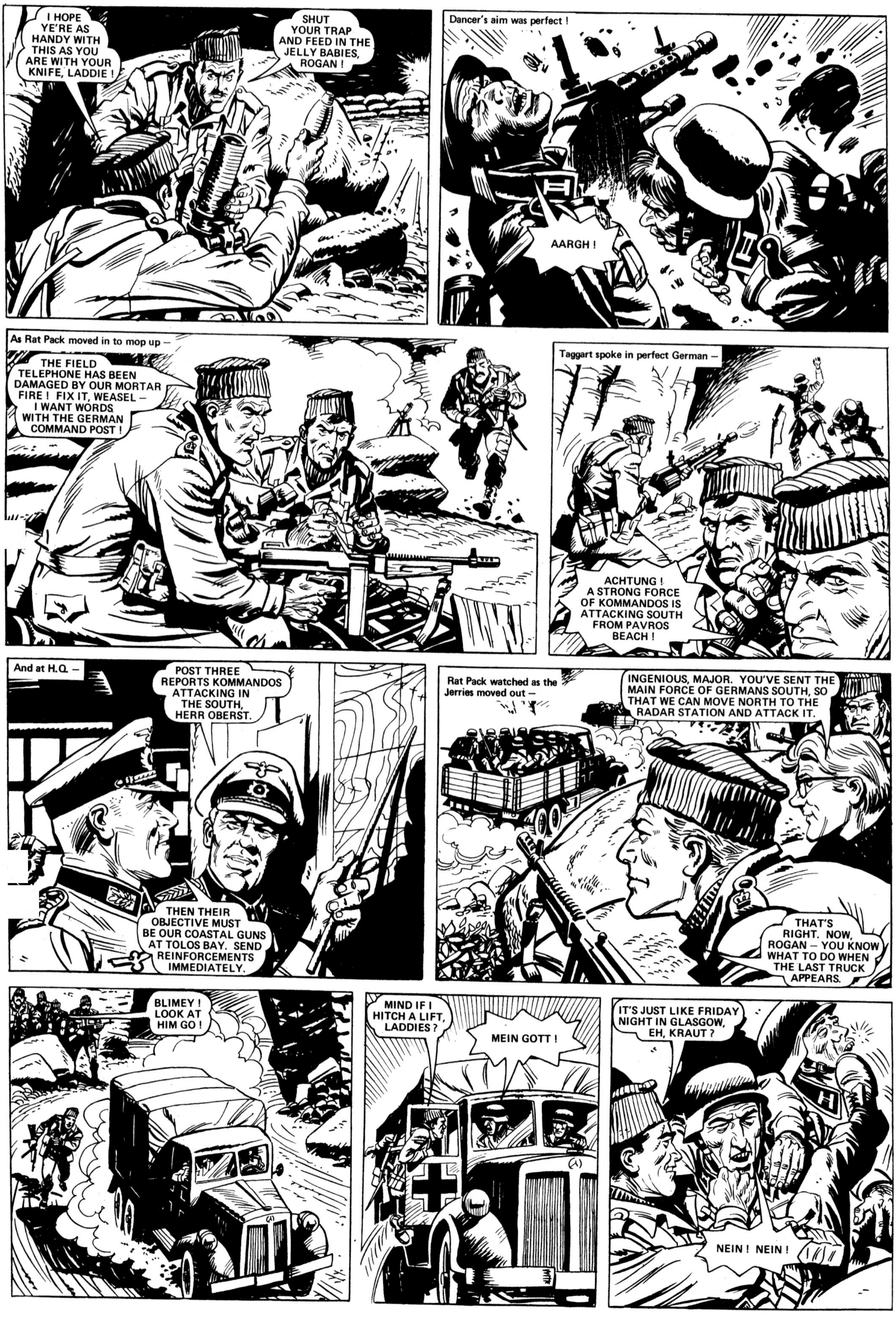
I HOPE YE'RE AS HANDY WITH THIS AS YOU ARE WITH YOUR KNIFE, LADDIE !
SHUT YOUR TRAP AND FEED IN THE JELLY BABIES, ROGAN !
Dancer's aim was perfect !
AARGH !
As Rat Pack moved in to mop up –
THE FIELD TELEPHONE HAS BEEN DAMAGED BY OUR MORTAR FIRE ! FIX IT, WEASEL – I WANT WORDS WITH THE GERMAN COMMAND POST !
Taggart spoke in perfect German –
ACHTUNG ! A STRONG FORCE OF KOMMANDOS IS ATTACKING SOUTH FROM PAVROS BEACH !
And at H.Q. –
POST THREE REPORTS KOMMANDOS ATTACKING IN THE SOUTH, HERR OBERST.
THEN THEIR OBJECTIVE MUST BE OUR COASTAL GUNS AT TOLOS BAY. SEND REINFORCEMENTS IMMEDIATELY.
Rat Pack watched as the Jerries moved out –
INGENIOUS, MAJOR. YOU'VE SENT THE MAIN FORCE OF GERMANS SOUTH, SO THAT WE CAN MOVE NORTH TO THE RADAR STATION AND ATTACK IT.
THAT'S RIGHT. NOW, ROGAN – YOU KNOW WHAT TO DO WHEN THE LAST TRUCK APPEARS.
BLIMEY ! LOOK AT HIM GO !
MIND IF I HITCH A LIFT, LADDIES ?
MEIN GOTT !
IT'S JUST LIKE FRIDAY NIGHT IN GLASGOW, EH, KRAUT ?
NEIN ! NEIN !

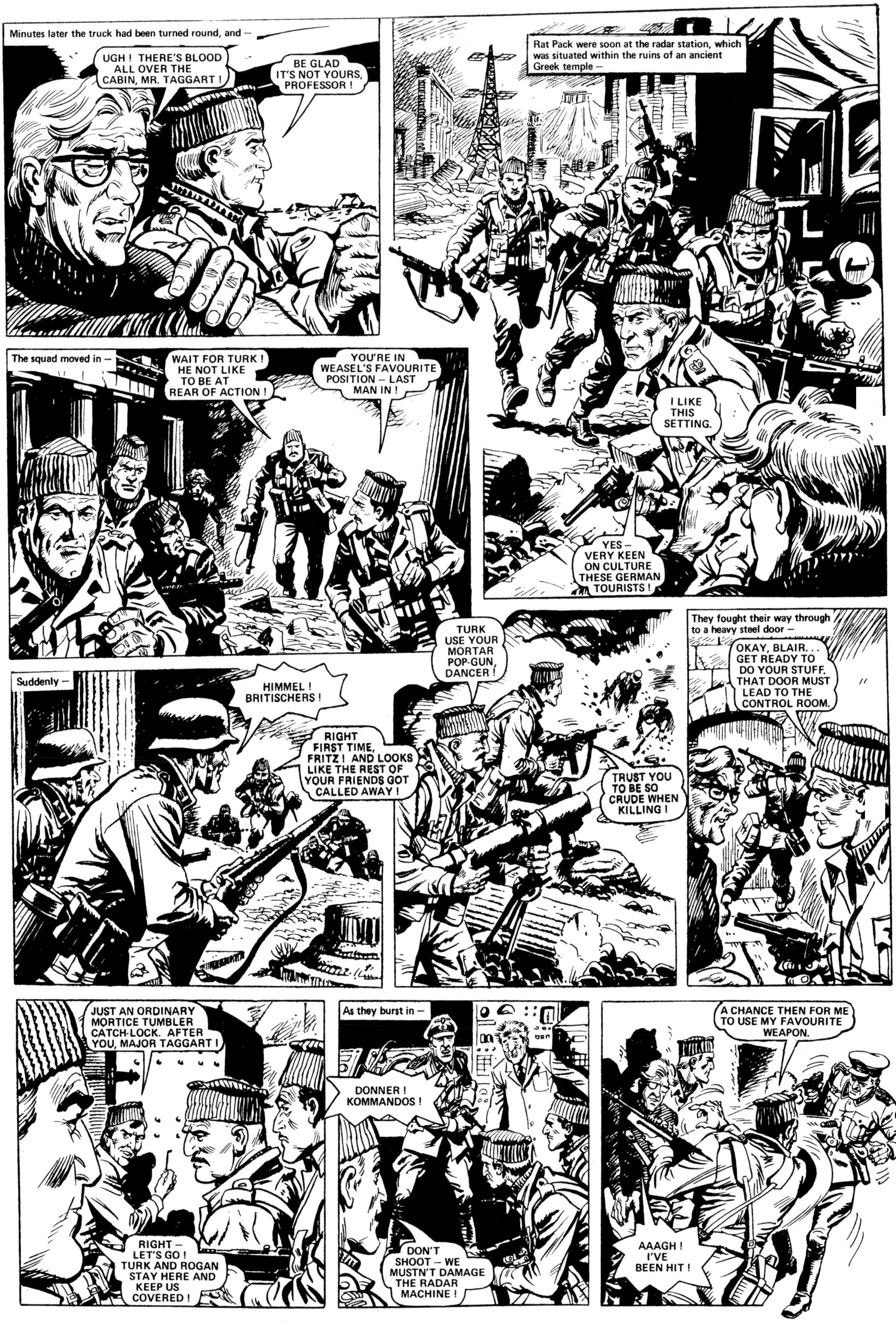

Minutes later the truck had been turned round, and –
UGH ! THERE'S BLOOD ALL OVER THE CABIN, MR. TAGGART !
BE GLAD IT'S NOT YOURS, PROFESSOR !
Rat Pack were soon at the radar station, which was situated within the ruins of an ancient Greek temple –
I LIKE THIS SETTING.
YES – VERY KEEN ON CULTURE THESE GERMAN TOURISTS !
The squad moved in –
WAIT FOR TURK ! HE NOT LIKE TO BE AT REAR OF ACTION !
YOU'RE IN WEASEL'S FAVOURITE POSITION – LAST MAN IN !
Suddenly –
HIMMEL ! BRITISCHERS !
RIGHT FIRST TIME, FRITZ ! AND LOOKS LIKE THE REST OF YOUR FRIENDS GOT CALLED AWAY !
TURK USE YOUR MORTAR POP-GUN, DANCER !
TRUST YOU TO BE SO CRUDE WHEN KILLING !
They fought their way through to a heavy steel door –
OKAY, BLAIR... GET READY TO DO YOUR STUFF. THAT DOOR MUST LEAD TO THE CONTROL ROOM.
JUST AN ORDINARY MORTICE TUMBLER CATCH-LOCK. AFTER YOU, MAJOR TAGGART !
RIGHT – LET'S GO ! TURK AND ROGAN STAY HERE AND KEEP US COVERED !
As they burst in –
DONNER ! KOMMANDOS !
DON'T SHOOT – WE MUSTN'T DAMAGE THE RADAR MACHINE !
A CHANCE THEN FOR ME TO USE MY FAVOURITE WEAPON.
AAAGH ! I'VE BEEN HIT !

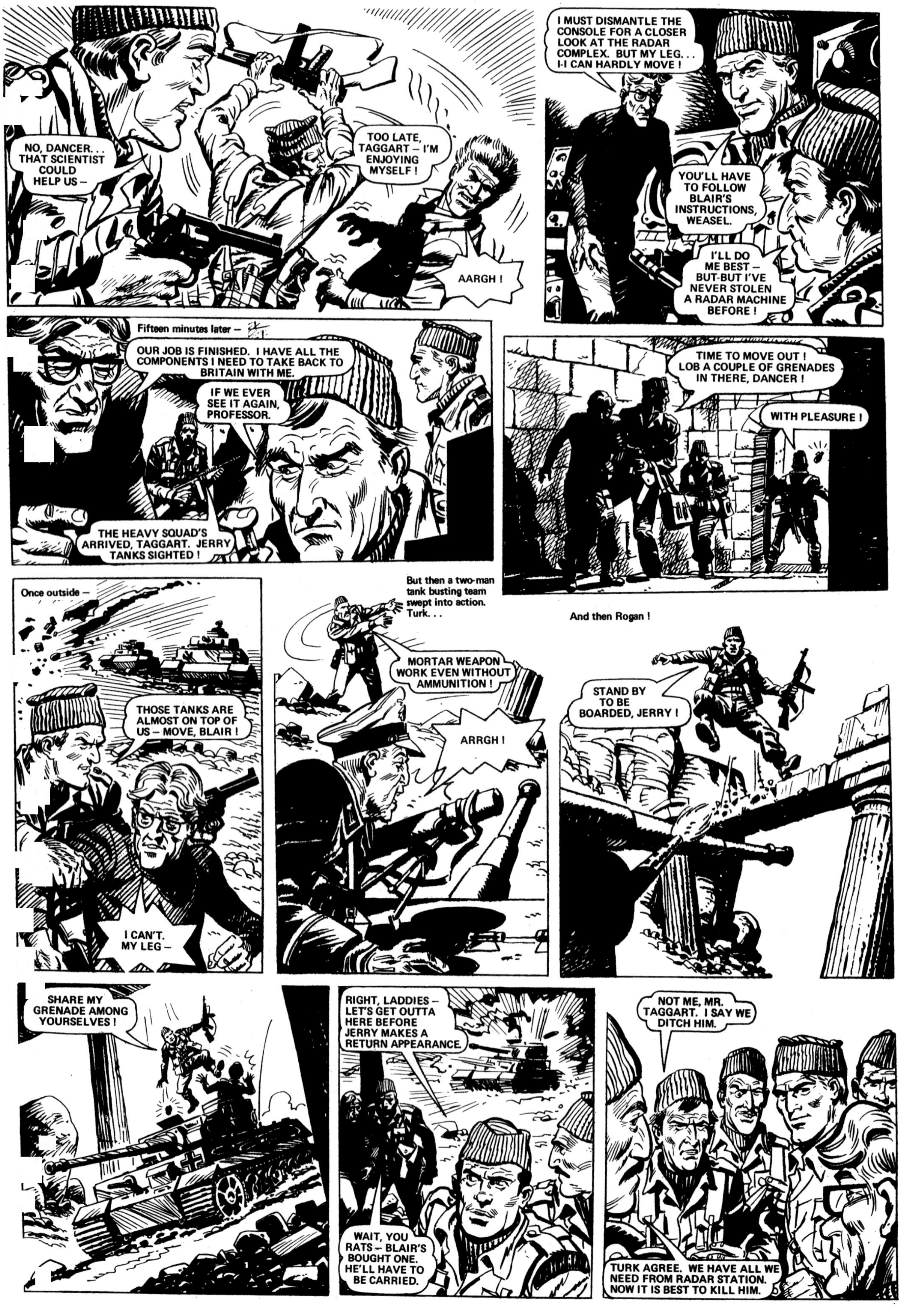
NO, DANCER... THAT SCIENTIST COULD HELP US –
TOO LATE, TAGGART – I'M ENJOYING MYSELF !
AARGH !
I MUST DISMANTLE THE CONSOLE FOR A CLOSER LOOK AT THE RADAR COMPLEX. BUT MY LEG... I-I CAN HARDLY MOVE !
YOU'LL HAVE TO FOLLOW BLAIR'S INSTRUCTIONS, WEASEL.
I'LL DO ME BEST – BUT-BUT I'VE NEVER STOLEN A RADAR MACHINE BEFORE !
Fifteen minutes later –
OUR JOB IS FINISHED. I HAVE ALL THE COMPONENTS I NEED TO TAKE BACK TO BRITAIN WITH ME.
IF WE EVER SEE IT AGAIN, PROFESSOR.
THE HEAVY SQUAD'S ARRIVED, TAGGART. JERRY TANKS SIGHTED !
TIME TO MOVE OUT ! LOB A COUPLE OF GRENADES IN THERE, DANCER !
WITH PLEASURE !
Once outside –
THOSE TANKS ARE ALMOST ON TOP OF US – MOVE, BLAIR !
I CAN'T. MY LEG –
But then a two-man tank busting team swept into action. Turk...
MORTAR WEAPON WORK EVEN WITHOUT AMMUNITION !
ARRGH !
And then Rogan !
STAND BY TO BE BOARDED, JERRY !
SHARE MY GRENADE AMONG YOURSELVES !
RIGHT, LADDIES – LET'S GET OUTTA HERE BEFORE JERRY MAKES A RETURN APPEARANCE.
WAIT, YOU RATS – BLAIR'S BOUGHT ONE. HE'LL HAVE TO BE CARRIED.
NOT ME, MR. TAGGART. I SAY WE DITCH HIM.
TURK AGREE. WE HAVE ALL WE NEED FROM RADAR STATION. NOW IT IS BEST TO KILL HIM.

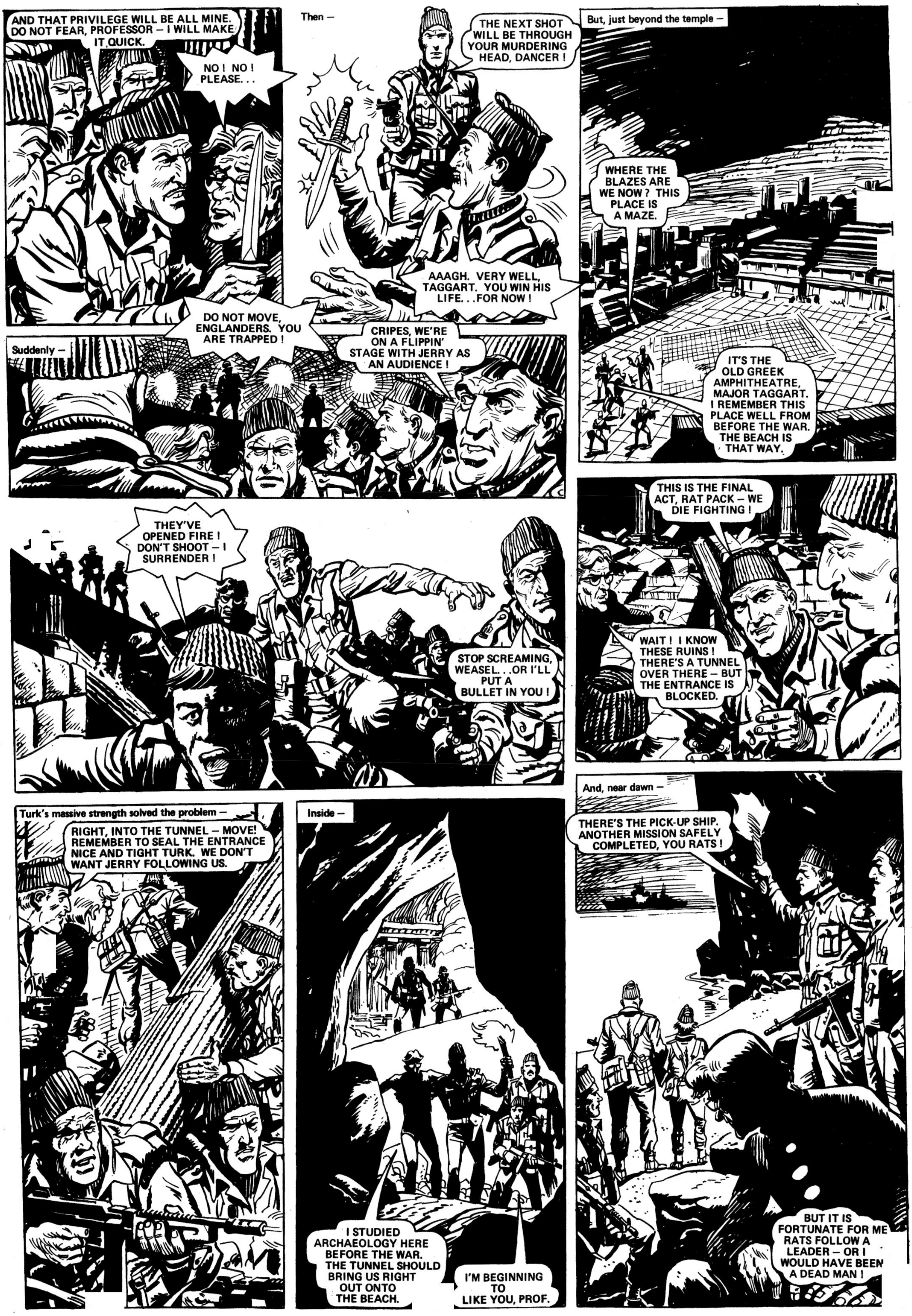
AND THAT PRIVILEGE WILL BE ALL MINE. DO NOT FEAR, PROFESSOR – I WILL MAKE IT QUICK.
NO ! NO ! PLEASE. . .
Then –
THE NEXT SHOT WILL BE THROUGH YOUR MURDERING HEAD, DANCER !
AAAGH. VERY WELL, TAGGART. YOU WIN HIS LIFE. . .FOR NOW !
Suddenly –
DO NOT MOVE, ENGLANDERS. YOU ARE TRAPPED !
CRIPES, WE'RE ON A FLIPPIN' STAGE WITH JERRY AS AN AUDIENCE !
But, just beyond the temple –
WHERE THE BLAZES ARE WE NOW ? THIS PLACE IS A MAZE.
IT'S THE OLD GREEK AMPHITHEATRE, MAJOR TAGGART. I REMEMBER THIS PLACE WELL FROM BEFORE THE WAR. THE BEACH IS THAT WAY.
THEY'VE OPENED FIRE ! DON'T SHOOT – I SURRENDER !
STOP SCREAMING, WEASEL. . .OR I'LL PUT A BULLET IN YOU !
THIS IS THE FINAL ACT, RAT PACK – WE DIE FIGHTING !
WAIT ! I KNOW THESE RUINS ! THERE'S A TUNNEL OVER THERE – BUT THE ENTRANCE IS BLOCKED.
Turk's massive strength solved the problem –
RIGHT, INTO THE TUNNEL – MOVE! REMEMBER TO SEAL THE ENTRANCE NICE AND TIGHT TURK. WE DON'T WANT JERRY FOLLOWING US.
Inside –
I STUDIED ARCHAEOLOGY HERE BEFORE THE WAR. THE TUNNEL SHOULD BRING US RIGHT OUT ONTO THE BEACH.
I'M BEGINNING TO LIKE YOU, PROF.
And, near dawn –
THERE'S THE PICK-UP SHIP. ANOTHER MISSION SAFELY COMPLETED, YOU RATS !
BUT IT IS FORTUNATE FOR ME RATS FOLLOW A LEADER – OR I WOULD HAVE BEEN A DEAD MAN !

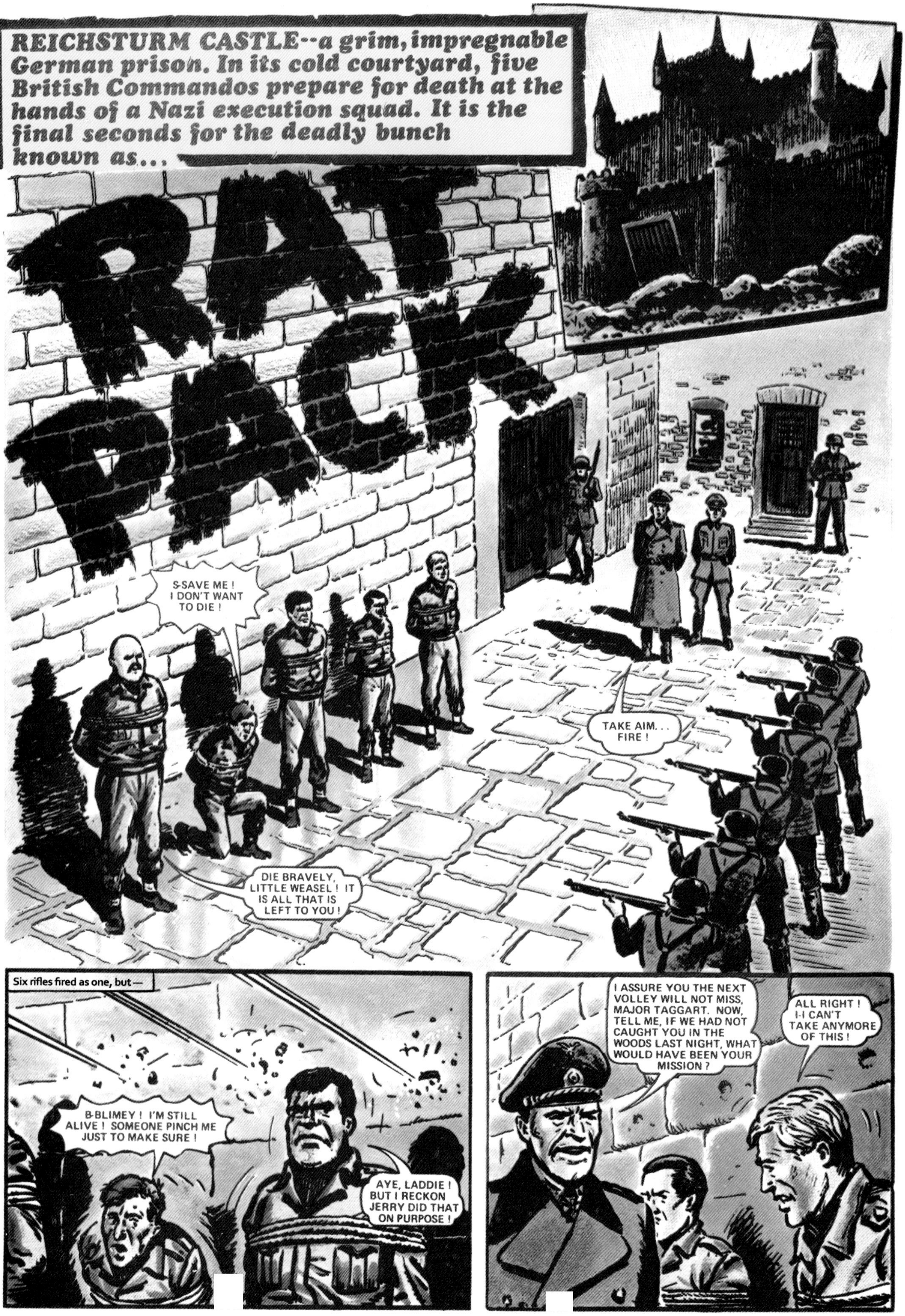
REICHSTURM CASTLE--a grim, impregnable German prison. In its cold courtyard, five British Commandos prepare for death at the hands of a Nazi execution squad. It is the final seconds for the deadly bunch known as...
RAT PACK
S-SAVE ME ! I DON'T WANT TO DIE !
TAKE AIM. . . FIRE !
DIE BRAVELY, LITTLE WEASEL ! IT IS ALL THAT IS LEFT TO YOU !
Six rifles fired as one, but —
B-BLIMEY ! I'M STILL ALIVE ! SOMEONE PINCH ME JUST TO MAKE SURE !
AYE, LADDIE ! BUT I RECKON JERRY DID THAT ON PURPOSE !
I ASSURE YOU THE NEXT VOLLEY WILL NOT MISS, MAJOR TAGGART. NOW, TELL ME, IF WE HAD NOT CAUGHT YOU IN THE WOODS LAST NIGHT, WHAT WOULD HAVE BEEN YOUR MISSION ?
ALL RIGHT ! I-I CAN'T TAKE ANYMORE OF THIS !

Later, in the prison commandant's office —

GOOD. YOU HAVE DONE WELL!

I HAVE BROKEN THEM – THE FAMOUS RAT PACK WILL CONFESS ALL WHEN THE GESTAPO ARRIVE.

But in Rat Pack's cell —

THEY FELL FOR IT – OUR PLAN TO DELIBERATELY BE ARRESTED, SO WE COULD GET INTO THIS CASTLE, HAS WORKED. NOW WE MUST COMPLETE OUR REAL MISSION HERE FAST – BEFORE SOME OF YOU START SQUEALING UNDER GESTAPO TORTURE.

MIGHT BE WORTH IT FOR US TO HEAR YOU SQUEALING FIRST, TAGGART!

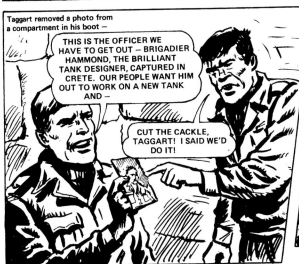

Taggart removed a photo from a compartment in his boot —

THIS IS THE OFFICER WE HAVE TO GET OUT – BRIGADIER HAMMOND, THE BRILLIANT TANK DESIGNER, CAPTURED IN CRETE. OUR PEOPLE WANT HIM OUT TO WORK ON A NEW TANK AND –

CUT THE CACKLE, TAGGART! I SAID WE'D DO IT!

YES – YOU TALKED US INTO THIS MISSION, ROGAN.

AND NOW LOOK WHAT A FLIPPIN' MESS WE'RE IN – LET'S GET 'IM!

GET OFF ME, YOU CRAZY FOOLS!

THATS FROM ME, ROGAN!

THAT'S THE STUFF, YOU TWO! HOLD HIM DOWN, SO I CAN PUT THE BOOT IN!

CUT IT OUT – ALL OF YOU!

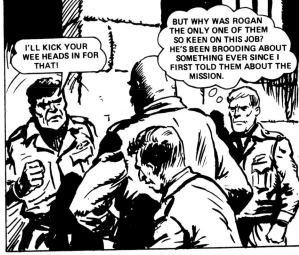

I'LL KICK YOUR WEE HEADS IN FOR THAT!

BUT WHY WAS ROGAN THE ONLY ONE OF THEM SO KEEN ON THIS JOB? HE'S BEEN BROODING ABOUT SOMETHING EVER SINCE I FIRST TOLD THEM ABOUT THE MISSION.

HEY – WHAT'S THAT TAPPING COMING FROM THE WATER PIPE – ?

IT – IT SOUNDS LIKE MORSE CODE, MR. TAGGART.

IT'S SOME OF THE BRITISH PRISONERS – USING A PIPE TAPPING TELEPHONE – THEY'RE ASKING – WHO - - - ARE - - - WE - - - ?

TELL THEM! THEN ASK THEM WHEREABOUTS IN THE CASTLE THE BRIGADIER'S IMPRISONED.

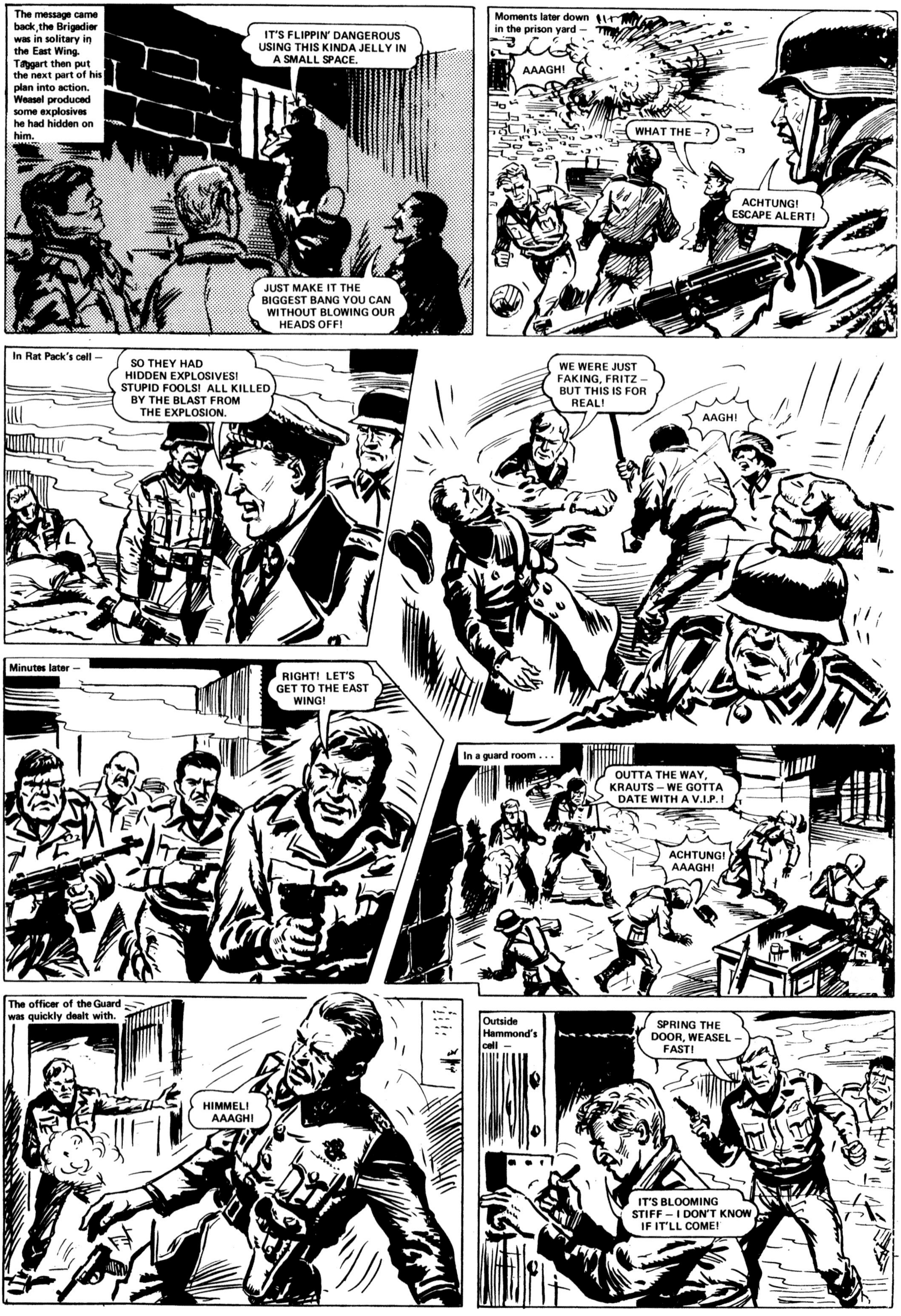
The message came back, the Brigadier was in solitary in the East Wing. Taggart then put the next part of his plan into action. Weasel produced some explosives he had hidden on him.
IT'S FLIPPIN' DANGEROUS USING THIS KINDA JELLY IN A SMALL SPACE.
JUST MAKE IT THE BIGGEST BANG YOU CAN WITHOUT BLOWING OUR HEADS OFF!
Moments later down in the prison yard —
AAAGH!
WHAT THE — ?
ACHTUNG! ESCAPE ALERT!
In Rat Pack's cell —
SO THEY HAD HIDDEN EXPLOSIVES! STUPID FOOLS! ALL KILLED BY THE BLAST FROM THE EXPLOSION.
WE WERE JUST FAKING, FRITZ — BUT THIS IS FOR REAL!
AAGH!
Minutes later —
RIGHT! LET'S GET TO THE EAST WING!
In a guard room . . .
OUTTA THE WAY, KRAUTS — WE GOTTA DATE WITH A V.I.P. !
ACHTUNG! AAAGH!
The officer of the Guard was quickly dealt with.
HIMMEL! AAAGH!
Outside Hammond's cell —
SPRING THE DOOR, WEASEL — FAST!
IT'S BLOOMING STIFF — I DON'T KNOW IF IT'LL COME!

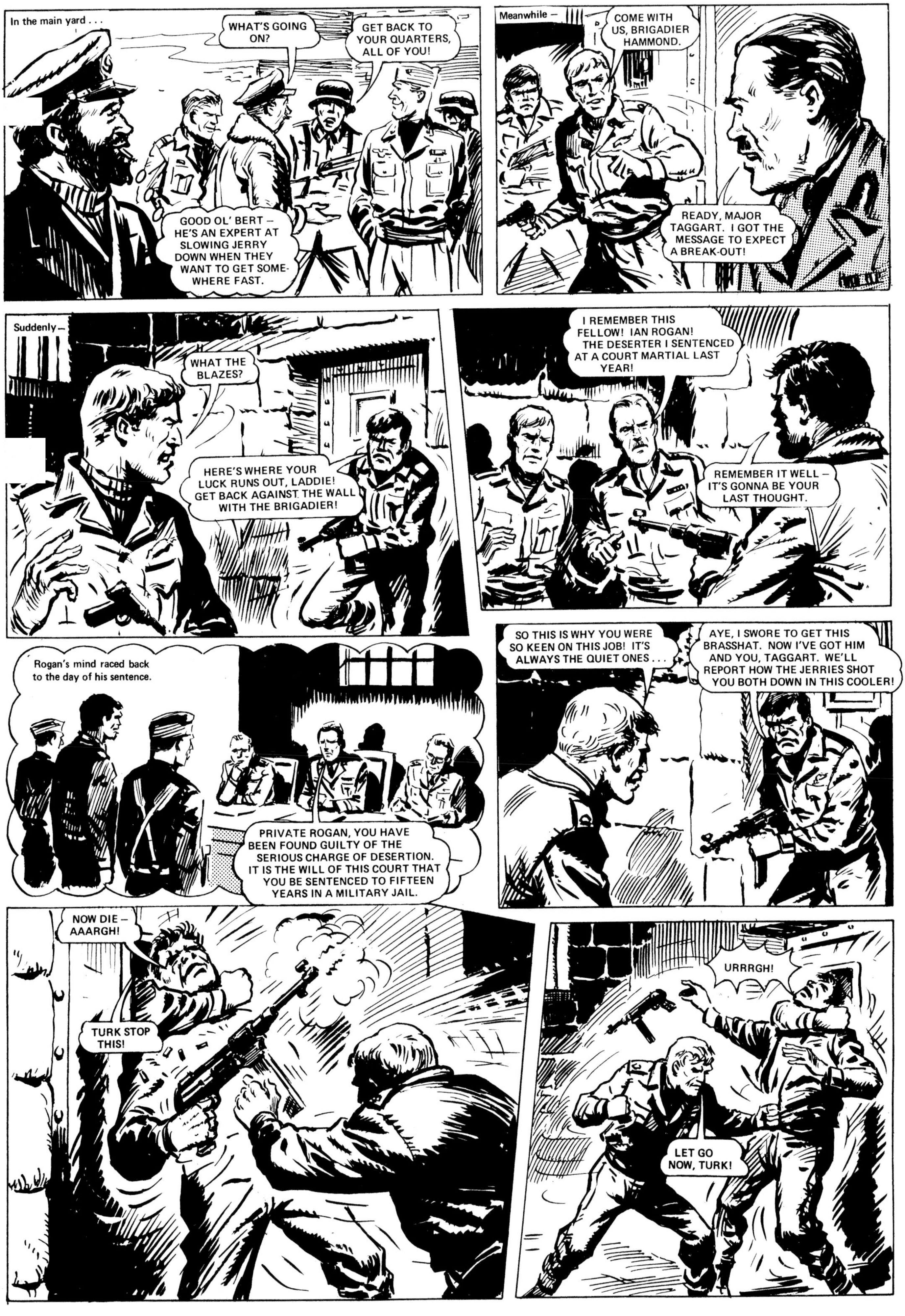
In the main yard . . .
WHAT'S GOING ON?
GET BACK TO YOUR QUARTERS, ALL OF YOU!
GOOD OL' BERT — HE'S AN EXPERT AT SLOWING JERRY DOWN WHEN THEY WANT TO GET SOMEWHERE FAST.
Meanwhile —
COME WITH US, BRIGADIER HAMMOND.
READY, MAJOR TAGGART. I GOT THE MESSAGE TO EXPECT A BREAK-OUT!
Suddenly —
WHAT THE BLAZES?
HERE'S WHERE YOUR LUCK RUNS OUT, LADDIE! GET BACK AGAINST THE WALL WITH THE BRIGADIER!
I REMEMBER THIS FELLOW! IAN ROGAN! THE DESERTER I SENTENCED AT A COURT MARTIAL LAST YEAR!
REMEMBER IT WELL — IT'S GONNA BE YOUR LAST THOUGHT.
Rogan's mind raced back to the day of his sentence.
PRIVATE ROGAN, YOU HAVE BEEN FOUND GUILTY OF THE SERIOUS CHARGE OF DESERTION. IT IS THE WILL OF THIS COURT THAT YOU BE SENTENCED TO FIFTEEN YEARS IN A MILITARY JAIL.
SO THIS IS WHY YOU WERE SO KEEN ON THIS JOB! IT'S ALWAYS THE QUIET ONES . . .
AYE, I SWORE TO GET THIS BRASSHAT. NOW I'VE GOT HIM AND YOU, TAGGART. WE'LL REPORT HOW THE JERRIES SHOT YOU BOTH DOWN IN THIS COOLER!
NOW DIE — AAARGH!
TURK STOP THIS!
URRRGH!
LET GO NOW, TURK!

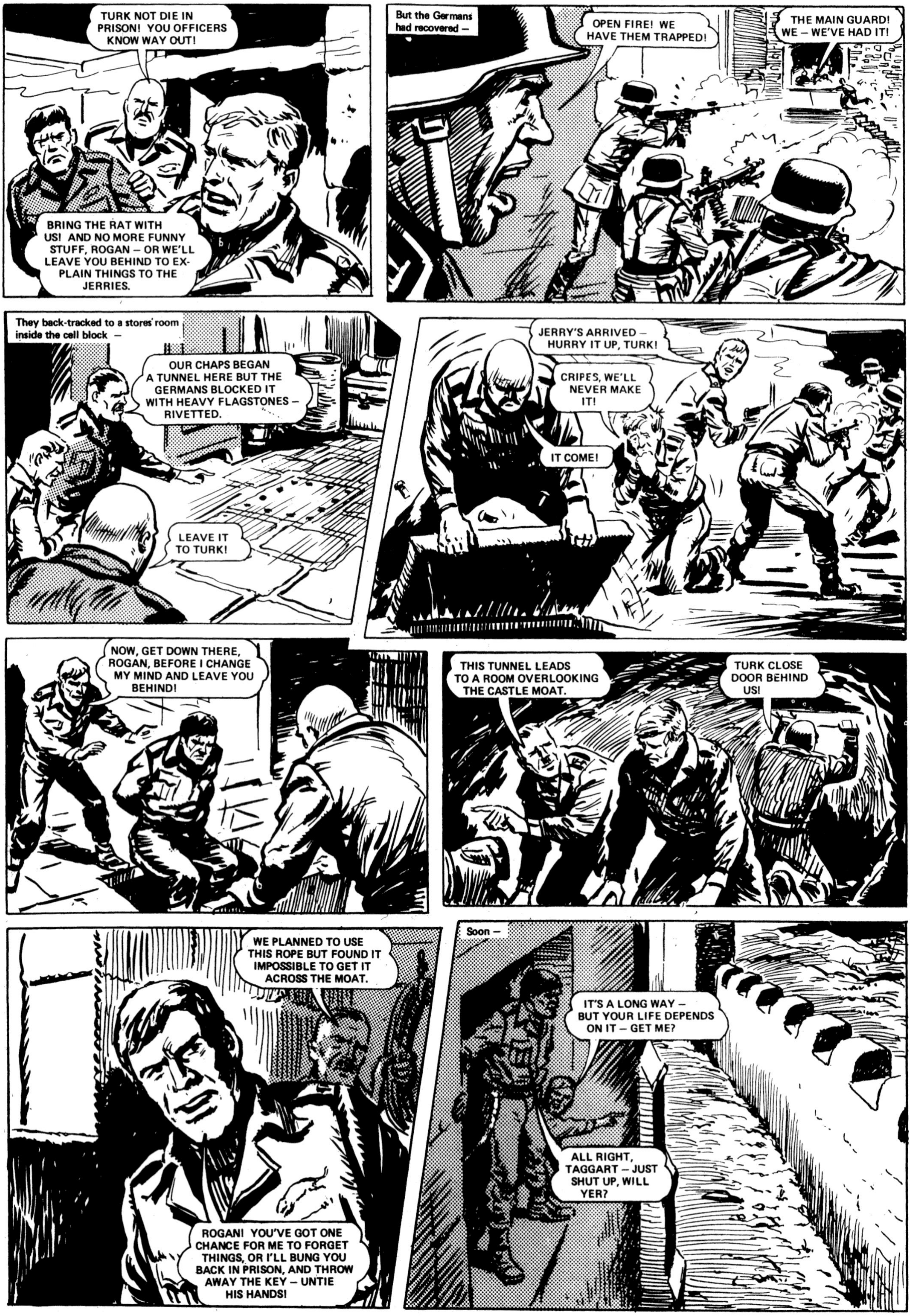
TURK NOT DIE IN PRISON! YOU OFFICERS KNOW WAY OUT!
BRING THE RAT WITH US! AND NO MORE FUNNY STUFF, ROGAN – OR WE'LL LEAVE YOU BEHIND TO EXPLAIN THINGS TO THE JERRIES.
But the Germans had recovered –
OPEN FIRE! WE HAVE THEM TRAPPED!
THE MAIN GUARD! WE – WE'VE HAD IT!
They back-tracked to a stores' room inside the cell block –
OUR CHAPS BEGAN A TUNNEL HERE BUT THE GERMANS BLOCKED IT WITH HEAVY FLAGSTONES – RIVETTED.
LEAVE IT TO TURK!
JERRY'S ARRIVED – HURRY IT UP, TURK!
CRIPES, WE'LL NEVER MAKE IT!
IT COME!
NOW, GET DOWN THERE, ROGAN, BEFORE I CHANGE MY MIND AND LEAVE YOU BEHIND!
THIS TUNNEL LEADS TO A ROOM OVERLOOKING THE CASTLE MOAT.
TURK CLOSE DOOR BEHIND US!
WE PLANNED TO USE THIS ROPE BUT FOUND IT IMPOSSIBLE TO GET IT ACROSS THE MOAT.
ROGAN! YOU'VE GOT ONE CHANCE FOR ME TO FORGET THINGS, OR I'LL BUNG YOU BACK IN PRISON, AND THROW AWAY THE KEY – UNTIE HIS HANDS!
Soon –
IT'S A LONG WAY – BUT YOUR LIFE DEPENDS ON IT – GET ME?
ALL RIGHT, TAGGART – JUST SHUT UP, WILL YER?

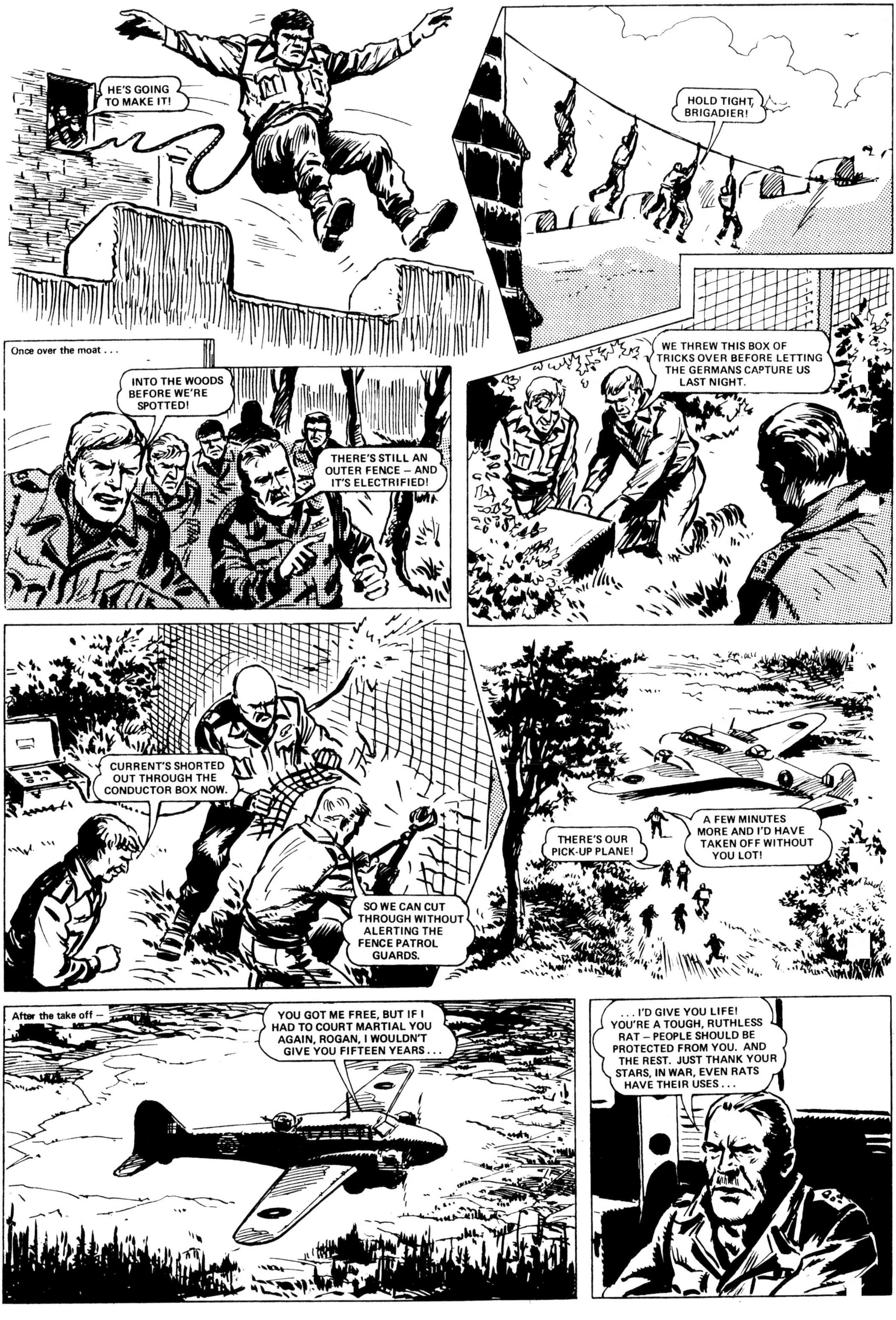
HE'S GOING TO MAKE IT!
HOLD TIGHT, BRIGADIER!
Once over the moat . . .
INTO THE WOODS BEFORE WE'RE SPOTTED!
THERE'S STILL AN OUTER FENCE – AND IT'S ELECTRIFIED!
WE THREW THIS BOX OF TRICKS OVER BEFORE LETTING THE GERMANS CAPTURE US LAST NIGHT.
CURRENT'S SHORTED OUT THROUGH THE CONDUCTOR BOX NOW.
SO WE CAN CUT THROUGH WITHOUT ALERTING THE FENCE PATROL GUARDS.
THERE'S OUR PICK-UP PLANE!
A FEW MINUTES MORE AND I'D HAVE TAKEN OFF WITHOUT YOU LOT!
After the take off –
YOU GOT ME FREE, BUT IF I HAD TO COURT MARTIAL YOU AGAIN, ROGAN, I WOULDN'T GIVE YOU FIFTEEN YEARS . . .
. . . I'D GIVE YOU LIFE! YOU'RE A TOUGH, RUTHLESS RAT – PEOPLE SHOULD BE PROTECTED FROM YOU. AND THE REST. JUST THANK YOUR STARS, IN WAR, EVEN RATS HAVE THEIR USES . . .

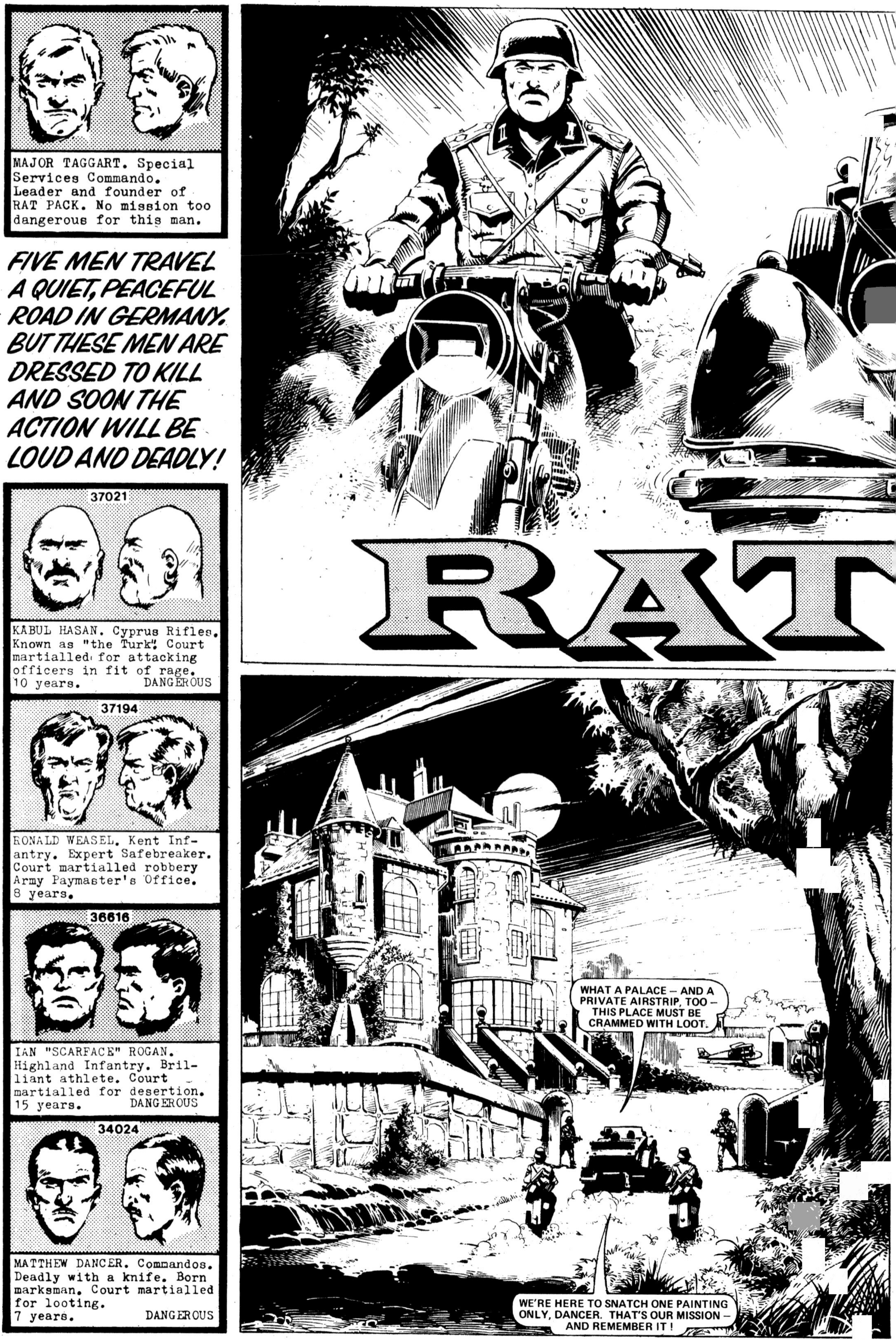
MAJOR TAGGART. Special Services Commando. Leader and founder of RAT PACK. No mission too dangerous for this man.
FIVE MEN TRAVEL A QUIET, PEACEFUL ROAD IN GERMANY. BUT THESE MEN ARE DRESSED TO KILL AND SOON THE ACTION WILL BE LOUD AND DEADLY!
37021
KABUL HASAN. Cyprus Rifles. Known as "the Turk". Court martialled for attacking officers in fit of rage. 10 years. DANGEROUS
37194
RONALD WEASEL. Kent Infantry. Expert Safebreaker. Court martialled robbery Army Paymaster's Office. 8 years.
36616
IAN "SCARFACE" ROGAN. Highland Infantry. Brilliant athlete. Court martialled for desertion. 15 years. DANGEROUS
34024
MATTHEW DANCER. Commandos. Deadly with a knife. Born marksman. Court martialled for looting. 7 years. DANGEROUS
RAT
WHAT A PALACE – AND A PRIVATE AIRSTRIP, TOO – THIS PLACE MUST BE CRAMMED WITH LOOT.
WE'RE HERE TO SNATCH ONE PAINTING ONLY, DANCER. THAT'S OUR MISSION – AND REMEMBER IT!

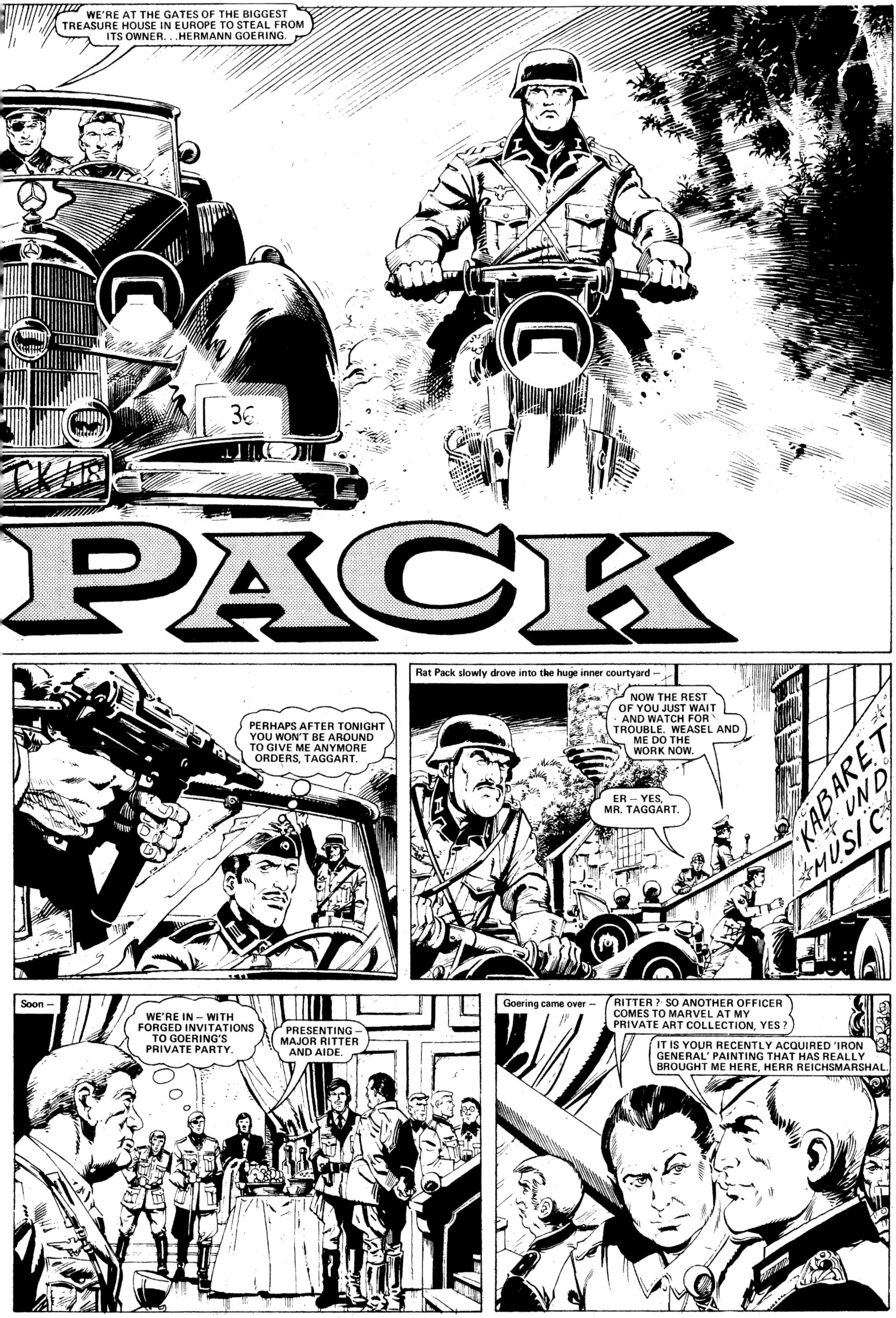

WE'RE AT THE GATES OF THE BIGGEST TREASURE HOUSE IN EUROPE TO STEAL FROM ITS OWNER. . .HERMANN GOERING.
PACK
PERHAPS AFTER TONIGHT YOU WON'T BE AROUND TO GIVE ME ANYMORE ORDERS, TAGGART.
Rat Pack slowly drove into the huge inner courtyard –
NOW THE REST OF YOU JUST WAIT AND WATCH FOR TROUBLE. WEASEL AND ME DO THE WORK NOW.
ER – YES, MR. TAGGART.
KABARET UND MUSIC
Soon –
WE'RE IN – WITH FORGED INVITATIONS TO GOERING'S PRIVATE PARTY.
PRESENTING – MAJOR RITTER AND AIDE.
Goering came over –
RITTER? SO ANOTHER OFFICER COMES TO MARVEL AT MY PRIVATE ART COLLECTION, YES?
IT IS YOUR RECENTLY ACQUIRED 'IRON GENERAL' PAINTING THAT HAS REALLY BROUGHT ME HERE, HERR REICHSMARSHAL.

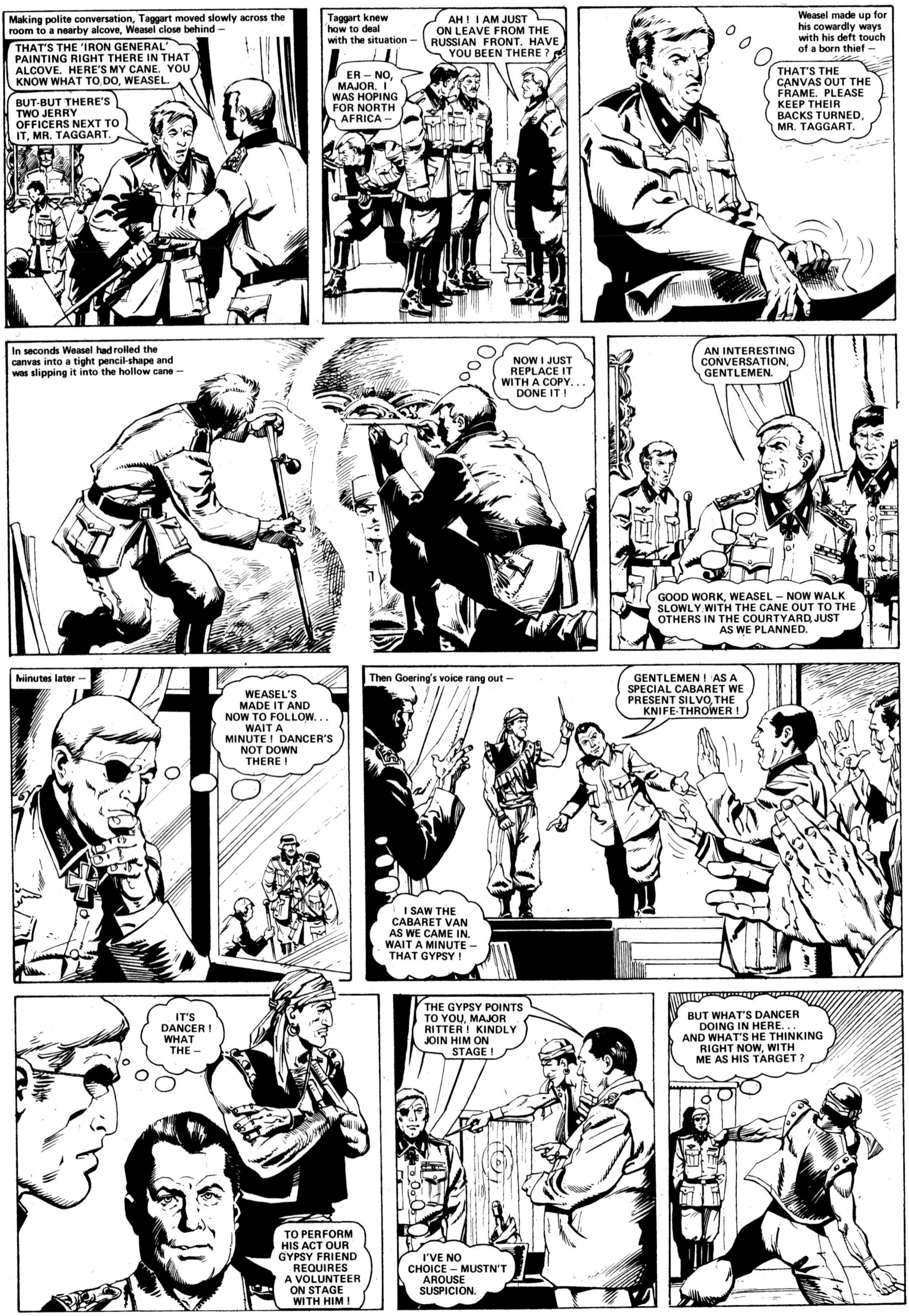
Making polite conversation, Taggart moved slowly across the room to a nearby alcove, Weasel close behind –
THAT'S THE 'IRON GENERAL' PAINTING RIGHT THERE IN THAT ALCOVE. HERE'S MY CANE. YOU KNOW WHAT TO DO, WEASEL.
BUT-BUT THERE'S TWO JERRY OFFICERS NEXT TO IT, MR. TAGGART.
Taggart knew how to deal with the situation –
AH! I AM JUST ON LEAVE FROM THE RUSSIAN FRONT. HAVE YOU BEEN THERE?
ER – NO, MAJOR. I WAS HOPING FOR NORTH AFRICA –
Weasel made up for his cowardly ways with his deft touch of a born thief –
THAT'S THE CANVAS OUT THE FRAME. PLEASE KEEP THEIR BACKS TURNED, MR. TAGGART.
In seconds Weasel had rolled the canvas into a tight pencil-shape and was slipping it into the hollow cane –
NOW I JUST REPLACE IT WITH A COPY... DONE IT!
AN INTERESTING CONVERSATION, GENTLEMEN.
GOOD WORK, WEASEL – NOW WALK SLOWLY WITH THE CANE OUT TO THE OTHERS IN THE COURTYARD, JUST AS WE PLANNED.
Minutes later –
WEASEL'S MADE IT AND NOW TO FOLLOW... WAIT A MINUTE! DANCER'S NOT DOWN THERE!
Then Goering's voice rang out –
GENTLEMEN! AS A SPECIAL CABARET WE PRESENT SILVO, THE KNIFE-THROWER!
I SAW THE CABARET VAN AS WE CAME IN. WAIT A MINUTE – THAT GYPSY!
IT'S DANCER! WHAT THE –
TO PERFORM HIS ACT OUR GYPSY FRIEND REQUIRES A VOLUNTEER ON STAGE WITH HIM!
THE GYPSY POINTS TO YOU, MAJOR RITTER! KINDLY JOIN HIM ON STAGE!
I'VE NO CHOICE – MUSTN'T AROUSE SUSPICION.
BUT WHAT'S DANCER DOING IN HERE... AND WHAT'S HE THINKING RIGHT NOW, WITH ME AS HIS TARGET?

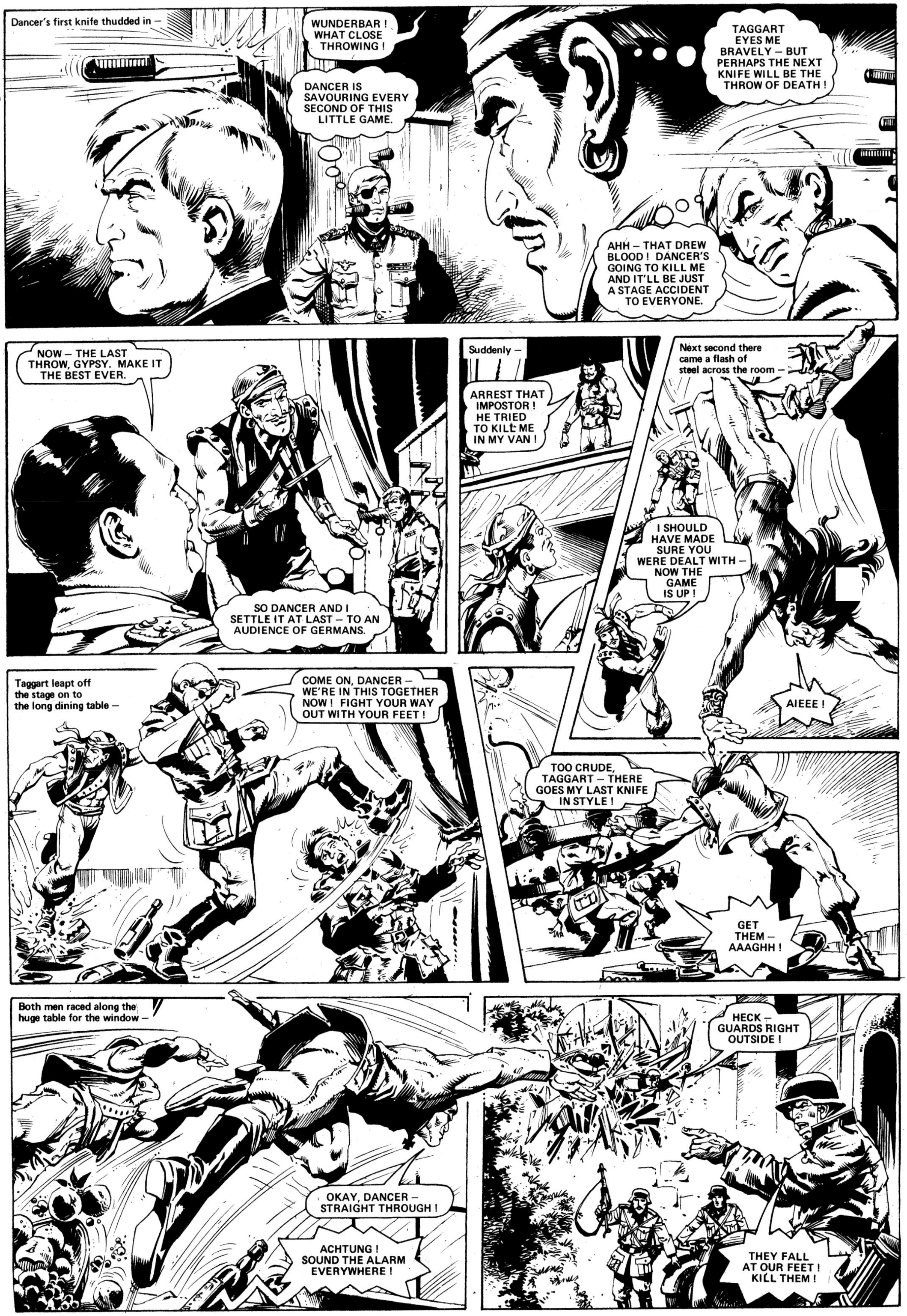

Dancer's first knife thudded in –
WUNDERBAR ! WHAT CLOSE THROWING !
DANCER IS SAVOURING EVERY SECOND OF THIS LITTLE GAME.
TAGGART EYES ME BRAVELY – BUT PERHAPS THE NEXT KNIFE WILL BE THE THROW OF DEATH !
AHH – THAT DREW BLOOD ! DANCER'S GOING TO KILL ME AND IT'LL BE JUST A STAGE ACCIDENT TO EVERYONE.
NOW – THE LAST THROW, GYPSY. MAKE IT THE BEST EVER.
SO DANCER AND I SETTLE IT AT LAST – TO AN AUDIENCE OF GERMANS.
Suddenly –
ARREST THAT IMPOSTOR ! HE TRIED TO KILL ME IN MY VAN !
Next second there came a flash of steel across the room –
I SHOULD HAVE MADE SURE YOU WERE DEALT WITH – NOW THE GAME IS UP !
AIEEE !
Taggart leapt off the stage on to the long dining table –
COME ON, DANCER – WE'RE IN THIS TOGETHER NOW ! FIGHT YOUR WAY OUT WITH YOUR FEET !
TOO CRUDE, TAGGART – THERE GOES MY LAST KNIFE IN STYLE !
GET THEM – AAAGHH !
Both men raced along the huge table for the window –
OKAY, DANCER – STRAIGHT THROUGH !
ACHTUNG ! SOUND THE ALARM EVERYWHERE !
HECK – GUARDS RIGHT OUTSIDE !
THEY FALL AT OUR FEET ! KILL THEM !

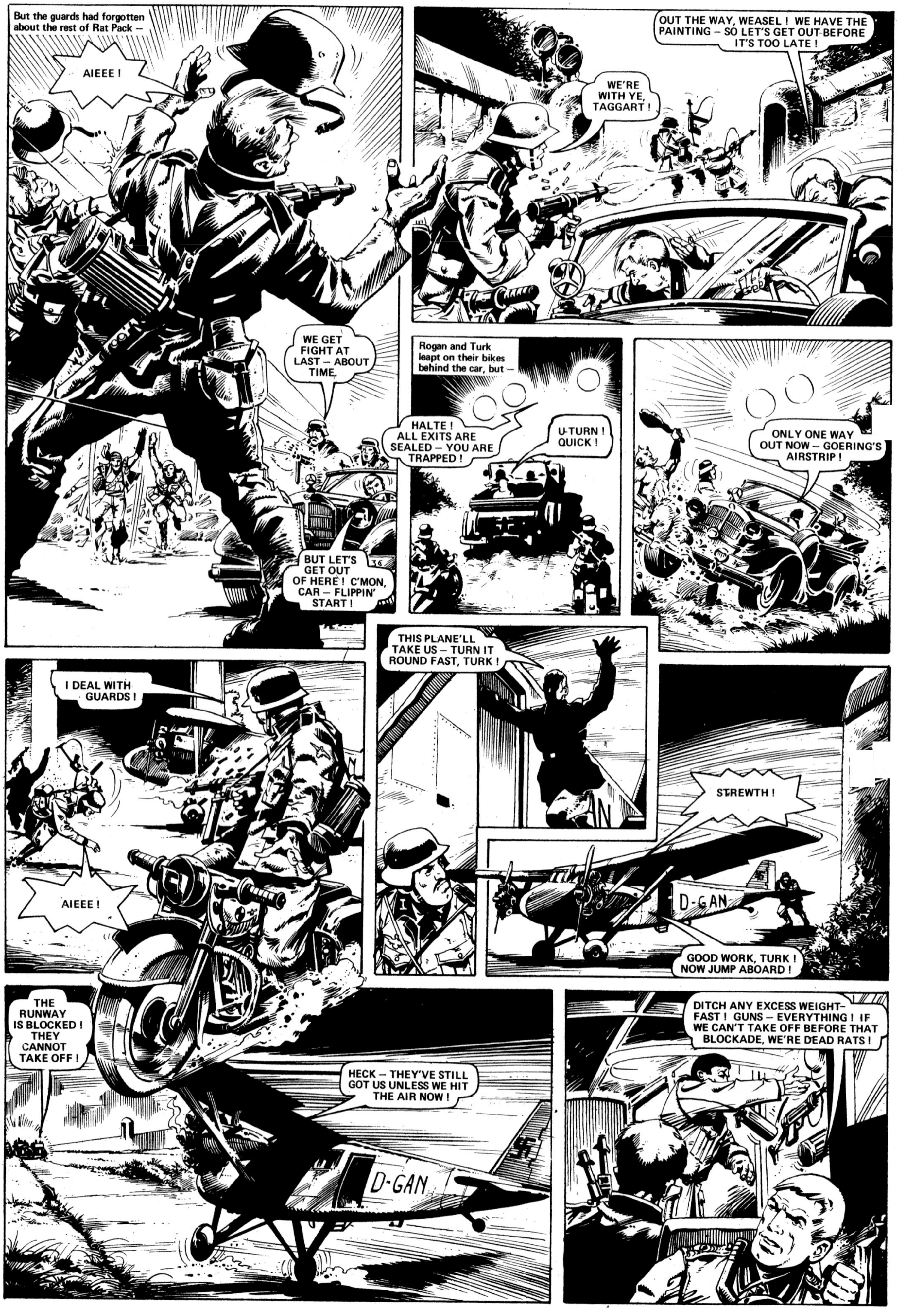
But the guards had forgotten about the rest of Rat Pack –
AIEEE !
WE GET FIGHT AT LAST – ABOUT TIME.
BUT LET'S GET OUT OF HERE ! C'MON, CAR – FLIPPIN' START !
OUT THE WAY, WEASEL ! WE HAVE THE PAINTING – SO LET'S GET OUT BEFORE IT'S TOO LATE !
WE'RE WITH YE, TAGGART !
Rogan and Turk leapt on their bikes behind the car, but –
HALTE ! ALL EXITS ARE SEALED – YOU ARE TRAPPED !
U-TURN ! QUICK !
ONLY ONE WAY OUT NOW – GOERING'S AIRSTRIP !
I DEAL WITH GUARDS !
AIEEE !
THIS PLANE'LL TAKE US – TURN IT ROUND FAST, TURK !
STREWTH !
D-GAN
GOOD WORK, TURK ! NOW JUMP ABOARD !
THE RUNWAY IS BLOCKED ! THEY CANNOT TAKE OFF !
HECK – THEY'VE STILL GOT US UNLESS WE HIT THE AIR NOW !
D-GAN
DITCH ANY EXCESS WEIGHT– FAST ! GUNS – EVERYTHING ! IF WE CAN'T TAKE OFF BEFORE THAT BLOCKADE, WE'RE DEAD RATS !

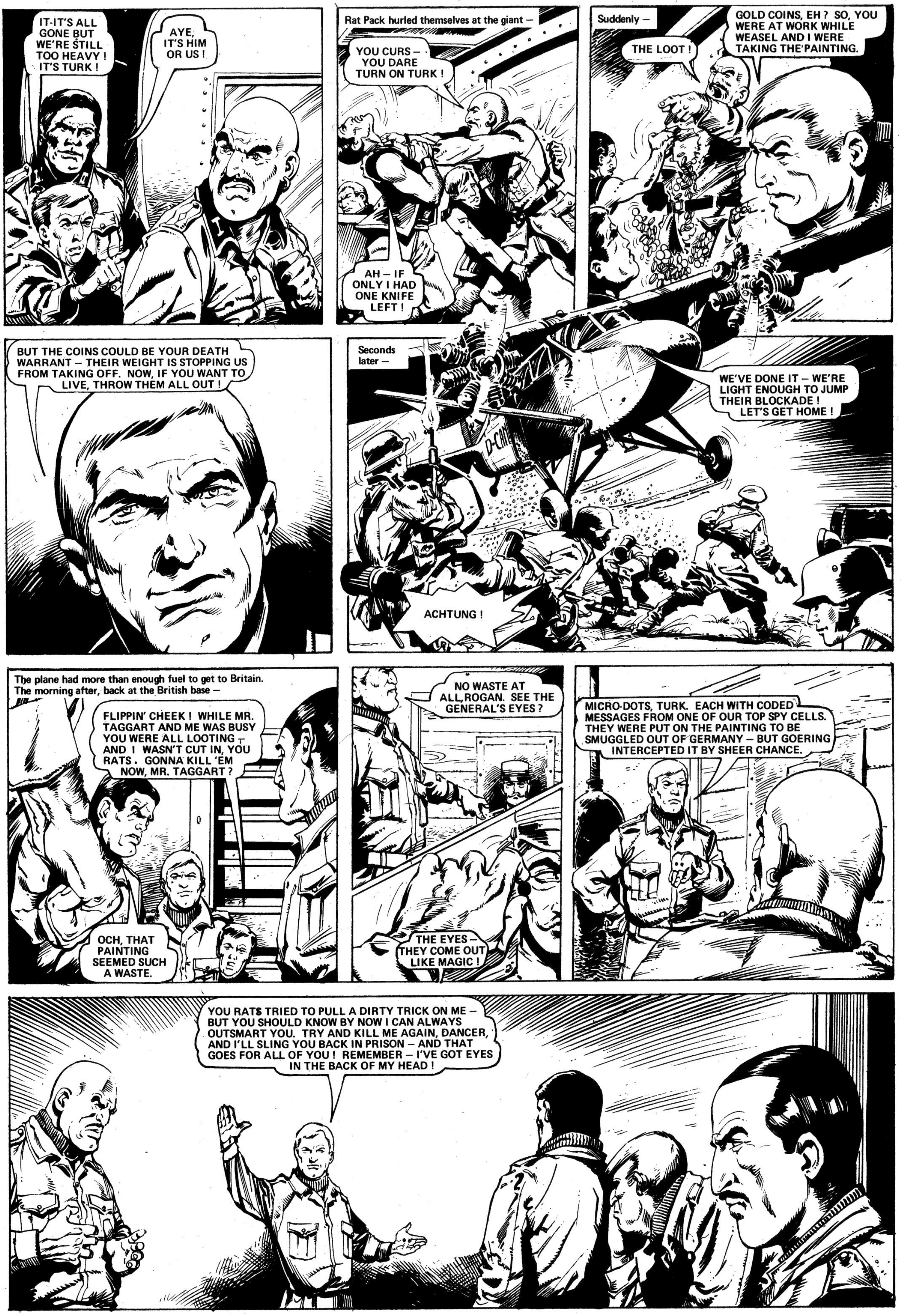

IT-IT'S ALL GONE BUT WE'RE STILL TOO HEAVY ! IT'S TURK !
AYE, IT'S HIM OR US !
Rat Pack hurled themselves at the giant –
YOU CURS – YOU DARE TURN ON TURK !
AH – IF ONLY I HAD ONE KNIFE LEFT !
Suddenly –
THE LOOT !
GOLD COINS, EH ? SO, YOU WERE AT WORK WHILE WEASEL AND I WERE TAKING THE PAINTING.
BUT THE COINS COULD BE YOUR DEATH WARRANT – THEIR WEIGHT IS STOPPING US FROM TAKING OFF. NOW, IF YOU WANT TO LIVE, THROW THEM ALL OUT !
Seconds later –
WE'VE DONE IT – WE'RE LIGHT ENOUGH TO JUMP THEIR BLOCKADE ! LET'S GET HOME !
ACHTUNG !
The plane had more than enough fuel to get to Britain. The morning after, back at the British base –
FLIPPIN' CHEEK ! WHILE MR. TAGGART AND ME WAS BUSY YOU WERE ALL LOOTING – AND I WASN'T CUT IN, YOU RATS. GONNA KILL 'EM NOW, MR. TAGGART ?
OCH, THAT PAINTING SEEMED SUCH A WASTE.
NO WASTE AT ALL, ROGAN. SEE THE GENERAL'S EYES ?
THE EYES – THEY COME OUT LIKE MAGIC !
MICRO-DOTS, TURK. EACH WITH CODED MESSAGES FROM ONE OF OUR TOP SPY CELLS. THEY WERE PUT ON THE PAINTING TO BE SMUGGLED OUT OF GERMANY – BUT GOERING INTERCEPTED IT BY SHEER CHANCE.
YOU RATS TRIED TO PULL A DIRTY TRICK ON ME – BUT YOU SHOULD KNOW BY NOW I CAN ALWAYS OUTSMART YOU. TRY AND KILL ME AGAIN, DANCER, AND I'LL SLING YOU BACK IN PRISON – AND THAT GOES FOR ALL OF YOU ! REMEMBER – I'VE GOT EYES IN THE BACK OF MY HEAD !

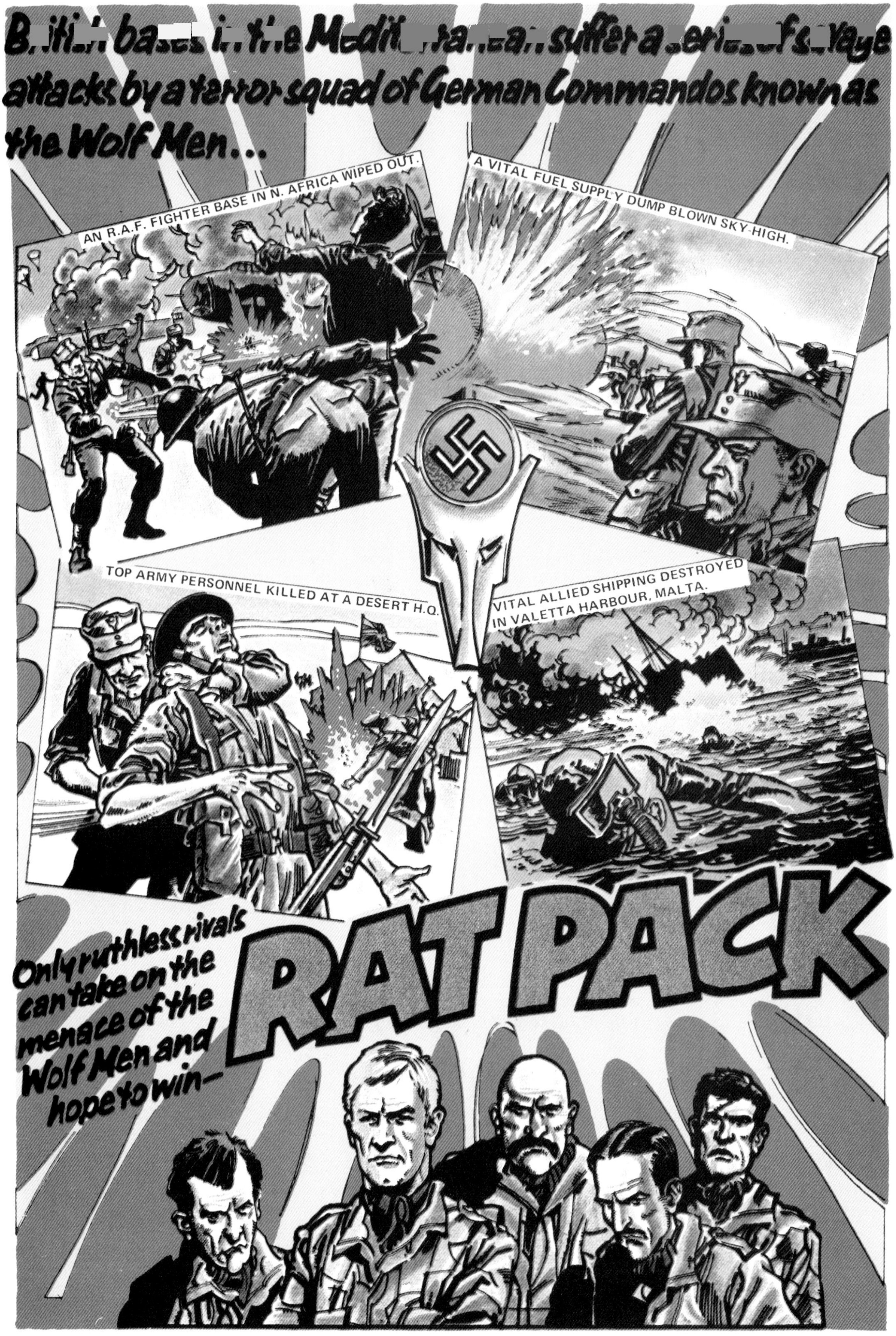
British bases in the Mediterranean suffer a series of savage attacks by a terror squad of German Commandos known as the Wolf Men...
AN R.A.F. FIGHTER BASE IN N. AFRICA WIPED OUT.
A VITAL FUEL SUPPLY DUMP BLOWN SKY-HIGH.
TOP ARMY PERSONNEL KILLED AT A DESERT H.Q.
VITAL ALLIED SHIPPING DESTROYED IN VALETTA HARBOUR, MALTA.
Only ruthless rivals can take on the menace of the Wolf Men and hope to win–
RAT PACK

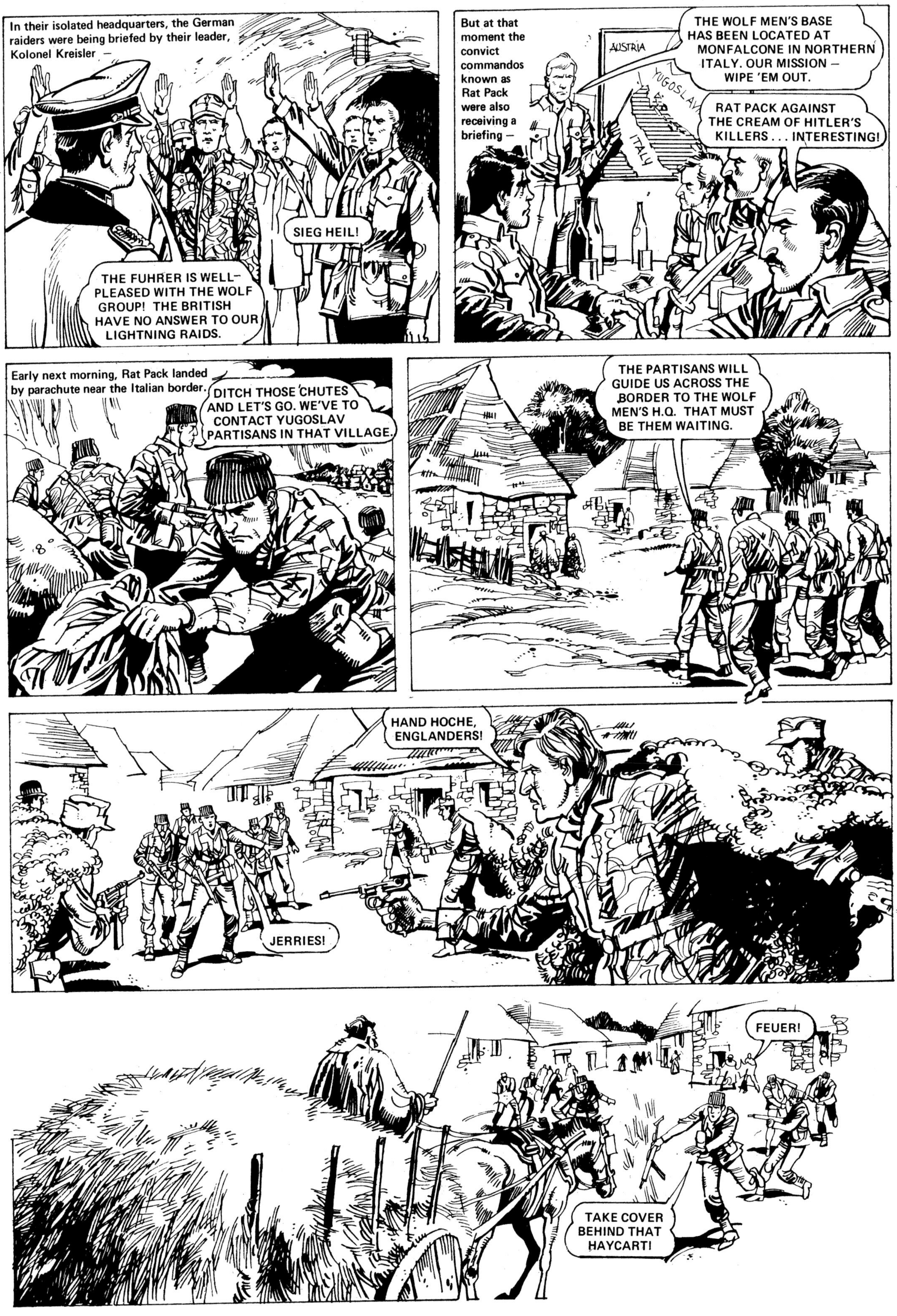
In their isolated headquarters, the German raiders were being briefed by their leader, Kolonel Kreisler –
SIEG HEIL!
THE FUHRER IS WELL-PLEASED WITH THE WOLF GROUP! THE BRITISH HAVE NO ANSWER TO OUR LIGHTNING RAIDS.
But at that moment the convict commandos known as Rat Pack were also receiving a briefing –
AUSTRIA
YUGOSLAV
ITALY
THE WOLF MEN'S BASE HAS BEEN LOCATED AT MONFALCONE IN NORTHERN ITALY. OUR MISSION – WIPE 'EM OUT.
RAT PACK AGAINST THE CREAM OF HITLER'S KILLERS . . . INTERESTING!
Early next morning, Rat Pack landed by parachute near the Italian border.
DITCH THOSE 'CHUTES AND LET'S GO. WE'VE TO CONTACT YUGOSLAV PARTISANS IN THAT VILLAGE.
THE PARTISANS WILL GUIDE US ACROSS THE BORDER TO THE WOLF MEN'S H.Q. THAT MUST BE THEM WAITING.
HAND HOCHE, ENGLANDERS!
JERRIES!
FEUER!
TAKE COVER BEHIND THAT HAYCART!

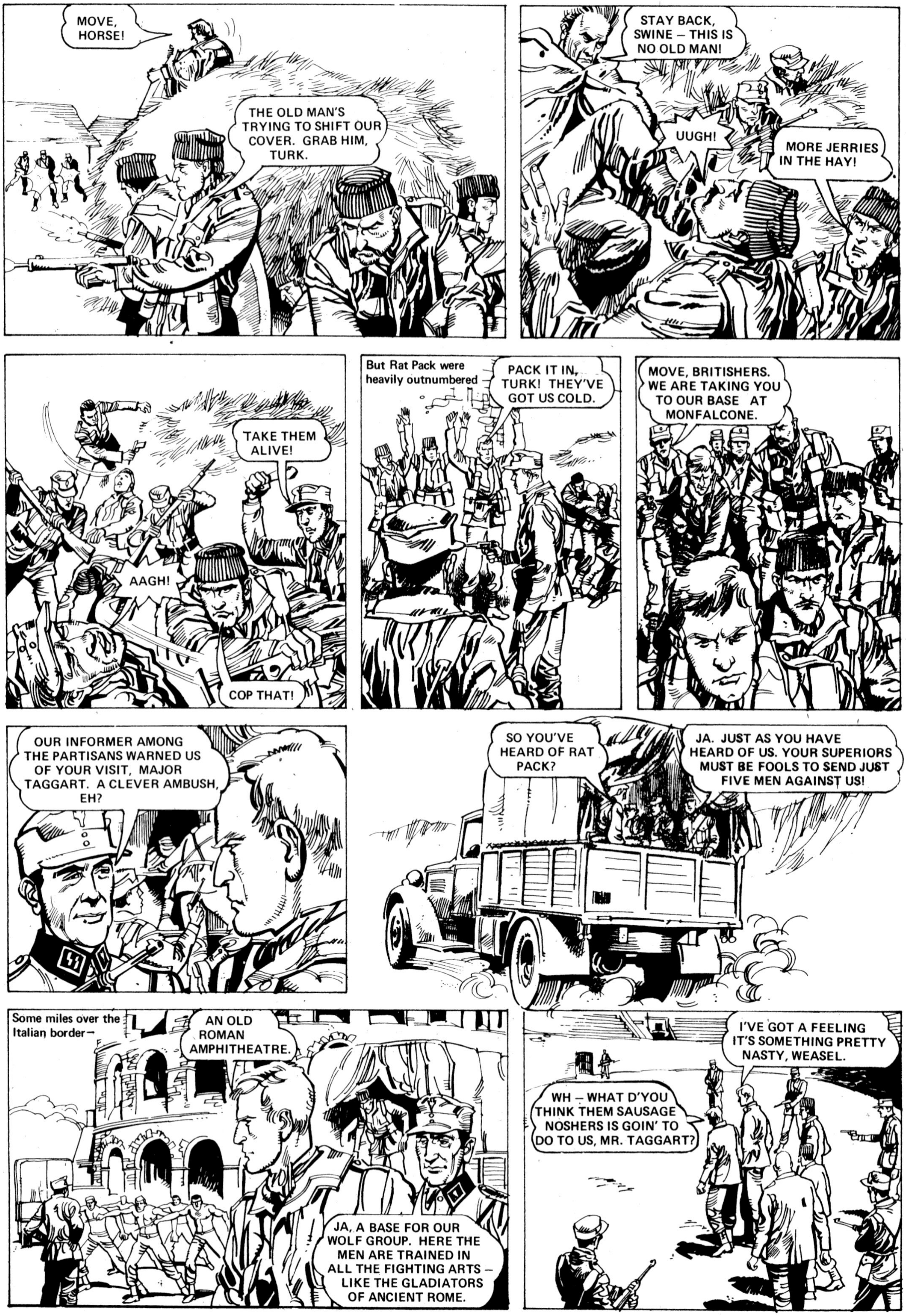

MOVE, HORSE!
THE OLD MAN'S TRYING TO SHIFT OUR COVER. GRAB HIM, TURK.
STAY BACK, SWINE – THIS IS NO OLD MAN!
UUGH!
MORE JERRIES IN THE HAY!
TAKE THEM ALIVE!
AAGH!
COP THAT!
But Rat Pack were heavily outnumbered –
PACK IT IN, TURK! THEY'VE GOT US COLD.
MOVE, BRITISHERS. WE ARE TAKING YOU TO OUR BASE AT MONFALCONE.
OUR INFORMER AMONG THE PARTISANS WARNED US OF YOUR VISIT, MAJOR TAGGART. A CLEVER AMBUSH, EH?
SO YOU'VE HEARD OF RAT PACK?
JA. JUST AS YOU HAVE HEARD OF US. YOUR SUPERIORS MUST BE FOOLS TO SEND JUST FIVE MEN AGAINST US!
Some miles over the Italian border –
AN OLD ROMAN AMPHITHEATRE.
JA, A BASE FOR OUR WOLF GROUP. HERE THE MEN ARE TRAINED IN ALL THE FIGHTING ARTS – LIKE THE GLADIATORS OF ANCIENT ROME.
I'VE GOT A FEELING IT'S SOMETHING PRETTY NASTY, WEASEL.
WH – WHAT D'YOU THINK THEM SAUSAGE NOSHERS IS GOIN' TO DO TO US, MR. TAGGART?

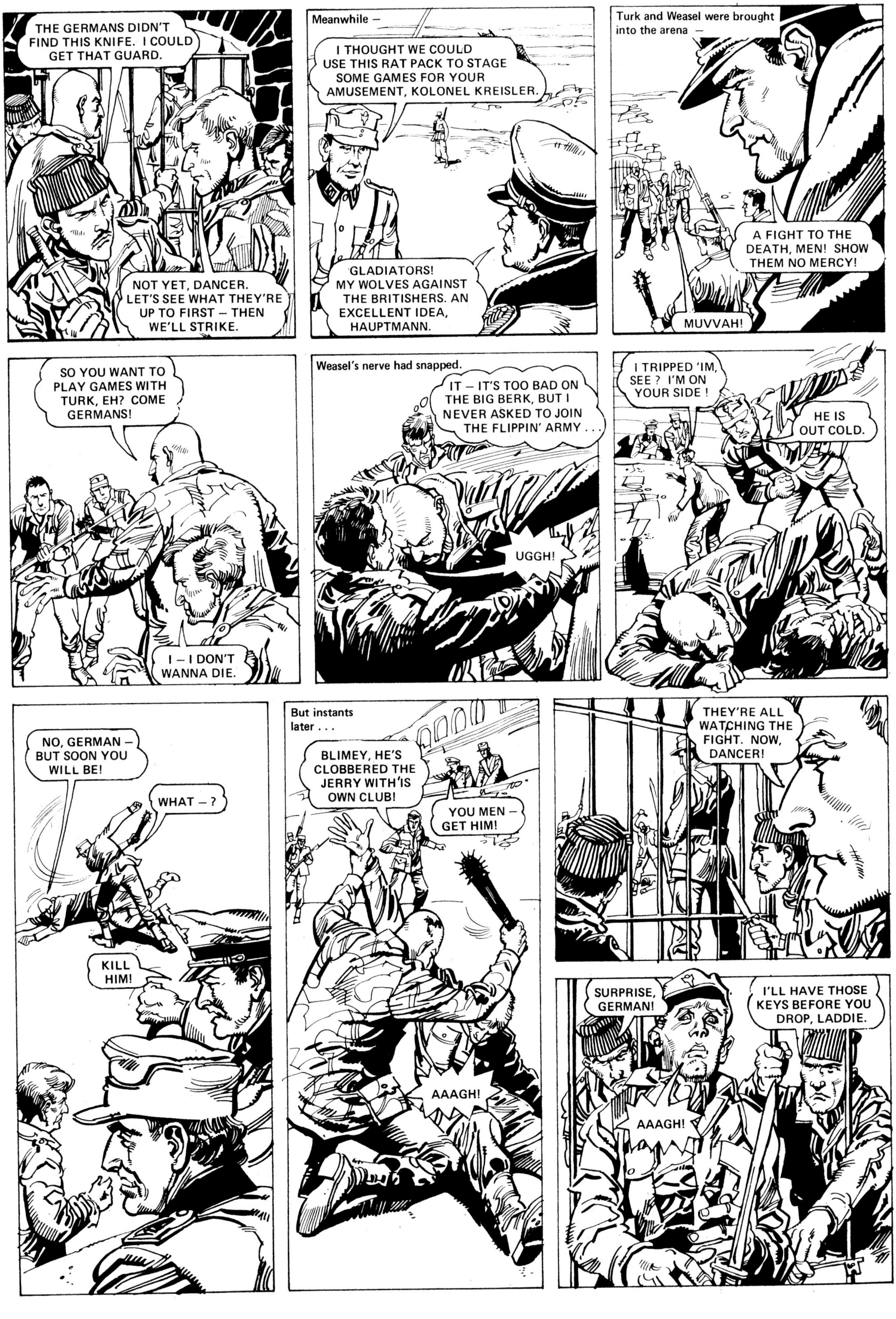
THE GERMANS DIDN'T FIND THIS KNIFE. I COULD GET THAT GUARD.
NOT YET, DANCER. LET'S SEE WHAT THEY'RE UP TO FIRST – THEN WE'LL STRIKE.
Meanwhile –
I THOUGHT WE COULD USE THIS RAT PACK TO STAGE SOME GAMES FOR YOUR AMUSEMENT, KOLONEL KREISLER.
GLADIATORS! MY WOLVES AGAINST THE BRITISHERS. AN EXCELLENT IDEA, HAUPTMANN.
Turk and Weasel were brought into the arena –
A FIGHT TO THE DEATH, MEN! SHOW THEM NO MERCY!
MUVVAH!
SO YOU WANT TO PLAY GAMES WITH TURK, EH? COME GERMANS!
I – I DON'T WANNA DIE.
Weasel's nerve had snapped.
IT – IT'S TOO BAD ON THE BIG BERK, BUT I NEVER ASKED TO JOIN THE FLIPPIN' ARMY . . .
UGGH!
I TRIPPED 'IM, SEE ? I'M ON YOUR SIDE !
HE IS OUT COLD.
NO, GERMAN – BUT SOON YOU WILL BE!
WHAT – ?
KILL HIM!
But instants later . . .
BLIMEY, HE'S CLOBBERED THE JERRY WITH 'IS OWN CLUB!
YOU MEN – GET HIM!
AAAGH!
THEY'RE ALL WATCHING THE FIGHT. NOW, DANCER!
SURPRISE, GERMAN!
I'LL HAVE THOSE KEYS BEFORE YOU DROP, LADDIE.
AAAGH!

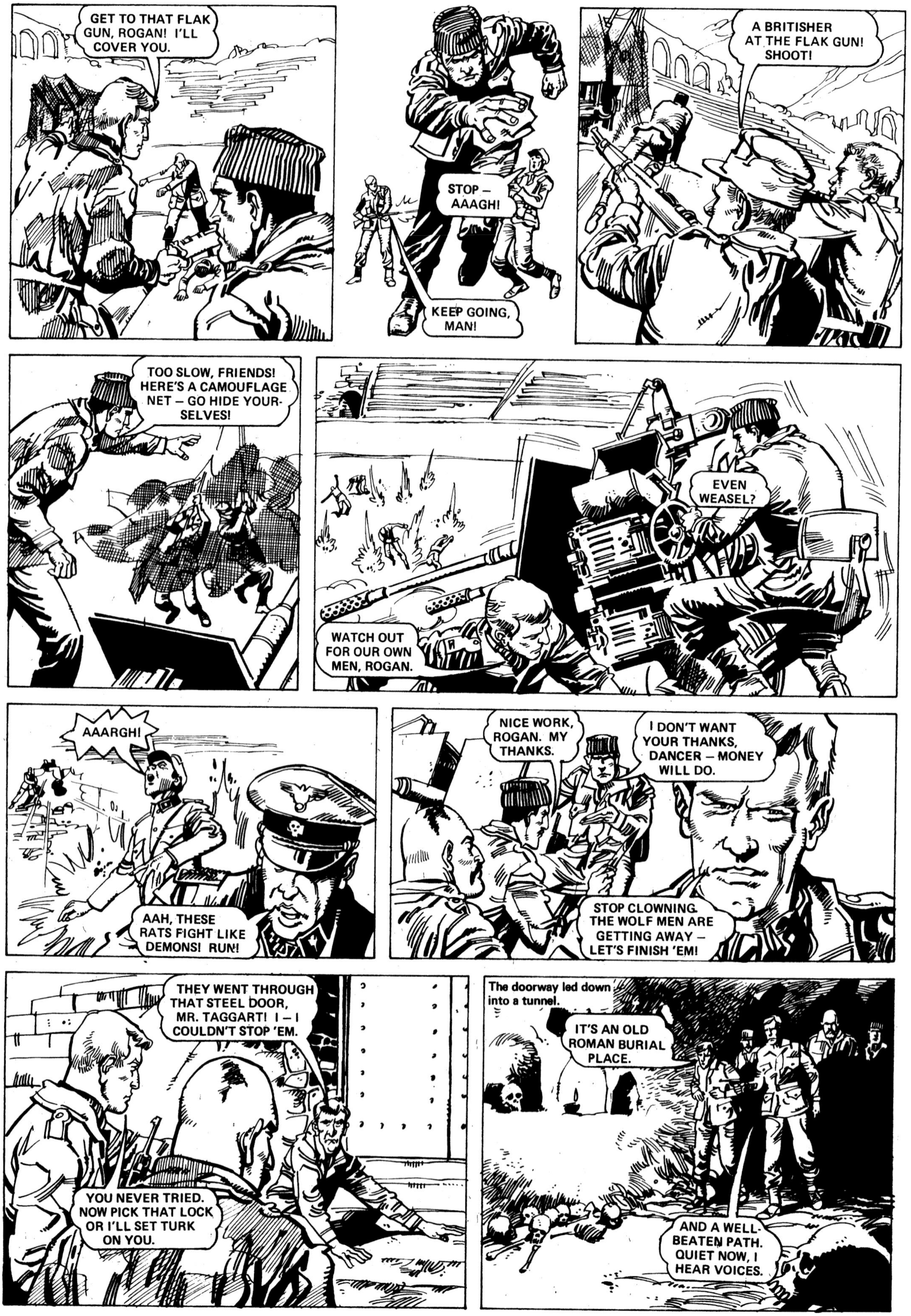

GET TO THAT FLAK GUN, ROGAN! I'LL COVER YOU.
STOP — AAAGH!
KEEP GOING, MAN!
A BRITISHER AT THE FLAK GUN! SHOOT!
TOO SLOW, FRIENDS! HERE'S A CAMOUFLAGE NET — GO HIDE YOURSELVES!
EVEN WEASEL?
WATCH OUT FOR OUR OWN MEN, ROGAN.
AAARGH!
AAH, THESE RATS FIGHT LIKE DEMONS! RUN!
NICE WORK, ROGAN. MY THANKS.
I DON'T WANT YOUR THANKS, DANCER — MONEY WILL DO.
STOP CLOWNING. THE WOLF MEN ARE GETTING AWAY — LET'S FINISH 'EM!
THEY WENT THROUGH THAT STEEL DOOR, MR. TAGGART! I — I COULDN'T STOP 'EM.
YOU NEVER TRIED. NOW PICK THAT LOCK OR I'LL SET TURK ON YOU.
The doorway led down into a tunnel.
IT'S AN OLD ROMAN BURIAL PLACE.
AND A WELL-BEATEN PATH. QUIET NOW, I HEAR VOICES.

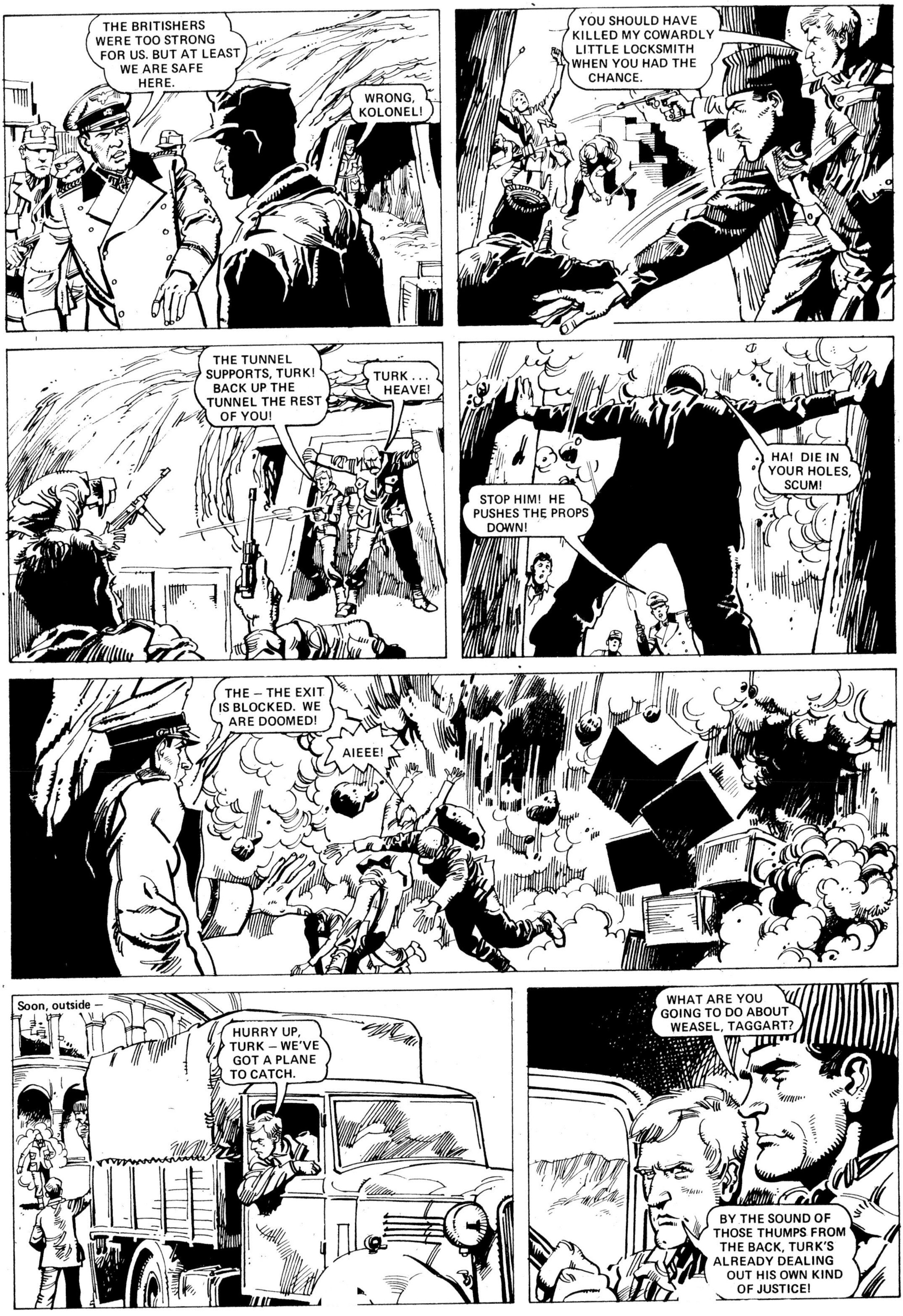

THE BRITISHERS WERE TOO STRONG FOR US. BUT AT LEAST WE ARE SAFE HERE.
WRONG, KOLONEL!
YOU SHOULD HAVE KILLED MY COWARDLY LITTLE LOCKSMITH WHEN YOU HAD THE CHANCE.
THE TUNNEL SUPPORTS, TURK! BACK UP THE TUNNEL THE REST OF YOU!
TURK . . . HEAVE!
HA! DIE IN YOUR HOLES, SCUM!
STOP HIM! HE PUSHES THE PROPS DOWN!
THE – THE EXIT IS BLOCKED. WE ARE DOOMED!
AIEEE!
Soon, outside –
HURRY UP, TURK – WE'VE GOT A PLANE TO CATCH.
WHAT ARE YOU GOING TO DO ABOUT WEASEL, TAGGART?
BY THE SOUND OF THOSE THUMPS FROM THE BACK, TURK'S ALREADY DEALING OUT HIS OWN KIND OF JUSTICE!

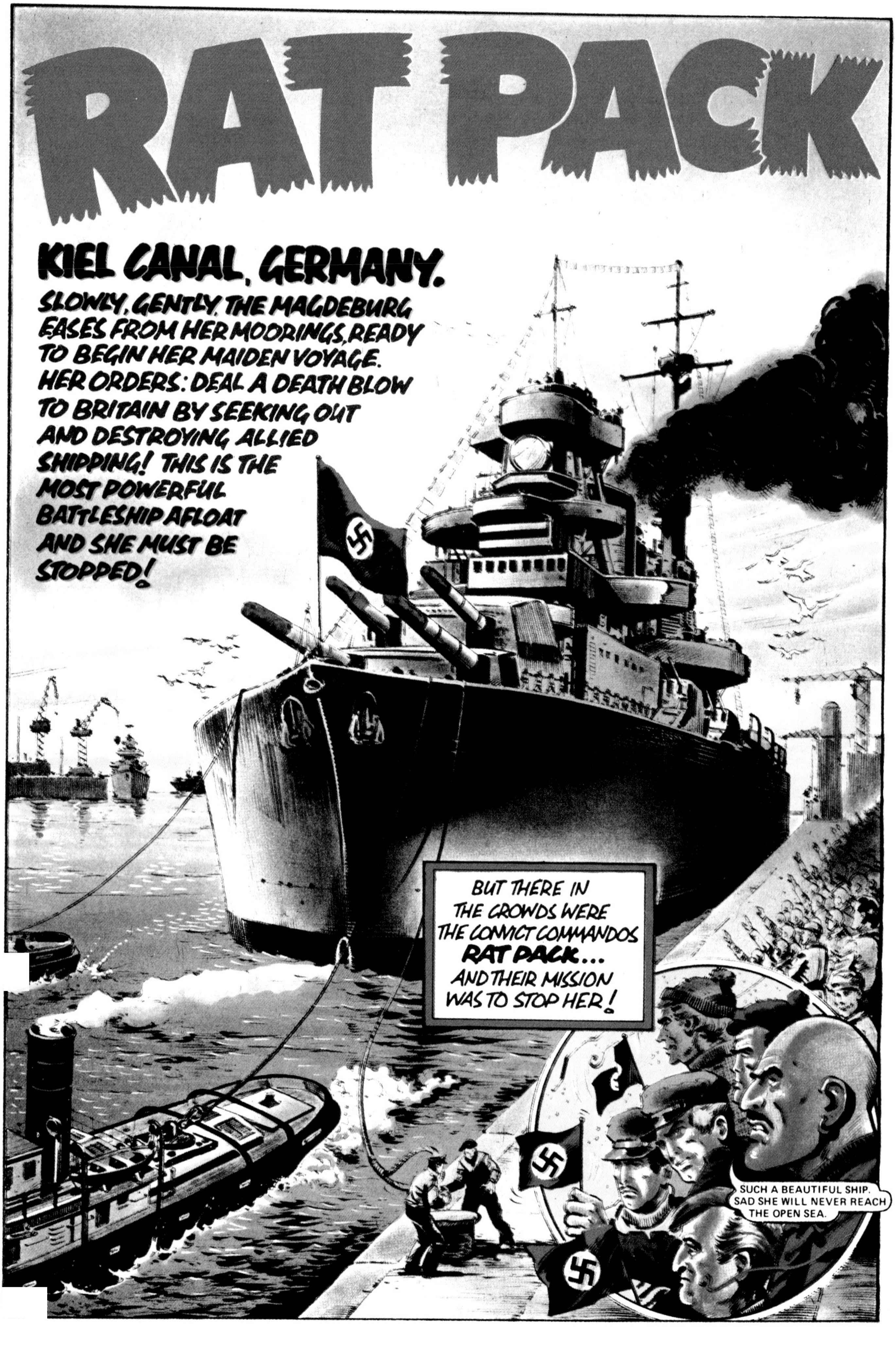
RAT PACK
KIEL CANAL, GERMANY.
SLOWLY, GENTLY, THE MAGDEBURG EASES FROM HER MOORINGS, READY TO BEGIN HER MAIDEN VOYAGE. HER ORDERS: DEAL A DEATH BLOW TO BRITAIN BY SEEKING OUT AND DESTROYING ALLIED SHIPPING! THIS IS THE MOST POWERFUL BATTLESHIP AFLOAT AND SHE MUST BE STOPPED!
BUT THERE IN THE CROWDS WERE THE CONVICT COMMANDOS RAT PACK... AND THEIR MISSION WAS TO STOP HER!
SUCH A BEAUTIFUL SHIP. SAD SHE WILL NEVER REACH THE OPEN SEA.

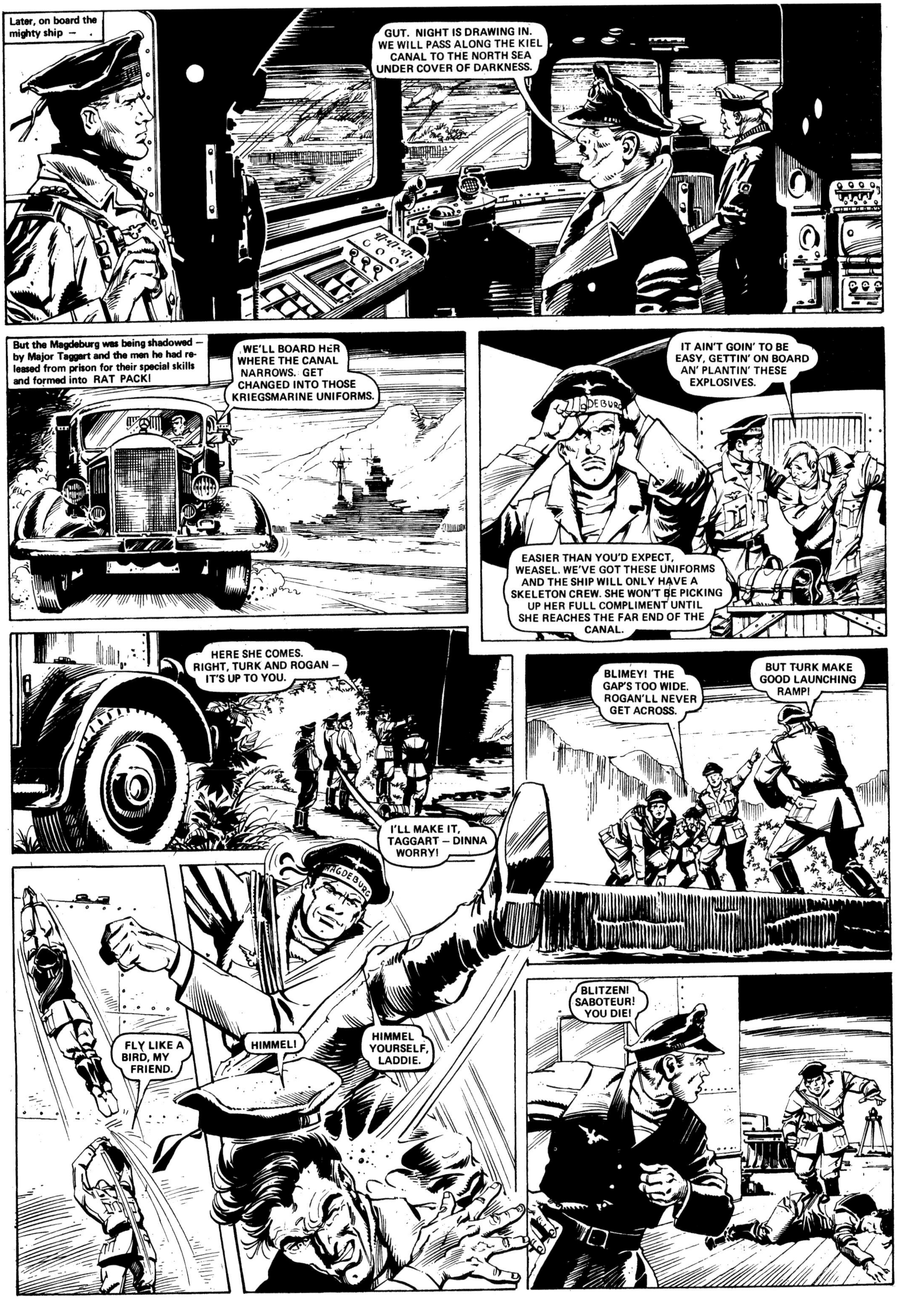

Later, on board the mighty ship –
GUT. NIGHT IS DRAWING IN. WE WILL PASS ALONG THE KIEL CANAL TO THE NORTH SEA UNDER COVER OF DARKNESS.
But the Magdeburg was being shadowed – by Major Taggart and the men he had released from prison for their special skills and formed into RAT PACK!
WE'LL BOARD HER WHERE THE CANAL NARROWS. GET CHANGED INTO THOSE KRIEGSMARINE UNIFORMS.
IT AIN'T GOIN' TO BE EASY, GETTIN' ON BOARD AN' PLANTIN' THESE EXPLOSIVES.
EASIER THAN YOU'D EXPECT, WEASEL. WE'VE GOT THESE UNIFORMS AND THE SHIP WILL ONLY HAVE A SKELETON CREW. SHE WON'T BE PICKING UP HER FULL COMPLIMENT UNTIL SHE REACHES THE FAR END OF THE CANAL.
HERE SHE COMES. RIGHT, TURK AND ROGAN – IT'S UP TO YOU.
BLIMEY! THE GAP'S TOO WIDE. ROGAN'LL NEVER GET ACROSS.
BUT TURK MAKE GOOD LAUNCHING RAMP!
I'LL MAKE IT, TAGGART – DINNA WORRY!
FLY LIKE A BIRD, MY FRIEND.
HIMMEL!
HIMMEL YOURSELF, LADDIE.
BLITZEN! SABOTEUR! YOU DIE!

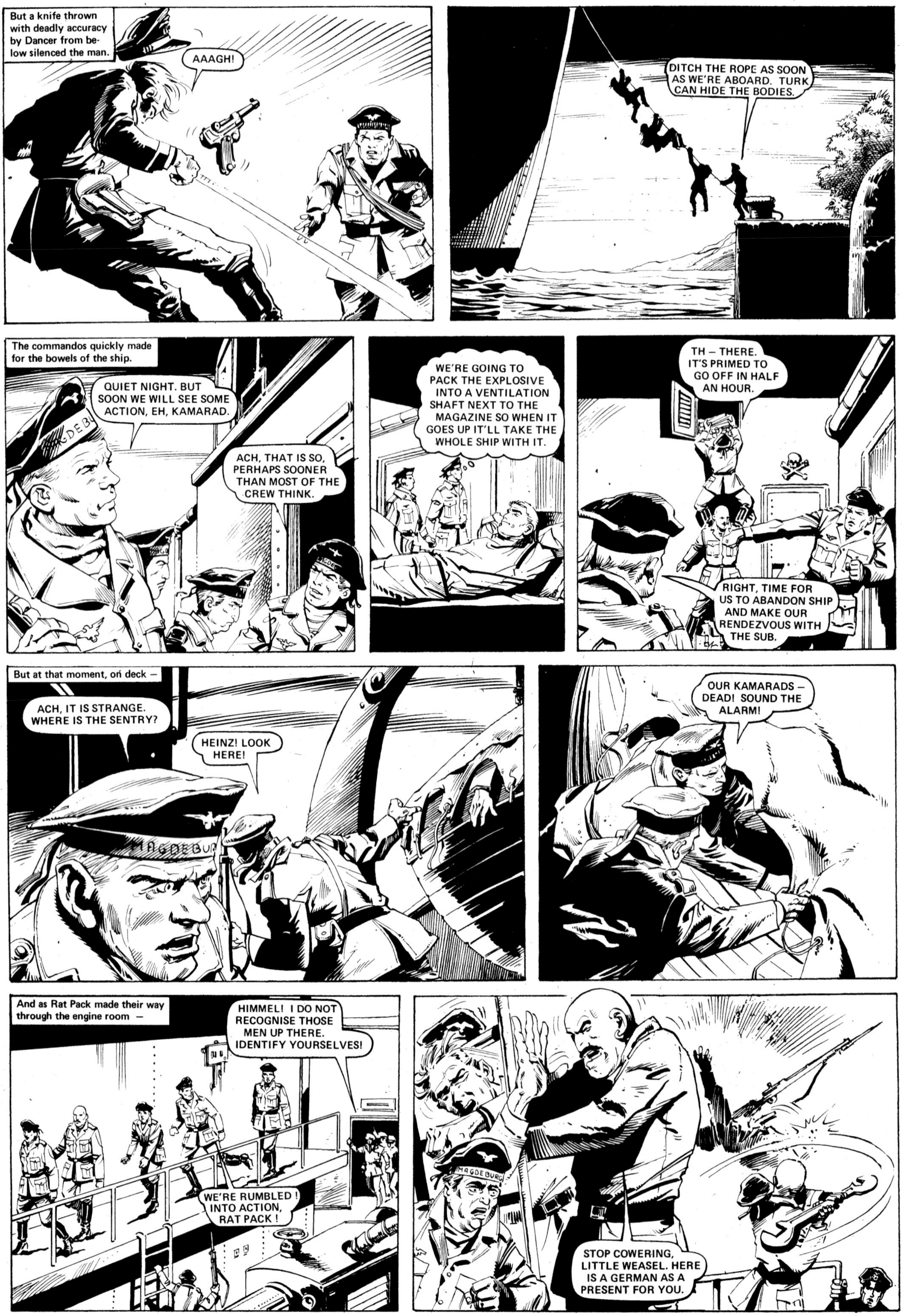
But a knife thrown with deadly accuracy by Dancer from below silenced the man.
AAAGH!
DITCH THE ROPE AS SOON AS WE'RE ABOARD. TURK CAN HIDE THE BODIES.
The commandos quickly made for the bowels of the ship.
QUIET NIGHT. BUT SOON WE WILL SEE SOME ACTION, EH, KAMARAD.
ACH, THAT IS SO, PERHAPS SOONER THAN MOST OF THE CREW THINK.
WE'RE GOING TO PACK THE EXPLOSIVE INTO A VENTILATION SHAFT NEXT TO THE MAGAZINE SO WHEN IT GOES UP IT'LL TAKE THE WHOLE SHIP WITH IT.
TH – THERE. IT'S PRIMED TO GO OFF IN HALF AN HOUR.
RIGHT, TIME FOR US TO ABANDON SHIP AND MAKE OUR RENDEZVOUS WITH THE SUB.
But at that moment, on deck –
ACH, IT IS STRANGE. WHERE IS THE SENTRY?
HEINZ! LOOK HERE!
MAGDEBURG
OUR KAMARADS – DEAD! SOUND THE ALARM!
And as Rat Pack made their way through the engine room –
HIMMEL! I DO NOT RECOGNISE THOSE MEN UP THERE. IDENTIFY YOURSELVES!
WE'RE RUMBLED! INTO ACTION, RAT PACK!
MAGDEBURG
STOP COWERING, LITTLE WEASEL. HERE IS A GERMAN AS A PRESENT FOR YOU.

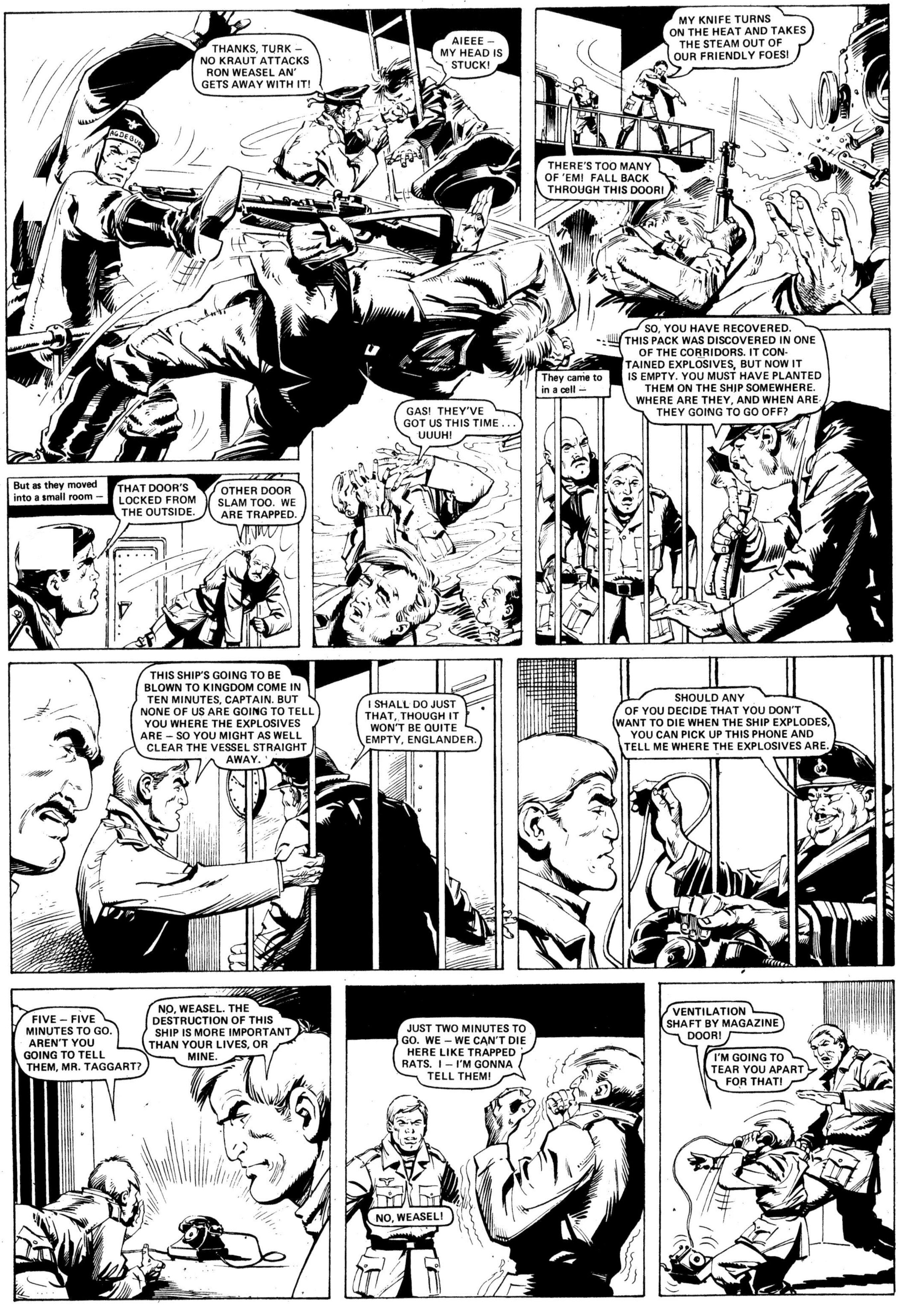

THANKS, TURK — NO KRAUT ATTACKS RON WEASEL AN' GETS AWAY WITH IT!
AIEEE — MY HEAD IS STUCK!
MY KNIFE TURNS ON THE HEAT AND TAKES THE STEAM OUT OF OUR FRIENDLY FOES!
THERE'S TOO MANY OF 'EM! FALL BACK THROUGH THIS DOOR!
But as they moved into a small room —
THAT DOOR'S LOCKED FROM THE OUTSIDE.
OTHER DOOR SLAM TOO. WE ARE TRAPPED.
GAS! THEY'VE GOT US THIS TIME . . . UUUH!
They came to in a cell —
SO, YOU HAVE RECOVERED. THIS PACK WAS DISCOVERED IN ONE OF THE CORRIDORS. IT CONTAINED EXPLOSIVES, BUT NOW IT IS EMPTY. YOU MUST HAVE PLANTED THEM ON THE SHIP SOMEWHERE. WHERE ARE THEY, AND WHEN ARE THEY GOING TO GO OFF?
THIS SHIP'S GOING TO BE BLOWN TO KINGDOM COME IN TEN MINUTES, CAPTAIN. BUT NONE OF US ARE GOING TO TELL YOU WHERE THE EXPLOSIVES ARE — SO YOU MIGHT AS WELL CLEAR THE VESSEL STRAIGHT AWAY.
I SHALL DO JUST THAT, THOUGH IT WON'T BE QUITE EMPTY, ENGLANDER.
SHOULD ANY OF YOU DECIDE THAT YOU DON'T WANT TO DIE WHEN THE SHIP EXPLODES, YOU CAN PICK UP THIS PHONE AND TELL ME WHERE THE EXPLOSIVES ARE.
FIVE — FIVE MINUTES TO GO. AREN'T YOU GOING TO TELL THEM, MR. TAGGART?
NO, WEASEL. THE DESTRUCTION OF THIS SHIP IS MORE IMPORTANT THAN YOUR LIVES, OR MINE.
JUST TWO MINUTES TO GO. WE — WE CAN'T DIE HERE LIKE TRAPPED RATS. I — I'M GONNA TELL THEM!
NO, WEASEL!
VENTILATION SHAFT BY MAGAZINE DOOR!
I'M GOING TO TEAR YOU APART FOR THAT!

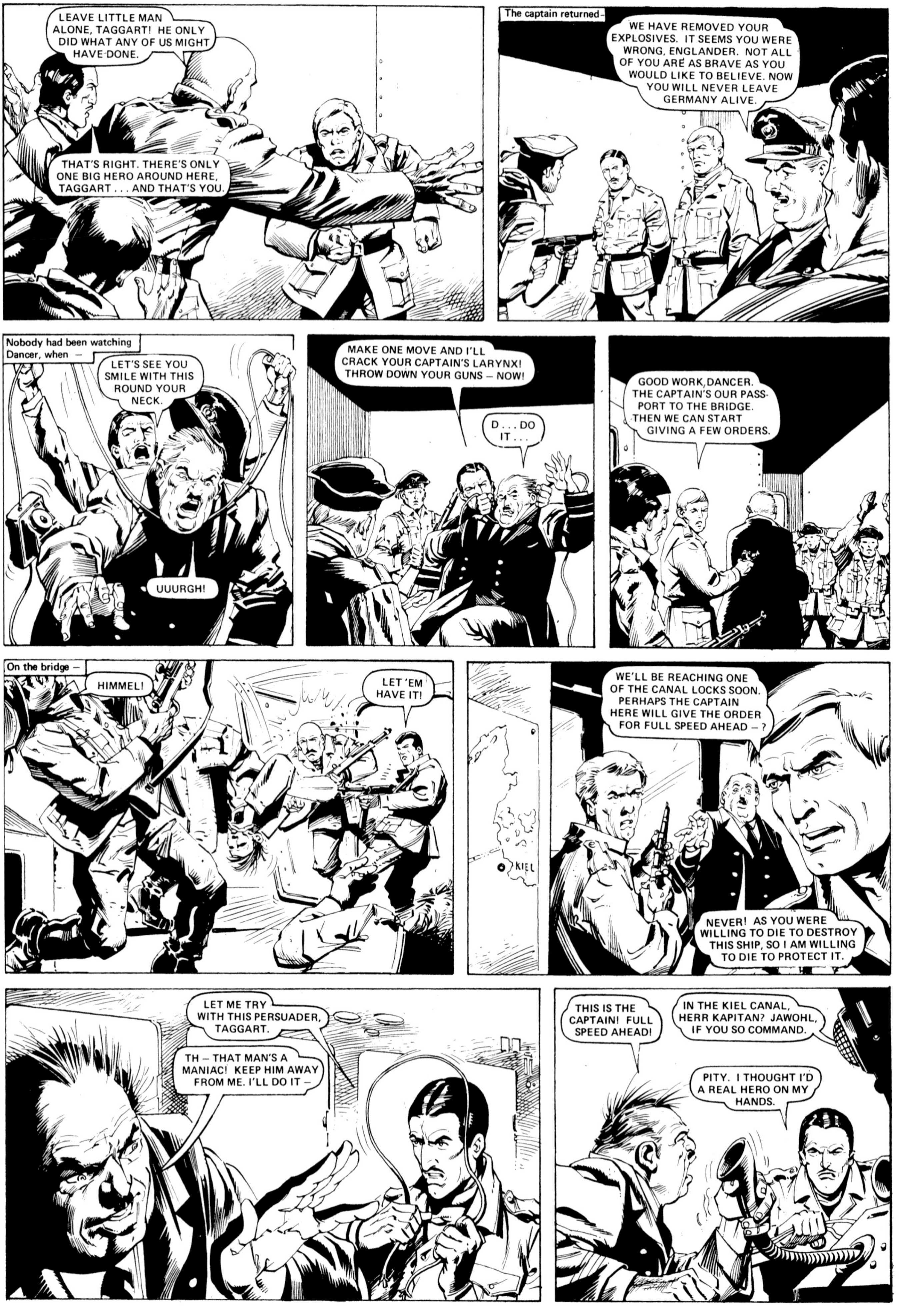
LEAVE LITTLE MAN ALONE, TAGGART! HE ONLY DID WHAT ANY OF US MIGHT HAVE DONE.
THAT'S RIGHT. THERE'S ONLY ONE BIG HERO AROUND HERE, TAGGART . . . AND THAT'S YOU.
The captain returned –
WE HAVE REMOVED YOUR EXPLOSIVES. IT SEEMS YOU WERE WRONG, ENGLANDER. NOT ALL OF YOU ARE AS BRAVE AS YOU WOULD LIKE TO BELIEVE. NOW YOU WILL NEVER LEAVE GERMANY ALIVE.
Nobody had been watching Dancer, when –
LET'S SEE YOU SMILE WITH THIS ROUND YOUR NECK.
UUURGH!
MAKE ONE MOVE AND I'LL CRACK YOUR CAPTAIN'S LARYNX! THROW DOWN YOUR GUNS – NOW!
D . . . DO IT . . .
GOOD WORK, DANCER. THE CAPTAIN'S OUR PASS-PORT TO THE BRIDGE. THEN WE CAN START GIVING A FEW ORDERS.
On the bridge –
HIMMEL!
LET 'EM HAVE IT!
KIEL
WE'LL BE REACHING ONE OF THE CANAL LOCKS SOON. PERHAPS THE CAPTAIN HERE WILL GIVE THE ORDER FOR FULL SPEED AHEAD – ?
NEVER! AS YOU WERE WILLING TO DIE TO DESTROY THIS SHIP, SO I AM WILLING TO DIE TO PROTECT IT.
LET ME TRY WITH THIS PERSUADER, TAGGART.
TH – THAT MAN'S A MANIAC! KEEP HIM AWAY FROM ME. I'LL DO IT –
THIS IS THE CAPTAIN! FULL SPEED AHEAD!
IN THE KIEL CANAL, HERR KAPITAN? JAWOHL, IF YOU SO COMMAND.
PITY. I THOUGHT I'D A REAL HERO ON MY HANDS.

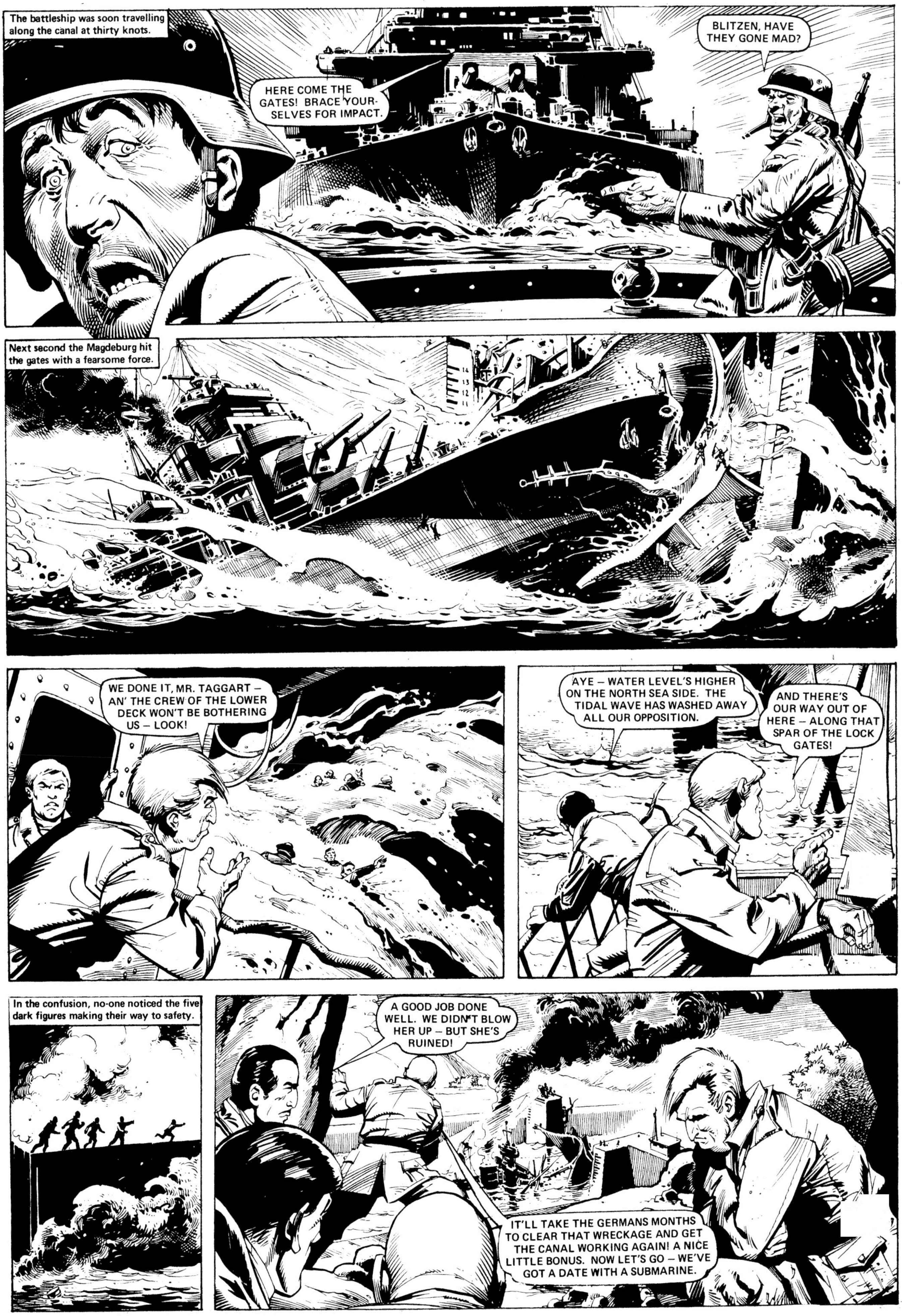
The battleship was soon travelling along the canal at thirty knots.
HERE COME THE GATES! BRACE YOURSELVES FOR IMPACT.
BLITZEN, HAVE THEY GONE MAD?
Next second the Magdeburg hit the gates with a fearsome force.
WE DONE IT, MR. TAGGART – AN' THE CREW OF THE LOWER DECK WON'T BE BOTHERING US – LOOK!
AYE – WATER LEVEL'S HIGHER ON THE NORTH SEA SIDE. THE TIDAL WAVE HAS WASHED AWAY ALL OUR OPPOSITION.
AND THERE'S OUR WAY OUT OF HERE – ALONG THAT SPAR OF THE LOCK GATES!
In the confusion, no-one noticed the five dark figures making their way to safety.
A GOOD JOB DONE WELL. WE DIDN'T BLOW HER UP – BUT SHE'S RUINED!
IT'LL TAKE THE GERMANS MONTHS TO CLEAR THAT WRECKAGE AND GET THE CANAL WORKING AGAIN! A NICE LITTLE BONUS. NOW LET'S GO – WE'VE GOT A DATE WITH A SUBMARINE.

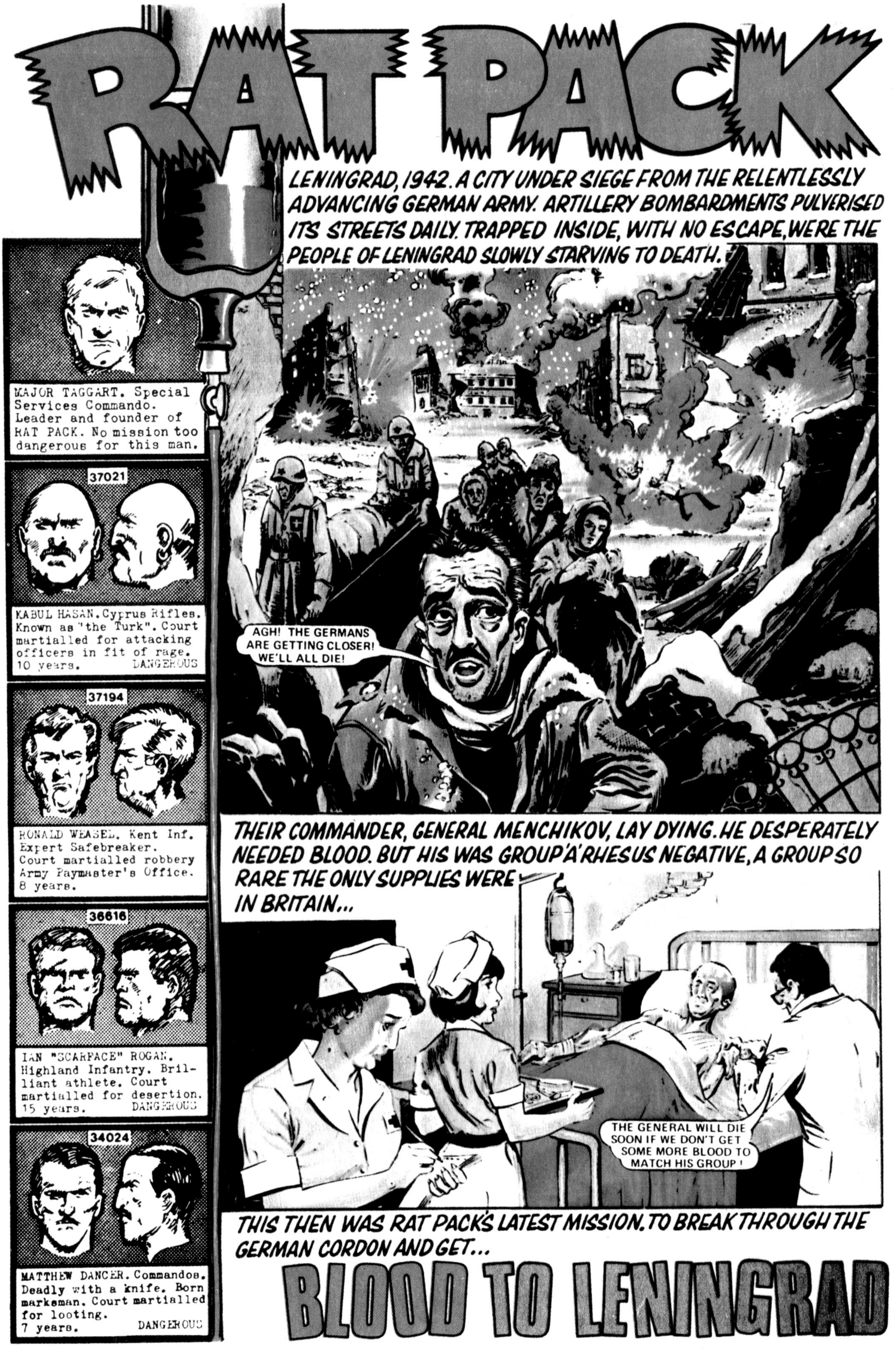
RAT PACK
LENINGRAD, 1942. A CITY UNDER SIEGE FROM THE RELENTLESSLY ADVANCING GERMAN ARMY. ARTILLERY BOMBARDMENTS PULVERISED ITS STREETS DAILY. TRAPPED INSIDE, WITH NO ESCAPE, WERE THE PEOPLE OF LENINGRAD SLOWLY STARVING TO DEATH.
MAJOR TAGGART. Special Services Commando. Leader and founder of RAT PACK. No mission too dangerous for this man.
37021
KABUL HASAN. Cyprus Rifles. Known as "the Turk". Court martialled for attacking officers in fit of rage. 10 years. DANGEROUS
37194
RONALD WEASEL. Kent Inf. Expert Safebreaker. Court martialled robbery Army Paymaster's Office. 8 years.
36616
IAN "SCARFACE" ROGAN. Highland Infantry. Brilliant athlete. Court martialled for desertion. 15 years. DANGEROUS
34024
MATTHEW DANCER. Commandos. Deadly with a knife. Born marksman. Court martialled for looting. 7 years. DANGEROUS
AGH! THE GERMANS ARE GETTING CLOSER! WE'LL ALL DIE!
THEIR COMMANDER, GENERAL MENCHIKOV, LAY DYING. HE DESPERATELY NEEDED BLOOD. BUT HIS WAS GROUP 'A' RHESUS NEGATIVE, A GROUP SO RARE THE ONLY SUPPLIES WERE IN BRITAIN...
THE GENERAL WILL DIE SOON IF WE DON'T GET SOME MORE BLOOD TO MATCH HIS GROUP!
THIS THEN WAS RAT PACK'S LATEST MISSION. TO BREAK THROUGH THE GERMAN CORDON AND GET...
BLOOD TO LENINGRAD

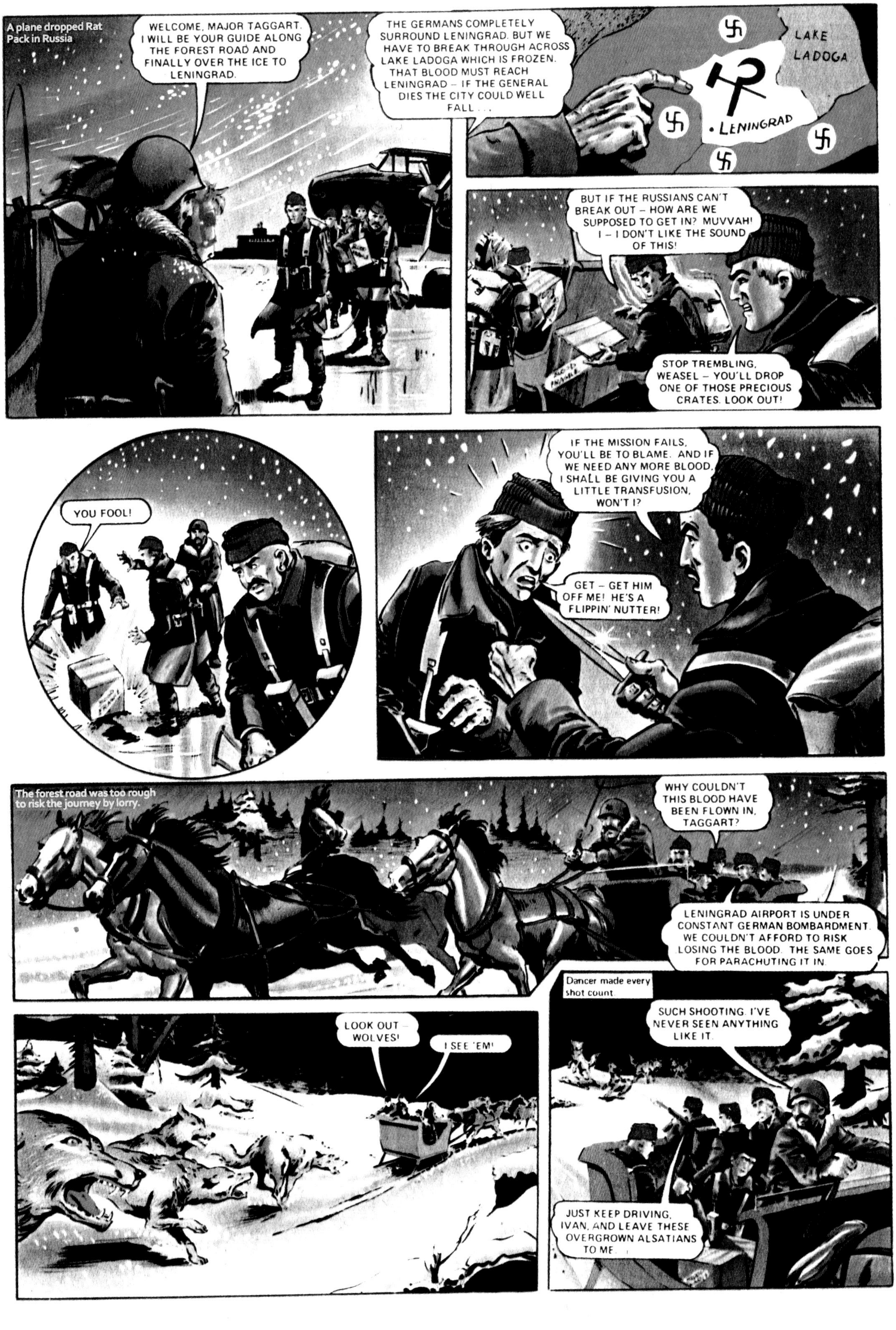

A plane dropped Rat Pack in Russia
WELCOME, MAJOR TAGGART. I WILL BE YOUR GUIDE ALONG THE FOREST ROAD AND FINALLY OVER THE ICE TO LENINGRAD.
THE GERMANS COMPLETELY SURROUND LENINGRAD. BUT WE HAVE TO BREAK THROUGH ACROSS LAKE LADOGA WHICH IS FROZEN. THAT BLOOD MUST REACH LENINGRAD – IF THE GENERAL DIES THE CITY COULD WELL FALL . . .
LAKE LADOGA
• LENINGRAD
BUT IF THE RUSSIANS CAN'T BREAK OUT – HOW ARE WE SUPPOSED TO GET IN? MUVVAH! I – I DON'T LIKE THE SOUND OF THIS!
STOP TREMBLING, WEASEL – YOU'LL DROP ONE OF THOSE PRECIOUS CRATES. LOOK OUT!
YOU FOOL!
IF THE MISSION FAILS, YOU'LL BE TO BLAME. AND IF WE NEED ANY MORE BLOOD, I SHALL BE GIVING YOU A LITTLE TRANSFUSION, WON'T I?
GET – GET HIM OFF ME! HE'S A FLIPPIN' NUTTER!
The forest road was too rough to risk the journey by lorry.
WHY COULDN'T THIS BLOOD HAVE BEEN FLOWN IN, TAGGART?
LENINGRAD AIRPORT IS UNDER CONSTANT GERMAN BOMBARDMENT. WE COULDN'T AFFORD TO RISK LOSING THE BLOOD. THE SAME GOES FOR PARACHUTING IT IN.
LOOK OUT – WOLVES!
I SEE 'EM!
Dancer made every shot count.
SUCH SHOOTING. I'VE NEVER SEEN ANYTHING LIKE IT.
JUST KEEP DRIVING, IVAN, AND LEAVE THESE OVERGROWN ALSATIANS TO ME . . .

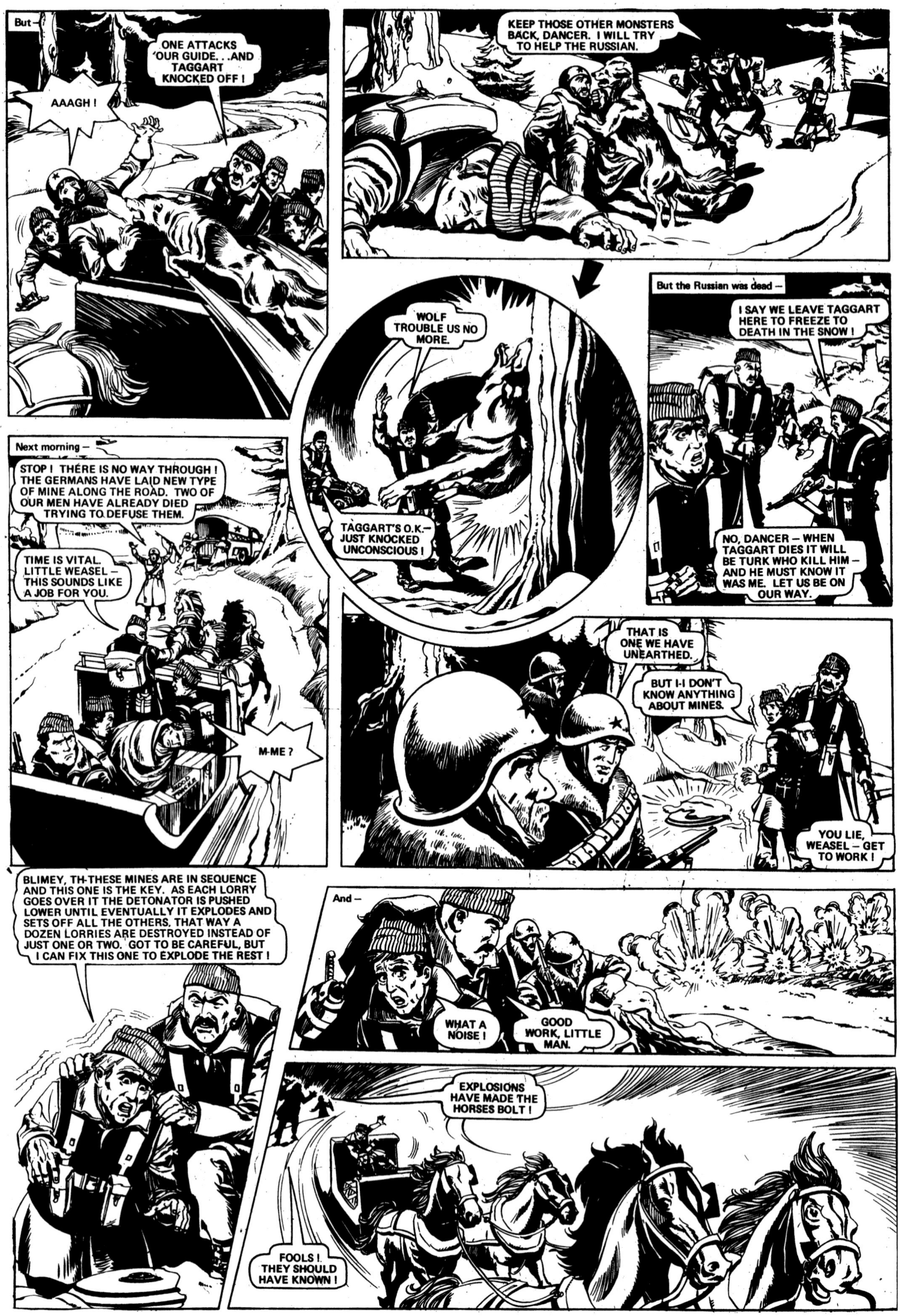
But –
AAAGH !
ONE ATTACKS OUR GUIDE. . .AND TAGGART KNOCKED OFF !
KEEP THOSE OTHER MONSTERS BACK, DANCER. I WILL TRY TO HELP THE RUSSIAN.
WOLF TROUBLE US NO MORE.
TAGGART'S O.K.– JUST KNOCKED UNCONSCIOUS !
But the Russian was dead –
I SAY WE LEAVE TAGGART HERE TO FREEZE TO DEATH IN THE SNOW !
NO, DANCER – WHEN TAGGART DIES IT WILL BE TURK WHO KILL HIM – AND HE MUST KNOW IT WAS ME. LET US BE ON OUR WAY.
Next morning –
STOP ! THERE IS NO WAY THROUGH ! THE GERMANS HAVE LAID NEW TYPE OF MINE ALONG THE ROAD. TWO OF OUR MEN HAVE ALREADY DIED TRYING TO DEFUSE THEM.
TIME IS VITAL. LITTLE WEASEL – THIS SOUNDS LIKE A JOB FOR YOU.
M-ME ?
THAT IS ONE WE HAVE UNEARTHED.
BUT I-I DON'T KNOW ANYTHING ABOUT MINES.
YOU LIE, WEASEL – GET TO WORK !
BLIMEY, TH-THESE MINES ARE IN SEQUENCE AND THIS ONE IS THE KEY. AS EACH LORRY GOES OVER IT THE DETONATOR IS PUSHED LOWER UNTIL EVENTUALLY IT EXPLODES AND SETS OFF ALL THE OTHERS. THAT WAY A DOZEN LORRIES ARE DESTROYED INSTEAD OF JUST ONE OR TWO. GOT TO BE CAREFUL, BUT I CAN FIX THIS ONE TO EXPLODE THE REST !
And –
WHAT A NOISE !
GOOD WORK, LITTLE MAN.
EXPLOSIONS HAVE MADE THE HORSES BOLT !
FOOLS ! THEY SHOULD HAVE KNOWN !

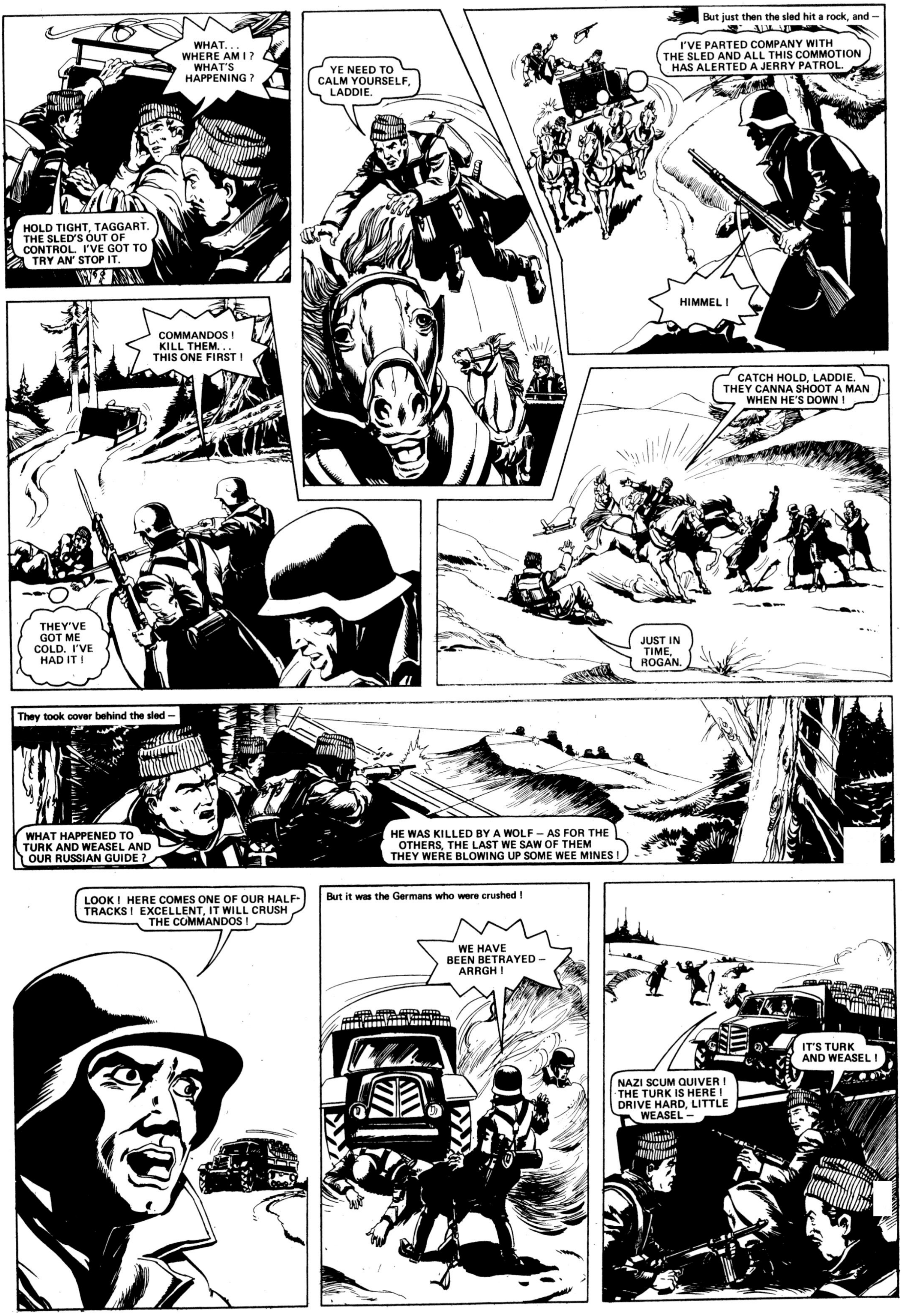
WHAT... WHERE AM I ? WHAT'S HAPPENING ?
HOLD TIGHT, TAGGART. THE SLED'S OUT OF CONTROL. I'VE GOT TO TRY AN' STOP IT.
YE NEED TO CALM YOURSELF, LADDIE.
But just then the sled hit a rock, and —
I'VE PARTED COMPANY WITH THE SLED AND ALL THIS COMMOTION HAS ALERTED A JERRY PATROL.
HIMMEL !
COMMANDOS ! KILL THEM... THIS ONE FIRST !
THEY'VE GOT ME COLD. I'VE HAD IT !
CATCH HOLD, LADDIE. THEY CANNA SHOOT A MAN WHEN HE'S DOWN !
JUST IN TIME, ROGAN.
They took cover behind the sled —
WHAT HAPPENED TO TURK AND WEASEL AND OUR RUSSIAN GUIDE ?
HE WAS KILLED BY A WOLF — AS FOR THE OTHERS, THE LAST WE SAW OF THEM THEY WERE BLOWING UP SOME WEE MINES !
LOOK ! HERE COMES ONE OF OUR HALF-TRACKS ! EXCELLENT, IT WILL CRUSH THE COMMANDOS !
But it was the Germans who were crushed !
WE HAVE BEEN BETRAYED — ARRGH !
IT'S TURK AND WEASEL !
NAZI SCUM QUIVER ! THE TURK IS HERE ! DRIVE HARD, LITTLE WEASEL —

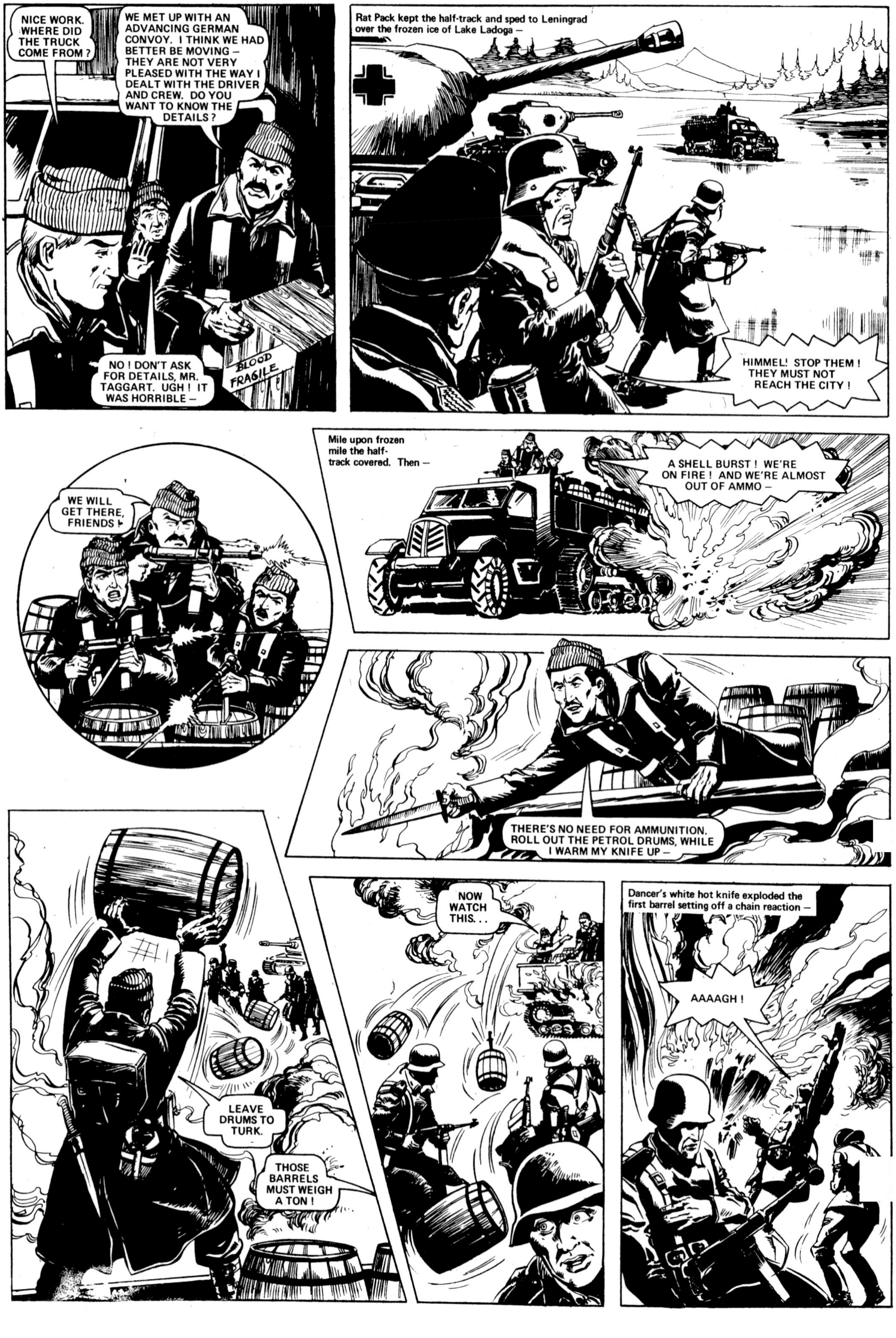
NICE WORK. WHERE DID THE TRUCK COME FROM?
WE MET UP WITH AN ADVANCING GERMAN CONVOY. I THINK WE HAD BETTER BE MOVING – THEY ARE NOT VERY PLEASED WITH THE WAY I DEALT WITH THE DRIVER AND CREW. DO YOU WANT TO KNOW THE DETAILS?
NO! DON'T ASK FOR DETAILS, MR. TAGGART. UGH! IT WAS HORRIBLE –
BLOOD
FRAGILE
Rat Pack kept the half-track and sped to Leningrad over the frozen ice of Lake Ladoga –
HIMMEL! STOP THEM! THEY MUST NOT REACH THE CITY!
WE WILL GET THERE, FRIENDS!
Mile upon frozen mile the half-track covered. Then –
A SHELL BURST! WE'RE ON FIRE! AND WE'RE ALMOST OUT OF AMMO –
THERE'S NO NEED FOR AMMUNITION. ROLL OUT THE PETROL DRUMS, WHILE I WARM MY KNIFE UP –
LEAVE DRUMS TO TURK.
THOSE BARRELS MUST WEIGH A TON!
NOW WATCH THIS...
Dancer's white hot knife exploded the first barrel setting off a chain reaction –
AAAAGH!

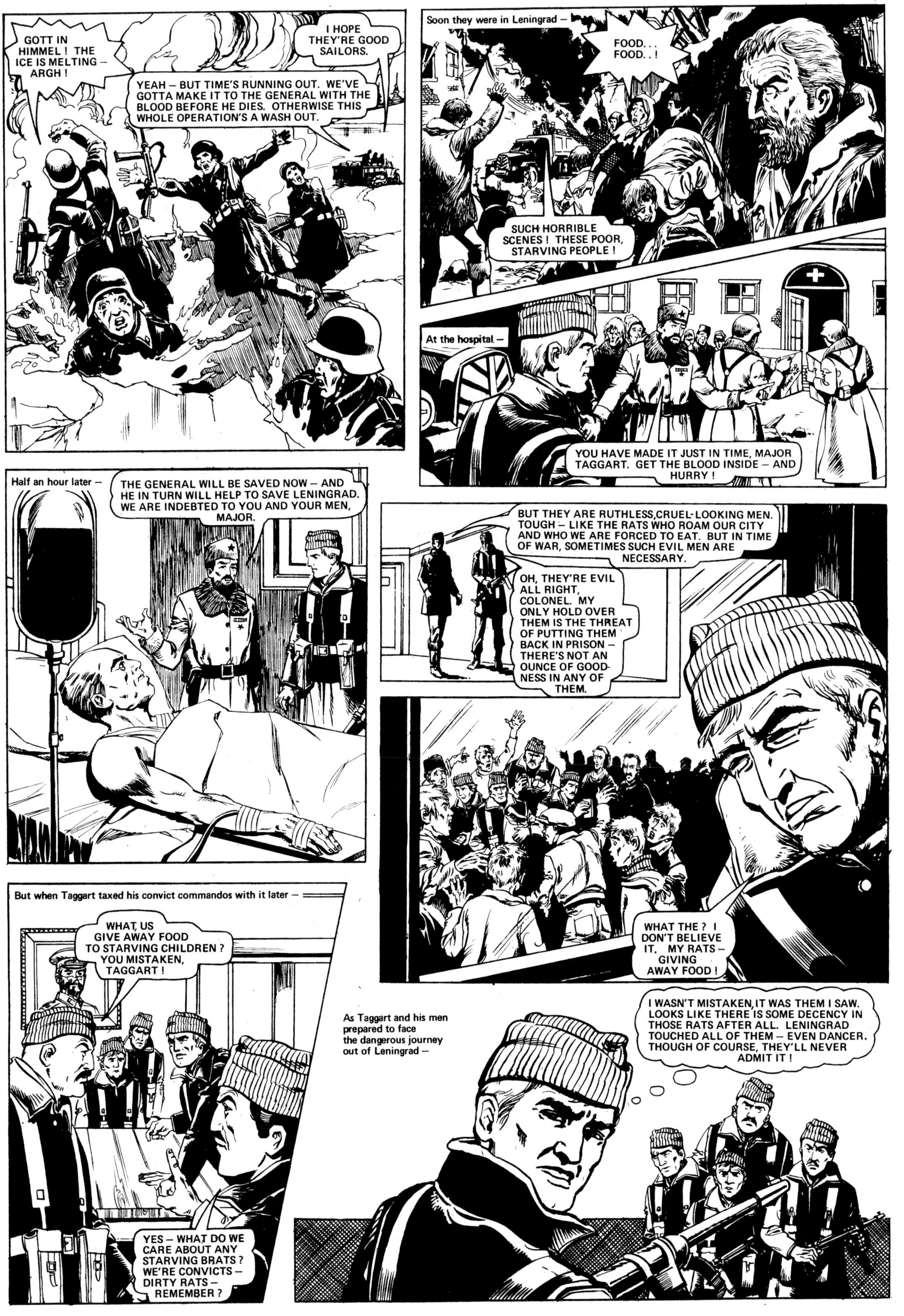
GOTT IN HIMMEL ! THE ICE IS MELTING – ARGH !
I HOPE THEY'RE GOOD SAILORS.
YEAH – BUT TIME'S RUNNING OUT. WE'VE GOTTA MAKE IT TO THE GENERAL WITH THE BLOOD BEFORE HE DIES. OTHERWISE THIS WHOLE OPERATION'S A WASH OUT.
Soon they were in Leningrad –
FOOD. . . FOOD. . !
SUCH HORRIBLE SCENES ! THESE POOR, STARVING PEOPLE !
At the hospital –
YOU HAVE MADE IT JUST IN TIME, MAJOR TAGGART. GET THE BLOOD INSIDE – AND HURRY !
Half an hour later –
THE GENERAL WILL BE SAVED NOW – AND HE IN TURN WILL HELP TO SAVE LENINGRAD. WE ARE INDEBTED TO YOU AND YOUR MEN, MAJOR.
BUT THEY ARE RUTHLESS,CRUEL-LOOKING MEN. TOUGH – LIKE THE RATS WHO ROAM OUR CITY AND WHO WE ARE FORCED TO EAT. BUT IN TIME OF WAR, SOMETIMES SUCH EVIL MEN ARE NECESSARY.
OH, THEY'RE EVIL ALL RIGHT, COLONEL. MY ONLY HOLD OVER THEM IS THE THREAT OF PUTTING THEM BACK IN PRISON – THERE'S NOT AN OUNCE OF GOODNESS IN ANY OF THEM.
WHAT THE ? I DON'T BELIEVE IT. MY RATS – GIVING AWAY FOOD !
But when Taggart taxed his convict commandos with it later –
WHAT, US GIVE AWAY FOOD TO STARVING CHILDREN ? YOU MISTAKEN, TAGGART !
YES – WHAT DO WE CARE ABOUT ANY STARVING BRATS ? WE'RE CONVICTS – DIRTY RATS – REMEMBER ?
As Taggart and his men prepared to face the dangerous journey out of Leningrad –
I WASN'T MISTAKEN, IT WAS THEM I SAW. LOOKS LIKE THERE IS SOME DECENCY IN THOSE RATS AFTER ALL. LENINGRAD TOUCHED ALL OF THEM – EVEN DANCER. THOUGH OF COURSE, THEY'LL NEVER ADMIT IT !

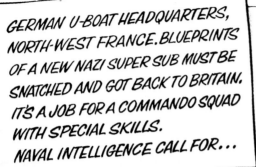

GERMAN U-BOAT HEADQUARTERS, NORTH-WEST FRANCE. BLUEPRINTS OF A NEW NAZI SUPER SUB MUST BE SNATCHED AND GOT BACK TO BRITAIN. IT'S A JOB FOR A COMMANDO SQUAD WITH SPECIAL SKILLS. NAVAL INTELLIGENCE CALL FOR...

RAT

BLIMEY — THERE MUST BE AN EASIER WAY TO EARN A LIVIN'!

THERE IS, WEASEL — BUT IT GOT YOU LOT IN PRISON. NOW MOVE!

But another obstacle soon faced Major Taggart and his convict commandos —

A BIG DITCH YOU HAVE FOUND FOR US, TAGGART! WHAT DO WE DO NOW — FLY?

WE HAVEN'T TIME TO BY-PASS, TURK!

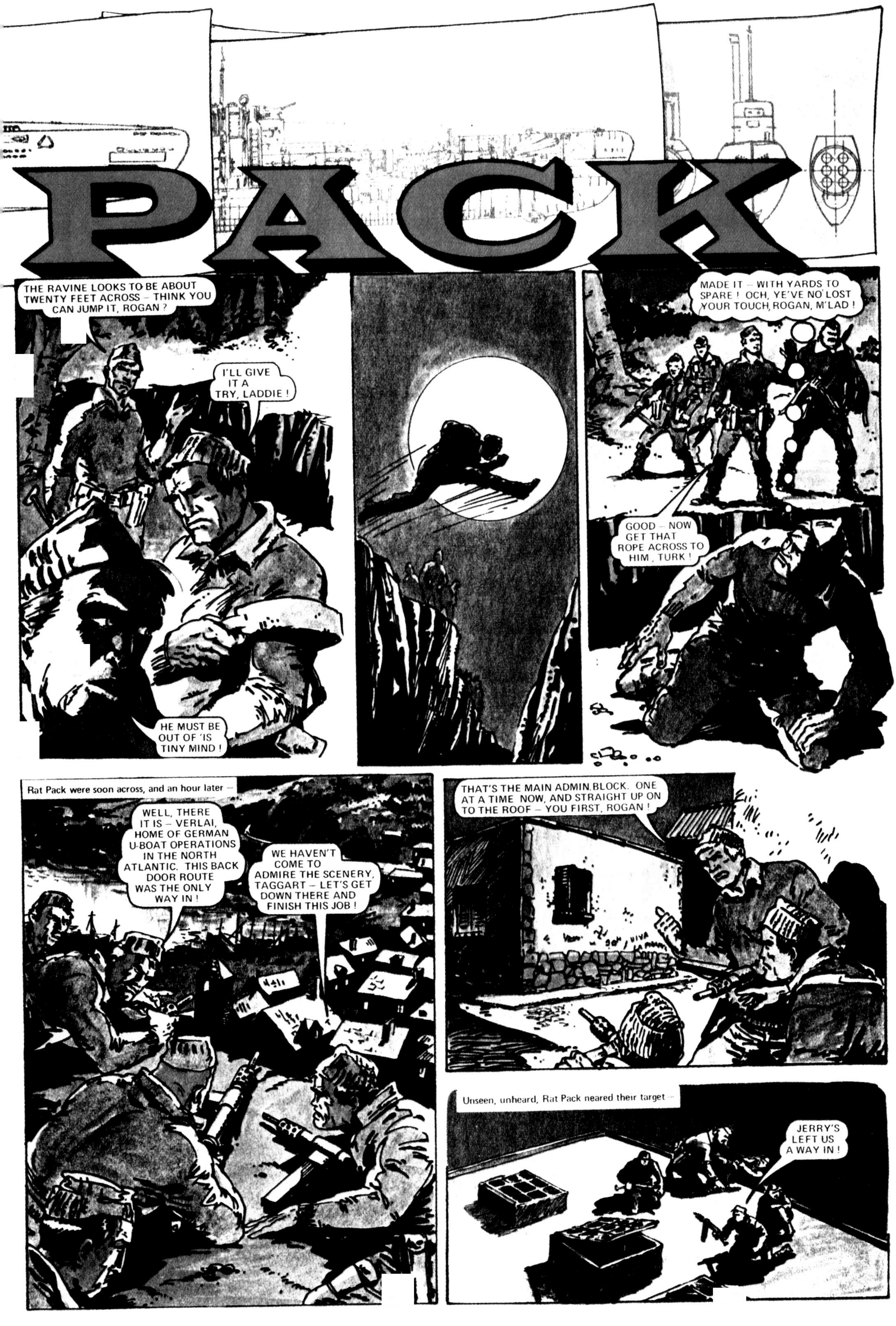
PACK
THE RAVINE LOOKS TO BE ABOUT TWENTY FEET ACROSS – THINK YOU CAN JUMP IT, ROGAN?
I'LL GIVE IT A TRY, LADDIE!
HE MUST BE OUT OF 'IS TINY MIND!
MADE IT – WITH YARDS TO SPARE! OCH, YE'VE NO' LOST YOUR TOUCH, ROGAN, M'LAD!
GOOD – NOW GET THAT ROPE ACROSS TO HIM, TURK!
Rat Pack were soon across, and an hour later –
WELL, THERE IT IS – VERLAI, HOME OF GERMAN U-BOAT OPERATIONS IN THE NORTH ATLANTIC. THIS BACK DOOR ROUTE WAS THE ONLY WAY IN!
WE HAVEN'T COME TO ADMIRE THE SCENERY, TAGGART – LET'S GET DOWN THERE AND FINISH THIS JOB!
THAT'S THE MAIN ADMIN. BLOCK. ONE AT A TIME NOW, AND STRAIGHT UP ON TO THE ROOF – YOU FIRST, ROGAN!
Unseen, unheard, Rat Pack neared their target –
JERRY'S LEFT US A WAY IN!

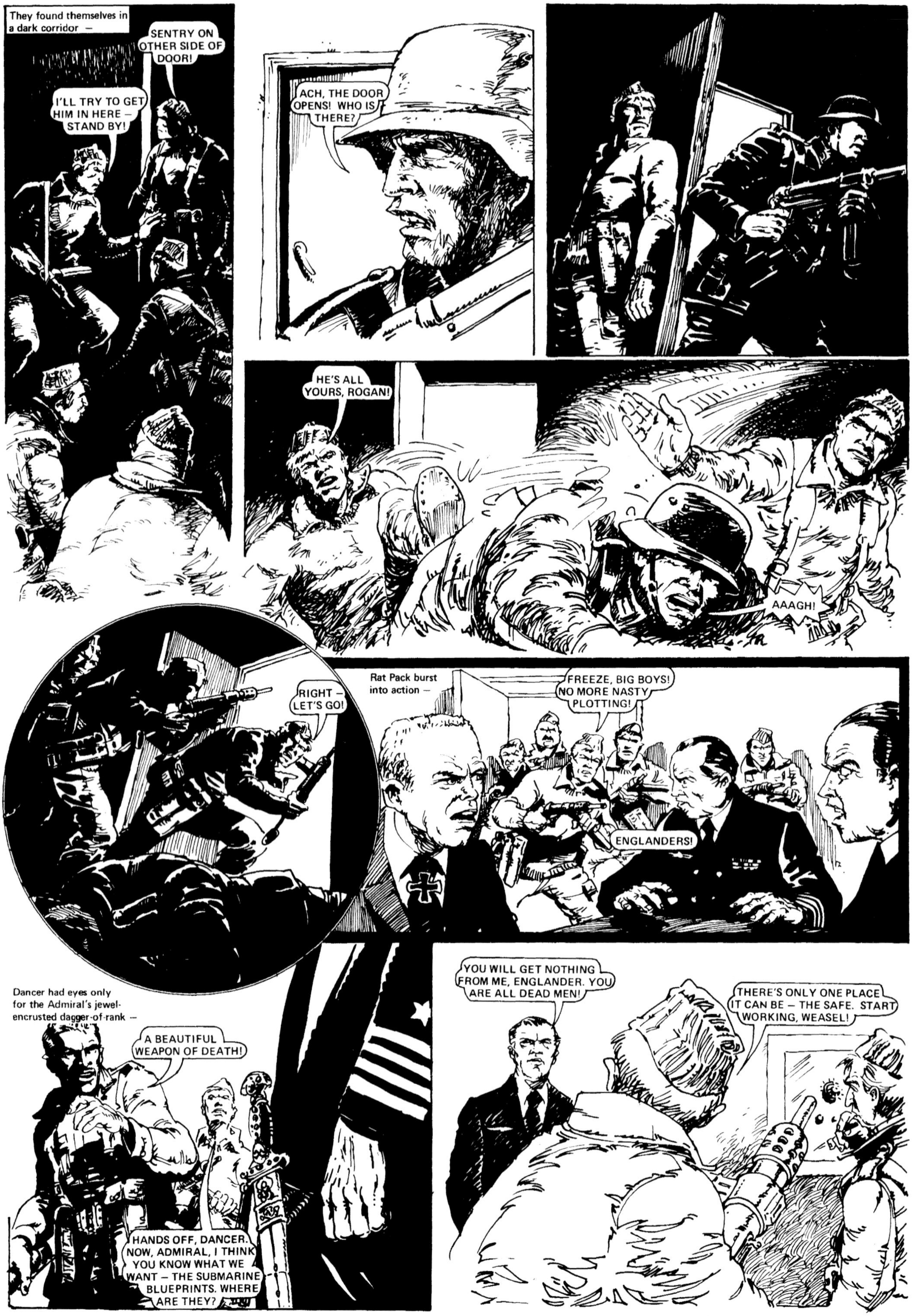
They found themselves in a dark corridor –
SENTRY ON OTHER SIDE OF DOOR!
I'LL TRY TO GET HIM IN HERE – STAND BY!
ACH, THE DOOR OPENS! WHO IS THERE?
HE'S ALL YOURS, ROGAN!
AAAGH!
RIGHT – LET'S GO!
Rat Pack burst into action –
FREEZE, BIG BOYS! NO MORE NASTY PLOTTING!
ENGLANDERS!
Dancer had eyes only for the Admiral's jewel-encrusted dagger-of-rank –
A BEAUTIFUL WEAPON OF DEATH!
HANDS OFF, DANCER. NOW, ADMIRAL, I THINK YOU KNOW WHAT WE WANT – THE SUBMARINE BLUEPRINTS. WHERE ARE THEY?
YOU WILL GET NOTHING FROM ME, ENGLANDER. YOU ARE ALL DEAD MEN!
THERE'S ONLY ONE PLACE IT CAN BE – THE SAFE. START WORKING, WEASEL!

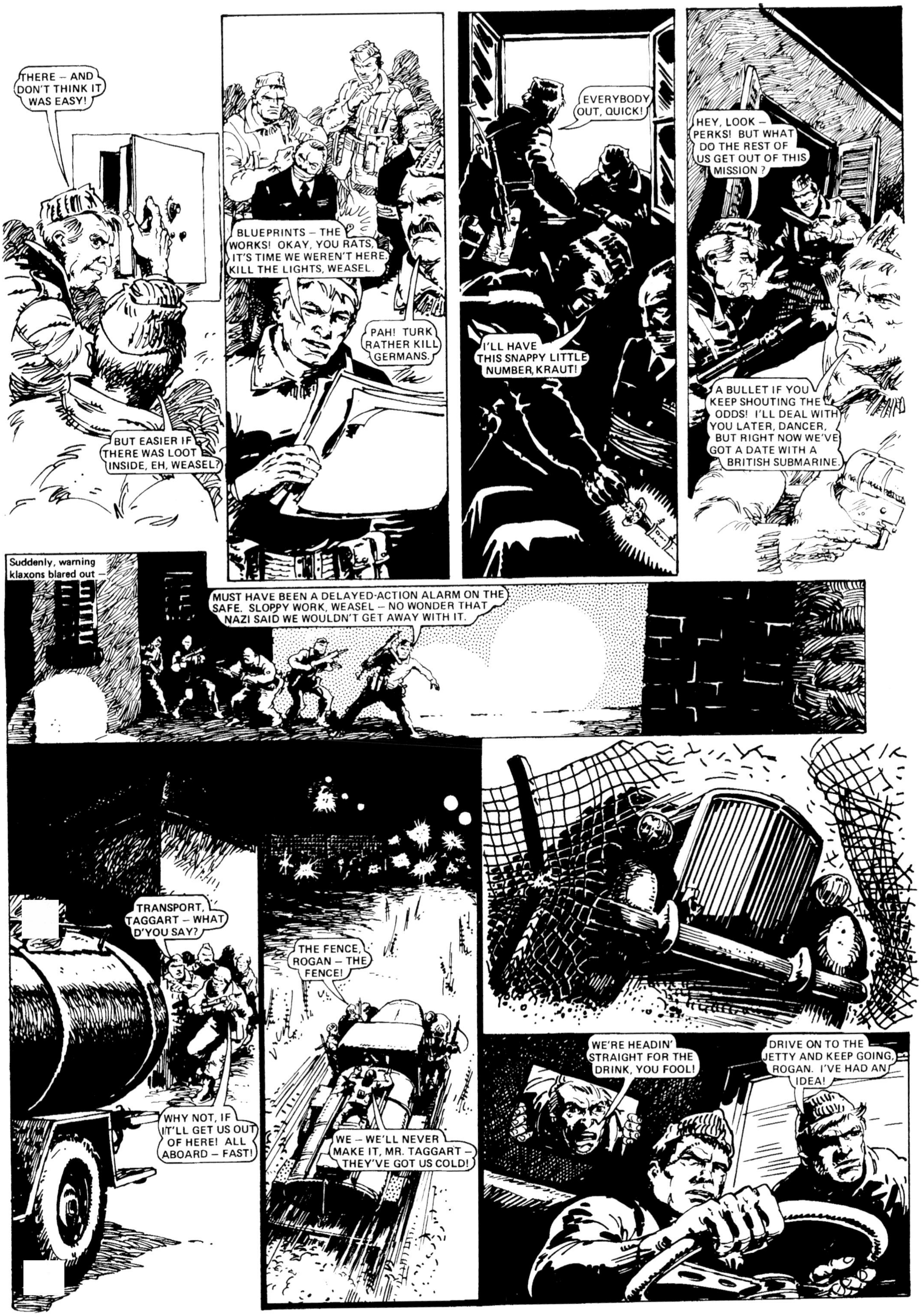
THERE – AND DON'T THINK IT WAS EASY!
BUT EASIER IF THERE WAS LOOT INSIDE, EH, WEASEL?
BLUEPRINTS – THE WORKS! OKAY, YOU RATS, IT'S TIME WE WEREN'T HERE. KILL THE LIGHTS, WEASEL.
PAH! TURK RATHER KILL GERMANS.
EVERYBODY OUT, QUICK!
I'LL HAVE THIS SNAPPY LITTLE NUMBER, KRAUT!
HEY, LOOK – PERKS! BUT WHAT DO THE REST OF US GET OUT OF THIS MISSION ?
A BULLET IF YOU KEEP SHOUTING THE ODDS! I'LL DEAL WITH YOU LATER, DANCER, BUT RIGHT NOW WE'VE GOT A DATE WITH A BRITISH SUBMARINE.
Suddenly, warning klaxons blared out –
MUST HAVE BEEN A DELAYED-ACTION ALARM ON THE SAFE. SLOPPY WORK, WEASEL – NO WONDER THAT NAZI SAID WE WOULDN'T GET AWAY WITH IT.
TRANSPORT, TAGGART – WHAT D'YOU SAY?
WHY NOT, IF IT'LL GET US OUT OF HERE! ALL ABOARD – FAST!
THE FENCE, ROGAN – THE FENCE!
WE – WE'LL NEVER MAKE IT, MR. TAGGART – THEY'VE GOT US COLD!
WE'RE HEADIN' STRAIGHT FOR THE DRINK, YOU FOOL!
DRIVE ON TO THE JETTY AND KEEP GOING, ROGAN. I'VE HAD AN IDEA!

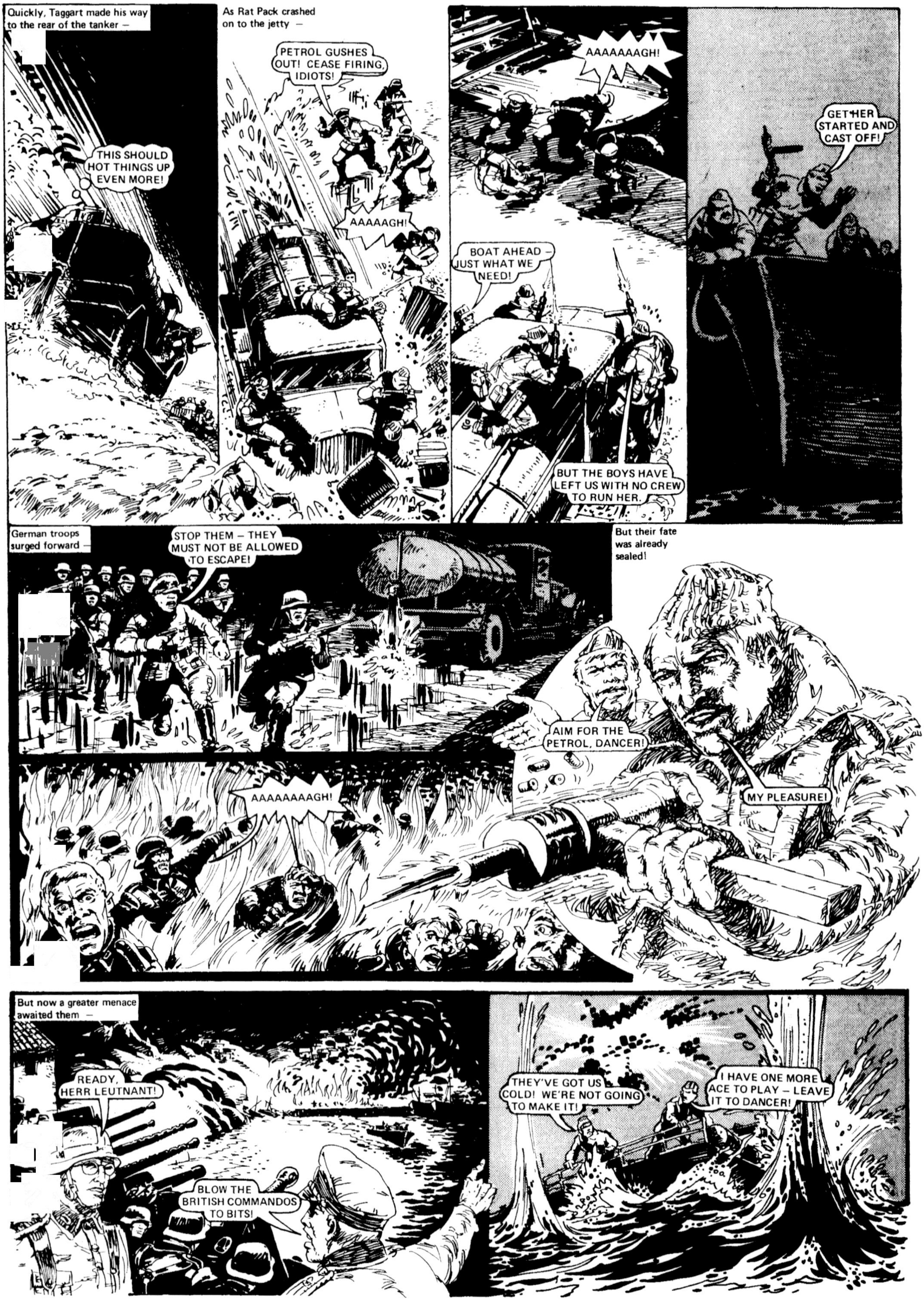

Quickly, Taggart made his way to the rear of the tanker –
THIS SHOULD HOT THINGS UP EVEN MORE!
As Rat Pack crashed on to the jetty –
PETROL GUSHES OUT! CEASE FIRING, IDIOTS!
AAAAAGH!
AAAAAAAGH!
BOAT AHEAD – JUST WHAT WE NEED!
BUT THE BOYS HAVE LEFT US WITH NO CREW TO RUN HER.
GET HER STARTED AND CAST OFF!
German troops surged forward –
STOP THEM – THEY MUST NOT BE ALLOWED TO ESCAPE!
But their fate was already sealed!
AIM FOR THE PETROL, DANCER!
MY PLEASURE!
AAAAAAAAGH!
But now a greater menace awaited them –
READY, HERR LEUTNANT!
BLOW THE BRITISH COMMANDOS TO BITS!
THEY'VE GOT US COLD! WE'RE NOT GOING TO MAKE IT!
I HAVE ONE MORE ACE TO PLAY – LEAVE IT TO DANCER!

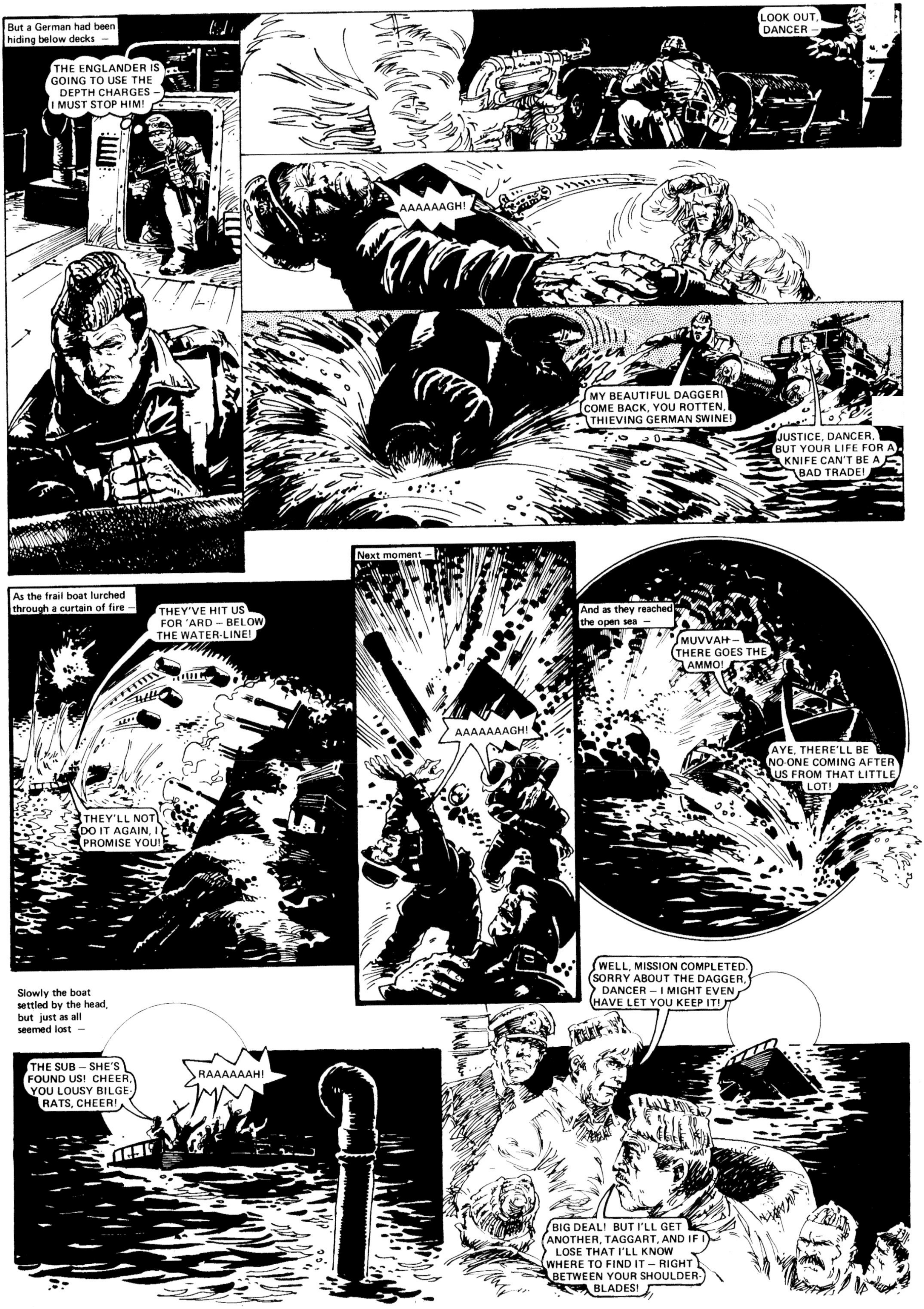

But a German had been hiding below decks —
THE ENGLANDER IS GOING TO USE THE DEPTH CHARGES — I MUST STOP HIM!
LOOK OUT, DANCER —
AAAAAAGH!
MY BEAUTIFUL DAGGER! COME BACK, YOU ROTTEN, THIEVING GERMAN SWINE!
JUSTICE, DANCER, BUT YOUR LIFE FOR A KNIFE CAN'T BE A BAD TRADE!
As the frail boat lurched through a curtain of fire —
THEY'VE HIT US FOR 'ARD — BELOW THE WATER-LINE!
THEY'LL NOT DO IT AGAIN, I PROMISE YOU!
Next moment —
AAAAAAAGH!
And as they reached the open sea —
MUVVAH — THERE GOES THE AMMO!
AYE, THERE'LL BE NO-ONE COMING AFTER US FROM THAT LITTLE LOT!
Slowly the boat settled by the head, but just as all seemed lost —
THE SUB — SHE'S FOUND US! CHEER, YOU LOUSY BILGE-RATS, CHEER!
RAAAAAAH!
WELL, MISSION COMPLETED. SORRY ABOUT THE DAGGER, DANCER — I MIGHT EVEN HAVE LET YOU KEEP IT!
BIG DEAL! BUT I'LL GET ANOTHER, TAGGART, AND IF I LOSE THAT I'LL KNOW WHERE TO FIND IT — RIGHT BETWEEN YOUR SHOULDER-BLADES!

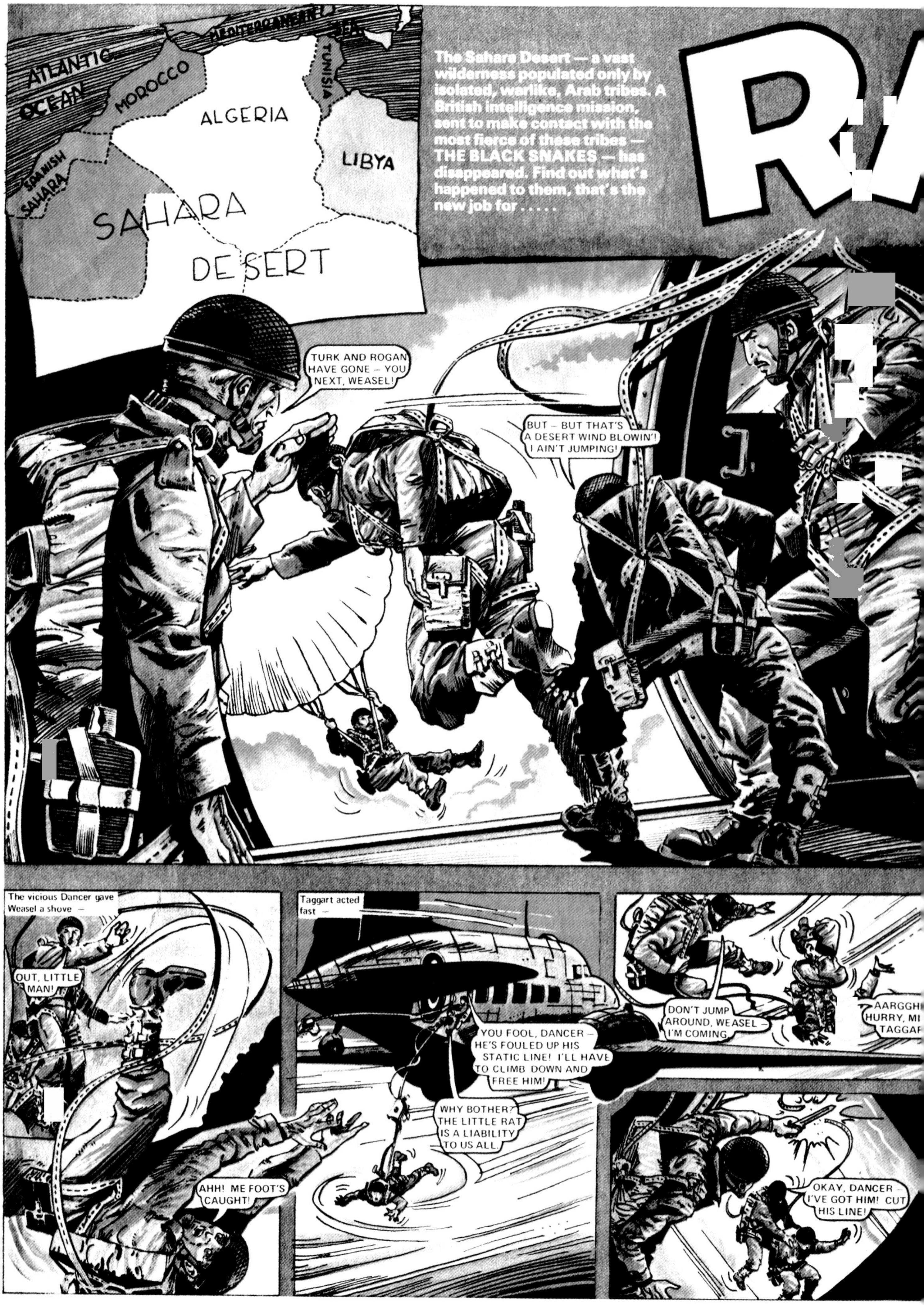

MEDITERRANEAN SEA
ATLANTIC OCEAN
MOROCCO
ALGERIA
TUNISIA
LIBYA
SPANISH SAHARA
SAHARA DESERT
The Sahara Desert — a vast wilderness populated only by isolated, warlike, Arab tribes. A British intelligence mission, sent to make contact with the most fierce of these tribes — THE BLACK SNAKES — has disappeared. Find out what's happened to them, that's the new job for . . . . .
RA
TURK AND ROGAN HAVE GONE – YOU NEXT, WEASEL!
BUT – BUT THAT'S A DESERT WIND BLOWIN'! I AIN'T JUMPING!
The vicious Dancer gave Weasel a shove –
OUT, LITTLE MAN!
AHH! ME FOOT'S CAUGHT!
Taggart acted fast –
YOU FOOL, DANCER – HE'S FOULED UP HIS STATIC LINE! I'LL HAVE TO CLIMB DOWN AND FREE HIM!
WHY BOTHER? THE LITTLE RAT IS A LIABILITY TO US ALL.
DON'T JUMP AROUND, WEASEL – I'M COMING
AARGGH
HURRY, MI
TAGGAR
OKAY, DANCER – I'VE GOT HIM! CUT HIS LINE!

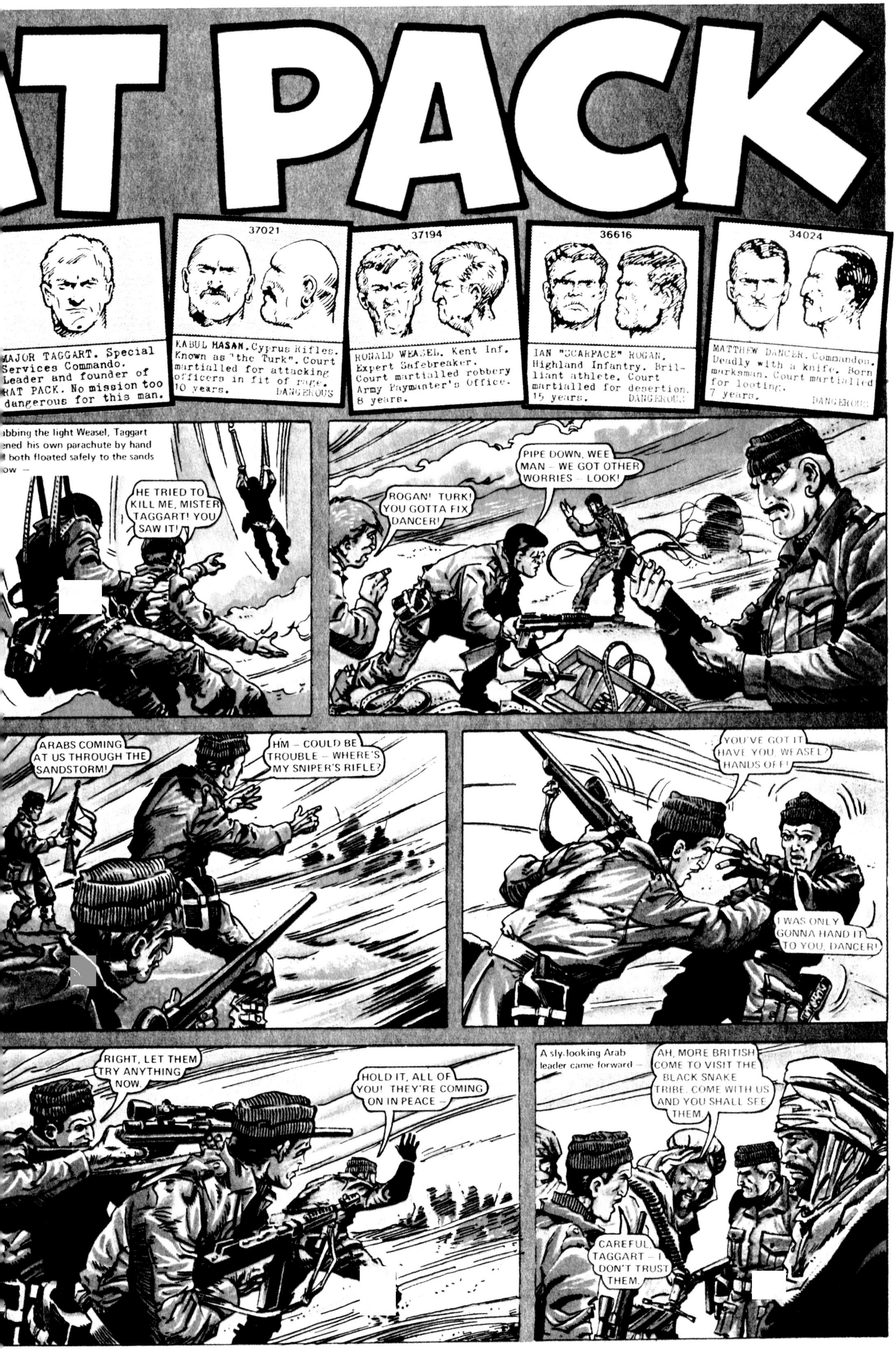
AT PACK
37021
37194
36616
34024
MAJOR TAGGART. Special Services Commando. Leader and founder of RAT PACK. No mission too dangerous for this man.
KABUL HASAN. Cyprus Rifles. Known as "the Turk". Court martialled for attacking officers in fit of rage. 10 years. DANGEROUS
RONALD WEASEL. Kent Inf. Expert Safebreaker. Court martialled robbery Army Paymaster's Office. 8 years.
IAN "SCARFACE" ROGAN. Highland Infantry. Brilliant athlete. Court martialled for desertion. 15 years. DANGEROUS
MATTHEW DANCER. Commandos. Deadly with a knife. Born marksman. Court martialled for looting. 7 years. DANGEROUS
abbing the light Weasel, Taggart ened his own parachute by hand both floated safely to the sands ow –
HE TRIED TO KILL ME, MISTER TAGGART! YOU SAW IT!
ROGAN! TURK! YOU GOTTA FIX DANCER!
PIPE DOWN, WEE MAN – WE GOT OTHER WORRIES – LOOK!
ARABS COMING AT US THROUGH THE SANDSTORM!
HM – COULD BE TROUBLE – WHERE'S MY SNIPER'S RIFLE?
YOU'VE GOT IT HAVE YOU, WEASEL? HANDS OFF!
I WAS ONLY GONNA HAND IT TO YOU, DANCER!
RIGHT, LET THEM TRY ANYTHING NOW.
HOLD IT, ALL OF YOU! THEY'RE COMING ON IN PEACE –
A sly-looking Arab leader came forward –
AH, MORE BRITISH COME TO VISIT THE BLACK SNAKE TRIBE. COME WITH US AND YOU SHALL SEE THEM.
CAREFUL, TAGGART – I DON'T TRUST THEM.

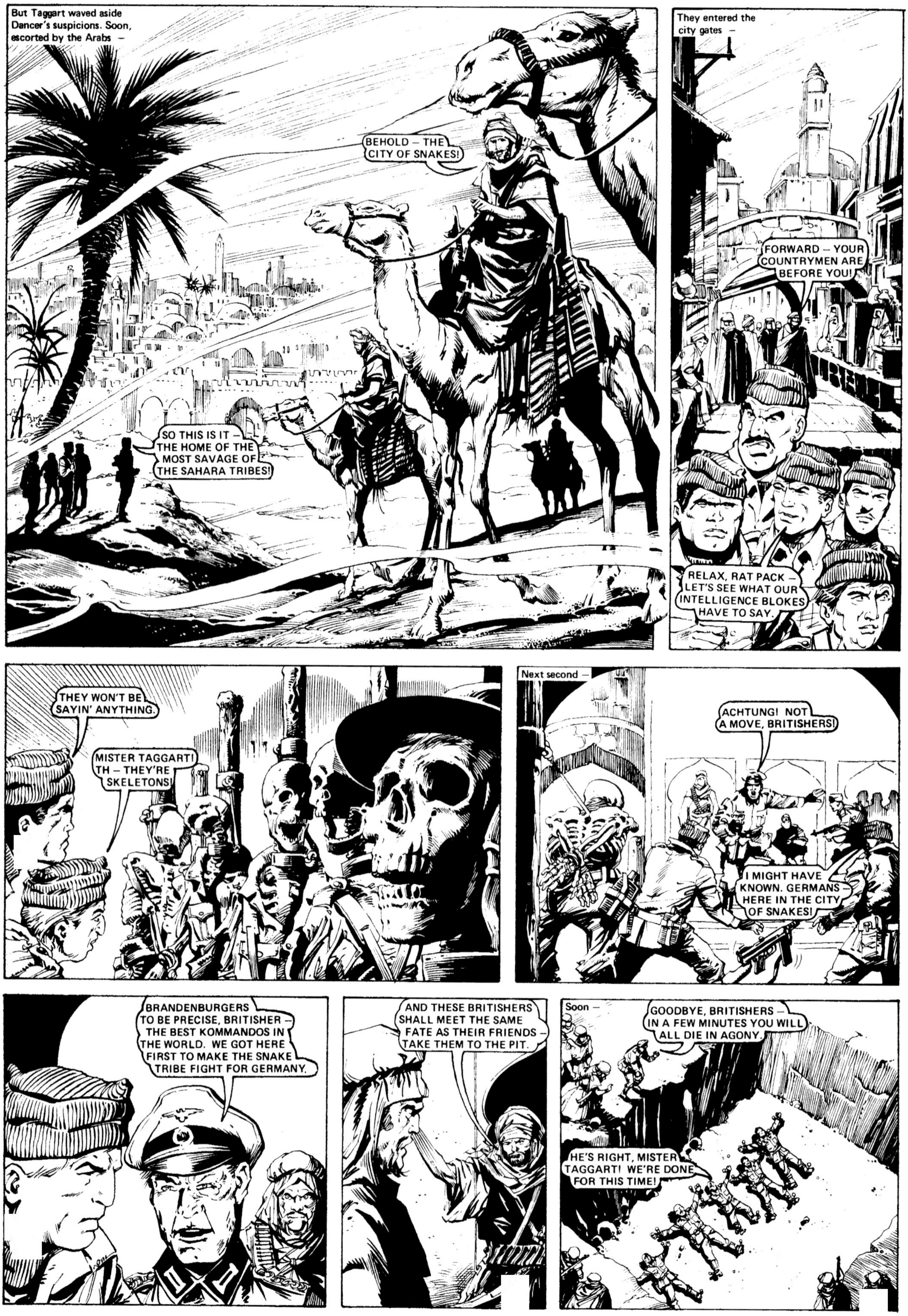
But Taggart waved aside Dancer's suspicions. Soon, escorted by the Arabs –
BEHOLD – THE CITY OF SNAKES!
SO THIS IS IT – THE HOME OF THE MOST SAVAGE OF THE SAHARA TRIBES!
They entered the city gates –
FORWARD – YOUR COUNTRYMEN ARE BEFORE YOU!
RELAX, RAT PACK – LET'S SEE WHAT OUR INTELLIGENCE BLOKES HAVE TO SAY.
THEY WON'T BE SAYIN' ANYTHING.
MISTER TAGGART! TH – THEY'RE SKELETONS!
Next second –
ACHTUNG! NOT A MOVE, BRITISHERS!
I MIGHT HAVE KNOWN. GERMANS – HERE IN THE CITY OF SNAKES!
BRANDENBURGERS TO BE PRECISE, BRITISHER – THE BEST KOMMANDOS IN THE WORLD. WE GOT HERE FIRST TO MAKE THE SNAKE TRIBE FIGHT FOR GERMANY.
AND THESE BRITISHERS SHALL MEET THE SAME FATE AS THEIR FRIENDS – TAKE THEM TO THE PIT.
Soon –
GOODBYE, BRITISHERS – IN A FEW MINUTES YOU WILL ALL DIE IN AGONY.
HE'S RIGHT, MISTER TAGGART! WE'RE DONE FOR THIS TIME!

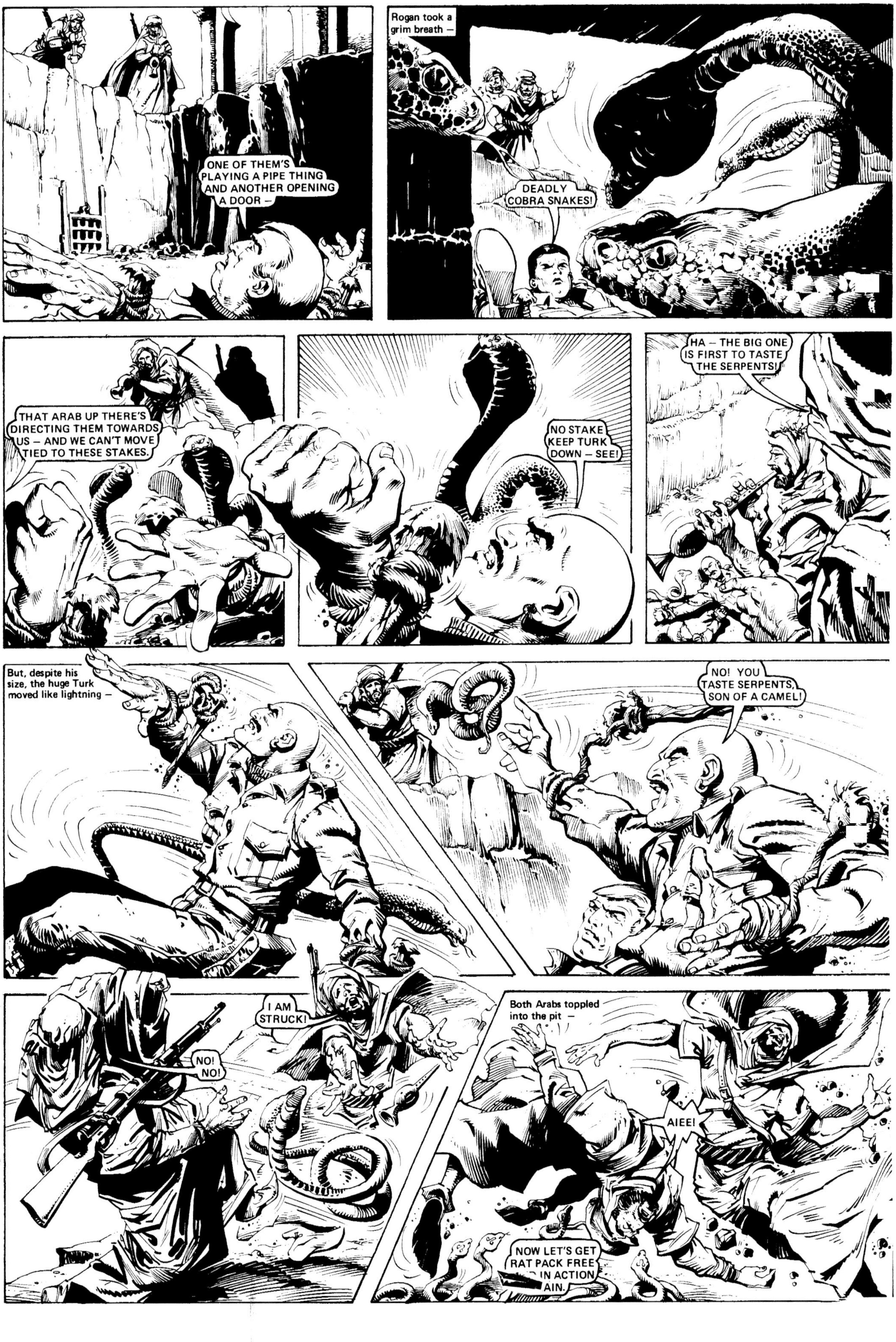
ONE OF THEM'S PLAYING A PIPE THING AND ANOTHER OPENING A DOOR –
Rogan took a grim breath –
DEADLY COBRA SNAKES!
THAT ARAB UP THERE'S DIRECTING THEM TOWARDS US – AND WE CAN'T MOVE TIED TO THESE STAKES.
NO STAKE KEEP TURK DOWN – SEE!
HA – THE BIG ONE IS FIRST TO TASTE THE SERPENTS!
But, despite his size, the huge Turk moved like lightning –
NO! YOU TASTE SERPENTS, SON OF A CAMEL!
I AM STRUCK!
NO! NO!
Both Arabs toppled into the pit –
AIEE!
NOW LET'S GET RAT PACK FREE
IN ACTION
AIN.

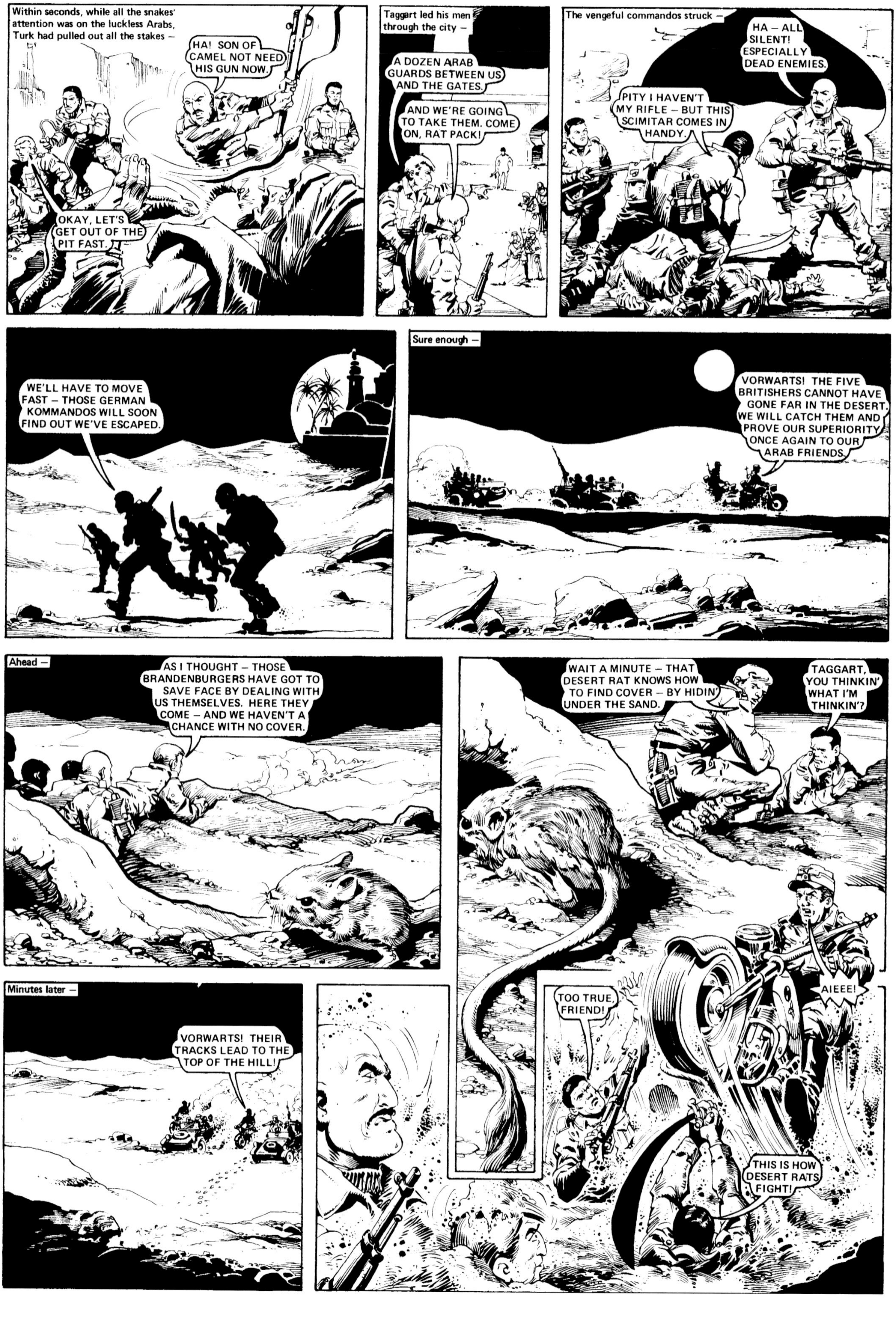

Within seconds, while all the snakes' attention was on the luckless Arabs, Turk had pulled out all the stakes –
HA! SON OF CAMEL NOT NEED HIS GUN NOW.
OKAY, LET'S GET OUT OF THE PIT FAST.
Taggart led his men through the city –
A DOZEN ARAB GUARDS BETWEEN US AND THE GATES.
AND WE'RE GOING TO TAKE THEM. COME ON, RAT PACK!
The vengeful commandos struck –
HA – ALL SILENT! ESPECIALLY DEAD ENEMIES.
PITY I HAVEN'T MY RIFLE – BUT THIS SCIMITAR COMES IN HANDY.
WE'LL HAVE TO MOVE FAST – THOSE GERMAN KOMMANDOS WILL SOON FIND OUT WE'VE ESCAPED.
Sure enough –
VORWARTS! THE FIVE BRITISHERS CANNOT HAVE GONE FAR IN THE DESERT. WE WILL CATCH THEM AND PROVE OUR SUPERIORITY ONCE AGAIN TO OUR ARAB FRIENDS.
Ahead –
AS I THOUGHT – THOSE BRANDENBURGERS HAVE GOT TO SAVE FACE BY DEALING WITH US THEMSELVES. HERE THEY COME – AND WE HAVEN'T A CHANCE WITH NO COVER.
WAIT A MINUTE – THAT DESERT RAT KNOWS HOW TO FIND COVER – BY HIDIN' UNDER THE SAND.
TAGGART, YOU THINKIN' WHAT I'M THINKIN'?
Minutes later –
VORWARTS! THEIR TRACKS LEAD TO THE TOP OF THE HILL!
TOO TRUE, FRIEND!
AIEEE!
THIS IS HOW DESERT RATS FIGHT!

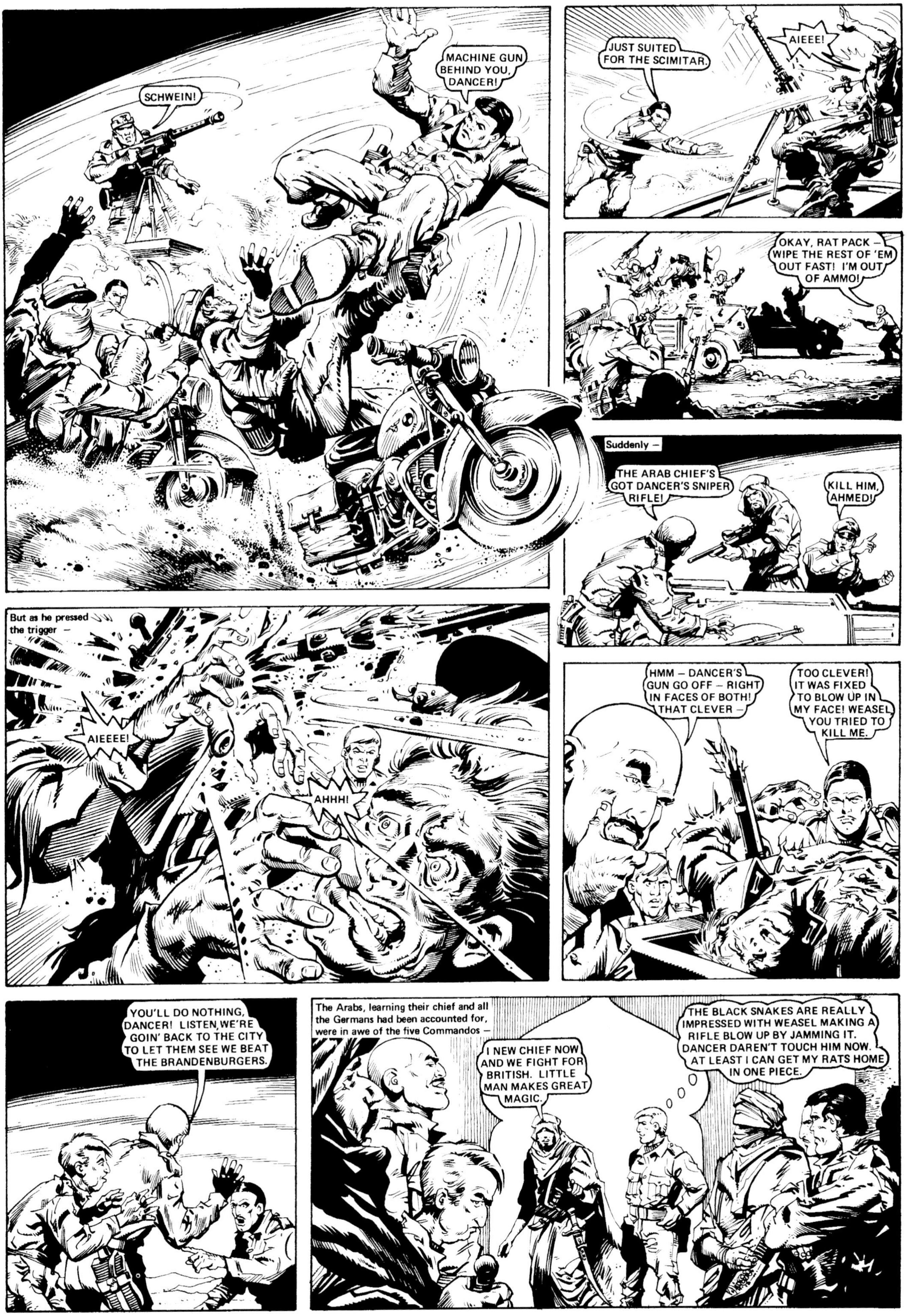

MACHINE GUN BEHIND YOU, DANCER!
SCHWEIN!
JUST SUITED FOR THE SCIMITAR.
AIEEE!
OKAY, RAT PACK – WIPE THE REST OF 'EM OUT FAST! I'M OUT OF AMMO!
Suddenly –
THE ARAB CHIEF'S GOT DANCER'S SNIPER RIFLE!
KILL HIM, AHMED!
But as he pressed the trigger –
AIEEEE!
AHHH!
HMM – DANCER'S GUN GO OFF – RIGHT IN FACES OF BOTH! THAT CLEVER –
TOO CLEVER! IT WAS FIXED TO BLOW UP IN MY FACE! WEASEL, YOU TRIED TO KILL ME.
YOU'LL DO NOTHING, DANCER! LISTEN, WE'RE GOIN' BACK TO THE CITY TO LET THEM SEE WE BEAT THE BRANDENBURGERS.
The Arabs, learning their chief and all the Germans had been accounted for, were in awe of the five Commandos –
I NEW CHIEF NOW AND WE FIGHT FOR BRITISH. LITTLE MAN MAKES GREAT MAGIC.
THE BLACK SNAKES ARE REALLY IMPRESSED WITH WEASEL MAKING A RIFLE BLOW UP BY JAMMING IT. DANCER DAREN'T TOUCH HIM NOW. AT LEAST I CAN GET MY RATS HOME IN ONE PIECE.

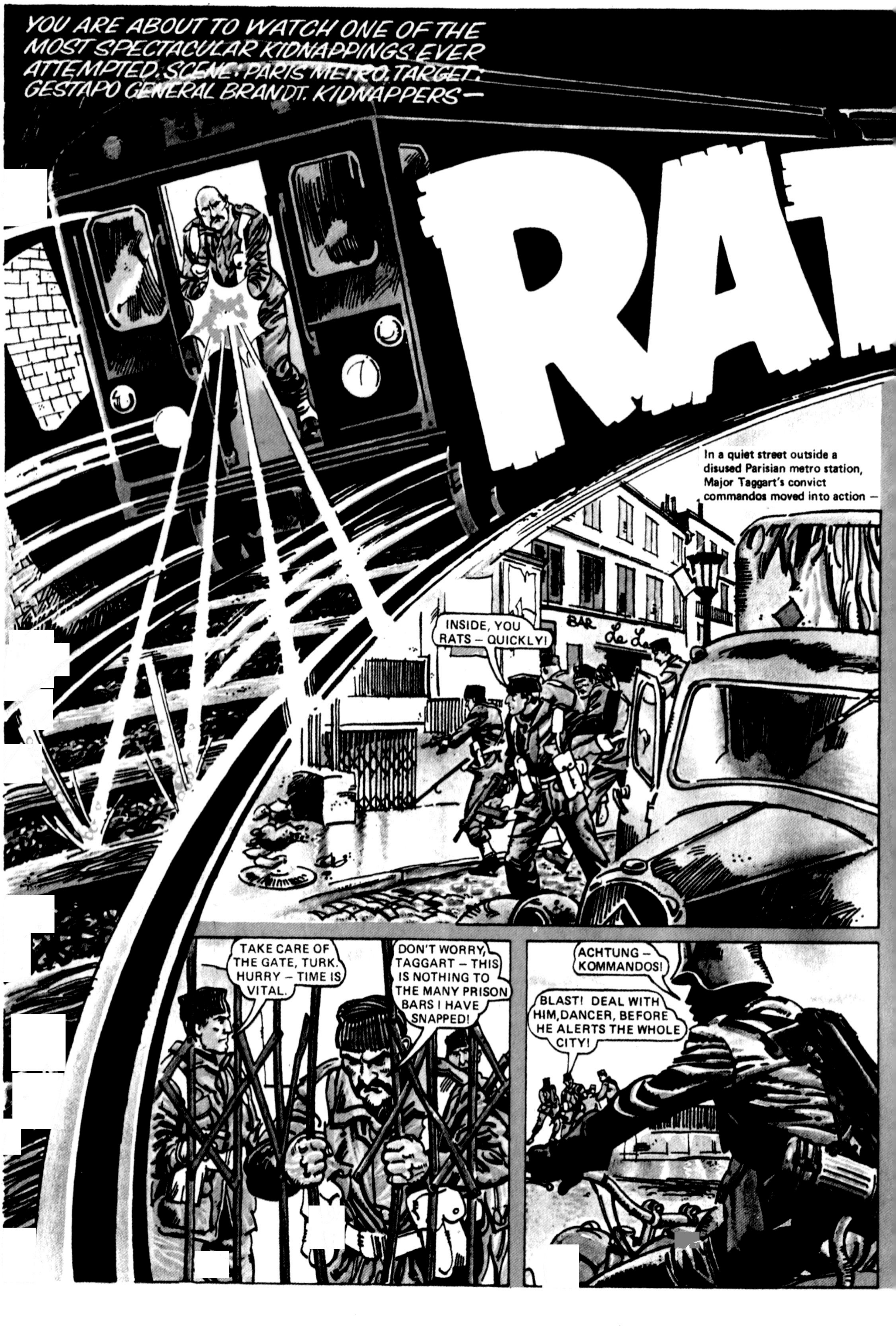

YOU ARE ABOUT TO WATCH ONE OF THE MOST SPECTACULAR KIDNAPPINGS EVER ATTEMPTED. SCENE: PARIS METRO. TARGET: GESTAPO GENERAL BRANDT. KIDNAPPERS—
RA
In a quiet street outside a disused Parisian metro station, Major Taggart's convict commandos moved into action –
INSIDE, YOU RATS – QUICKLY!
BAR
TAKE CARE OF THE GATE, TURK. HURRY – TIME IS VITAL.
DON'T WORRY, TAGGART – THIS IS NOTHING TO THE MANY PRISON BARS I HAVE SNAPPED!
ACHTUNG – KOMMANDOS!
BLAST! DEAL WITH HIM, DANCER, BEFORE HE ALERTS THE WHOLE CITY!

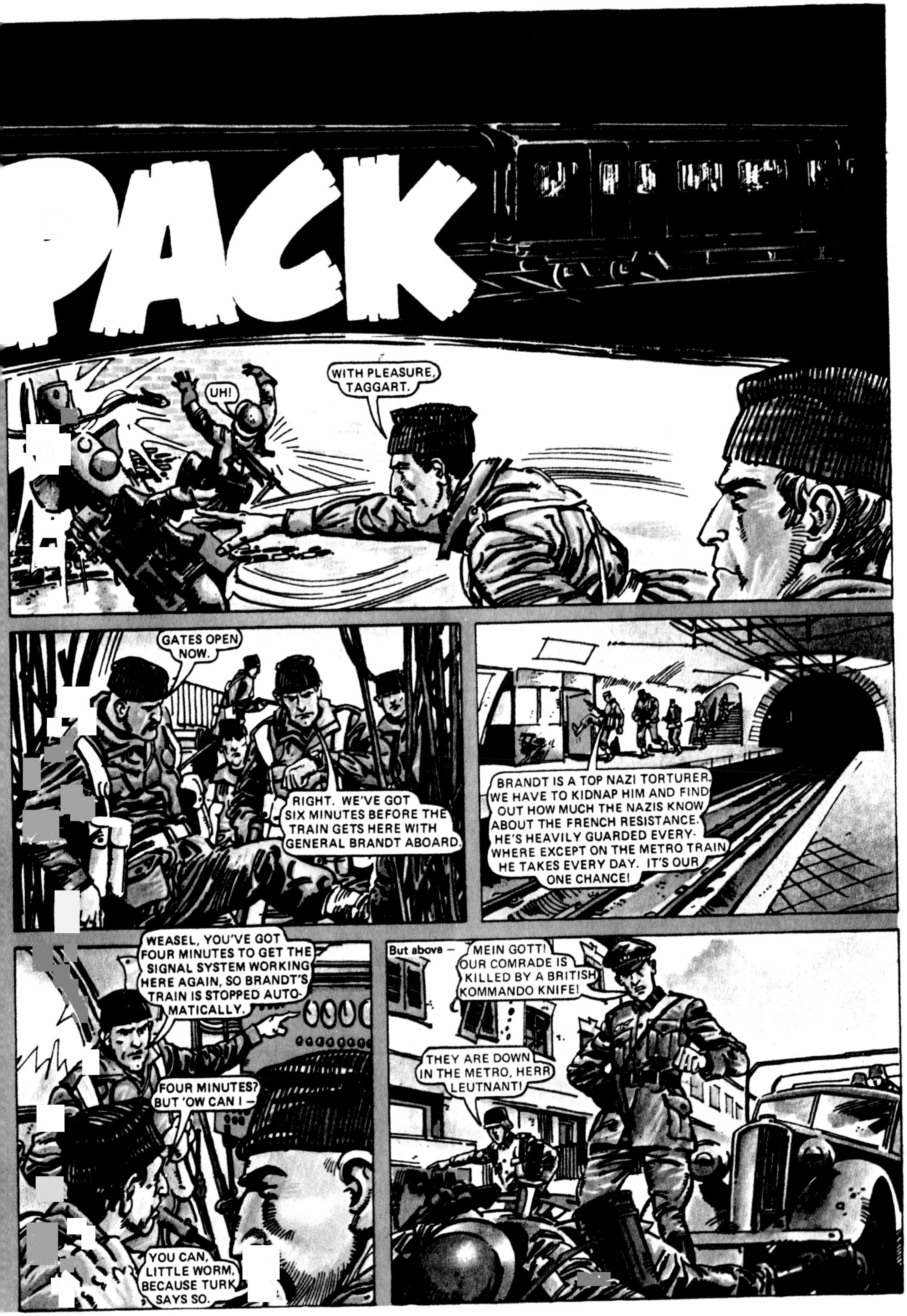
PACK
UH!
WITH PLEASURE, TAGGART.
GATES OPEN NOW.
RIGHT. WE'VE GOT SIX MINUTES BEFORE THE TRAIN GETS HERE WITH GENERAL BRANDT ABOARD.
BRANDT IS A TOP NAZI TORTURER. WE HAVE TO KIDNAP HIM AND FIND OUT HOW MUCH THE NAZIS KNOW ABOUT THE FRENCH RESISTANCE. HE'S HEAVILY GUARDED EVERY-WHERE EXCEPT ON THE METRO TRAIN HE TAKES EVERY DAY. IT'S OUR ONE CHANCE!
WEASEL, YOU'VE GOT FOUR MINUTES TO GET THE SIGNAL SYSTEM WORKING HERE AGAIN, SO BRANDT'S TRAIN IS STOPPED AUTO-MATICALLY.
FOUR MINUTES? BUT 'OW CAN I —
YOU CAN, LITTLE WORM, BECAUSE TURK SAYS SO.
But above —
MEIN GOTT! OUR COMRADE IS KILLED BY A BRITISH KOMMANDO KNIFE!
THEY ARE DOWN IN THE METRO, HERR LEUTNANT!

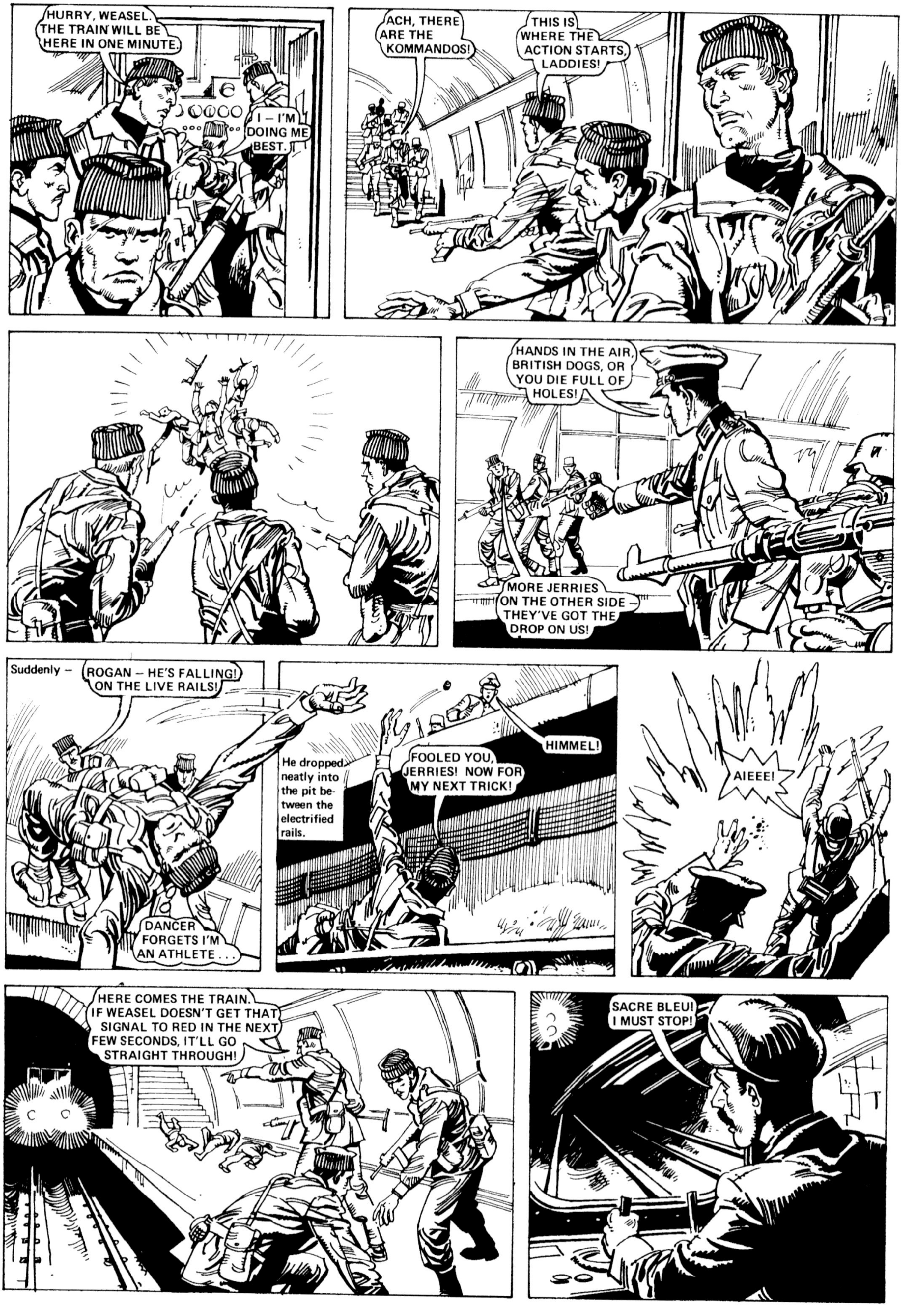
HURRY, WEASEL. THE TRAIN WILL BE HERE IN ONE MINUTE.
I – I'M DOING ME BEST.
ACH, THERE ARE THE KOMMANDOS!
THIS IS WHERE THE ACTION STARTS, LADDIES!
HANDS IN THE AIR, BRITISH DOGS, OR YOU DIE FULL OF HOLES!
MORE JERRIES ON THE OTHER SIDE – THEY'VE GOT THE DROP ON US!
Suddenly –
ROGAN – HE'S FALLING! ON THE LIVE RAILS!
DANCER FORGETS I'M AN ATHLETE . . .
He dropped neatly into the pit between the electrified rails.
FOOLED YOU, JERRIES! NOW FOR MY NEXT TRICK!
HIMMEL!
AIEEE!
HERE COMES THE TRAIN. IF WEASEL DOESN'T GET THAT SIGNAL TO RED IN THE NEXT FEW SECONDS, IT'LL GO STRAIGHT THROUGH!
SACRE BLEU! I MUST STOP!

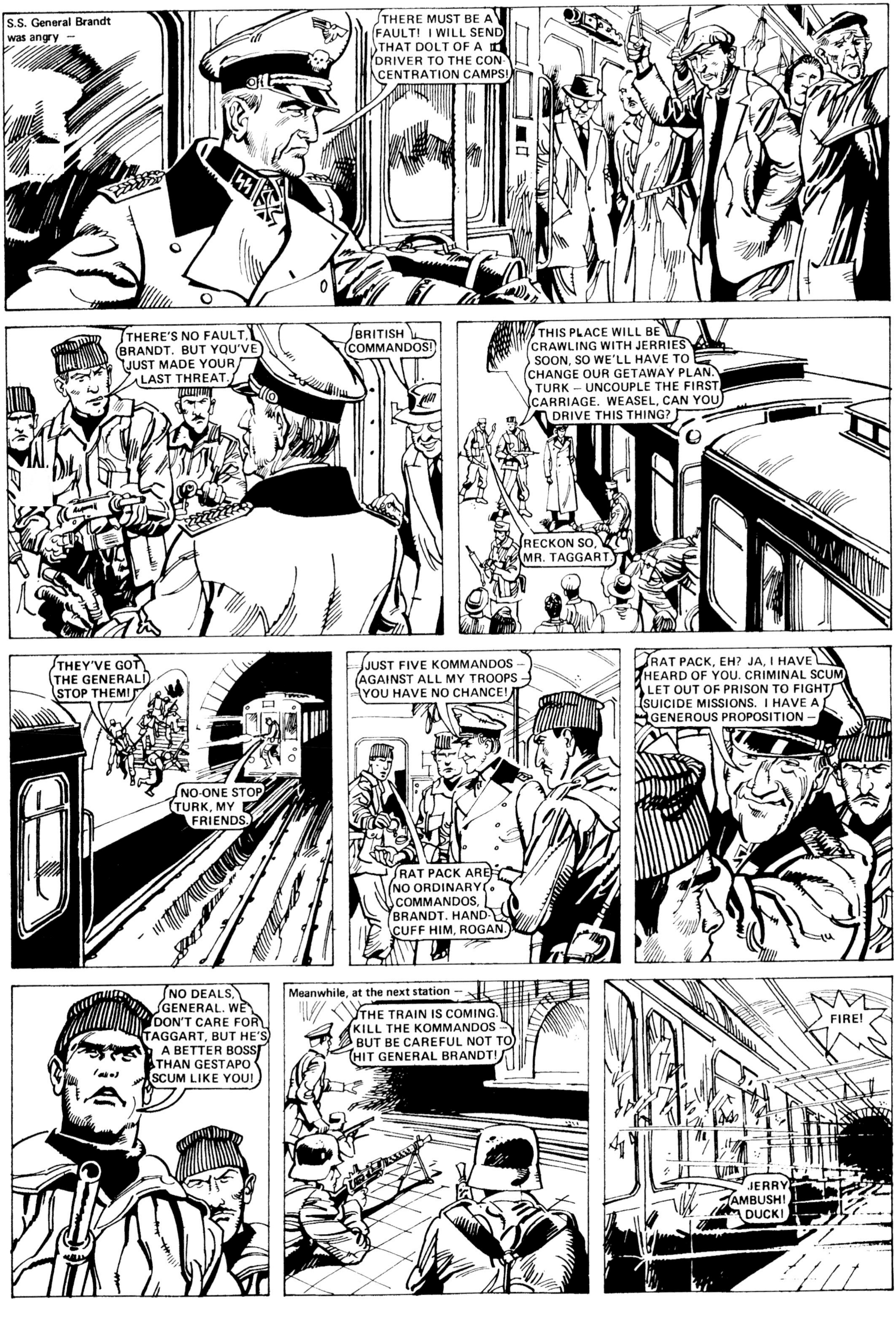
S.S. General Brandt was angry —
THERE MUST BE A FAULT! I WILL SEND THAT DOLT OF A DRIVER TO THE CONCENTRATION CAMPS!
THERE'S NO FAULT, BRANDT. BUT YOU'VE JUST MADE YOUR LAST THREAT.
BRITISH COMMANDOS!
THIS PLACE WILL BE CRAWLING WITH JERRIES SOON, SO WE'LL HAVE TO CHANGE OUR GETAWAY PLAN. TURK — UNCOUPLE THE FIRST CARRIAGE. WEASEL, CAN YOU DRIVE THIS THING?
RECKON SO, MR. TAGGART.
THEY'VE GOT THE GENERAL! STOP THEM!
NO-ONE STOP TURK, MY FRIENDS.
JUST FIVE KOMMANDOS — AGAINST ALL MY TROOPS — YOU HAVE NO CHANCE!
RAT PACK ARE NO ORDINARY COMMANDOS, BRANDT. HANDCUFF HIM, ROGAN.
RAT PACK, EH? JA, I HAVE HEARD OF YOU. CRIMINAL SCUM LET OUT OF PRISON TO FIGHT SUICIDE MISSIONS. I HAVE A GENEROUS PROPOSITION —
NO DEALS, GENERAL. WE DON'T CARE FOR TAGGART, BUT HE'S A BETTER BOSS THAN GESTAPO SCUM LIKE YOU!
Meanwhile, at the next station —
THE TRAIN IS COMING. KILL THE KOMMANDOS — BUT BE CAREFUL NOT TO HIT GENERAL BRANDT!
FIRE!
JERRY AMBUSH! DUCK!

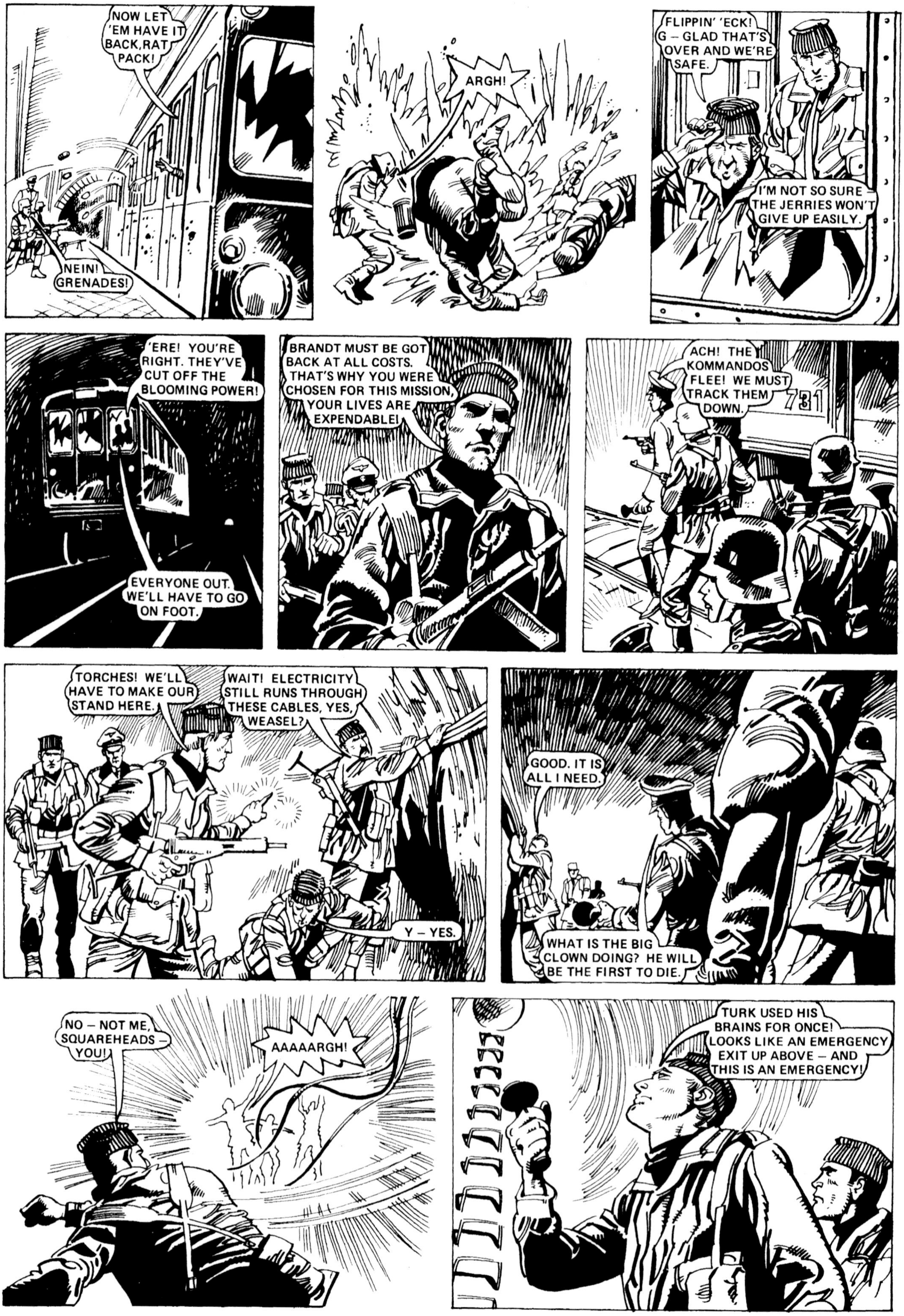
NOW LET 'EM HAVE IT BACK, RAT PACK!
NEIN! GRENADES!
ARGH!
FLIPPIN' 'ECK! G – GLAD THAT'S OVER AND WE'RE SAFE.
I'M NOT SO SURE – THE JERRIES WON'T GIVE UP EASILY.
'ERE! YOU'RE RIGHT. THEY'VE CUT OFF THE BLOOMING POWER!
EVERYONE OUT. WE'LL HAVE TO GO ON FOOT.
BRANDT MUST BE GOT BACK AT ALL COSTS. THAT'S WHY YOU WERE CHOSEN FOR THIS MISSION. YOUR LIVES ARE EXPENDABLE!
ACH! THE KOMMANDOS FLEE! WE MUST TRACK THEM DOWN.
731
TORCHES! WE'LL HAVE TO MAKE OUR STAND HERE.
WAIT! ELECTRICITY STILL RUNS THROUGH THESE CABLES, YES, WEASEL?
Y – YES.
GOOD. IT IS ALL I NEED.
WHAT IS THE BIG CLOWN DOING? HE WILL BE THE FIRST TO DIE.
NO – NOT ME, SQUAREHEADS – YOU!
AAAAARGH!
TURK USED HIS BRAINS FOR ONCE! LOOKS LIKE AN EMERGENCY EXIT UP ABOVE – AND THIS IS AN EMERGENCY!

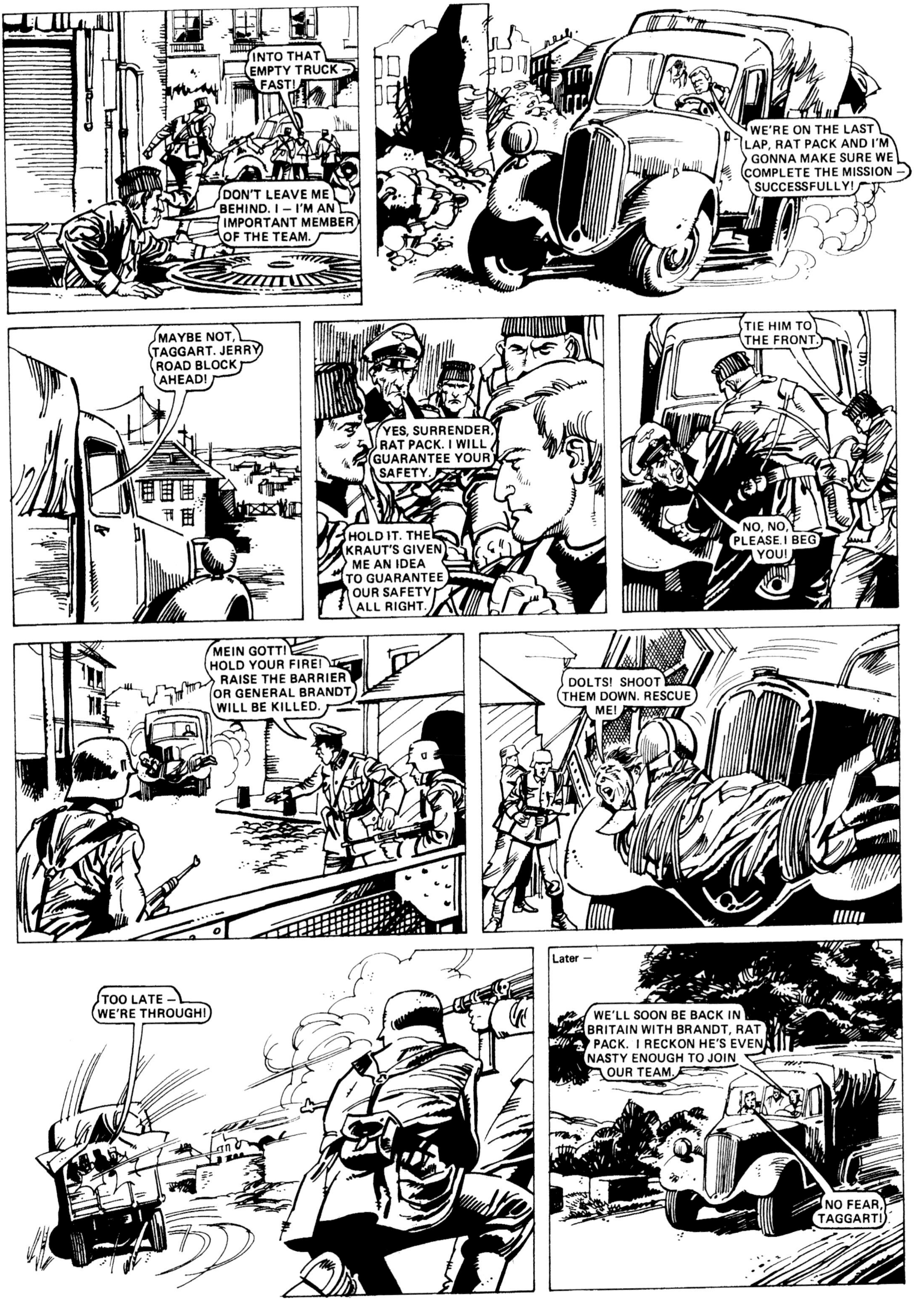
INTO THAT EMPTY TRUCK – FAST!
DON'T LEAVE ME BEHIND. I – I'M AN IMPORTANT MEMBER OF THE TEAM.
WE'RE ON THE LAST LAP, RAT PACK AND I'M GONNA MAKE SURE WE COMPLETE THE MISSION – SUCCESSFULLY!
MAYBE NOT, TAGGART. JERRY ROAD BLOCK AHEAD!
YES, SURRENDER, RAT PACK. I WILL GUARANTEE YOUR SAFETY.
HOLD IT. THE KRAUT'S GIVEN ME AN IDEA TO GUARANTEE OUR SAFETY ALL RIGHT.
TIE HIM TO THE FRONT.
NO, NO, PLEASE. I BEG YOU!
MEIN GOTT! HOLD YOUR FIRE! RAISE THE BARRIER OR GENERAL BRANDT WILL BE KILLED.
DOLTS! SHOOT THEM DOWN. RESCUE ME!
TOO LATE – WE'RE THROUGH!
Later –
WE'LL SOON BE BACK IN BRITAIN WITH BRANDT, RAT PACK. I RECKON HE'S EVEN NASTY ENOUGH TO JOIN OUR TEAM.
NO FEAR, TAGGART!

COVER GALLERY

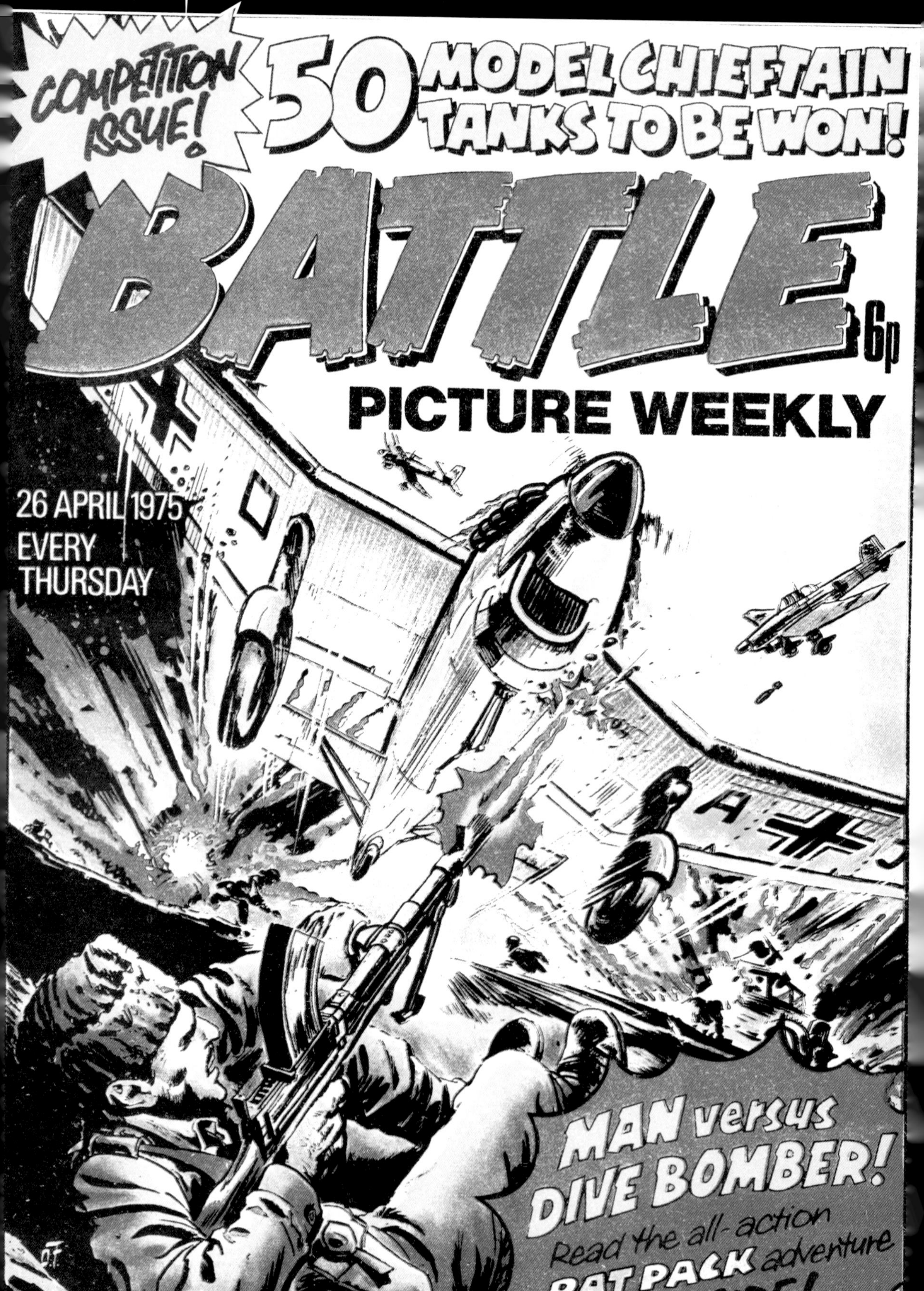
COMPETITION ISSUE!
50 MODEL CHIEFTAIN TANKS TO BE WON!
BATTLE 6p
PICTURE WEEKLY
26 APRIL 1975
EVERY THURSDAY
MAN versus DIVE BOMBER!
Read the all-action RAT PACK adventure INSIDE!

WIN A DAY OUT WITH THE ARMY!

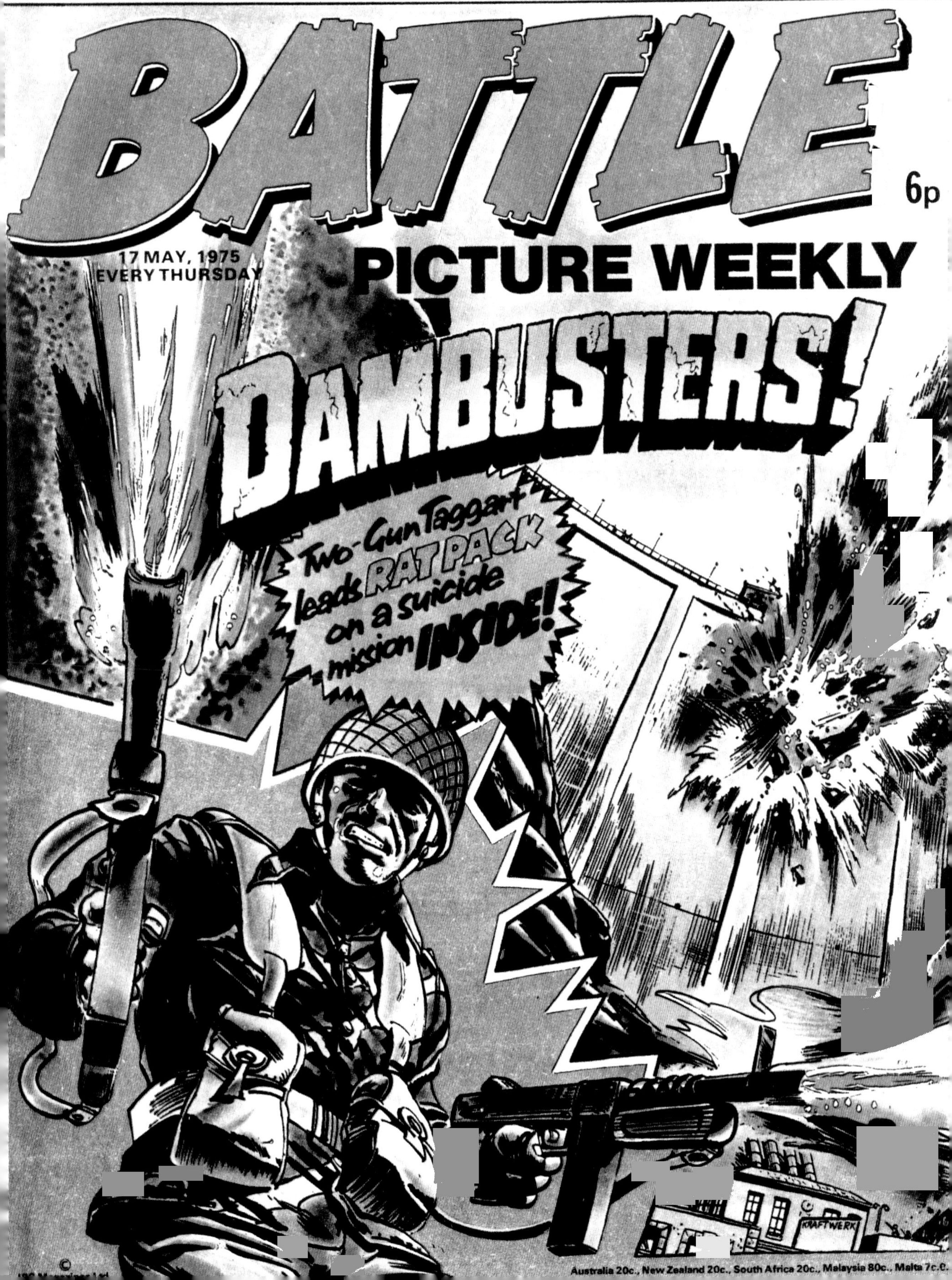

BATTLE
6p
17 MAY, 1975
EVERY THURSDAY
PICTURE WEEKLY
DAMBUSTERS!
Two-Gun Taggart leads RAT PACK on a suicide mission INSIDE!
KRAFTWERK
Australia 20c., New Zealand 20c., South Africa 20c., Malaysia 80c., Malta 7c.C.

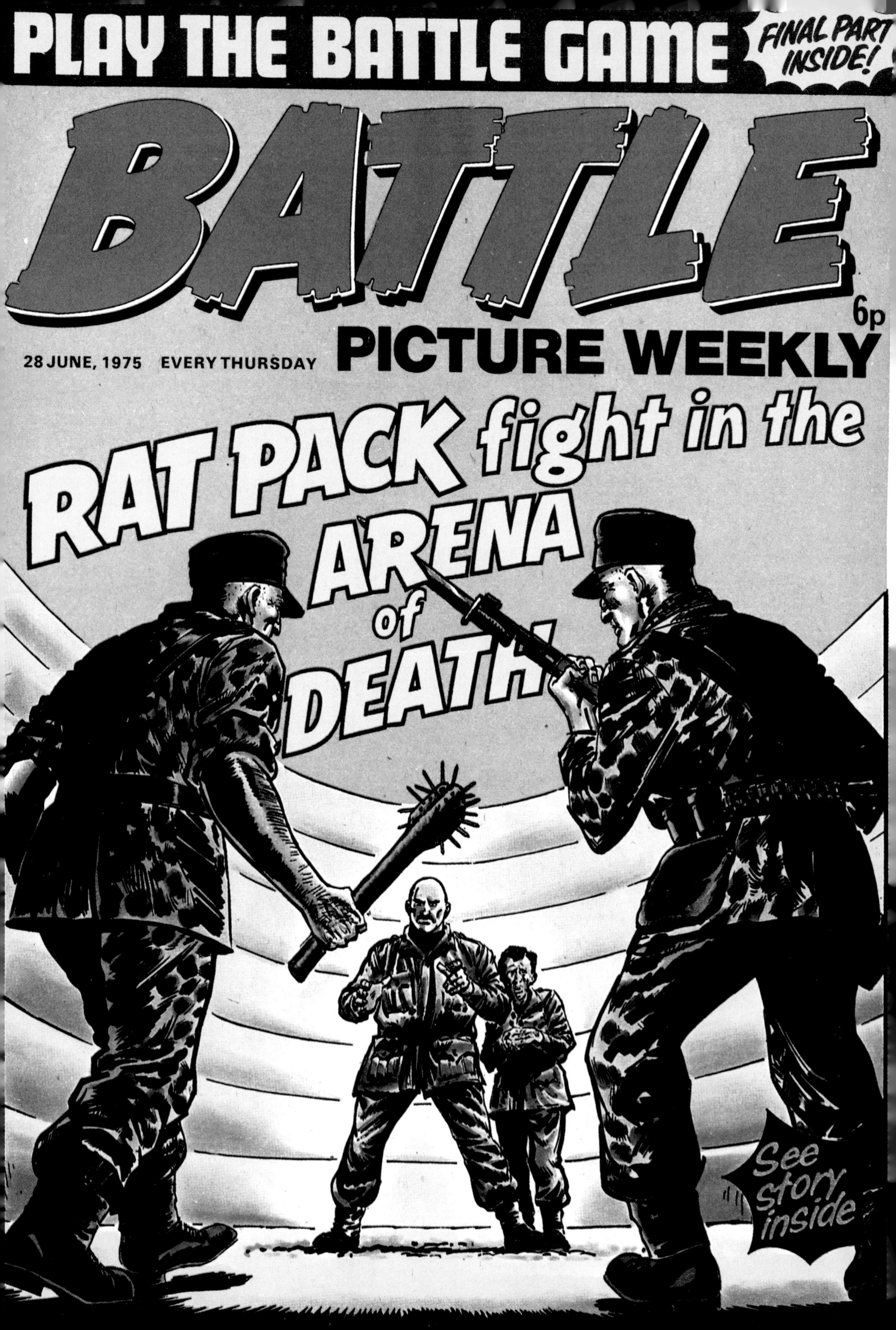
PLAY THE BATTLE GAME
FINAL PART INSIDE!
BATTLE
6p
28 JUNE, 1975 EVERY THURSDAY
PICTURE WEEKLY
RAT PACK fight in the ARENA of DEATH
See story inside

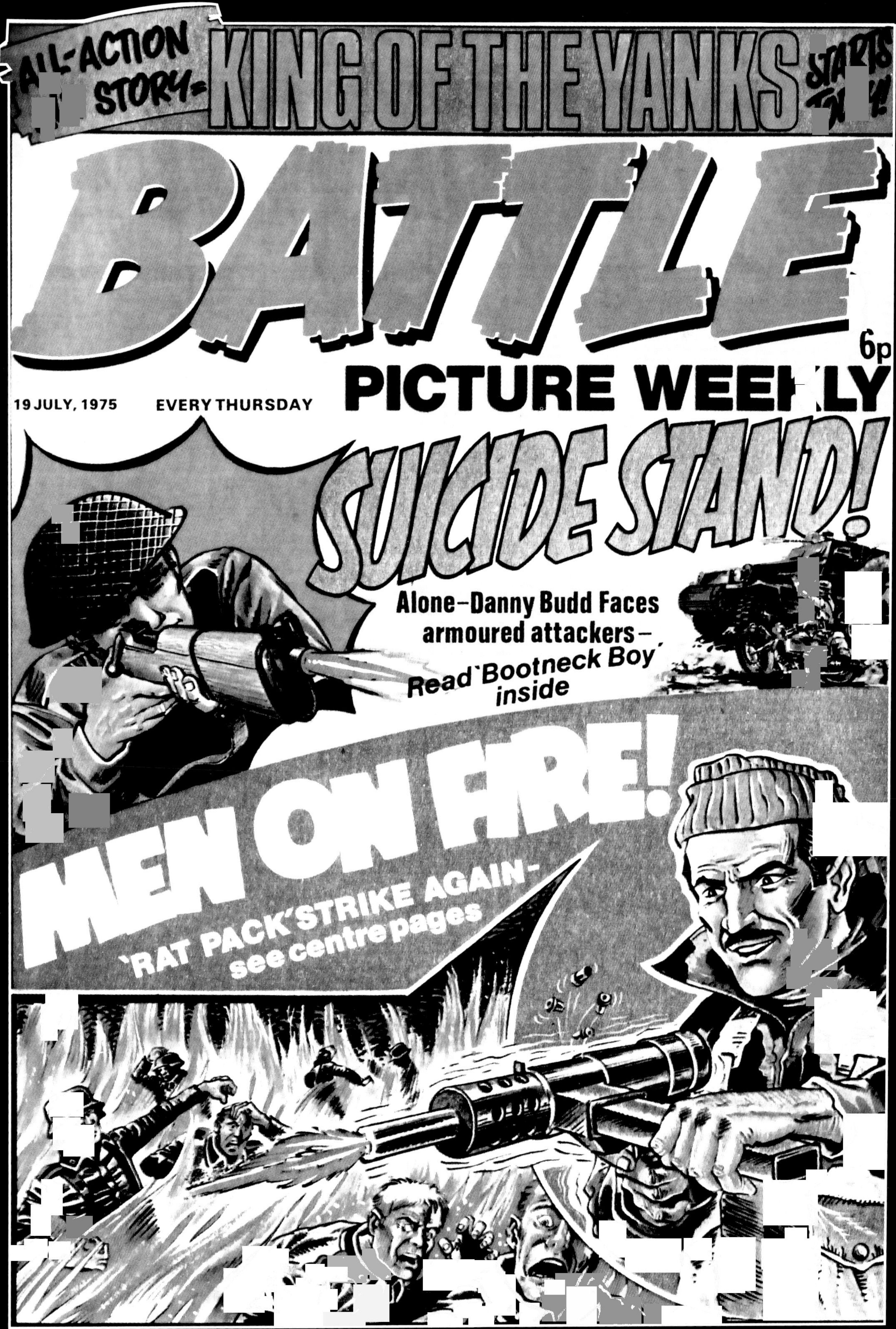

ALL-ACTION STORY
KING OF THE YANKS
BATTLE
6p
PICTURE WEEKLY
19 JULY, 1975
EVERY THURSDAY
SUICIDE STAND!
Alone–Danny Budd Faces armoured attackers–
Read 'Bootneck Boy' inside
MEN ON FIRE!
'RAT PACK' STRIKE AGAIN–
see centre pages

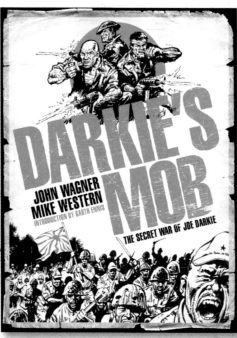

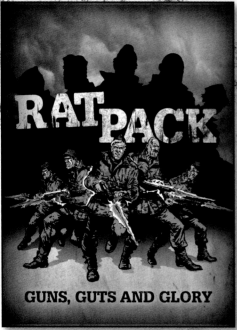

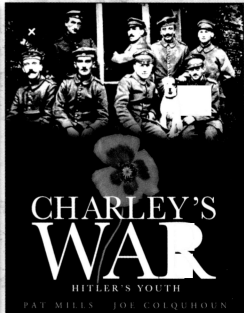